"Ever wonder what would happen if *Stranger Things* had a threesome with Stephen King's *The Body* and 1997 cult film *I Know What You Did Last Summer*? Levis Keltner's rollicking debut, *Into That Good Night*, is exactly the kind of novel such an unholy union would, and should, produce."

—David James Poissant, author of *The Heaven of Animals*

"An existential mystery, *Into That Good Night* explores the difference between what's right and what others tell us is right. This elegant, wise novel about adolescence and tribal loyalty makes us flinch with recognition about the difficult navigation into selfhood. Everyone's rite of passage isn't this dark, but this is everyone's rite of passage."

—Debra Monroe, author of *My Unsentimental Education*

"Levis Keltner's debut has echoes of William Golding and Ian McEwan. Haunting and moving, *Into That Good Night* is a dark twist on the coming-of-age narrative that you will not easily forget. This one will keep you reading well past your bedtime. Keltner is the real thing."

—William Jensen, author of *Cities of Men*

"If *The Breakfast Club* were a witchy murder mystery, you'd have *Into That Good Night*. With his shocking awareness of human nature and the forces that propel us through the dark absurdity of life, Levis Keltner will make you laugh, cry, and shudder in fear at the horrors we are all capable of."

—Tatiana Ryckman, author of *I Don't Think of You (Until I Do)*

INTO That GOOD Night

A NOVEL

LEVIS KELTNER

ARCADE PUBLISHING • NEW YORK

Arcade Publishing books may be purchased in bulk at special discounts for sales promotion, corporate gifts, fund-raising, or educational purposes. Special editions can also be created to specifications. For details, contact the Special Sales Department, Arcade Publishing, 307 West 36th Street, 11th Floor, New York, NY 10018 or arcade@skyhorsepublishing.com.

Arcade Publishing® is a registered trademark of Skyhorse Publishing, Inc.®, a Delaware corporation.

Visit our website at www.arcadepub.com.

10 9 8 7 6 5 4 3 2 1

Library of Congress Cataloging-in-Publication Data is available on file.

Cover design and illustration by Brent Bates

Print ISBN: 978-1-62872-844-6
Ebook ISBN: 978-1-62872-848-4

Printed in the United States of America

INTO *That* GOOD *Night*

"And we savor the distance. And we savor the forest. Tasting its many darknesses. And we love what is far. And we are called to the river's eternity. The black pomegranate on the table. Our pupils dilated: *look, look, oh look!*"

—Carole Maso, *Aureole*

"Accepting the limits of one's ability is individuality. Accepting the limits of one's experience is adulthood."

—Elsa Marne, *Borta Bra Men*

"Between our dreams and actions lies this world."

—Bruce Springsteen

PROLOGUE

Without the Summerson girl, we might never have recovered from the tragedy of young John Walker. The winter after his diagnosis, she was found stabbed to death in the woods outside of town.

A group of seniors trekked the rim of the moraine that morning, for which they'd been training several weeks, led by a zealous woman who reaffirmed over their huffs and grunts that none would live forever. Thirty minutes into the hike, the leader had stopped to count the line, neatly outfitted with walking sticks, hiking boots, and flannel shirts, except for one woman who'd insisted on wearing a white knit sweater and who, after second count, had definitely gone missing. With much confusion, then some relief, the group turned back. The woman stood in the brush along the rim. She faced the valley and looked aside only to smile pleasantly, as if not having noticed they'd gone. A sheep lay down in the mud, she said. Her straying would make them late to lunch, the leader scolded to salvage the expedition, and the senile or stubborn woman rejoined the line. Embarrassment fogged what she'd seen, as she groaned and recalled how her daughter had gone from blonde to dark-headed as a child, before the accident, rest her soul, and why was she missing her now? The woman then wheeled around and pointed below at Bachelor's Grove and said, "A sheep's stuck in the mud!" after which others saw it through the bare branches. She might've said "sheet." Reports were mixed, and the woman herself couldn't remember when questioned, though either metaphor revealed to be apt, as Erika's body was caked to the ground but for some dry blonde hair that waved in the wind.

Palos Hills police were left with scant evidence, as much to blame on the unusually heavy rains as the officers' inexperience with murders. Public commiseration over John's treatments and his decline in spirit then competed with rumors of suspects responsible for the sixth grader's death, of campfire devil worship, and of the gangster past of the otherwise unremarkable Chicago suburb. Eventually, like even the best stories, John's was retired and almost completely forgotten.

I

1

"John Walker is not dead."

The limp American flag spoke from the windowless corner of the classroom. Breathless, students endured the dramatic pause. A/C blared against their adolescent bodies to render all a crisp sixty-six. From the opposing window, a parallelogram of daylight shivered on the flag. Despite that, despite the blowing and the words, it didn't wave.

Hidden behind the tall stripes, the speaker crackled: "After Sunday's on-field diagnosis ... rushed to the hospital early this morning...."

The principal delivered the news as if a president had been shot. Students were led (again) in the Pledge of Allegiance. They chanted, hands over hearts, over a backbeat of whimpers and sniffles.

Afterward, a guy on the baseball team dribbled tears on his desk. The math teacher drew a triangle, stopped before the final points met. She set the chalk on the ledge with the uncertainty of trying a puzzle piece. The room wasn't silent so much as hollow, inside them and out—except for Doug.

Doug Horolez could laugh, climb a desk, spit. That's how much he didn't care the guy was dying. Of course, he would never do those things. Not because it would do no good. Doug had long been a no-body. He was too meek for clubs, and as for sports, not once had he hit a pitch during a gym unit—he'd been hit twice, jerks being what they were. As a dork, an outcast, to disrespect John Walker would rip him completely from the social fabric of Palos Hills Junior High. Doug hated that he still cared what others thought, but he didn't make the world. In fact, he barely understood it.

Before the interruption, math class had been interesting for the first time all year. The lecture had derailed on Pythagoras, the ancient Greek with a conical beard who'd founded a cult around truths he'd uncovered about shapes, with far-out rites, like abstaining from beans and purifying his followers' souls with music. That's what the teacher said, anyway, and Doug absorbed every detail. He'd wanted to raise his hand (he didn't) to ask how a guy invents a difficult-to-recall equation and gets people to adore him that much. He saw a glimmer of an answer now—the same way a town worships a Little League baseball star.

He dared only to glance at the others, each suffering in private hells of bewilderment and desolation. Was it his imagination or had the boy cast a spell on them so potent it was impossible not to care? Doug felt it, too—a sense that a defining moment in someone else's life was defining his own. Meaningless details were heightened: the shirt tag (XL) up on Ronnie Mickle's blotchy neck, the thick weave of the (sickly) yellow-green curtains, the summer paint (already) peeling away from the window glass—insignificant things made memorable, overwhelming, larger than himself. Doug never felt smaller in his desk. He wondered if affection, too, weren't an equation, if he had so little because another boy had so much.

·

"Cancer," said Sweatpants Kid at lunch.

"That's gross," said the kid who looked like a poorly aged woman, half a baloney sandwich in his mouth.

"Dying," said Whiskers. Today's black T-shirt read ABOMINATION.

"Dead Man Walker," Doug blurted, reflectively though aloud—a learned defense. If others thought his contribution to a conversation worthless, they had the option to regard the comment as obtuse mumbling so it could be appropriately ignored.

The lunchroom rejects' faces blanked as the nickname dropped on their fallow fields of possibility.

Whiskers showed teeth like a donkey. He laughed and then sang with a country lilt, "He's a Dead Man *Walk*er."

Each repeated the line around the table, trying it on. Doug could almost hear something click on inside them. They weren't friends, only outliers corralled by the shortage of table space. It was unusual they were even talking—more proof of the boy's charisma-based magic. But right then, a circle of laughter united them against John, the Dead Man. Doug had done that.

A moment later, their eyes dimmed and the boys munched again with their mundane fantasies in isolation. Doug wouldn't so much as smirk and jinx his tiny win. Tiny to the world. The last time he'd left school so proud he'd learned to tie his shoelaces.

•

Doug had one above-average thing in his life. E. Summerson was his best friend. E. was a girl and therefore worth more to him than a lineup of high-fiving male buddies. She was his only friend and all he needed for a long time.

They'd met in the sixth grade in the band director's office, a utility closet connected to the music room. It had no windows. Bare pipe ran overhead. A plain desk occupied most of the space with pistachio shells and paper cups crumpled into lumpy white shits all over the desktop, except for two bare spots where the director sulked on his elbows whenever Doug wheezed the chorus of "Greensleeves" like a congested mallard. There was no formal door, only a pair of folding doors, behind which large instruments were locked at night, the timpani and chimes and tattered bones of a xylophone let out to roam by day, which left the tang of wood glue in the air, Doug noticed, as the fog of the man's putrid breath cleared. One door was shut, the other left open by the director, who'd gone out. Doug was alone to make a hard decision in the dim light that reached in from the music room and sliced across the toes of his gym shoes.

Doug clung to the water cooler by the desk like a defeated man. He took in all the details, maybe the last he would see of the place, not out of nostalgia, but for an answer that perhaps lurked in the room. He looked at the cup, reflecting glossy in his hand, unable to recall how it'd gotten there or to will himself a sip.

"Mr. Cremini?" a girl said as she came in.

She'd mistaken Doug for the band director. A false mustache and he could've passed as the man on Halloween. Their resemblance ran deeper than the predominant prescription glasses and short-sleeved

4

button up. The twelve-year-old unconsciously emulated his stooped posture, a single blow from broken, a monster shying in the dark.

"Where's Roger?" she asked, clarinet held like a club.

Backlit in the doorway, Emily Summerson had a dawn glow. They'd gone to different elementary schools, but the sway of her long red hair in the hallways caught his attention on the first day of junior high, and he'd admired the girl from a distance ever since. Emily was special. She went friendless with confidence. Not because she was the only natural ginger at school or some other physical or social abnormality, it seemed, but by choice, in preference to the company of others. She was also the one girl Doug wouldn't masturbate to—couldn't. To touch her, even in his imagination, felt vile without some kind of prior approval.

Emily's posture straightened, to exert dominance or to appear lovelier or both. Breasts stuck up as if two action figures had pitched tents beneath her shirt. Doug dove into his paper cup.

"Cremini needed more nuts," he said after a gulp.

Her neck blushed up to her ears. Doug hadn't intended to insinuate the band director was in need of manhood and to insult him.

Emily was in the room now. She asked what he was doing.

"Quitting … I guess," he said. It wasn't the whole truth. The director had told him he stunk at the oboe, that he couldn't believe the grade school music teacher had passed him on, and he recommended that Doug give up before he'd wasted his life on a lot of hot air.

The girl was slouching again. She straightened when he looked over to read the impression his decision made on her. This time he saw beyond her chest, down to the intention of her straightening—by some miracle she was seeing him, like he wasn't a piece of furniture, a nonentity. They were here, in the room, *together*.

5

Under his stupefied gaze, Emily sank into the folding chair and dissembled her clarinet, which she cleaned with precision like a trusty firearm. Between swabs, she glanced up, as if finding him, or at least his situation, curious, maybe even interesting. She was expecting him to explain or add another witticism. If he wasn't a band geek with band friends, what would a guy like Doug do? Who was he? That was the question that threatened to send him into an existential crisis. Director Cremini had provided Doug a way out of geekdom, sure, but to what?

Doug had no better answer for the girl, no cool reply. He knew he should ask her something. He could only think to ask what she was doing here, which was obvious. The book on her clarinet case—he gestured at it with his empty cup and, with great relief, asked what she was reading.

"A Salinger," Emily said, pausing in her work. She'd read it a bunch of times, but "needed to give it up." This would be her last time.

She asked who he read, and Doug muttered in not so many words that he read all sorts of stuff, everything, except not Salinger, only because he hadn't gotten to it—*him(?)* yet with all the other reading he got to, but that he, Doug, was looking forward to it because … *Salinger*, and he would have plenty of time now because he wouldn't be in band, in fact that's all he would do now really is read, Salinger.

After a thoughtful glance at the tattered cover, she held out the book to him.

"Wow. You sure? Thanks, Emily," he said and winced. He sounded like a stalker, knowing her name before she'd introduced herself.

"I prefer E.," she corrected. She added that, when he'd finished the book, she'd be curious to hear what he thought. The way she said it was less like an invitation and more like a test—he could pass or fail. Her clarinet was assembled and in her hands, poised to play. To avoid displeasing her or looking like a fool in talking with the band director, Doug fled before the man returned. He figured the director would assume he'd quit, feel like he'd saved a kid. For a few hours, Doug felt saved.

He struggled with the book for a few days, terrified that he wouldn't "get it" and blow his chance with the one girl who'd acknowledged his existence, and not just any girl, either. Every time he began from the beginning, full of cold sunlight and ... Doug couldn't get it—the plot, the relationship between characters (lovers or brother and sister?), the Meaning. Doug was too distracted by his fantasies. He saw her hands holding the book under his. Before every reading, he set his glasses in a safe spot and, with abandon, buried his nose between the pages and inhaled until his lungs were hard balloons full of the shared experience of this object she had cherished, kept on her nightstand or inches from her face for years.

After a week of floundering around page fifteen, Doug avoided the challenge by saying hi after school and following her to the public library. E. didn't mention the book. She didn't say anything after a quizzical hello, but continued to walk with a sense of purpose to the library. There, she nodded at the librarians and went up the stairs where she curled in a cushion-topped chair beneath a skylight, maybe waiting for him to interrupt, pull her out of herself and her routine. Others might've been intimidated enough to retreat, which Doug considered many times as an honorable course of action. He clung on, battered by doubt, to this impression of her, that she savored aloneness, and that, so long as he respected her space, she wouldn't mind him lingering within reach. Doug didn't say anything. He did his homework, then he stared at his work until she got up and smoothed her hair. She gave him a small, though steady smile and explained she had to leave for dinner but feel free to stay. She didn't chase him off the next day when he appeared, and even asked about the short stack of books under his arm. He kept coming.

Two years had passed like this.

•

One of the rejects must've tried the nickname on the other dorks, geeks, and freaks of Palos Hills to dip a toe in a sliver of spotlight. Whiskers, Doug figured, for shock value, or the kid who looked like a poorly aged woman, blabbing about the "barftastic burn." They'd all, in fact, repeated it. "Dead Man Walker"—it was hardly funny; harmless, no harm intended at least. It wasn't slander, each outcast independently relying on the joke as a flimsy, one-use charm, a temporary +1 to Charisma, of which they'd relished every moment. Most listeners hadn't laughed. Still, the nickname fed on their worries about John and his condition, and rooted in the minds of kids who hoped his fate didn't befall them unless it meant being similarly idolized, going out in a blaze of (seemingly) everlasting glory.

That November, Doug witnessed a fight at recess over the one thing he'd ever invented. A jock pinned some nerd's arm so smoothly that no one shouted or scattered. The nerd kneeled in the sooty crust along the iced schoolyard. His brow trembled as if under moral dilemma. Those nearby turned to spectate. "Say it again, dickhead," the jock dared. "What he do?" a prep in the crowd asked matter-of-factly. "Said he wanted to die," another kid, the jock's crony, answered and blew into his pink hands. Both were on the baseball team. "You shouldn't treat people that way," a girl said behind them. It was the girl of the religion that makes girls wear denim skirts year-round. "He said John's a dead man," the jock said and shoved the nerd face-first into the muck. A punk kid stepped forward but didn't say anything. "Dead Man Walker," the crony repeated. No one helped the nerd up. He didn't move, either, and lay facedown after everyone had left until a teacher asked why he was doing that. "It was my fault," he said and lied that he'd fainted. Doug was embarrassed for the kid, who went to the nurse's office limping to convince everyone he'd paid dearly enough for his transgression. Mostly, Doug was glad it wasn't him.

"The Dead Man" spread fast after the fight, despite Doug's usual bad luck. Kids whispered it in the hallways and in classrooms when teachers foolishly turned their backs. John's loyal followers reacted with distaste: *How could anyone disrespect a sick kid? After all he'd done.* By some natural law of human argument, a fringe subculture of peer critics emerged to counter: *Had they ever asked him for anything? What had he given them other than hope? Hope* was the loyalists' rebuttal, what Palos Hills so desperately needed since his diagnosis. Fall semester ended in stalemate. Students on both sides subsisted on rumors as to whether the boy would return one hundred percent or be dead before winter break.

By then, the nickname's acridity dipped into fondness as everyone at school used it, pleasantly or unpleasantly. And wasn't that just like John, the boy they'd loved, even loved to hate? Dead Man Walker became a stand-in for the boy, a capsule of sentiment, a bubble of John-ness bearing his image, warped, though not yet burst.

Doug smiled coolly whenever overhearing the nickname, pleased yet stunned that so many kids found something he'd said remotely funny or apt, though no credit was ever given. No harm done, he figured. By spring it would sputter out, and the guy could take a blow while he was down. He'd probably be back up in a few months, anyhow, possessing more influence and happiness at fourteen than Doug would ever know.

•

E. and Doug read upstairs in her bedroom a few evenings a week under condition the door remained open. They were "just friends," she'd affirmed to her family after her younger sister had complained of the injustice of E. being allowed to bring home a boy. The open door rule wasn't once followed or enforced, such faith the Summersons had in their daughter or such little threat they saw in Doug.

The family lived in a brick two-story in upper Palos that appeared old enough to have been the first home on the block. E's window overlooked the tree-lined Octavia Street and, though she'd taken down the curtains to sync her sleep pattern to the natural cycle of the seasons, as the greatest minds in history had lived, her room seemed a secluded corner suspended in time, where there was only E. and her ramparts of books and sometimes her jester-knight, Doug. The air was distinctly dry—a rug on the hardwood permanently stained from one of Doug's nosebleeds—with ceilings that slanted to a high peak. Though equipped with modern amenities, she lit candles, even with the stand-up lamp on, and burned incense, sandalwood or some other contemplative fragrance. Time was not suspended there, however, and Doug spent too many of those evenings overly conscious of his luck, so the visits never felt real enough, and week after week he went home with a hole widening in his heart that started the size of a pinprick, then the puncture a juice box straw makes, which grew, gradually, nightly, until it gaped and was impossible to keep any satisfying bit of her with him, sealed away and not sloshing about. Instead he had less of her and was a mess of newer and more terrible emotions until near her again.

As the daylight drained from the walls, from the pages, from E.'s hair, they would read and work for hours, legs up a wall or in bed stiffly on top of the comforter or whirling an inch a minute in the desk chair or basking under the tall window. Never would the kids read side by side and rarely in the same spot, except for when Doug managed to make himself small on the foot of the bed. He truly hated reading and spent all his time at home on video games. Yet with E., he endured several slim fiction classics, which devolved into genre classics, and soon hardcore fantasy, paladins hacking through crypts teeming with undead, mighty heroes traversing cold wastes against impossible odds. Doug battled boredom for her. Sometimes the kids would discuss what they'd read, though she mostly did the talking while he kept it going with questions, listening for the roundness of pleasure in her voice, appreciating even sour smiles at the expense of asking something boneheaded, convinced his devotion was a form of love.

Junior high passed with Doug giving little thought to what was next, the next stage of life, that there were stages. He made no new friends. He skimmed dozens of books beyond his comprehension. He'd masturbated to hundreds of girls and none of them were E. Their time together blurred into a precious investment, in long anticipation of something great, which remained years later as proof of his constancy, then proof of his idiocy, then of just having grown up. Several of their inside jokes and intimate conversations, glimpses of what E. was deep down, beneath her influences, lasted decades. Because of what would happen next, however, one conversation stood out among the rest.

"I wish I were an only child," E. had said.

In the adjoining bedroom, her sister Erika and her best friend were shrieking lyrics to a pop song. "*I wanna. I wanna, wanna …*" was all Doug could catch. There was some rhythmic thumping that might've been jumping on the bed. E. had gotten a noise cancellation system for Christmas, but it was no match against the preteens. The peaks of their laughter sawed through the walls.

"Oh, yeah." Doug couldn't say more to make E. believe he understood. He and his six-year-old brother used to play together, but the year he met E., Doug lost interest. Like his parents, his little brother wasn't bad or annoying, just around. "They have fun together, at least … I guess."

E. asked him to please fucking pound the wall. Doug followed her order with two upbeat knocks. The girls beat back, and he jumped.

"Maybe they'll just disappear," E. said.

"Dead Man Walker style," Doug muttered.

"Who-style?"

He couldn't tell if she were joking. E. looked at him deadpan. A book entitled *Meditations* bobbed in her hand as if she were waiting for a punch line.

It was possible she'd gone through every announcement and award ceremony over the last few years with her head between two pages. She could be the one person who didn't think much of the boy either way, obsessively, or at all.

Doug started to explain: the Dead Man, John Walker, cancer, the fall of a local legend.

E. went to her long mirror, which was covered with an old bed sheet. Doug hadn't asked why. A bottom corner peeked out at them, flashed S-O-S in candlelight. E. tugged the sheet over the glass completely, then stepped back to admire her work.

"There're worse ways to die," she said.

Her sister's room went oddly silent. They turned their heads, not for too long.

E. picked another book from her fresh-borrows stack and fluffed her pillow. She hefted the open end so it packed deep into the case, which she reshaped into a cylinder before smashing it against her back and the headboard.

"I came up with that ... you know?" Doug said. "The nickname."

E. snorted.

He thought maybe she'd read a funny line in *The Art of War*. No, she looked down at him with a haughty grin as if to say, "That's what he deserves." Or, "That's what false greatness deserves—mockery." He interpreted either as her approval. Unless her laughter was directed at himself, for taking pride in something so trivial.

She didn't say anything more about it and became serious, stern. She asked what he was reading.

"Oh ... *this?*"

Doug began to talk up the sci-fi novel in his lap, written at no higher than an eighth-grade reading level, though still he struggled with its more convoluted sentences. He soon wasn't hearing the bullshit coming out of his mouth, like how one of the book's layers was this really crazy commentary on good and evil being just layers of evil. Something changed in E.'s face. One moment she was listening, the next she'd phased out. Her eyes refocused, if it were possible, and no longer looked outward, but in, her pupils tracking ideas that popped dazzlingly as fireworks inside her brain. She smiled, not to him or

13

anything he said, but vaguely, in refrain of hearing him or expressing herself, cardboard-cutout attention, a stand-in for the girl.

He'd bored her, was his first thought. Wasn't smart enough. He might never be.

Doug wondered if she were even conscious of slipping behind the cover of her mental landscape. He hoped not.

She was still physically there, in the room, of course. He asked about her new book.

E. blinked. Her gaze gathered intention as she found him among her stacks, an old friend in kid years. A minute later, she'd returned and discussed the benefits and drawbacks of high ground guerrilla warfare.

One day, she would wake to him like this and more—smile not vaguely, not amused or merely fond, but fortunate to have him near. That's what Doug believed, anyway. They just needed a little more time.

•

A week after the murder, E. messaged: "SAVE ME FROM MOTH-ER." It was the first he'd heard from the girl since, "Dingbat got herself hurt," and fifteen minutes later, "*Dead." Doug sent frantic questions, then condolences that'd provoked no reply.

The wake and funeral passed without invite. In the weeklong silence, he'd had his dad drop him off at the mall, alone, where he didn't see the holiday storefronts—trees, deer, and mannequins in tight silver foil lost amid spills of paper snow—so intently he tried to imagine losing a family member. His sole reference was a pet turtle that'd dried up like beef jerky and which had made him disappointed in himself and sort of relieved too because he was always doing too much or too little and hurting the creature and feeling terrible about it and unable to communicate how sorry he was. E. would better cope with much greater loss, Doug was sure. Nevertheless, she might be changed. Their relationship might change. He'd bought her a gift that day, which he later wrapped in white tissue paper and too much Scotch tape, and swore that he would support her in any way possible and no matter what. Ready for her summons, he dunked the gift into his backpack seconds after she'd messaged and came lightning-quick on his Huffy.

That evening, Mrs. Summerson never looked more pleased to welcome him into their home. She'd always regarded the boy coldly, beneath her daughter, called him "Douglas." This time, she took his coat and said to never mind the slush he'd trekked in, just go on up to her, please, go up to her daughter's bedroom where the door was locked.

Doug risked it. The woman didn't have blood on her hands. She wasn't a friendly lady, but he didn't really think she … No suspects had been officially named. Wasn't it always the parents?

Her slippered feet shuffled behind him to the stairs. Doug took two steps, then turned and asked Mrs. Summerson if she was OK.

An un-tucked nightshirt hung over her work slacks. She seemed to have aged twenty years. Her typically powder-white face was gray but for the purple stamp of sleeplessness around her eyes, large with gratitude. Her hands trembled and were clasped together as if holding themselves back from seizing him.

"If I can do—um—anything," Doug said, referring to her daughter, whom he knew wouldn't ask for water in the desert from the woman if it necessitated a sincere, heart-to-heart discussion.

Mrs. Summerson pulled him close. She squeezed for an uncomfortably long time. The forty-year-old's breasts ballooned against his meager body. Doug put a hand on her back and eased into the strangeness.

Mr. Summerson wasn't in the living room in front of the TV news. The house was quiet enough to hear the heater tick. Down the hall, only the kitchen was lit. The man wasn't home. That he could be anywhere but with his family bothered Doug. There was some reasonable explanation, surely. And what'd he know about being a husband and losing a child? The more he thought of the man, Doug felt worse about not checking in with E. daily, two or three times, at least. He should've come over sooner, shown up to the wake, even if she hadn't returned his messages. If she hadn't liked it, well, that was fine because E. needed him even if she didn't know what to ask for, even if he wouldn't know what to say. But he hadn't. He'd blown his best chance to prove how much he cared. Maybe there was still time.

Mrs. Summerson shuddered with heartbreak. After a minute, Doug touched her hair to stroke it, as in to comfort her. He must've seen people do that in movies. The woman froze. He'd crossed some invisible line or she had. Either way, she turned her head, as if not clutching him but an oozing troll she couldn't bear the sight of. With a flick of her hand she shooed the boy, unable to look at him while waiting for him to go. Doug was too embarrassed to apologize, and he went upstairs, cursing his awkwardness.

E. said to hurry up and let him in. She relocked the door and, without another word, sat in bed with her legs folded and read with Zen-like focus. After minutes of waiting in the desk chair for her to finish her paragraph and then her page and then her chapter, Doug opened his backpack and rolled the papered gift, weighty and awkward as a bowling ball, crinkling from one hand to the other. He quickly berated himself for bringing a gift, which now seemed grossly insensitive, as if her sister's death were cause for celebration. Frustration and desperation to do one thing right for somebody racked the boy.

"How are things?" he said.

"Mother's been talking at my door all day about counseling," E. said, calmly, reasonably, violence tucked in behind her curls of enunciation. "Clearly, she needs the therapist. Have you seen her? Her face is a mess. She's inconsolable, disturbed. Did she ask you for anything? To 'save my soul'? I don't think she's bathed. Did you smell her? She's as stale as she looks. It didn't rain on you, coming over? Do you want my sister's Xbox?" Her gaze never lifted from the page.

Doug wanted to say more than, "No." He didn't. He set the gift in the trashcan.

That was the last they'd talked about Erika.

2

Doug Horolez was the first to learn why John H. Walker had reappeared at school that spring, half dead and nearly forgotten. On the last Friday of April, the Dead Man pointed him out after social studies among thirty kids who scattered to make class by the bell. Doug's brain flatlined from fear. John waved him over, mouthed, "*You*." At last, it was time to pay for having defied the order of the social universe and inched up his esteem at a dying star's expense. The guy must've somehow traced the nickname back to its source and come to drag him down to the underworld in retribution. What else would John Walker want with someone who couldn't fit in with the band kids? Doug hesitated to join the guy in the pale light that filtered through the tall, clouded windowpane at the end of the hall. Shuffling his feet, mind thawing after a lecture on Manifest Destiny, Doug speculated if he could swing at someone to save his life, a dying guy no less, who he couldn't even see clearly. Doug would've sworn that his glasses had begun to fog after a panicked spike in body temperature and burst of perspiration. Or maybe it was the glare that lent John's figure a misty outline. Not fast enough to run away and no friends to go to anyway, Doug walked into the light.

John patted the kid's shoulder softly as if to say, "It's all right, bud." It was the same stiff-armed reassurance that John's father gave when a teammate had botched a play or threw a game. The dork's mouth hung open beneath his glasses revealing a pair of maroon and wet lips. His gawking persisted as John talked, so that it seemed the kid wasn't receiving a single word of it. He needed to reach Doug now. To utter a single sentence in a manner casual enough to mask his deep fatigue took great effort. John sighed to release his frustration with his own limits and explained again, more slowly this time, that he needed Doug to introduce him to Erika Summerson's older sister.

The chance that the much leaner, but potentially still a powerhouse John Walker might have a crush on E. was ridiculous, Doug told himself. The girl was irregular, a goth-y first-chair clarinet player predisposed to long and determined silences. Not only was she beak-nosed (*in a smartish way*), acned (*not too-too badly*), and decidedly unathletic (*sports were awful, anyway*), but her preference for the company of books over people—and the fact her sister was now famously dead—had forever cast the girl as a social pariah. Not that she minded, which was what Doug admired most about E. She was easily the most fearless person he'd ever met and would never go for a jock who tried so hard to be liked. Yet jealousy made Doug hesitate, second-guess how best to answer the guy. "She wouldn't waste a glance on a guy like you," was what he wanted to say, but he wasn't comfortable pre-judging someone he didn't really know. Also, the remark could come across as defensive and lead John to perceive him as an obstacle to be stepped over, possibly on—not worth the risk. Doug closed his lips to swallow, throat parched though his mouth a pool of saliva. He clutched the back of his neck with one hand, fingers tugging at the fuzzy hairs, like he did during tests or whenever his parents suggested that he try to make more friends at school, as he struggled to find the right words to satisfy the predicament.

"I know Emily doesn't speak to anyone but you since ..." John started. "Hey, it would mean a lot to me, buddy."

Buddy? Though they were the same year in school, the Dead Man hadn't once said hi or seemed interested in his rare though valid contributions in English class or passed him the ball during a stupid gym basketball game, where winning didn't even matter. It was true E. didn't talk about her younger sister and had become more hermit-like, having fallen into a monkish vow of silence with everybody except Doug. Even then, he wouldn't describe E. as chatty. She only talked about big ideas. Recently she'd been reading brain-science stuff, which Doug struggled to follow whenever she explained it, but didn't get too bummed when he couldn't. He just enjoyed hearing her be excited about things. Her ability to be impenetrable matched Doug's one stalwart quality—patience. He figured E.'s silence was her way of coping with the trauma of having a sibling hacked so awfully across the stomach that the girl had been found in roughly two pieces (or so the rumor went). She made it seem, however, as if she weren't speaking simply because she'd been given the best excuse in the world to withdraw from people for good. Doug didn't understand John's request and couldn't imagine any reason why she would talk more openly with the guy. Maybe his was some kind of kooky deathbed wish. Doug found himself unable to say no, at the same time curious and afraid of what he wanted.

"I—I could."

"Today. At the library."

"Ah … OK."

Doug wasn't oblivious to the pathetic dribble of his voice. The starts and stops made others treat him as indecisive or foggy-brained, neither of which he believed was true. If anything, too many thoughts popped into his mind. Most were purely dumb, but some were smart, too. They all rushed in at once and he became uncertain of where to start. The task of communicating a complete idea with all notable threads seemed impossible and created the awkward gaps in his speech. Doug also fought hard to parse what he wanted to say from what he knew he *should* say to avoid causing upsets and arguments, any conflicts at all, really, and the result was the irritating meekness of his voice. For example, how was it that John knew the public library was E.'s after-school hangout? He wanted to ask, but didn't, to avoid seeming accusatory or overly protective.

What he said was, "You be there, too."

Doug blushed at the stupidity of attempting to sound as assertive as this guy he could never hope to compete against. John nodded in acknowledgment, closing both eyes for a moment—*in embarrassment for him?* The guy returned to the land of the living with his poster boy smirk that made most people believe him earnest and good-natured—*to release the tension between them?* The smile looked pretty phony to Doug. This close, he noticed a tightness around John's eyes that said his confidence could crumble in an instant. Yeah, so Dead Man Walker was freakily good at baseball and had assistant-coached the school's Special Olympics team and volunteered at the animal shelter over summer breaks—he could do it all. But he didn't know everything. He didn't know what it was like to be nobody. He never would.

John didn't turn away to the window, like he wanted, while waiting for Doug to leave, despite how taxing it was to present a pleasing mask. Fortunately, the bell rang, signaling the start of next period, and the dork sprinted off, spilling his books after ten feet. Unobserved in the otherwise empty hallway, John relaxed for a few breaths and allowed the pain seething in his bones to surface. It consumed his features and twisted them into a haggard wince. He would need his strength for the more important work ahead. John disappeared down the stairwell before Doug could glance back and see him changed, any less capable of greatness than ever.

3

Before fourteen-year-old John H. Walker became a wonder, he'd been a lean powerhouse of a third baseman with great potential. *Potential* was the word his parents and coaches used most to describe the boy and what'd led him to expect a life more extraordinary than his peers. In only a few short years, the legend grew greater than the boy. So when a shattered femur after a standard dive revealed the malignant tumor thriving above his kneecap and doctors said he'd have to give up baseball for good, John mentally collapsed. For most of that summer and first semester of eighth grade, he lay prone by his family's pool beside a glass of lukewarm lemonade, crushed by the opposite of potential.

•

In November, City Council mistook his withdrawal as solely symptomatic of his worsening sickness and they held a candlelight benefit for childhood cancer in his honor. An intermittent and icy rain plagued Peaks Park that evening, as residents packed around the tented stage or else huddled beneath the skeletal trees, dismal as winter birds. The mayor held his opening speech until well after dark. He let the heartwarming music repeat until its lyrics seemed to mock the sincerity of attending, and a few fights broke out over accusations of encroachment on another's dry space. The mayor watched the clock more than the restless crowd, desperate for their homebred symbol of eminent greatness to materialize like a vision of the Virgin. At some point, he prayed for mercy, then made a speech, the slogan "keep the fire burning" (it was an election year; the job market what it was), and all were asked to light candles during a moment of silence, mostly spent sparking lighters against the wind. Then the school band played jittery renditions of interfaith songs, including a Kwanzaa tune that the many white, working-class folks in the audience were curious to hear when announced, big-hearted in that moment, full of the potential to be more than what they were, which really impressed themselves. The mayor, however, interrupted the band, spotting John's parents as they arrived late and sat among the other speakers. Palos Hills' star had refused to shine on them that night. The mayor asked the Walkers to say a few words of assurance, but there was some confusion with the band, who abruptly resumed "Celebrate Kwanzaa" over his encouragements for them to take the stage, only to be cut short again by the mayor's insults. The rain worsened after that and snuffed the vigil, and residents went home feeling childhood cancer was only the beginning (Of? No one dared ask).

Photos of the event, which John's parents afterward subjected their son to, of familiar faces bound in scarves, huddled together against the winter chill, a candle in every glove, confirmed the boy's suspicion that the town was mostly mourning for itself. He couldn't recall one of those kids entrusting him with confidences, like real friends do, or needing him for anything except to outperform them on the field. In all their bent necks and solemn faces, John saw a lot of hangers-on crowding around the flickering light.

•

Corroborating rumors he had six months to live, John Walker withdrew from school and social engagements entirely. As the Palos Pirates suffered all-time lows in the preseason, messages from his baseball buddies went unanswered urging him to appear at crucial games. His coach's calls rang to voicemail insisting the kid drop by one lousy practice.

John refused to answer. He would not have been himself. At home, while the hall clock struck midnight and the icy rain scrubbed the world clean of all that would not persist, to think of anything but his present condition felt false, pathetic, the return of the fiction of his potential, what'd made him a star by age ten—sought after by opposing coaches, beloved by his teachers, and talked about respectfully by other kids' parents—and, for a few terrific years, what'd imbued John with the charisma responsible for his many friends and fans, for all of his hometown fame—all meaningless. Post-diagnosis, that giant, terminally wounded word—potential—ravaged his mind, clobbered every dream on the horizon, and brought his entire future down with it.

Down he remained, crushed and unresponsive in bed or between the paper-stiff sheets of various hospital beds at Palos Community, Advocate Christ, the Comprehensive Cancer Center at the University of Chicago, and lastly the Cardinal Bernadin Cancer Center at

Loyola. You might not have noticed him, he was so flat, a bump in the covers, plagued by recurring nightmares of dissolving—muscles first, then his bones, made granular, would crumble into his organs and form tiny pools, gray as mercury, until all just evaporated, he did, left not a stain. John awoke terrified. He could barely sit up, he was so badly beaten. His mind raged against the reality that a boy who could dance on the field lay nailed to the earth. Though his anger was superficial compared to the loss of who he'd been, being angry was the one thing left in John's power to do exquisitely. So, in the Get Well Soon messages his mother read, he heard Get Well Now. And when the team and town sounded frustrated that his condition had worsened, as if owed his company to raise their spirits and to make them feel like winners again, John gave them what he was left with—nothing.

•

John's parents tolerated their son's reclusion, believing it best to allow him time to cope with his disillusionment over youth not equating invincibility. This lesson came with age to every child, they rationalized. It'd only come early to John in a grander form, as had most things. He would be as good as ever in a year's time, they assured friends of the family—stopped on the doormat or, if insistent, ushered into a corner of the front room on a firm sofa unused until now, shielded from a view of the inner rooms by two venetian dividers; and never invited into the kitchen to see the cookbooks and pale and gnarled vegetables and vials of powders and musty-smelling drops for several homeopathic remedies; and never ever allowed upstairs where they might peer under the single lamp covered with great-grandmother's shawl and glimpse the pill bottles and wilted bouquets and the unresponsive face of their son. He would enter high school on schedule, better than before, ego tempered after learning what was of most value in life. Though, if asked, neither would've been able to pin down exactly what that meant.

Just as they'd carted John to games and practices and award ceremonies, the Walkers wheeled him to screenings and treatments and specialists. These were joyless, hours-long visits in acrid waiting rooms and doctors' offices and adjoining rooms, clean but for the feeling that someone had left moments before, with doctors who were too jovial to have faced cancer, unless they cured it without fail. Mostly, they talked with well-meaning nurses in what looked like Easter-colored children's pajamas, who translated the jargon and quick handshakes of the doctors as gradual improvement. The Walkers left and arrived again beaming, in deliberation over which private high school to enroll him in next fall and then which universities to apply to, with names so long polished they glowed, that would admit their boy with full-ride scholarships and a difficult though flattering bidding war. They lived in shock during that time, their marriage no great meeting of souls but a highly efficient system of realizing a single, shared goal—to give their only son the world. All they'd worked so hard to build teetered on his health. So they remained affixed with hope to the utter success that all previous signs had confirmed that their progeny was destined to become.

John, however, interpreted the space they provided as willful obliviousness to the gravity of his illness, maybe out of fear of jinxing his recovery, maybe out of neglect. The isolation allowed his head to settle, to cool until cold, until the boy became grateful that his parents had helped him accept what he would henceforth be forever: a nobody, nothing.

•

The boy reappeared at school sporadically after winter break. Teachers didn't seem to care if "Walker, John" produced homework. When he did, they might pause to gleam with pity or admiration, sometimes both, at his efforts. They'd then carry on as if he were invisible, already dead, the specter in the desk an occasional reminder of what'd already come to pass. Soon, those who'd begun to believe John overvalued for being merely a handsome and respectful boy and a fine athlete were quick to criticize that he hadn't entirely ceased to be special, he'd only entered a new phase of specialness—a transparency or, as these peer critics called it, "the ghosting of John Walker." He came as he pleased, filled a desk midday without saying a word, remaining a period or two, or else the wavy image of him spectated from the high bleachers during gym class, only to vanish before the bell. Running into ex-teammates still required an awkward exchange of too-gentle high-fives. Catching him down one of the building's long hallways, a desperate-to-be-noticed girl might occasionally squeal, "Walk this way!" echoing his ballpark anthem, currently in moratorium. In each case, the boy would smirk and decline invitations to meet later at a game with a stock excuse, "doctor's orders," which he did until he hadn't any remaining buddies, then barely any acquaintances, so that, if he were never to show up again, it might be years before any of his classmates recalled an inning he'd saved in a clincher, or that he'd never used others as the butts of his jokes, or the gorgeous contrast between his dark forehead and the corona of his hair in the summertime and ask, "What ever happened to that kid?"

4

Alone but never lonely, E. lived and learned within the maze of shelves at the Palos Hills Public Library. Her self-sufficiency wasn't so much a matter of having so many friends between the covers of the Fiction section. Not anymore—stories were kid stuff. Since puberty, the girl read only nonfiction and had matured as swiftly intellectually as physically. Nature had endowed E. with breasts by age ten, a gift she begrudgingly hid beneath baggy layers to keep her body from defining her. For this and family drama reasons, the local library had become her sanctuary. The stink of aged paper and walls of spines stood against time and the small-mindedness of Palos Hills, the brightest thinkers in human history her compatriots. Here she sought answers about the "grown-up" world that made little sense, such as the contradictions and failures in character and the general ignorance exhibited by most adults (e.g., why her very-much-not-in-love parents, who could live financially secure without each other, were still married; and generally, why people preoccupied themselves with inane distractions, a weakness for comforts and pleasures that became dependencies over time). E. pictured the road to understanding life profoundly as steep and narrow, a nearly impossible climb that required too much study to waste her time obsessing over boys in the brainless manner displayed by so many hetero girls her age—like her dead sister, (once) the world's most darling idiot. They'd gotten along well growing up and had played for hours, House and Doctor and such games, mostly dramatic dialogue about how to survive another brutal winter on the prairie and prevent the loss of the newborn to diphtheria, or about measuring the risks involved in a dangerous though necessary procedure that would leave the family destitute from medical bills alone—until Erika began playing games that involved much less talking with a neighbor boy down the street. The girl was lost to E. since. She tried not to let what'd happened (forever) keep her from reading, from moving upward. When she did think about it, though, E. determined that ignorance and love, or something like it, had killed her sister.

Not that E. didn't have urges that followed the absurd logic of what adults broadly labeled "hormones." She simply packed physical urges into tightly bound boxes in her mind and launched them into deep storage.

For instance, when Dougy sulked up the aisle followed by John "Dead Man" Walker, E. found herself struck by the lunacy of attraction. She denied her eyes the pleasure of lifting from the broad pages of her book, *Fundamentals of Abnormal Psychology*. She couldn't even ask why her friend was exhibiting symptoms of a depressive episode. Hormones compelled her attention past Dougy to tractor-beam on John's tragically beautiful face. It seemed that losing Erika was making her susceptible to sympathetic delusions. To gaze at the boy for more than an instant seemed liable to whip up an infatuation that would threaten the solitary life she had chosen, such was his extraordinary potency. E. plowed onto the next sentence. The next. Finding no relief, she risked another glimpse at the soon-to-be-ghost to understand his sudden supernatural grip on her better sense.

John was different than she remembered—Mr. School Spirit who, during those trivial end-of-the-year award ceremonies, received so many medals around his neck that he left looking like a gangster rapper. The version standing before her included the same strong jaw and boyish handsomeness. There was something new, too, a quality of weariness in his manner that E. interpreted as experience, perhaps even wisdom of the kind she sought. Its gravity sickened her. She focused on his negative qualities: the boy was cute, athletic, indistinguishably kind—otherwise generically all-American. She knew plenty of fictional characters that were more real than the sum of traits exemplified by John H. Walker. E. mostly despised what he represented in the community: a false sense of unity that rested on intrinsically worthless human abilities (hitting and catching a ball—to what benefit to the human race?). But no matter what E. told herself, desire pestered her to learn how facing death had contributed to his maturity. Was it superficial or authentic? What E. did know was that to depend on anybody for anything was foolish, and the only defense she had against that at the moment was holding the hardback book in front of her face.

"E. ... it's me—obviously," Dougy began in his cautious and lurching manner she'd found endearing, until now. Beside John—behind, really—a specimen of maleness with whom she shared no history or common interests, Dougy appeared a stunted and mostly defective member of his sex. E. adored her friend's quirks and valued his companionship, though her mere association with him now stung as a reflection of herself, of her rank or quality of femaleness, values she didn't know she had, shallow, repulsive, and undeniable. The intensity of E.'s embarrassment made her so disappointed in her psychological development that she tipped the spine of her book in his direction and said, "Dougy!" overcompensating with cheer.

"Um ... OK," Doug said, startled by E.'s warmth. He reached for his neck for the second time today to cope with his anxiety. He willed a stop to the defensive gesture and smiled to say he appreciated the change. Too slow—the college textbook again shielded her eyes. "Well, this is John. The—he's the kid ... who—"

John stepped forward. "Emily, you know things that could help a lot of people."

An appeal to her perceptiveness? The girl's pulse sped. She leaned in, feigning an even deeper interest in the page she'd flipped to, as if she hardly cared that the revised John Walker had a genuine interest in anything she'd discovered during her fourteen long years of studying human behavior. The open chapter was titled "Disorders of Sex and Gender," and E. blushed, whizzing through paragraphs about sexual dysfunction before the boy. She took comfort in knowing that, even if he could see over the book, he likely wouldn't notice her face redden, her cheeks so awash in acne that her otherwise pale skin sometimes matched her ginger hair. No—if she thought any more about her appearance and how the boy perceived her, her emotions would childishly dive into shame. Over what? John Walker wasn't special in the deep sense of the word.

His explanation for the visit iced her excitement. The Dead Man had come to discuss her actually dead little sister: "Who was Erika hanging out with the week of the incident?" "Who were her closest friends and enemies?"—questions like those the police had drilled E. over countless times. The answers were common knowledge at Palos Hills Junior High, Erika would've been proud to know. As if popularity were synonymous with respect, the girl had worked hard to become the most notorious socialite before the end of her first year. She'd snuck out of the house, showing skin like a high schooler despite her underdeveloped body, and had hung out with an older, eighth-grade crowd. She'd had an alcohol tolerance and several overlapping boyfriends, all action-packed into those first four months. E. was left to deal with the fallout. Instead of kids reaching out over Erika's passing, E. was harassed. Kids left notes in her locker, reading, "She was asking for it," "God does exist," and "Ding dong the whore is dead." The band kids had even ostracized her, all of whom she couldn't care less about. She didn't need condolences. What bothered her was the blame in their eyes, as if they believed she could've prevented the murder, or worse, that she had something to do with it. The notes had escalated to "Kill yourself next, Sataness!" by February, after two months of police work hadn't turned up conclusive evidence against a single suspect. She told herself that the accusatory looks and notes were partly inspired by the rumors of devil worship in the woods where Erika had been found, of which E. had long been an easy target because, quite simply, she wore a lot of black.

But most of their suspicion likely had to do with her inability to express much emotion over losing her sister. E. hadn't cried at the service or the burial. The spectacle attracted over a hundred people whose behavior upset E. more than anything, snapping photos around the funeral home and demanding more coffee and cookies from the staff when none of those kids could've said they'd loved Erika.

E. even struggled to say it. The girls had grown into antagonists, forever irreconcilable. When she thought of her sister allowing herself to be dumbly taken advantage of by older boys, or when she pictured the woman Erika might've become, then E. felt something. She wanted to hurt someone, waste them as her sister had been wasted. But she didn't feel the amazing emptiness she believed she should. Maybe there was something wrong with her. As with all mysteries, she'd turned to books for an answer. Until then, E. had nothing more to give to the living or the dead—or this boy in between, who couldn't possibly care for Erika any more than his fans.

"*Please—*" John said. No more than the girl's ginger dome and eyebrows were visible from behind the book. By her silence, he sensed her interest phasing into complete absorption of her reading, blocking him out, a stranger, unwelcome. Eager to be the first on the crime scene since the police had reopened the woods to the public this morning, and desperate for the lead he needed, John admitted, "I owe it to your sister to learn who did it."

The girl had visited him during his most difficult time in the hospital, he said. Just once, during his first and worst round of treatments. Every drop of the chemo blew fire into his veins until his fine muscle had evaporated down to the sinews. During that period, no visitors were allowed up to his room except family. But, one night, his nurse chased off a group of baseball buddies that'd come to celebrate their first win without him, and Erika, who was with them, had slipped by, determined to woo the guy she'd heard so much about, if not to leave dating the most popular boy in school, then maybe to brag about having made out on his deathbed. When John's clouded eyes opened, a girl was smiling, cross-legged at his feet. With some effort, he lifted his head and smiled back. No—she was crying, cheeks glossy from the light overhead. John's skeletal smile confirmed that his looks, strength, and vitality were completely spent, what'd made him adored was gone. The fight to restrain her emotions tensed Erika's face into a grimace. John hadn't feared death until that moment, witnessing the girl's revulsion to himself. She apologized: "I'm so sorry." John heard her grieving over the frailty of her own mortality after glimpsing what she too would become one day. Anger and hot breath swelled inside him, enough to spew a curse on her and the entire town. Sitting up loosened a pain in his chest, however, and he was forced to lie back, ego deflated. Erika's gaze hadn't dropped from his face, and her hand hesitated to touch his leg, which looked slim as a stick under the bed sheet. She reached out and squeezed his hand. "If it could be me," she said, "I would do that for you." The girl was no longer crying. Her eyes were blotched with mascara in a clownish way that accentuated how very serious she was. Not John's mother and father, nor any of his family or friends had expressed anything so selfless. So, when he'd heard Erika had been killed, honoring her by solving her murder was all he could think of. It'd gotten him to stop feeling sorry for himself and out of bed to do something about it.

The boy had his head bowed before her. He'd spoken in short, simple sentences charged with emotion, which E. parsed for meaning. "Love" was the word that invaded her mind regarding the interchange between the Dead Man and her sister. It sounded as if they'd barely spent ten minutes together. If their special moment had dragged on for an hour or dipped into conversation before the nurse had returned and thrown Erika out, surely the boy would've realized that her sister wasn't a saint, and he wouldn't be here now. He must've heard about her first-semester exploits. Yet here he was, which proved John was as nonsensical as everybody else. Though not exceptional in judgment, the story did prove to E. that at least one of the boy's legendary attributes was true—he cared about more than himself.

What a story. Doug bounced his shoulders in a defeated manner behind John, as if to say, "Well, how in the hell am I supposed to compete with that?" If not for E.'s cheery hello, Doug might've pulled a shelf of books on himself to end his misery. For the first time in his life, he experienced a true pang of jealousy, not the common kind of another's charms and talents and accomplishments that he experienced daily and had grown numb to, but an unmistakable, personal kind of jealousy that deranged his thinking about his relationship with E. In the years he'd known her, Doug had never pushed for more than friendship. Neither of them had dated anyone, yet, and he'd been grateful for what intimacy they had. Dating wasn't E.'s thing. She put the development of her mind first—another of her traits he respected. How many people can say that? She made him want to be a better person and to play video games less to make time for books that she recommended, despite that he never finished them. He knew he would enjoy taking things further, though he didn't want to jeopardize their friendship. He didn't want to lose the only girl who'd ever paid him attention. Sometimes she would laugh at the bungling things he did or said, but that was OK because Doug liked to see her happy, which was a rare thing, he'd learned. Most importantly, she always came back. She called him to her place, up to her room, to be around him no matter what he did. That time together was rare, precious, too. Sure, E. could be cold, lost in her brainwork over big ideas, things that Doug sometimes couldn't begin to understand, and sometimes she used her disinterest to keep people at bay that she didn't respect, which was what he hoped she was doing with Dead Man Walker. "You had your chance, *buddy*, move along," he wanted to say. But Doug wasn't one hundred percent positive that was what she wanted, and jealousy made him afraid of messing up with John around. Instead, he reseated his glasses on his nose and waited for someone else to break the silence.

"Did Erika go to the woods on certain days of the week or month? Was it always at night? Any little thing—"

"I can't help you," E. said. The boy was making her uncomfortable in so many ways. She wanted him out of her mental space where no visitors were allowed—not her mother, though the woman often tried; not even Dougy, though he was good company. Yes, it was a defense mechanism to prevent others a glimpse of the general disorder of society that was reflected in her personality—the frivolity, the shortcomings, the contradictions, the flaws and resulting failures—issues that E. could handle alone. No one had posed even a mild threat of drawing out her mess into the world. What would happen if her defenses lowered and the charismatic Dead Man lay siege to her mind with his pained eyes and his goodness? He might even love her as easily as he'd loved her sister.

John couldn't understand the girl's indifference to his story and total self-absorption. She didn't care about finding her sister's murderer. In her position, he would do anything to aid an investigation, public or private. The loss wasn't real for her yet, he thought, at once conscious of his numbered days and bodily limits. John came forward and stood over her, then—to reach her, make the face of death real enough. The girl's forehead and the tops of her otherwise pale cheeks were reddened, as if with too much sun. Beneath, he saw a halting resemblance to Erika. E. wasn't as kidlike. Her distinguished nose and calculating eyes spoke of an adult intelligence years beyond him. His heroics seemed childish then, and John's advance yielded the opposite response he'd hoped for. E. reared the hardback as if she might hit him if he got any closer. Doug shuffled behind him, and John felt like what he was—an outsider between two friends, maybe more, whose lives he'd charged into. The self-consciousness of his illness began to spiral out of control and make him feel ghoulish, a persistent nightmare. He abruptly apologized and turned to leave.

E. saw the passion in his face drain. Complete emotional vacuity—all traces of life erased, exposing the corpse, the remains, as what was left of her sister had been called. She remembered the inert and waxen likeness of the girl's face framed by the half-closed casket and the way it—no longer she, but it—contrasted against the living hair, so golden, fanned out on white satin. Maybe we are objects, and life is the trick? she thought, seeing John go.

Corpse—grave—dirt....

That was how E. recalled the detail: her sister's manicured nails caked with dirt. The week before she'd died, Erika had taken a scrubber to her hands. E. had thought she was brushing her teeth and commented about taking off the enamel. On a few of those mornings, E. had washed silt from the basin of their shared bathroom sink. The observation couldn't mean much.

"Her fingernails were dirty," E. said. "On more than just one night."

E. didn't want to start caring about the boy and what he did or did not feel. The information was a small gift to make his transformation into it-ness easier. Her big mouth stopped the boy at the end of the aisle, who half turned to ask more from her.

"Brilliant." He was smirking. Benevolent again, he dumped gratitude on her. "Thank you, Emily—E. This is important."

"I—well, the dirt … maybe. But it's woods—really dirty," Doug stammered.

"Sure, buddy. On the bottom of your shoes. Unless—"

"She was digging," E. said. Suddenly her book felt very heavy. She set it down reluctantly.

"Right." John nodded with determination now.

So full of purpose so close to the grave, the boy was trying to make his last days mean something, E. saw. Maybe something of value could be learned from observing him, though not too closely.

"It could be something," he said. "It could be nothing. But we won't know until it's looked into, and I don't have the strength to do this alone."

John faced E. fully. Caught between them, Doug backed into a bookshelf, compelled to clear the aisle as if by the force of understanding that seemed to unite this stranger to his friend to the exclusion of himself. The thought of losing that bond to someone else—not just anyone, but John Walker, Palos's favorite damned-to-be dead kid—made his mouth spasm a series of panicky phrases, the sum of which made it known that, if E. decided to help for her sister's sake, she wouldn't have to do it without him.

"Help? Of course. Why wouldn't I? I might know a guy at school who we could—"

"Great," John cut him short, "but let's keep it between us for now."

"E.?" the Dead Man asked, proving to Doug how little he understood the girl, that he never would. Her choice was obvious: E. had closed her book.

5

The kids went to the woods while the sun was still up. At night, it was said, devil worshippers crept from behind trees, stalked in shadow to nab child sacrifices for their blood rites. If too old or un-virginal, they'd only chop off your big toe with a rusted knife. Nobody could walk with his big toe missing, know-it-all Ronny Mickle once had told Doug when they should've been studying for the Constitution test. Whenever he thought about the woods now, Doug couldn't get the image out of his mind: gleeful maniacs watching him crawl through the trees homeward, bleeding out to inevitably die in a fit of hopeless frustration. Maybe Ronny had made up the demented story after hearing how the police had found some kid's lost dog in a pit along one of the trails; dead, of course, three of its feet lopped off. Maybe that story, too, had been invented by another tall-tale teller or a parent to scare their kid from wandering into the woods at night. Either way, there was no getting around the case of Erika Summerson.

Tales of nighttime evils were told about the woods long before Erika's body had been found at Bachelor's Grove divided in two. Not that John or E. believed in these fantasies. John needed daylight to aid his search for clues, and E. was only glad not to have to stand close beside the boy in the dark. Doug, however, didn't not believe in devil worshippers and blood rites, and he was grateful to see the afternoon sun high above the woods at the end of the block of homes they walked. Even if the rumored hooded marauders weren't magical beings, but older kids playing dress-up and performing make-believe rituals past curfew, if his fourteen years' experience as an underdog had taught him anything, it was that ordinary people were capable of extraordinary wickedness.

The trail entrance at Oketo Street was still blocked with a long PHPD barricade. Alone, not one would have gone inside, their fear was so great. Doug feared crossing paths with a devil or lesser demon that would prove true his worst nightmares to date, the existence of uncompromising evil, which knowingly made him childish and further inferior to John. E. feared crossing a trace of her sister's murder. John feared finding nothing at all.

Wordlessly, together, they scaled the barricade. The kids scurried into the trail mouth to avoid notice by a passing car or kid from the neighborhood who might misunderstand their intention and phone 9-1-1. The police had announced an end to their regular surveillance of the woods this morning, proclaiming the trails safe for "adult-supervised activity"—John's green light for approaching her, E. assumed. The public backlash to their yet fruitless investigation would doubtless redouble. Since January, outraged members of the community, E.'s parents included, had petitioned to have the area bulldozed to protect the children of Palos Hills. They were going to build condos or something much less interesting.

The day was cool yet lovely while the sun was up. The sky was cloudless but for two scrawls, one in the shape of a hook and the other like three snowy peaks of an otherwise invisible mountain range. The breeze gave the kids goose bumps and gently stirred the leafing treetops. Shadows danced in slow motion along the path, as if in welcome. They hiked over a mile out to the ridge of the wooded moraine, carved out fifteen thousand years ago by glaciers during the last ice age. Sometimes a clearing in the trees would reveal sections of town from strange angles that made their home only vaguely familiar, a midwestern town, sure, but not their own.

The kids walked in a line. Doug kept close to E. in case an animal or devil worshipper sprung from the tree line. Not that E. needed protecting or that he would have the ability or courage to do anything but screech. But if something did happen and he wasn't there, John would be, and Doug's anxiety over losing her that way was presently greater than the loss of his own life, enough to get him to walk into this cursed place, likely the first people to enter since it'd reopened.

Doug had been in the woods once before. Not really in, he'd hid from kids in the weedy ditch along 115th. This was during a game of hide-and-seek, years ago, back in the fifth grade when being an odd duck could be overlooked for the sake of evenly numbered teams. The woods might've been out of bounds, but the boy didn't want to get caught again. As he'd stretched to lie flat, something crinkled behind his ear—a tightly folded note with a pull tab. Curious, he opened and smoothed the note. Doug held a pencil drawing of the Devil. The drawing was ornate, geometric: an inverted triangle head, larger triangle body. He couldn't redo the fold. Doug tossed the note. It returned on the wind and flapped against his neck. When he awoke, the street was empty of taggers. The drawing in his hands had protected him, he thought, impossible and terrifying if it was. He kept it in his back pocket, though he knew he shouldn't. For a week, whenever alone, he peeked to decipher the weird markings on the arms and chest. Never for long—he feared losing his soul. Then his mom washed his jeans. Doug was even more afraid that she would find it. The note was still in the pocket. It unfolded blank, and he was so relieved. Thinking of it now, Doug couldn't believe he'd ever taken such a risk. Maybe his boldness had washed out that day, too, as if with magic ink.

As they trekked deeper, the woods became denser. The trail narrowed. Doug gazed homeward, to a train bridge also visible from his bedroom window. What direction was his house? Which way would he run if they were separated? He couldn't say. An acute disorientation set in, as the immensity of the maze of trails gulped his reserves of comfort.

Then he walked into E.

She'd stopped at John's signal, and she and Doug smashed and tumbled to the ground. They landed entwined, face-to-face in the middle of the trail.

It wasn't the fall, but the feel of her beneath him that bewildered Doug. They'd never been so close. He experienced the intimate lines of E.'s chest and hips through the swath of black cloth, and the fragile weight of each part, at once with maximum body contact. Her jolts and squirms combined with all he knew of E. to allow him to glimpse—or to believe he was glimpsing—her essence, the miracle of her, wonderfully alive. Doug felt wonderful, too, then. How many times had he dreamed of them touching like this and told himself to forget it, that being her friend was good enough. It wasn't even close

43

to this feeling. Doug wanted to be her boyfriend—an undeniable and visceral fact whose comprehension took a moment before he could wonder if she were thinking the same. He looked into her eyes for an answer. She winced, forehead wrinkling, theirs having dashed on the way down.

"E.—I really—"

"You're really all over me."

The pressure she exerted, faintly pushing his chest to get him up, expressed little more than her physical discomfort, though Doug was launched aside by the force of his conscience and hope to never displease her. Kneeling, he helped E. to her feet. Above him, she brushed herself off and thanked Doug with a glance, not the monumental exchange of unspoken, though palpable desire he wanted her to feel.

John stood before an offshoot of the trail that dipped between two trees. Their tops were arched to form a sort of shaded gateway down into the moraine and to Bachelor's Grove. John had sipped beers a few times at friends' houses to see what the big deal was, though he'd never partied in the woods. Before Erika, some guys on the team came regularly and had invited him out. They were the kids who played for the perks of baseball. John was committed to the game itself, and though his refusals had made him appear not yet grown up, a trip to Bachelor's Grove represented the ultimate junior high transgression. Its initiation seemed to require a change in priorities that John hadn't been comfortable making. He wasn't sure how much his choice owed to wanting to preserve his reputation as "one of the good guys" and how much owed to fear of the other, wilder side of sports which relieved guys of the unyielding control needed to perform at one's natural best, as if he might lose it or some other important but inexpressible thing down that path, the one beneath his feet, forever.

E. touched one of the trees, traced the artful curve of the branches. They looked dead. They weren't budding, and a few of last year's leaves clung to the bark. Dark and crumpled, they didn't tremble in the wind. She hadn't peered ahead, yet, down inside the grim archway. She kept trained on her immediate surroundings—the knots in the smooth bark, the slowly dying breeze, the dank odor of drying mud. The physicality of the woods staved her anxiety, minus history, minus Erika. Many times E. had pictured the murder scene. She didn't want to. She hated to think of it—a losing struggle in the dark, futile screams against the intention of the knife—*Who did Erika cry out to before …?* She shoved the torturous thought from her mind. E. didn't know how she would react once they reached the spot—an uncomfortable notion, and more so in front of these boys.

"This leads to the Grove." John hung his head to show respect to Erika, whether the gesture meant anything to E. or not.

"Yeah … Sad. I—" Doug stopped short, didn't attempt to match John's showy sympathy. Frankly, Doug didn't understand the first thing about being dead, being almost dead, or being somebody with a dead person in the family. Not much had happened in his life, which really wasn't his fault. Doug's dad had lost his computer programmer job last year, and both parents sat their son down and swore to him that nothing would change right away other than his mom being gone more for work. Both pairs of his grandparents were still alive, including one grandfather who always roughed his hair and pinched his thighs and said, "Ham bone! Ham bone!" which made his family laugh. Then he wanted them to be dead. Not really. Maybe. He wasn't sure. For Doug, death was as true as a rumor. He'd seen enough horror movies to know being killed was an excruciating event to be avoided, which characterized his relationship to it—abstract, yet observing. That was fine except again he felt excluded from some big secret shared by E. and the Dead Man.

John searched their faces as he would fresh recruits at summer training for signs of physical and mental exhaustion. They looked nervous, but able to push much further.

"Ready?" he said to rally them.

"Isn't there supposed to be an old graveyard down there?" Doug asked.

"The Devil in the Woods," John said.

"Ronny Mickle said hooded figures—"

"He says those things to scare you, Dougy," E. said, and John laughed.

Doug charged through the archway.

"Yeah—well, come on." He waved them forward. He didn't want to fight over E.'s attention, but it seemed the Dead Man wouldn't mosey along to the astral plane until this tribute to Erika was paid or the guy keeled over in the process.

"Go, Dougy," E. said, a nervous lilt in her voice.

She didn't smile at him, though. She looked shyly at the Dead Man, who smirked in return.

Doug told himself to be strong and, not really knowing where he was going, led them down a steep and staggered path overrun with raised roots. At times, the path was barely visible. The drop took several sharp turns through the trees as it wound into a shaded ravine. They were plummeting to the very bottom. The thought terrified Doug. The forest's belly was far from everything he'd known, no matter how miserable.

Abruptly, the path leveled. They followed the narrow ravine toward the valley. From the end, the kids looked out onto Bachelor's Grove.

The overhead canopy glowed dimly. The valley floor was shaggy with clover and fern. A running creek bisected the Grove. Past that, a gigantic and ancient-looking tree grew aslant from the base of the opposite wall. Without a word between them, the kids headed to the unusual tree.

The area appeared to be pristine woodlands, until they came upon several planks—a crude bridge, which they used to cross the creek. More signs of civilization appeared. To the right, an area of young trees was roped off with dirt-speckled police tape. E. went to them, leaving the boys, and allowed the sagging lines to stop her short. Inside, crudely hacked stumps crowded around a fire pit. Dead saplings wilted over the circle of stones, their tops crisp as marshmallow-roasting sticks upturned in the mud. Garbage littered the ground—pop bottles, chip bags, and objects indistinguishably charred. Partial shoe imprints, mostly gym shoes, were stamped around the stumps. The mess told of just how many kids Bachelor's Grove had lured before the murder.

E. caught herself searching the shoe prints for her sister's pink flats. E. wouldn't put it past Erika to have worn the flats in the woods in December. They'd complemented her every outfit for two months. She'd gotten the shoes on E.'s birthday. The girl had made their mother drive her and her BFF to the mall to buy Erika a present to feel better about watching E. open gifts later. A selfish-bitch move, in E.'s opinion. Except now, the act was clearly a cry for help. Though popular, Erika hadn't felt loved. The thought of spotting one of those pink plastic-y shoes, sticking up in the mud, threatened to shatter E.'s composure and make her cherish the thing forever. Nothing was to be learned from that sort of behavior, E. reprimanded. She turned her back on the debris. Behaving like her mother would only open herself up to needless pain and a lot of blubbering.

John came and stood beside her then and gazed with his world-weary and goddamn beautiful eyes at the scene of the crime. He didn't press her to talk about it, and E. was glad for that. Dougy came over, too, and stood on her other side. Good old Dougy, her closest friend ever. If that boy had a clue about what she was feeling, just one, so that she wouldn't have to say any of it to him, E. would sink into him for support, her body urging her to avoid the handsome ghost and this haunting world. E. took short, incremental breaths to restrain these and other pathetic notions flooding her brain, such as how stupid she was for having let these boys get even this close to the empty grave of her heart and how good it felt to have two people beside her that cared enough to be here with her now.

Doug had noticed E.'s body stiffen, and so he'd gone to her side in front of the creepy, roped-off murder scene. Despite that the woods around them teemed with wildlife, ghost girls and boys, and knife-wielding murderers, Doug's only concern at that moment was for E.'s well-being. She'd become so still and quiet that, this close to her, E. seemed to radiate cold. Her withdrawal was unlike when they read at the library, shunning the world for a few hours of respite. Here E. seemed to be imploding emotionally and renouncing life in the process. This was his second chance, he realized, to show how he felt for her in a way his intentions couldn't be misunderstood. Doug adjusted his glasses and contemplated taking her hand.

E. expected John to stalk inside and begin sleuthing where it'd happened, playing young Sherlock Holmes. The boy turned from the site and walked away. E. watched him retreat toward the Big Tree, and his absence allowed the weakened doors of her heart to close and lock again, pleasantly tight. Her sister was dead. Like John soon would be. Like she and even Dougy and the person or persons who'd murdered her sister would be one day. And everybody else, too. Those were the known facts. Case closed.

Something touched her hand—

Had he waited too long gathering the courage to grope past the boundaries of their friendship? Watching her gaze over her shoulder at the Dead Man, Doug thought, I'm what you need. Then he went all in. He clumsily missed, brushed her pinky knuckle with his fingertips. He'd meant to take her hand, as in to hold it to comfort her. He had no intention of intertwining her fingers with his. That would be taking things too far too fast, unless that was something she wanted. He would give her that and anything else she needed to be happy again, and to hear that she needed him as much.

E. spun and pushed him down hard. Doug grasped for the loose tape, and fell on his ass in the mud.

"What're you doing?" she demanded.

"You looked … I thought—and I wanted to—"

"Dougy, no."

"Do you … feel …? Because—"

"I don't feel anything, OK?" Her tone softened, seeing her friend beneath her and filthy. He didn't move. She thought he might cry. He was only trying to be there for her. But she couldn't help him up, couldn't touch his hand, yet. "Just let me be … me."

"I do," Doug said with defeat. His glasses had been thrown someplace, and he was glad that E.'s face was a red blur. He didn't want to see how badly he'd blown it.

"You do," she said lukewarmly. "That's why I appreciate you."

Her appreciation stung worse than the fall. The opportunity to express his feelings had passed. Yet Doug continued to try, speaking limply, losing at every word: "But maybe—maybe you'd like—with me—to be—"

"Dougy, I know. You want to help," she said, eager to leave the grossly sentimental moment behind. "I'm fine. OK?"

E. found and handed him his glasses. Before he could put them on, she called to John to wait up, something she never imagined doing in a million years. Wasn't the boy supposed to be "honoring Erika's memory" by investigating her murder like the well-meaning do-gooder he supposedly was? Just like that, she'd sealed away the exchange with Dougy to be forgotten.

Even through smudged lenses, E.'s weirded-out-ness was plain. She strode eagerly to John Walker, which made Doug want to throw himself down on purpose this time as a sacrifice to the Devil in the Woods. The only reason he'd tried so hard to connect—reconnect?—with E. was because of the Dead Man's interference. Doug had moved too quickly and now looked like a huge idiot—twice. His backside was covered in mud as if he'd shit himself with such force that it'd blown through his pants. Doug scraped at his rear with a long stick, squeegeeing and then flinging the loosened mud off the end, as if engaged in some primitive method of ass wiping. Never mind that he'd failed at the boldest thing he'd attempted in his life. E. hadn't outright rejected him, only the idea of being touched by him tenderly. His vision went blurry. This time it was tears of self-pity. Don't do that, he told himself. His pitifulness made him number two—two trillion. No, number one was her books and learning. That wouldn't change, that was E. And Doug was her closest friend, her number two. Not in the way he wanted, but a high number, still—really as good as one, considering E. was adamant in dealing with her feelings alone. There was no reason for that to change so long as he gave up trying to beat the Dead Man at his game. No one was better than Doug at his own—the long game. Good, he thought. Today he was the loser he'd always been, making fumbles that he and E. would laugh about one day, and John H. Walker was the adored star he'd always been, their fates as unalterable as Doug and E.'s bond, who they would be long after the guy died and left E. to Doug. Maybe then, when her sister and John were past, she'd choose a new life. Doug tightly retied the line of police tape that'd snapped during his fall, eager to leave this awful place and lurch on.

John stood beneath the Big Tree. It had an enormous base and was easily the largest they'd ever seen. Only hand in hand might the kids have been able to wrap their arms around its trunk. The tree grew so close against a sheer face of the moraine that it projected from the rock on a slant and a few hearty branches reached over their heads. The bark was ashen with exaggerated black ravines, as if carved instead of grown. There was altogether something satanic about it, Doug thought.

John wasn't actually looking at the tree towering above them, but at a meter-deep hole beside a mound of dirt, ten or fifteen paces in front of it.

"That's not where they found her," he said.

He glanced aside at Doug, who hadn't even asked—some kind of show-off-y alpha move. The guy squatted at the edge of the hole. Doug wanted to kick him in.

"Yeah … obviously. She wouldn't fit. I mean, not unless—"

"This dig could be four months old."

"The murder weapon could be buried here," E. suggested.

"Half-buried?" John scooped soil from the mound and dusted his hands over the hole.

Doug hated to see her play detective with the Dead Man. E. had responded with her usual malaise, probably wishing John would shut up already to have another hour at the library before dinner. Still, she was playing, which wasn't like her, especially since losing Erika. Doug was beginning to believe that the guy really did have mind control powers. Their being out here was proof enough. Luckily, he was probably so used to others joining the cult of himself that he didn't notice that a girl too deep and fearless and real, too out of his league, was bothering to pay him attention.

"Well, let's—I'm not scared." With his mud-smeared stick, Doug prodded inside the hole.

E. grabbed his arm. "Dougy, I don't want to see it."

"They weren't burying anything." John stood and scanned the area around the tree. He pointed out several other mounds, as old looking, thirty or so feet apart. "I think they were digging for something."

"They?" Doug said. "The police?"

"No," was all John answered. He looked to E. to comment.

"Digging for what? Gold? China?" she said skeptically. John had possessed plenty of physical power before his sickness, sure. But in E.'s world, people weren't blessed with brains and brawn—most weren't given either—and she was glad for the studiousness bestowed on her. The boy sounded so confident, though. Not cocky, more like he'd been thinking hard about the murder for a long time.

John hesitated before doing what he did next. He would need the help of a team to continue The Work and, without E., Doug was as good as gone, too. He clawed up a handful of dirt and showed his soiled fingernails.

"Whatever it was," he said, "Erika knew."

Darkness rimmed John's eyes. The boy appeared undead with his withered-corpse hand and fingernails bared as if come to drag them into his grave.

Doug stepped between him and E.

"We don't care about what some killers wanted," Doug said, consciously speaking for E. He was glad when she didn't object.

"Whatever it was—whatever's here, Erika cared a lot about it," John reasoned. "You said you'd help me. Help me find what she was looking for. Not for me, but for her."

"You said it could be nothing." E. drew away from the hole, suddenly faint and unwilling to ask for a hand. She leaned against the rugged trunk of the Big Tree for support against a tide of rising guilt. Glimpses of her sister invaded her mind: the girl in her underwear on all fours in the night, clawing ravenously into the earth for … what? E. responded slowly, through the haze of the vision. "You want us to dig in the woods? That's crazy. Erika—she wouldn't do that. She was crazy, but like normal crazy. I would've noticed. I'm not the worst sister ever."

John shook his head. "It must've been a secret she kept from everyone. Of course you'd have helped. She was your sister. But you couldn't, and now you have a chance to do something about it. You said her hands were dirty for about a week, right? Help me for a week. We'll start Monday after school. After we've found it, you can leave this place, having done her proud."

"If we find it," Doug said.

John didn't acknowledge him. The guy had his eyes closed, as if listening intently to the forest canopy, which had begun to rustle high above.

"A week. Then you're on your own," E. said from the deepening shade of the tree. Sunlight flooded the valley. She turned her head.

"The Work begins," the Dead Man said. He smiled, luminous in a misty beam. To Doug, he appeared translucent, actually supernatural.

That was the first time Doug truly feared him. The boy grinned as if he'd willed the Grove to glow. Doug wondered what John Walker was capable of, or believed himself to be.

Doug looked to E. to share his terrible unease. Against the glare and through the dark, however, his friend was so very hard to see.

6

*A*lthough on a high ridge that overlooked the badlands of Jakar'tep, and the dust of the Rymer Road lay unbeaten by horse hooves below, and the sculpted hills cut back to the wound-pink rock unpeopled, and the desert over his armored shoulder retreated into pixel gusts that closed on the horizon like a sleepy lid over the mean and bloody eye of the sun, Dorion knew no peace.

The southern pass to Galador was quick, but risky. Death struck wild past its rolling plains and the capital's spires, where Emamor, his love, suffered under a wasting curse. He'd recovered the bones of a Harradorian saint, lead-heavy and lost in a caravan sieged by the Lupine Raiders. Dorion had barely survived the fight. He was no tactician or master swordsman. He wasn't quick or clever. He stuck out a challenge. He cared. But would it be enough to save her?

His bay horse shifted and whinnied, so close to the edge. Dorion dismissed the mount and began an angled descent of the ridge face, deliberate in his footing, to the valley floor....

Doug tried not to recall his descent into the woods, what they'd done, what he'd agreed to do next week.

He caught his breath halfway down the slope and peered over a sheer face into a nest of scorpions, small as fire ants from this height. Vertigo pitched his balance—Dorion stumbled back—his burlap mantle caught the wind and billowed. Until then, it had kept his breastplate from glinting across the many miles of desert. If he crossed a battle-hardened warrior, with no place to run, fatigued as he was, chances were that he'd end this quest in the belly of the fat vulture that sunned on a boulder not far off.…

Doug was a clumsy gamer, over-reactive to the adrenaline of combat. He spasmed, popped random actions—once, he blew a lively lute while repeatedly skewered until blood sputtered forth in lieu of music—or else he covered his eyes IRL and waited to be dead. Sometimes, he didn't want to run away anymore. He wanted to slay others' players, counter their flashiest moves and bring them to their knees, begging *p-p-p-p-please*, before he split into their juicy brains—or not—just to be great at something, or better than most. Doug would settle for as good in a make-believe world that didn't matter but to a few thousand other dorks across the globe. But he never won duels. Not one. Hacked to pieces, he gawked up at his opponents, who glistened with his blood, large with victory before the game blacked out and reset. He wasn't one of these guys, didn't belong here, Doug told himself, regretting that he'd ever wanted to be anything at all.

The breeze seeped in—sand flew from the steel joints around his knees and the grooved plates over his shoulders—it cooled him, body and spirit. Dorion wasn't home, yet. He stood and—

"With two growing boys?" his mother retorted in the kitchen. Bottles clinked—his father pulled a cold one from the fridge. The man stammered a reply that Doug didn't care to hear.

Doug rubbed his eyes, itchy from hours of vigilant questing. Why stop? E. hadn't messaged back. His parents hadn't settled whether to sell the house. The thought made his heart sink. They would live someplace, he would still have a home, a family, right? He disliked how unwelcome these discussions made the house, enough that Doug couldn't go in to grab a snack or speak to them for the rest of the night. Dad still hadn't found a job, his mother worked two, and they fought more about most things. They didn't ever really fight. They insisted on points the other hadn't considered until one locked themselves in their bedroom to wonder why they even tried.

Doug turned up the volume—*The hollow wind in his ears, the bored squawks of the vulture....*

Odd—the bird didn't flap away as Dorion passed. Its beak clicked the stone. It peered over the edge of a hundred-foot fissure in the rock. Had the bird dropped its dinner? Dorion shimmied alongside the boulder down to the split's base. He would fish the morsel out, however slight, low on life and, he hoped, more clever than the bird.

The gap was too narrow to squeeze more than an arm inside. Maybe with his sword—

About ten feet in, the darkness stirred. Someone was in there—a long-haired warrior in ragged leather, stiffly upright, arms pinned at her/his sides. Head turned, the lodged character stared at him blankly—

HELP, the player typed.

How s/he'd survived the fall, Doug couldn't guess. S/he hopped a few inches off the ground, but otherwise couldn't budge. Maybe a klutz like himself. After several in-game hours, the character would starve.

Dorion—Doug typed back, How?

HELP ME.

The player hopped again, crunched gravel, otherwise silent. S/he didn't have a mic. Doug tossed his remaining, low-level rations inside. They lodged at knee height a few feet in. The character hopped again, then continually as Doug backed away.

An Oil Snake slipped between Dorion's boots into the stone gap. It was thick—a level 3 mother. The snake pushed its head in and lost the rest of its bulge in the shadows. It slithered without pause, hungrily, toward the trapped warrior. Dorion could save her/him.

He pulled his sword. In an impressively wide arc he chopped at the tail—struck sand.

HELP ME. HELP ME. HELP ME.

The player kept hopping as Doug powered off his console.

His finger remained over the button for a few moments, then felt gross there. Yet he couldn't move. That was make-believe, he told himself, a game. What'd happened didn't matter. The character would respawn. The player, unharmed, would quest another day. Doug pulled at the fuzzy hairs standing up on back of his neck. He considered an older game to take his mind off it, something less real, reflex against a dumb AI.

"I got *downsized*—our *life* got downsized," his dad moaned.

"But with two growing boys?" his mother returned.

Doug went to his bedroom. Cornered by despair, he was left to think about last night.

On the walk home after Bachelor's Grove, E. had talked nonstop about the Dead Man. She'd started with his arrogance in believing that Erika had been so interested in him. Then she began trying to figure him out.

"Why is he really doing this, Dougy?" she'd said at one point.

"Because the guy has a deadly serious hard-on for your sister," was what he'd wanted to say, his jealousy bristling. Still sore from failure, Doug didn't risk further rejection. The way she talked about the Dead Man, wondered about him … Why didn't she try to figure him out like that? He didn't say anything about that, either, just nodded beside her in the dark, hoping she would acknowledge that he'd walked past his house to make sure she got home safe after such a creepshow of a day. After all, the killer could've been there, seen them in the woods, and followed in the shadows. On his walk back, Doug could become the second kid whose guts suffered that wretched blade. "Don't step on a crack," was all she'd said and, for three-quarters of a block, stepped on all the cracks, loped from one to the next, and at last smacked the pavement with both feet. "What was that for?" Doug had asked. She'd never been so animated. "Why not?" she'd said like a challenge and not really knowing herself. E. smoothed her hair and went the rest unenthused as usual. When she rose to her front door, Doug braved one stair for a smile and a word of thanks, maybe even a kiss, some acknowledgment of his thoughtfulness, for being courageous for her all day. "Don't forget your dad's shovels Monday," she'd said, closed the door, and turned off the porch light. That night, curled in bed, Doug had cried, face red in his pillow though no sound escaped, throat clenched, and willing out his heart sickness. The pain of being unwanted, of having no one to share his thoughts and feelings with, of being deeply alone, he experienced bodily as though a disease. When it didn't help, he'd willed out his love for E., instead. But he'd taken that wish back a second later and lived with it numb as a block of ice in his chest all the next morning and night.

Doug weaved his bedroom curtains between each of his fingers and clutched them as hard as he could to keep from being pulled under another crying fit. The street was empty. He gazed at the sky. The moon was full. Then he couldn't wait a moment longer for E. to return his many messages about how selfish John was in his quest for Erika's killer, putting their lives in danger.

Look at that moon, he sent. He stared dumbly at the screen, waiting.

She might turn to her bedroom window. They might see it at the same time. Wouldn't that be something?

The moon wasn't yellow, but silver. A mirror in the sky. It was late. Exhausted, his mind wandered....

Could she see him reflected, around the curve of the Earth? Would she like what she saw?

Messages: 0.

Doug was only looking back at himself.

7

They returned to the woods Monday after school. John reared his spade to break earth near the Big Tree, when four kids appeared up the path. They came over the creek with shovels and buckets and a competitive strut as if come to bury someone, and quickly. The tallest had a basketball under his arm and looked up in awe and said, "That's one big motherfucking tree." John met the newcomers—all familiar from the halls at school—with a round of formal handshakes. He led first name introductions: "Greg, Tiffany, Josué, Alex, meet the rest of our team." Then he detailed the first of three tasks before the group—which, John added without explanation, should never be named. By the light of Erika's memory, they'd assembled to dig holes on the Big Tree side of the creek, approximately three feet in depth, no different than the model holes discovered Friday. Any found objects could be evidence and should be reported to the group immediately. He didn't elaborate on what their second or third tasks might be.

The Dead Man's leadership gnawed at Doug's timidity enough that he very seriously considered asking him to quit showing off. Doug couldn't tell if the guy was deliberately out to steal E., if that's all the investigation was about, because surely his assertiveness was warping her better judgment. To make matters worse, Doug's forehead had broken a sweat and he fought to keep his glasses from slipping off his nose after realizing two more girls would be in the group. Tiffany Dennys was Erika's closest friend and well known as the hottest eighth grader. She was so hot that she was, like, painful to look at, too hot to be yanking roots with her angelic hands and sculpted nails. Alex Karahalios was the opposite—preppy, a stout, shorthaired tomboy with sandy freckles on her cheeks—also amazingly cute. Doug's heart buzzed with guilty pleasure at the thought of spending time with girls superficially prettier than E., which was meaningless beside her intellectual integrity, of course. He tried to will away the guilt, but didn't possess the same powers as John to make things appear when and how he desired. If he did have such talent, John's disappearance would've been his first act.

None of the newcomers were truly stranger than Doug or E., only unusual as a group. They were so different from one another that it seemed more likely that John had drafted an Erika sympathizer from each clique at school than that they were friends. Doug considered this a stratagem to discourage mutiny before the week's end. To have convinced seven kids into a wild ghost chase in Bachelor's Grove couldn't have been simple, and to keep them working diligently for an entire week would prove a challenge, even for a megalomaniac. Doug looked forward to seeing the guy squirm, show weakness, and fail just once. John had likely employed the same tactic on the others that he'd used on E. and himself—sympathy for the last wishes of a soon-to-be-dead guy plus sentiment for the dead girl he was obsessed with. And if something terrible happened out here in the middle of nowhere? It wasn't like John would be around long enough to pay the consequences. All it would take was one kid to squeal to a buddy or a parent, and they'd be in huge trouble, maybe jailed. Doug especially worried about Alex. She was an eighth grader who was a sixth grader age-wise, known for skipping grades and taking the school mathletes team to state. She was also a notorious tattletale on principle. For his own sake as much as everyone else's caught up in John's scheme, Doug waited until the group had spread around the Grove to dig before confronting the Dead Man about her.

"We're missing one," John said, too lost in thought to notice Doug at his side. His hands sagged on his hips in the manner of a coach disappointed with himself. A glimmer of a smile chased the grimness out of his features. "I guess she wasn't ready. Eh, it's perfect. Seven—my old lucky number."

"Hey, Dead—whoa. I'm … John—you're John. Obviously. I mean—hey," Doug stammered. His confidence buckled under the mess his mouth made. Saliva drowned his tongue though his throat was parched.

"There a problem already?" The guy's hands replanted higher on his hips.

Doug apologized for the interruption. He kept his lips parted, mouth-breathing noisily as he asked was it really such a good idea to have Alex here? What they were doing—disrupting a crime scene—most likely, it wasn't legal.

"Alex approached me in the cafeteria." The guy's face softened, humored by the recollection. "She said it was obvious I'd been planning something 'of great importance' for a few weeks, and wanted in.

63

That really surprised me. It's the kind of light you don't say no to, no matter what you think you know."

"So you don't care … I mean, if we get caught? My parents will kill me."

"Dying isn't a joke, buddy. It's the hardest inning you'll ever play." He squinted as if back on the field, against the stadium lights. "It's just you out there—a one-on-one in the rain. And the big guy is batting to take your head off. Except you're on the field with me now."

John seemed to have hit his head this morning. He was probably on some hardcore painkillers and dizzied by visions that flashed behind his eyeballs. He'd probably been up all night, Doug could picture it, the guy tirelessly planning how to catch Erika's murderer and to restore his lost fame.

"But we're not …" Doug stopped, feeling foolish for believing he could talk such a person out of anything. "Forget it."

John seized his arm. It was a tough guy gesture. There was something desperate in it, too.

"Talk to me, Doug. Do you prefer Douglas? Or is it Dougy, like E. calls you? I want to hear what you're not saying."

"Just … Doug," he said. The Dead Man's grip surprised and spooked him, yet Doug caved to his earnestness. No one had ever asked before what he liked to be called. His throat still felt irritated, unsatisfied. He tried to slow down. "If it's so … serious—I mean dying … why are we here?… is what I'm saying."

John released him and patted his shoulder in the fatherly manner he'd assumed Friday in the hallway.

"That's easy—to make a play that matters before the game ends."

Doug stepped out from under his hand.

"But if something happens. If. Something … bad—"

"I won't let it. Not to you or any member of the team. Our team. That's a promise. We've made the right moves so far. I plan to keep us playing smart. I know we don't know each other very well, yet, but I hope you trust when I say that I couldn't live with myself, otherwise."

This last "promising his safety" bit whupped Doug, crushed his apprehensions, and, without an equally clever rebuttal, he thanked John—like the weakling he was—and sulked to a lone spot across the Grove to bury his shame from E. and everyone. The Dead Man was completely full of himself, a real wacko. He did seem to mean to do right. He spoke so confidently, almost ominously, as if able to peer into the future, which made resisting his assurances futile. Doug recalled him bathed in light on that first trip to the Grove, smiling as if having passed through the gates of Heaven. Doug seriously questioned then if John's having one foot in the grave allowed him access to stuff that most people didn't, or couldn't, understand, like powers. It seemed a fair trade for so soon departing the world. More likely, the guy was a charismatic bully on the verge of losing his mind after having lost his place in the world. Doug expected an equally bizarre answer from him about including Josué—a kid from Mexico who got suspensions a lot for school fights—and Greg—a kid from the city who hardly showed up to school at all. Though concerned, Doug didn't ask how the other newcomers cared enough about E.'s sister to be trusted, let alone to be following the cursed or blessed maniac into the wilderness. John was simply too commanding a presence for Doug to face in conversation. This was the kind of guy that made E.'s brain skip a beat? Doug would help until the end of the week. After that, he would have to make a tough choice: follow his friend deeper into the woods after the doomed guy or let her go and learn to live as a very lonely person.

After the kids had spread out over the area, Greg wandered over to the original crime scene and stepped over the police tape. Greg was taller than most kids and wore mesh shorts and his favorite gray basketball jersey that declared: STRONGER THAN FAILURE. He was in seventh grade and had wanted to ask Erika out since the first school assembly of the year. She'd been nearby chomping gum—which she wasn't supposed to have—and blowing big bubbles, and she gabbed to a friend like she could care less about the rules or school spirit, which Greg found sexy. He felt the same irreverence about dumb school. It was school. Erika did cheer, though. Greg knew she cheered because sometimes he'd go to a basketball game to measure up the players to later challenge them to a real street game, and he began to notice her warming up beside the bleachers, stretching her tanned legs, always a shade darker than the other girls'. Then a whistle would blow, and she'd spring in front of the first row, kicking her white shoes up past her head and doing shakes and twists and leaps and things Greg wouldn't have been able to dream up with those gold pompoms zigging and her blonde hair zagging. That shit had put him into a trance. He typically never stayed for a whole game, but he stayed to the very end of every one starring Erika Summerson front and center. Then he'd pretended to be busy talking with friends on his phone—though only rereading an earlier text from his mom that she'd be home later than usual—while the kids and parents and next the players filed out of the gym doors. One night Greg watched Erika exit the locker room, a gym bag over her shoulder and still sexy as hell in the sweats she'd thrown on. And off she went with some guys on the other team, which sucked, but it was also an amazingly tough thing for a girl to do. "Erika … Erika …" he'd later repeated in the dark on the way back to lower Palos under the too-quiet, leafless boughs of fall trees hanging over the sidewalk, not bouncing his ball, but clutching it to his chest. They were the same, he thought—two outlaws among so many ass-kissers. She was the girl for him. Greg didn't do well at tests and homework and so couldn't play on the team, not that he'd want to put up with that teamwork trash. He didn't hang out with the jock crowd, either, and never had the guts to stop the girl after a game and ask her out. And now ... a few muddy footprints from those spoiled, school-athlete motherfuckers and a burnt-out fire pit collecting dirty rainwater. He hefted the shovel blade closer to his hands. Greg was sure that, if he and Erika had been dating, he'd be raging and might not just want to kill some fools, but actually do it—kill and bury the bitches with the shovel right here.

"There's nothing over there," E. said to the tall basketball kid, despite the threatening manner with which he held his shovel, as if against all the ghosts of Bachelor's Grove. The boy was listening to music, and his ear buds blared, "*On to the next one. On to the next one....*" E. didn't like that a stranger was in the circle where her sister had been killed. Nor did she like that she didn't like it. E. didn't believe in anything, so how could she sympathize with trapped souls not appreciating the breathers that violated their place of death? She tried to picture the good times that must've been had here late into the night. Erika's shrieking laughter returned.... Ordinary woods lay beneath the trash of the scene—dirt, plants, trees, bugs—and all this would be woods again one day, E. reassured herself and grounded yet another irritating emotional flare-up.

Greg lowered the shovel. The kid took heaving breaths, and E. saw that he'd been thinking and feeling too much. Though tough acting, Greg's concern for her sister made him seem vulnerable in a way that E. bitterly understood. If he'd loved her, it must've been the kind of love familiar to her—the kind some fought brutally to keep, like her parents, who shouted and shoved and woke the neighbors and called the police on one another in the name of preserving senseless, but unmistakable love. It was easily more senseless how she was jealous of it. Not of their love necessarily, but of the fight for something bigger than oneself.

"You searched this area?" Greg said. "You sure?"

"John says he did."

"John says, huh."

"He also said, 'Our fate hangs in the Big Tree's branches,' or something, so—yeah."

"Kooky. But OK. Whatever the man says."

Greg had first heard about John H. Walker after Greg's mom remarried and they'd moved to an apartment in the burbs way back in the fourth grade. If he'd talked sports with any Palos Hills kids, they'd inevitably mention the guy and shamelessly compare his talent to Hall of Fame baseballers. Greg had thought the whole town pretty damn stupid until he saw Walker play. He was the real thing. The guy sprung like a snake and made flashy catches like the pros while the crowd oohed and aahed. So Walker was legit despite that he cared too much about his image and grades and all that. And their favorite sports were different. Still, it was kind of cool to see him turn up alone on Greg's court at Penny Park one November night, before Erika had died. The halogen floodlight mounted to the telephone pole behind the backboard had already whited-out the world beyond the court, right before Greg was about to head home, when the swings creaked. Greg saw nothing, then jumped—startled by the Dead Man on the sideline. Buried in a scarf and the hood of his parka, his face looked bloodless, zombiefied. The kid had cancer or something. Still, meeting Walker was worth skipping dinner for. They played HORSE. Greg won, but the game wasn't a sweep. Walker might've had a chance if he'd stopped gabbing and focused when he had the ball. Greg remembered the kid asking after the winning shot if there was anything he loved more than basketball. Greg had said no. Greg then mentioned Erika, like some big stalker. He kept shooting, stripped down to his jersey and shorts, his body heat worked up, trying hard not to listen too hard to the bundled kid on the sidelines pushing with the personal questions, as though somehow he knew how sick Greg's heart was for her, the guy saying, "Erika … Erika …" with these floats of white breath that Greg dodged on his way to the hoop, as if she would materialize out of one if the kid wasn't dying and had a few ounces better lung capacity. Greg couldn't shoot worth a shit, then, too afraid it could happen, which was dumb because of how badly he wished it would—until an hour later, when they were drinking hot Gatorade teas together—he and John H. Walker drinking Greg's own winter game elixir, no shit—outside of 7-Eleven, like buddies, and Greg admitted wanting to love someone as much as he loved the game. "Something bigger," Walker said and admitted he knew the feeling. Greg walked home that night with true respect for the kid, though feeling kinda that he'd gabbed and hardly let Walker speak, which wasn't his style. Sharing feelings wasn't his style. Still. So when the guy came up to him yesterday to say there might be a way to help Erika, he must've already known Greg would say yes.

The kids dug until daylight fled the crowns of the trees. All that time, they plodded with their long-handled shovels in the well-rooted earth while John went around saying, "Deeper. No—close. A little deeper." Each thanked him for his feedback to be kind. They figured his condition made physical labor risky—everyone except E.

Between her warring compulsions to stare all evening at the site of her sister's murder or at the Dead Man, E. chose what she hoped to be the lesser emotional risk. John had ambled all afternoon from digger to digger, hands in his pockets, a boy playing a much older man, burdened, almost crippled by his self-imposed responsibility. His kindness toward everyone was grating, made him seem daft, she thought, like he might be only a boy scout, doing the right thing for no reason other than an obligation to goodness. Then she witnessed him vulnerable. During a moment when he believed no one was watching—her attention went to him after every sling of dirt—John had closed his eyes in the shade of the Big Tree. His brows clenched as he wrestled with something inside himself, and he summoned the strength to win. For lack of a more dignified word, his struggle was "sexy." E.'s body had urged her to him then—Did he need water? A hand to keep him steady? Flaky stuff like that. E. knew she was overextending her empathy and needed another way to distract herself before she did something she would later regret. All weekend, she'd run through Fromm's *The Art of Loving*, articles that debunked love into oxytocin and codependency, self-help books on common relationship pitfalls, and by Sunday she was annotating one of her mother's well-thumbed romance novels. Meanwhile, her desire grew hourly, a wildfire clearing the weightier aspects of her personality. Or was her attitude to it the problem? "The foundation of love is vulnerability," she'd read. E. couldn't risk more loss. Her sister … John had liked Erika so much. The same guy couldn't like her, too. Could he? John could hold himself upright just fine, she told herself. He cared. It was sweet. That was all there was to him. One week was all she would lend in return. After that, she wanted her life back.

Eventually, John caught her gaze. He came over with his head lowered, grinning, she thought, about having acquired yet another fan. E. cursed herself for acting adolescent. If she couldn't control her eyeballs, E. feared what else she'd fail to control if the boy got too close.

"How're you feeling about The Work?" he said. "It's going well, I think," he answered after a block of silence.

E. kept her eyes on the blade of her shovel. "Tired. Fine. Just— watch out." Her digging intensified, and a forceful pitch of dirt swept over John's shoes.

"I'll go. Don't want to disturb your flow."

"My flow is heavy as usual."

"That's great, E.," John said, nonplussed with a nod of encouragement. He didn't get the period joke, meaning it either wasn't funny or the boy was immune to humor. It frustrated her that she even cared which.

"It must be hard to be in this place," he said. "Thank you for trusting me this far."

"Hey, John—?" she said, unable to restrain from talking to the boy a moment longer— "I loved Erika. I wish that what'd happened to my sister never did. I do want to know what happened. And I'm grateful for your concern. But she was a crazy bitch, too. You know?"

"She had a wild soul."

"Sure. But you loved her. That's what this is about—right?"

"You could call it that."

"Because that's what it is? Was?"

"Lately, love has been feeling bigger than the word," he said.

"Tell me about it."

His tired eyes rounded into hopeful circles. "You know what I mean?"

"Oh, no way. I mean, you tell me about it—please." *And quit look-*

ing at me so damn sweetly while you talk about my sister. You make me want to die trying to be a monster like her.

"I guess we shared something. She was real in that moment at the hospital. She let me in and asked for nothing in return. That's the stuff worth fighting for, I think. But anybody could share that, if they were brave enough."

Over John's shoulder, Dougy spied from behind his upright shovel. He resembled a child that still believed covering one eye made him half invisible. In the way he clung to the top of the handle, wiltingly, E. saw how her talking to the boy injured him. Yesterday's awkward moment—Dougy's attempt to hold her hand—that was him trying to be "real," and she'd rejected him. Because she wanted someone else. Maybe she already was as careless as her little sister.

"Erika was a good person, too," John continued. *Too? As in, like you, E.?* "Something out here corrupted her."

"Boys with beer, maybe."

"Not someone, something. Erika didn't like whatever it was, and they—" John noticed E. had checked out—in too deep, really, watching his lips make passionate and determined words of gorgeous insight—and he stopped short. "I'm rambling, sorry. My mind has been—"

"No, I like hearing ..." *anything that comes out of your mouth, really.* "Your perspective is unique. Really. Talk to me, anytime." *So I can spew even more embarrassingly earnest sentiments like this.*

"I will," he said. And, by the simple pleasure in his smile, she knew that his weren't empty words.

After several hours of digging on that first day, the most remarkable thing the kids found in the dirt was an old chrome car door handle.

"Does this mean anything?" Greg asked.

"It's still too early." John looked up at the dying light.

He immediately asked the group to "gather 'round," which they did in a loose half-circle. "I mean, huddle," he said. They shuffled tighter. He led the group in a moment of silence devoted to remembering "the good in Erika." Mostly, the kids shifted uncomfortably from one foot to the other for an entire minute, slightly repulsed by the sweaty shoulders and BO and radiant body heat, and self-conscious of others listening to them breathe. John thanked everyone for his or her "strength" and wished all a safe journey home.

"Tomorrow?"

"Tomorrow," he said.

On the walk home with Dougy that evening, E. put aside her private joy, shining through the mire of reminiscences she'd managed to suppress that day, and didn't mention John or The Work. She asked Dougy, What videogames was he enjoying? Was he keeping up with his reading? He said he wasn't and described a game he'd started in which one constructed a house and trees and tools and, in time, an entire world out of tiny blocks, anything that you wanted living or dead, and it wasn't easy, as the sun and stars spun on forever and the undead rose at night. "So, there really is no point," she said. "The point is to make stuff," he said defensively, which did sound tedious—to what end? Still E. continued to ask about it, forgetting the details of the impressive objects he said that he'd built as soon as he'd mentioned them. Doug didn't seem moved by her efforts to be a better friend, nor did he walk her home. E. then recognized that he'd accompanied her home on that first, much scarier night and that he had every evening since what'd happened to Erika, to put her mother at ease about walking home and make her dreadfully early 6 p.m. curfew. Before E. could think to tell Dougy that he was appreciated, he'd said, "Goodnight, E.," and disappeared inside his small, poorly lit house. There was finality in his tone, like a goodbye from someone you wouldn't see all summer break and who might not be the same when they returned.

The sun had dropped behind the houses, and an insistent breeze blew against her back and urged E. down the empty sidewalk. Her life was changing at a manic speed, as if whizzing through space with no control over the destination.

E. stopped along some house's newly paved driveway. The asphalt warmed through her thin shoes. She didn't want to go home on time like usual. She pictured how her mother would freak when she got in just five minutes late. She ignored her nagging conscience. E. thought to go to the library, but it would close soon after she reached it. She remembered how questions seemed to have answers there, and ending one's ignorance seemed as easy as reading a well-written book (but only seemed, she thought). If she wanted, she could turn back to Dougy's, throw rocks at his window until he let her into his bedroom, maybe to watch a movie like they did on his birthdays. No, that would be cruel.

E. lifted one leg and enjoyed the feel of the cool wind that nudged her calf forward. She took a step and smiled. Perhaps she could learn some lesson by listening to her feelings. She took another step, off the curb this time, then another back onto the sidewalk. Then she drifted into the street until treading the yellow dashes there were no end of, with the sleepy road aimed into the night. This is how John must see the world, she thought and her whole body shivered.

E. stopped between lanes. Her destination lit up ahead as bright as oncoming headlights along the timeline in her mind. She saw what she wanted most: to date the Dead Man.

8

Only their second day in the woods and the kids' hands—puckered with tender, quarter-sized blisters—smarted against the unyielding handles of their shovels. They labored for several hours, digging and filling, in pairs.

When John had suggested they work in teams, Doug had elbowed through Greg and Josué and walked right up to Tiffany Dennys. He understood why she looked down on him initially—well, she was three inches taller. But he didn't let her hair flip and a less-than-pleased sigh daunt him. He reseated his glasses out of habit and pointed to, in his estimation, the best digging spot this side of the creek—in the shade, so they wouldn't become sunburned or dehydrated, and along a fallen tree, upon which they might rest at intervals. Through some miracle, she heard him and followed.

Her windbreaker came off at the spot, revealing her toned arms, tanned as incredibly evenly as her legs and ready to dig. He caught her scent, like stewed cherries over vanilla ice cream, and what little courage the boy had evaporated. Doug focused on the simple task of shoveling dirt.

An hour went by in silence until they rested a moment on the fallen tree, as if he'd ingeniously planned it that way. Tiffany gestured at the four other diggers, who were sweat-spotted in the sun. "Thank god you're a genius," she said. Years beside E. had made Doug painfully aware of his average intelligence, at best, but, yes, he wore glasses and had the runty, underdog look of a math or science geek. Still, he took the remark as a compliment. He certainly possessed assumptions about her intelligence that he'd resolved earlier to put aside.

He and Tiffany shared the pair of oversized yard gloves he'd brought—another genius move. His dad had two pairs, but he'd only stuffed the one into his backpack this morning after telling himself to stop caring about E. and to focus on himself until she began to miss him and returned. By lunch, he'd decided to give E. the gloves all week to prove how selflessly he cared for her. Surely that would stir her affection after their years together in a nonsexual friendship. But when he'd arrived at the Grove and E. was asking questions and proposing ideas that the Dead Man praised, which caused her to fall into orbit around him like a fertile planet to his sun, Doug's naivete came into tight focus, spiked his anger, and he wasn't his meek self again until he'd whisked away the hottest girl who'd ever graced the Grove to a shady corner of the valley.

The risk paid off. When Tiffany passed him the gloves, Doug wiped his palms on his pants to dry them before he slipped his hands inside, and he enjoyed the cool shock of her sweat on his skin. The pleasure was simple and perverse. To be able to say he'd sat a reach away from Tiffany Dennys, shooting the shit in Bachelor's Grove, restored a bit of his pride. Sharing her sweat, something so intimate, allowed Doug to try on a new fantasy: being one day worthy enough to hold such a girl's hand.

Tiffany didn't mind the genius. He was safe. And he'd pointed out a spot furthest from "the pit." That's what Rocky called the circle of stumps where he and his crew threw weird parties with the campfires that stunk up her clothes for days. They weren't the only people she'd partied with here, some older kids, too. But most guys, even the biggest on the football team, were scared of Bachelor's Grove. Maybe it was not knowing what was behind the trees and being almost lost in the middle of nowhere. Tiffany actually kinda liked it. In the middle of nowhere … The last night she'd spent in the woods, she'd repeated the saying, chanted it to feel more lost. People say it all the time, In the middle of nowhere … but lying outside the pit, a girl in the grass, searching for the stars past the treetops … She wanted to see them twinkle. Her dad had once told her that's how you tell the difference between a regular planet and a star. "And you're one of the stars," he'd said, dropping his clammy hand on the small of her back and raising a wave of goose bumps that burned up over her shoulders. To be out there—where?—far from Palos Hills and everyone she knew. Better to be gone a long time, maybe forever, and in some new place, outside of time, even, to be whatever she was and—"Wakey, wakey." Erika had pulled her by the ankle and stuck a beer in her hand as she sat up. "Be with us," Erika had said, pushing the can to her lips, and then—here she was, digging with the dork and his merry band of rejects, sweating her tits off. She'd owed Erika that much, to say yes to the still somewhat cute-ish Dead Man and to be here now. At least she still could sweat and run and try.

The day's heat had peaked, and Tiffany put her hair up, which exposed more of her face. Doug noticed her cheeks were uncommonly wide, almost muscular in a way that made her face mannish. Not that Tiffany wasn't still hot. She was debatably hotter with the added streak of athleticism, which Doug read as an aptitude for sexual prowess years beyond the average junior high kid. Barely average in every way imaginable himself, the revelation was paralyzing.

"What's up, genius?" Tiffany said as she maneuvered her bound hair into place above her head. She could feel the weak light of his gaze. That alone was enough for her to push the ignore button, but Tiffany was trying on a different life and continued to talk to him, the opposite of what she would normally do. It wasn't easy out here. Compared to the guys she was used to, though, he was harmless.

Doug lifted his eyes to the Big Tree like he wasn't gawking at her necessarily, but into general space and was maybe in the middle of a deep thought. This then luckily triggered an actually deep thought— just as Tiffany could only admire his mental features, Doug could only admire her physical features. He was enthralled by her, but not by who she was, only who she was insofar as she was this person more physically perfect than other people, which lent the girl an otherworldly presence, grounded in the body, her form so exquisite that the only explanation of her as a phenomenon seemed to be that he'd dreamed her into existence. How else could all her parts possess the splendor of a magical being, like a sexy elf or something, not like that creeping, mist-bodied specter, the Dead Man. Tiffany's fey beauty was a rare and precious thing. Doug allowed himself to accept that fact, which was difficult, because the times she'd been at E.'s house, hanging with Erika, he'd completely avoided Tiffany for this exact reason, never looking at her directly, always quick to duck and exit a room that she dominated, sensing what she was, but never allowing himself to behold it for fear, he now realized, of succumbing to her like so many fools and becoming another in a long line of fools suffering from fantasies that would never be fulfilled. Doug had no illusions about his place in the junior high social world, where, because of his manner and dress, he was nothing and Tiffany was everything that others wanted and wanted to be. She was no less striking in the woods, maybe more so, in a whole other dimension Doug would never have access to unless as some warty green troll at her beck and call, a hopeless position he'd resisted by making comments to E. about how superficial Tiffany and Erika were and then laughing when E. would go off on how totally meaningless those girls' lives were and that it would be no great loss if they died. What would E. think of him now? If looks alone were enough to make Doug want to be intimate with Tiffany, then E. would certainly deem him shallow, shallower than she already did because he didn't enjoy reading (how many yards of pages had he skimmed for a chance to sit inches beside E. in the good light, shoulder to shoulder, just once?). Doug didn't want to think about what she would think, but he had and couldn't unthink it now. This made him angry and precipitated into his best attempt to get to know Tiffany Dennys better.

"What would you be doing? If you weren't … here?" he asked.

"Listening to music in my room," she answered. "Why?"

"You could do anything," Doug blurted.

"You're thinking way too fast for me, genius. What?"

"That's—I mean, what would you do … if you could do anything? Right now."

"I'd rather be dancing, I guess."

"Dance here!" he said with such a force that his glasses half jolted off.

"OK … You got a little beer for me in that book bag?" she said, amused by the dork, but skeptical of his ability to keep up. He said no, but he did have a soda saved from lunch, and gave it to her without checking if she really wanted it or not. If he was trying to hit on her, he wasn't doing great. But if he was trying to get to know her, he was doing a lot better than most.

After a sip, Tiffany thanked him, though it wasn't diet, and talked about her dance experience. She did ballet as a girl, then cheer. She gave it up after Erika died. Doug didn't ask why. Tiffany appreciated that. She stretched one of her legs as she spoke, down the length of the tree and tried to point her toes against the restriction of her rubber boots. A mosquito landed just above her kneecap. She watched it stick her and suck all it wanted. She thought about tensing her thigh to make his head explode.

"What kind of dance would be good?… to you … to do out here."

"I don't know. Something nymph-y, maybe."

"What's a nymph? Like a dryad?"

"Nymph—nympho." He didn't laugh. "Never heard of it?"

Doug hadn't. She'd never heard of a dryad before. Both were surprised that the other's life experience had excluded them from such information.

"It's a mythological creature.…" He described the woodland spirit from one of his role-playing games. Instead of backing out of the topic, he explained the game, too, and risked sounding dorkier than he apparently looked to her.

"A nymph is mythological, too, I think," she said, stumbling over the big word and repressing commentary on the game. It sounded important to him and kinda interesting: shooting a bow, defending the forest from outsiders, living in the shadows of great trees. Tiffany had forgotten about the mosquito while he talked, and it was gone except for a red bump.

"What do they look like?" the genius asked. He seemed actually interested and no longer stole peeping glances. He blinked up at her straight on. He'd lost that sheepish, already-defeated self-consciousness guys got around her that was sweet but mostly annoying.

"Nymphs? Oh, I imagine they have long arms and legs and long hair."

"Like you! Obviously."

"And they like sex a lot."

"Like—"

Tiffany covered her mouth demurely as she laughed. "Boys are too much trouble."

"Some are," he said. Doug looked over to the Big Tree at Dead Man Walker. Greg and Alex were shoveling near the guy, but his back was turned on everyone. He looked up into the boughs, as if listening to someone high up. E. resumed digging when Doug glanced in her direction—she'd stopped to watch him and Tiffany. He hoped that she was a little jealous. He immediately took back that mean-spirited hope and hoped instead that she was content with her Dead Man and left him alone.

"Girls can be, too," Tiffany said after a moment.

"Let's stay away from them," Doug said, "the troublemakers."

"I like that idea," she said.

E. watched her friend shake hands with the blonde witch in a polite and gentlemanly manner that made the thing's orange face light up with mocking glee. A girl that vapid couldn't appreciate Doug's sincerity. E. had never cared for her sister's best friend. Her name alone made E. cringe. Doug must've made a joke, and Tiffany raised one of her razored talons to coyly cover her many rows of shark's teeth as she hee-hawed. Did she have a problem with teeth falling out? She couldn't possibly be self-conscious. She was a young boy's wet dream on two, very radiant—possibly radioactive after so much tanning— dream legs. Even Dougy, a boy who knew better, was staring at the side of her face as if he'd never seen a girl before. It hurt a little. Not that E. wasn't familiar with the absurdity of attraction. But it did seem as if he were making a show of it to try and wound her. Just days ago, the kid was literally tripping over himself to change their friend- ship into something more. Now he was coming to the woods alone and avoiding her—the only boy who'd ever treated her like a person and not a contagious disease. Weren't they still friends? Even if E. did resemble two or three other girls at school, at least she didn't resemble two or three dozen. At least she attempted authenticity. Individuality. Personality. *Dougy is still my friend. He has his own life, and I have to let him make mistakes.* The thought didn't return any comfort. Dougy needed someone to connect with on a deeper level, and at that range this girl would leave teeth marks on his heart. She was sincerely wor- ried for him. And for herself? There's John, she thought. Though she didn't have him yet, did she.

E. worked with Josué Ortiz, a stocky ESL seventh grader who didn't say anything. He didn't yesterday and hadn't today. Neither had she, brooding over Doug and Tiffany or eyeballing John, so the two were a fine match. E. was all smiles when John checked in. She couldn't restrain it. She tried, which, she imagined, lent her otherwise dour and reddened face a jack-o-lantern fright. John smiled back and assured that their hard work wouldn't be for nothing. E. could only mutely nod, thankfully unable to gush her thoughts and feelings. It'd been easier to communicate when she didn't care what he thought about her. She got a lot of digging done.

The kids by now had internalized their leader's very particular instructions (the ideal depth and diameter of holes, what soil types they were and weren't supposed to break into, how all rocks and roots and unearthed items were to be returned at precisely the depth they were found, etc.) and no longer paid close attention to his encouragements or heard much of anything but the occasional spade smack against stone and the incessant sawing of the insects.

"Quiet! Stop everything!" John called out in a hushed voice. He beckoned and had the group crouch around the trunk of the Big Tree. He pointed up at a clump of trees that appeared ready to topple over the western edge of the valley. "An outsider ..." he said. They watched for cops or hikers or kids who might've seen them. There was no one, or no one who dared descend into Bachelor's Grove. After ten minutes, the group set back to work, overly sensitive to scuttling in the underbrush and the branches stirring above. Their paranoia subsided after a few hours, and the kids went back to disbelieving anything would come of their labor, until Tiffany Dennys shrieked.

"Gah! I found something!"

E. wiped the sweat from her brow and rested against her shovel, skeptical, as the others ran over. E. had many reasons for not liking Tiffany. The girl had been her sister's closest friend, which meant them gabbing too loud in the house about X boy and Y girl who gave her Z look during study hall. Tiffany represented the kind of woman E. worked hard not to be—a person without a complex and mature inner life who cared solely about her looks and the attention of boys. Also, Tiffany and Erika had a falling out the week before it happened, so the police had heavily interrogated her. Still technically a suspect, she'd quit cheer and, according to rumors, hid in her bedroom after school, haunted by her guilt for killing Erika over some mystery boy. E. didn't believe Tiffany was the murderer. She was too dumb to get away with it this long. What bothered E. most was that the girl might have useful information lost in the black hole of her brain. Which, E. realized, was the mistake she'd made with Erika's dirty fingernails—if it meant anything. Ugh, just look at Tiffany. Hugging her shovel, she and the rubber ducky faces, printed on her yellow boots, peered fearfully into the hole. The girl was maybe half real. Why did she get to live and not Erika?

When the chatter surrounding Tiffany didn't clear and it seemed that the girl had found something of worth, E. came over using her upturned shovel like a walking stick and stopped beside John. Doug was hunkered beside the hole. At arm's length, he held up to the light what he'd picked out: a dull chrome slug—a bullet shell.

The kids deliberated over the find:

"Wait—she was stabbed, right?" Greg said.

"The dipshits still haven't found the murder weapon," Tiffany said.

"Erika didn't die like that," E. said.

The mention was enough to replay the gruesome scene that'd run through their minds after hearing the reports and rumors of reports and plain rumors and then rumors of rumors—the discovery of the body. One freakishly pale leg stretched casually, seen through the trees. A young girl in the grass … Smears of dried blood start past her muddied knees, thicken higher up, the more thigh that's revealed. Her bent elbow touches her hips, the other arm tangled in her soiled blonde hair. Her torso is at an extreme right angle to her hips, a wrong angle, like a snapped pencil and just as cleanly. How straight her back, how flat the shoulders lie. The wound gapes. Animals have picked her guts into a slop. Her voided eyes—

"Could be from a hunter's rifle," Alex said.

"Nobody hunts here," Tiffany said.

"Hunting isn't allowed in the woods?" E. said.

"Not in *these* woods, I don't think."

"That doesn't mean people don't do it."

"No rifle," Josué said, overtaken by excitement of his insight. He shook his head, raised and snugged his arms around the stock of an imaginary rifle. Then he dropped his shoulders and drew a six-shooter from his side. Bang, bang—he fanned gunfire into the woods around them. The guy blew the smoke from the barrel and twirled the gun around his index finger before holstering.

"You're on my team if we play charades," Alex said, having comprehended his gestures in context.

Josué ducked his head and smiled, embarrassed that he didn't catch the girl's whole meaning, but knowing the comment to be friendly from her tone. He understood a lot of what he heard in English, and read American comic books, and mostly lacked the confidence to express his ideas in words. He wished that he could explain to the kids at school how it was that he lived in the US and could not yet speak the language with great fluency. This had caused bullies to fight him. It was many bloody noses many times. Sometimes Josué won, but never against a group. Though he was getting more confident at punching and taking the punches. Some white kids and pochos watched these fights and did nothing. Doug was one of those who did nothing. He'd watched during one of the fistfights after school in the parking lot behind the library, the full glare of sunlight across those glasses and the pendejo's mouth open as if he would say stop if he were not so afraid of his world. The world. Josué understood this well. To stand alone. Now in the woods, it seemed Doug feared him, the way he stood out of reach. Or perhaps the pendejo was ashamed of his own cowardice. He perhaps deserved a smack for this, but Josué had been taught that this work was best left in the hands of God. John was different. The sick kid stopped the fight at Erika's funeral against the angry boys in the parking lot that said he didn't belong, helped him up from the ground. Josué took his hand, though distrustful of what John would believe him indebted to. "We're all of us here because we loved Erika in some way," he'd said to the bullies, and they'd turned their backs. The words were much truer here. It would be wrong not to help, though would he be only a laborer or part of something?

"There weren't any cowboys in Illinois," Tiffany said, pronouncing the s. "Wait—"

"Read a book," E. said. "He's saying the bullet comes from a hand-gun."

"Oh. Well, you don't have to be a stuck-up bitch about it."

"Anytime—really."

Greg spurted laughter. "Shots definitely fired here," he said.

Everyone stepped back from the two girls except John. He lowered his head, eyes closed as if listening to a faint cry on the wind.

"I'm sorry about your sister, OK?" Tiffany said.

"Don't be. Unless you did it."

"I'm here, aren't I? Obviously, I didn't do it."

"Oh, obviously."

Tiffany looked to Doug. Jaw clenched, he glared at E. Behind his thick lenses, his eyes appeared wet, and he trembled with concentrated anger. The freak must've broke the dork's heart and was now coming back for more blood. By fourteen, this was a tired story for

Tiffany. She'd broken boys' hearts and at least one girl's and had her own broken almost as many times. So she understood E.'s lashing out, not wanting a guy because you knew it wouldn't work, but not wanting anyone else to have him either. She and the freak were both, in Doug's words, "troublemakers." Tiffany didn't want to be one anymore. That was why she'd dropped out of her old friend circle and from cheer. She wanted a second shot at being good. Not good looking, or good at dancing, or good at giving BJs. She wanted actual goodness in her life. Great restraint was not in her nature, however, especially when some ugly bitch in a shlumpy outfit came around clawing and pissing like she was God's gift. Strangely, John's presence helped. Something about the Dead Man, across from her with his eyes shut as if he'd fallen asleep standing up, and the stiffness of his body, tamped her rage. Instead of slapping the girl upside the head, Tiffany said:

"Erika made her own bed. Here more than once. Yeah—I'm here because I feel like shit. I wish I'd done more for her while she was alive. But I didn't and—guess what?—neither did you."

"I know and—"

"And now you want to be queen of the geeks. Well, I recommend not making out with the whole bunch like your sister would've."

Tiffany walked off. Her shovel thudded at E.'s feet and struck shame into her heart. E. knew that Tiffany didn't deserve antagonism, yet still she wanted to bare her teeth and throw dirt and whoop to drive the girl out. That's what E. felt, not what she wanted, and she too was surprised when her mouth opened and the melodrama she'd long criticized paraded out. She sounded like her parents: needlessly defensive, petty, immature. Worse, she was doing it in front of John. Listening to her feelings also had urged her to care about him, to touch his shoulder, and to say something to redeem herself. She didn't. The boy cringed with his arms crossed over his stomach as if the disturbance had physically wounded him.

"OK," she said. "I'm being stupid."

"Whatever." Tiffany headed for her purse. She pitched Doug's yard gloves up and over her billowing hair. He watched the girl's shadow float across the grass.

"Forgive me, everyone," E. said.

"Don't apologize to me." Greg waved her away with a scissor-like motion, making it clear he wouldn't get caught in the middle. Their bickering made him regret coming out here. Greg heard enough of it at home between his mom and stepdad. John had assured him his time wouldn't be wasted, confident that his investigation would uncover the killer. Now look at the drama—surprise, surprise. So, the kid had a shred of undisclosed info the police didn't have. What'd he think would turn up that months of police work hadn't? Anyway, Greg was no cop. Far from it.

Dougy's gaze floundered back to E. He didn't appear upset so much as defeated, submitting himself so that she might land the killing stroke for his faithlessness. E.'s eyes watered suddenly, as though knocked in the nose. The intensity of her shame was upsetting, yet that distaste was powerless against its breaking wave. She shielded her face at the thought of hurting her friend over something so childish as jealousy, that she'd never been any wiser than other people, only more alone, with less opportunity to exhibit her psychological shortcomings.

"Dougy, I'm sorry." She spoke through her hands. There was more she wanted to say, not in front of the group. A second thud sounded at her feet. E. dabbed her tears with her shirt collar to find John collapsed into the hole.

The kids hoisted the boy out and laid him on his back. "Don't be dead, dude," Greg said. John looked unconscious. E. shook him. His eyelids popped open. He softly begged for water as if a child in need of help to break a fever. E. brought the bottle to his lips. Doug wasn't resentful. He was glad the dying kid had someone at his side. John kept his gaze at kneecap level, and Doug would've sworn that, when the guy clenched his eyelids, he was going to sob from embarrassment. Muddied, at the mercy of others, their hometown hero had never looked more beaten and he must've felt that. John looked up at the faces of the kids close around him, Tiffany included. His head bobbed back, as if still faint. He smiled a weak version of his classic grin. Their memories filled in the rest.

"Friends," he said cheerily, drunk with exhaustion.

The group shifted noncommittally, but they nodded, without glancing up at one another.

"My friends," he said again.

Despite how little each kid actually knew him, John spoke with such sincerity that only Alex didn't feel it instantly, owing to the distraction of calculating how much time it would take to carry John to Palos Community Hospital versus calling an ambulance crew to the location if his condition worsened: *Yes, another dead kid. Same spot, no coincidence. While conducting an illegal private investigation ...* As if listening in on the imagined 9-1-1 call, John wore a humored smile, appreciative of the concern, then grateful for them all. He hadn't ever been knocked down before, they realized. Publicly beat on, but never beaten. Of all the people in Palos Hills, they were at his side. John H.

Walker was just a kid after all. He needed help sometimes, same as them.

Still, too many hands helped him to his feet and dusted him off, and too many questions were asked about his condition for him to be average, what he might've liked to feel. John claimed to be simply in need of bed rest. He wasn't keeping down much food these days, he admitted. Josué immediately gave him a hard lemon candy for his blood sugar, a bag of which he kept in his pocket after an aunt had begged God to banish them from the house, otherwise, she'd claimed, diabetes would make her face pucker permanently. John turned the tiny lemon in his fingers as if familiar, a memento returned, and popped it into his mouth with a warm "This means a lot," and a handshake that lingered on well past awkward. Josué's grin said he didn't much mind. The ghost of the legend yet wore his sheen of specialness. While in his presence, they did, too.

For John's sake, the kids hiked up out of the moraine for the first time as a group instead of trickling street-side singly. Down the walking trails, they smelled the spicy weeds and wild blossoms. They spotted the birds in the branches and the low sun in the sky, and returned to the sidewalk pace of small suburban life on a mild spring day. Each kid talked about what he or she would do with the rest of it. Generally, that was dinner and watch something or videogames. Only Josué would be eating with his family. Greg would be in bed before his mom came home and would stop at McDonalds on the way. E. hated TV—no offense, she said. Only Alex mentioned homework, studying for an honors algebra test. All of which recalled their many differences. The group fell quiet again as they struggled to imagine hanging out under normal circumstances. Part of them wanted to believe they could be friends, yet they knew it could never happen in any place but the woods.

The kids said bye where the trail along the elevated train tracks splintered and let out behind a derelict baseball diamond, the community recreation center's parking lot, and, further up, the yellow-bricked building itself. They decided to come and go this way from now on to avoid being seen by traffic near the trailhead.

Good call, John added, because of the regular police patrol.

Just then, a squad car turned onto 115th a few blocks up. It sidled along the woods in their direction. The kids squatted, though too far off to be spotted. "Oh, shit! I'm too young to go to jail," someone joked. "I'm too horny to shower with sex offenders!" mocked another. "Shut up, you jackasses," was the last word. They hooted with laughter, and the fear of being caught dissipated, even the consequences—parental guilt? a minor criminal record? military school?—seemed inconsequential. The rules and laws of the adult world were make-believe they could shed like a dream, but only from this distance, playing as they were on the edge of belief and disbelief. Hearts thumping, they caught a waft of hot asphalt and the citrusy scent of cut lawns out there, on the other side. They'd been wrong earlier. Time didn't move slowly in Palos Hills, but mechanically. For how many hours had they escaped today? The woods had granted that illusion, unadulterated time, the privilege of childhood, without delineation of weekdays or weekends or chores or homework or tests or big games, babysitting and "work around the house," marks of greater responsibility a little further down the timeline—and then? They still had summers to idle away, at least. That refuge would very soon be eclipsed by high school and the looming uncertainty of their futures. Because who knew how long it went on. Because Erika. All at once, they became serious. The police weren't looking for them, but a child killer.

The squad car U-turned in the rec center parking lot. They watched it double back, up 115th and out of sight. They were alone again as a group.

Before they disbanded, Tiffany unzipped Doug's backpack and stuffed in the yard gloves. She'd picked them up from where they'd landed. She thanked him again.

"You'll be back? Tomorrow?" he asked.

"Not even you could stop me, genius," she said haughtily, chin pointed up the street. She let a playful smile slip.

E. started to apologize to her for earlier. "Hey, I lost it a little, and I—"

"I know—I *know*." Tiffany snatched E. in a hug. She followed Greg out across the parking lot before the freak could say more.

E. insisted on seeing John home safely. Doug didn't moan from heartache. He did that locked in his bedroom, later. Instead, he donated his bike for the week so she could speed him home on the handlebars, somewhat selflessly, conscious of appearing selfless but still feeling bad for the guy. John accepted his help, touched Doug's shoulder in thanks without saying anything, the pain he wrestled with showing in his hunch and tepid gait. What was the allure of a guy like that? John's renowned handsomeness had faded. Doug could still catch it, but only in glimpses, the way he sometimes spotted the smartass young man his grandfather must've been when he told a joke after a few beers. To want a relationship with John despite his eminent death, was sympathy enough? Maybe what the guy represented turned her on. E. liked big ideas. Or maybe he allowed her the opportunity to care about something bigger than herself. Doug wanted companionship and something big, too, one day.

As the pair rolled down 115th, his heart went limp. E. didn't look back.

Doug tailed the rest glumly to the end of the trail where the trees thinned to full daylight behind the rec center. Ecstatic shrieks sounded from the playground, where children cried for the day to never end.

Doug had let E. go. He was kept standing by the residual rush of success with Tiffany Dennys. What would come of it? The question drowned out all thoughts of lesser excitement, which happened to be any other thought he was capable of at that moment. If Doug kept doing well, maybe the very popular non-nerd could be his first real date. His first kiss. She could be patronizing him, acting sweet and nice because she hadn't much to lose. But maybe not. Wisps of much larger fantasies whirled in his head composed of pristine snapshots of her arms, her laugh, her boldness. Doug withheld from entertaining them. He feared jinxing his luck and the slap of disappointment. The result was that his head felt full of fizz. Anxious and desperate to be distracted, he walked beside Josué in a half-gestured conversation about videogames each played, the boys followed closely by Alex, silent and ever watchful.

Their favorite videogame of all time was the same. Doug didn't know why this came as a surprise. He was captivated as J. described the epic end game scene Doug had yet to reach, the battle in Jakar'tep against the Great Snake in the statuary of the Old Gods, stone giants that rose on all sides as if bearing The Void upon their shoulders, where one's story-companion at last succumbs to not just any curse, but possession by Balagal, and when a player must choose his or her fate: to forever banish the demon's soul with magic or to rid the vile serpent with steel.

Josué slashed the air between them—cried out in delivery of the final blow. Doug flinched, and Josué could tell he'd scared the kid. He smacked the pendejo on the back to say it was OK, to lighten up, but also toughen up a little, too, eh? And the boys laughed to rid themselves of the discomfort.

Doug was fairly sure J. would never really hurt him. He was friendly and not ignorant as expected. His precision of expression and clarity of thought were arguably better than Doug's, which surprised Doug as much as when J. had chopped the air between them. Why? Because he'd underestimated the guy and believed him dangerous, though he didn't start the fistfights he got suspensions for at school, and because of how he looked, not stout in the middle and lean in the limbs with an easy smile, but foreign, dark-complexioned, Mexican. Doug wasn't racist—was he? He'd flinched and laughed and kept laughing to expel the anxiety of difference. He couldn't. He'd never helped J.—wouldn't risk to pronounce the kid's name—for fear of what? Doug probably deserved to be hit. He talked about his current favorite game instead, building a world block by block, etc., which J. had heard of and was excited to try. At every pause in the conversation, Doug tried and failed to put himself in Josué's shoes: another landscape, language, family, food, traditions—problems—memories—dreams? What he'd assumed was the world wasn't all or even most of it. Doug felt white for the first time, and a panicked burst of perspiration and shame over that fact, beside the other boy's daily reminders of what he was and wasn't.

So when Alex tapped his shoulder before they broke from the tree line and said, "Please, would you allow me to date your find?" hand open to take the bullet shell, Doug stared dumbly for a moment, as if the question were in another language.

His reaction was understandable, Alex thought; they hadn't known each other long enough to have developed faith in the other's abilities. Or he too suspected foul play. Alex had estimated the probability of at least one member of the group being involved in the murder of the twelve-year-old Erika Summerson as moderately high. All knew the victim and were potentially motivated by social-sexual jealousy and/or betrayal. Contrary to Tiffany Dennys's earlier defense of her presence on the team exonerating her from being a suspect, Alex had watched enough *Real Crime* documentaries in the last forty-eight hours in preparation for this investigation to know that murderers often return to the scene of a crime to tamper with evidence, posture as an innocent, and/or generally mislead an investigation. Doug, for instance, could be the murderer, which would easily explain his leading Tiffany Dennys to dig exactly where the bullet casing was found as well as his eagerness to pick it up—to give false cause to the presence of his fingerprints and/or to pocket and "accidentally" lose it later. Any unwillingness on his part to hand the object over might incriminate him further. Alex therefore clarified:

"Despite the reported cause of death, we need to conclusively rule out the bullet as evidence. I'll inventory it and do what research I can so that we might put this heartless child slasher behind bars. Unless you have any reason not to give it to me?"

"Oh, date it," he said and gave over the shell. "Sure—I mean … of course." Doug was still wary as to whether Alex could be trusted to keep their work secret. What would stop her from running the evidence straight to the police? Well, if the group got in trouble now, they would surely all go down together, her included.

Alex parted with the boys at Depot Street, where they waved and took the pedestrian tunnel beneath the elevated tracks to the lower part of town. Their voices elongated, bounced excitedly off the concrete walls as they passed through to the arc of light on the other side, talking about girls, specifically Tiffany Dennys, who, though pleasing enough to behold, was, in Alex's opinion, too much of a drama queen to waste time courting. Alex let both suspects return to their regular lives, this time without trailing Doug, as on that first night that John had led him and E. down into the woods. As long as Dennys was alive, it seemed, he wasn't going anywhere. Alex climbed the commuter stairs and walked on the tracks across 111th Street. It was the shortest line home and, anyway, Alex avoided those who attracted or created drama. Achieving mastery of advanced mathematics was a challenging enough pursuit, and the attention necessary to do one thing brilliantly required the keeping of a well-ordered life. Distancing oneself from conflict had led Alex to being labeled as a tattletale, which had stunted the acquisition of acquaintances beyond fellow mathletes, who were united by purpose more than affinity. Skipping grades had further complicated junior high. For one, Alex did not share the interests of older boys and girls. Elder mathletes saw placement in state competitions as opportunities to flirt and make out with each other during the long bus trips, rather than opportunities to exhibit one's intellectual fitness. Alex was curious about sex only as an intellectual problem. Who to like and how to express that sentiment seemed so much less complicated than what kids seemed to make of it due to sex's exaggerated role. Perhaps they too hid a good deal of their true feelings and acted out simply to conform. Alex had given that up, conforming, after coming to Palos Hills Junior High and meeting Mrs. Shepard, the school gym teacher and volleyball coach, easily the most captivating person in the building. Within days of witnessing the well-muscled spark of positive energy that was Mrs. Shepard, Alex got a similar bowl haircut and began dressing in smart, boyish clothes. Alex would've tried out for the volleyball team if athletic. Ever since, the primary goal of dressing had become identity expression—studious, fastidious, affable—not the attraction of mates. This attitude, that life should be lived with clear purpose to accomplish some meaningful goal, was the deepest divide between Alex and other students. In that regard, math was much less a challenge than navigating the social world of junior high. Alex very much desired to be accepted and respected, but sought that validation in terms of intellectual aptitude. Like the great Marie Curie, Alex hoped to make a discovery worthy of praise and, one day, perhaps even love. At one time, John Walker held that throne for so many people. What fair-weather fans didn't see was his unyielding brilliance. He refused to play the part others expected: the sickly boy in a hospital robe and wheelchair, who was to accept their pity and flowers and roll into the sunset without a squeak. His strength had been robbed, yet the passion of the great sportsman remained. Alex saw it—altered in form, but indestructible—when he sporadically reappeared at school, then noticed a pattern to his visitations that corresponded to watching those within Erika's intimate circle. He was at work again, plotting his last earthly exploit, maybe only to reclaim his place in people's hearts. Whatever the motive, Alex wanted in, in a big way.

The sun dropped behind 111th, and the melt of orange and gold silhouetted the last hill that marked the very edge of Palos Hills, made gorgeous thanks to atmospheric pollution, and halted Alex in the crunchy rocks between the parallel tracks. Beauty seemed simple, looking over the town, a product not so much of being alone—Alex was always alone—but of being. In time, the pinks shied into purples. A cooler breeze swept by, signaling night. Looking back, one could see its purplish shade falling from the east of town. Somewhere out there lived a killer, a person capable of turning a young girl inside out and red all over and going on with life quietly. Until he or she killed again.

"I'm going to find you," Alex whispered, eyes closed as if praying beside Yiaya, except not hollow-hearted, a show to please Grandmother, but brimming with faith in the power of deductive reasoning.

Someone coughed close by. On both sides, the tracks were empty, shadow-tipped peaks stretched against rocks that glowed neon white in the new dark. Alex listened for a clue. The stranger thrashed through the brush below. Here, past the intersection of 111th and Harlem, the concrete train bridge was a grassy wall of dirt that carried the tracks through upper and lower Palos Hills. The fear the situation induced was laughable. The probability of facing the child killer in this manner was infinitesimal. Likely a fellow kid rushed to make curfew or a fellow explorer took to the tracks to enjoy the night in solitude.

Alex did not wait to find out and ran hard.

Before sliding down to the street, Alex glanced back. A thin rectangle of a figure of indiscernible age stood in the middle of the tracks and gazed in Alex's direction.

Turning the front door lock that night felt good. Only then did a laugh escape Alex over the stranger. And another at E. and Tiffany's fight in the woods, and the troubles they would inevitably face tomorrow. And lastly at how irrational one human being's actions could make a community. Such potent, perilous influence.

9

The kids came prepared to make their third day of excavating clues at Bachelor's Grove more pleasant than before.

E. and John showed up on Doug's bike—the Dead Man pedaling on the weakest gear and E. upright on the back pegs with her backpack jiggling, full of bottled waters. The group laughed at how the heck they'd got the bike down the ravine, then cheered as the pair crossed the valley in slo-mo, John eager and determined to reach the creek. E. looked more tired than he did. Her under-eyes were the color of ripe plums. She yawned, happily, as if having cruised all night and never having let go of his shoulders, too thrilled by the company to sleep, ready to meet whatever obstacles life brought next so long as they did it together.

That's what love looks like, Doug thought. He felt queasy. E. had found the one boy who fascinated her enough to make her act like everybody else. And it seemed the Dead Man had found a groupie to entertain him until his final days. What more could she mean to a guy like John H. Walker, who at one time could've had any girl in town? Doug was left with nothing, of course. A lesson in maintaining his dignity, maybe.

It wasn't easy to watch them murmuring to each other as they dismounted and came over the creek planks toward Doug and the rest waiting around the Big Tree. Alex had refused to share research about the chrome shell discovered here yesterday until John arrived. Another groupie, Doug had thought, envy pricking his heart, which he plunged into soothing visions of Tiffany Dennys's face turned to him in full glow. All he could really think about at school was being near the girl again and pleasing her. Sure, Tiffany wasn't smart or serious or deep. But she seemed a good person—good enough if more loyal than Mrs. Dead Man. Tiffany, however, hadn't yet arrived.

"We've got a lot of work ahead of us," John announced to the group. He recapped yesterday's progress and detailed the sections of the Grove yet unearthed. He clapped his hands to get them moving, not allowing Doug to get a word in about waiting for Tiffany. Doug suspected John was trying to keep anyone from commenting on how he'd recovered from yesterday, from bringing any attention to his weakness and subsequent surge of vitality. To push E. on the back of Doug's bicycle just to be cute, either the guy had faked yesterday or was so doped up on painkillers that he didn't know how he'd gotten here. Neither explanation comforted Doug.

"John?" Alex jumped in. "I have information on the bullet that Doug and Tiffany discovered, relevant to the dig. I would like to share this information with you now."

"Please, share it with the group," John said. "We're in this together."

Alex reported on the find: Firstly, it wasn't a bullet, but a casing, a shell. The bullet was the part of a cartridge that flew out and killed people, in this instance, at approximately one thousand feet per second. The find was a .38 caliber Super casing from the '70s or '80s. The rim of the case was stamped with most of that information and Alex had just looked up the manufacturer and saw when the company was in business. Of course, the person could've fired an old cartridge at a later date, but either way it was a pistol round, not from a rifle. That said, Erika Summerson wasn't shot, at least not publicly reported to be shot.

"I appreciate your hustle on this, Alex," John said.

"Thank you, sir."

Doug could've puked.

Feeling he was missing something, Greg said, "So, this tells us—"

"Nada?" Josué said.

"Not a thing," Doug affirmed.

"There's more here than we can imagine right now," John said.

Everyone nodded thoughtfully, even the real genius, who was clearly Alex. E. didn't voice a word of criticism about yesterday being a waste of time. She beamed at John with ravenous adoration, as if nothing in the world would please her more than biting the guy's head clean off. The Dead Man seemed to have put the group under a spell of lunacy. Doug wasn't wholly immune to its influence. Yesterday, after John had asked the group if they were hot, a cool breeze blew in, and later, a limb of the Big Tree had been squeaking for an hour and the Dead Man looked up and began muttering to it, talking with the tree until, a minute later, it ceased. These were a series of coincidences, which nevertheless made a weakness invade Doug's guts and settle down into his balls with a cold pang of fragility. The others had glanced at one another for confirmation that these small miracles were indeed happening, yet they couldn't look each other in the eyes.

To do so would acknowledge what they'd witnessed, actual miracles. Instead of recognizing John as crazy and that no one was going to find anything but trouble, the effect was greater faith in what was possible. The police had combed the area for months, and they were just kids, not trained detectives. Their only advantage was having larger imaginations, easily a disadvantage under the wrong influence. They were honoring Erika's memory, that's all.

Not all. Doug had stumbled into a one-in-a-million chance to woo someone as valuable as he wished to feel. Tiffany still hadn't come through the trees, though. The wait was torturous. He didn't ask everyone to wait as they grabbed shovels. He wouldn't reveal his weakness to the group, unlike John, who'd exposed his yesterday. Doug doggedly held out to prove himself the better man.

Though the kids' blisters were still raw, with John's encouragement, they raised their shovel blades in a shaky salute and set out in teams of two. That day, they uncovered a mess of scrap metal: an old car antenna, a dash knob, and a few chrome bits of auto body. Alex plotted these finds on a 3D grid of the area made of graph paper turned on a 45-degree angle, which of course greatly impressed everyone. They soon isolated the area of highest debris deeper in the ground and closest to the base of the Big Tree, as if at one time the stony trunk was the cause of a devastating auto wreck later buried. The advantage of this knowledge, John touted, was an increased ability to discern objects that were unusual and relevant to the crime.

More bullshit to keep us pacified, Doug thought. No one asked how a car got down here, let alone gathered enough speed to smash into a tree. Doug didn't mention it to avoid sounding antagonistic.

The Dead Man supervised the kids' work, aided by his assistants, Alex and E. The girls spent most of their time refilling and replacing water bottles, ensuring that John and their lackey diggers were properly hydrated. Doug kept himself from souring over the unequal distribution of labor by picturing the guy as a senile pharaoh perpetually dissatisfied with sites chosen for his burial chamber. After taking his orders to stop what he was doing and do it in another spot, then again told to stop and do it someplace else, Doug couldn't restrain his frustration and muttered, "So long as we bury you, eventually." He was relieved when John didn't turn to confront him.

About an hour before sunset, John suggested that the group get to know one another. He directed Greg and Josué and Doug to carry over large rocks and a section of fallen trunk, which they did, panting as they dropped the crude seats in a semicircle around the hole first discovered in front of the Big Tree. For a few minutes, the kids spoke short, unconnected declaratives at one another. The silence between their attempts at conversation lengthened. The beat of Greg's headphones became noticeable, and he turned them off to not be rude. Then it was really quiet. Each kid kept their gaze on the empty pit, as if on one's desk to avoid being called on by a teacher.

"Is this all we have to say to one another?" John asked, more of an observation than a question.

Greg and Josué immediately began to perspire harder than while digging. To speak a single word seemed the hardest task they'd been charged with all day.

"No partying without me!" short yet sharply echoed off the rock face encircling the Grove, making the place seem isolated and far removed from the world. Whether they liked Tiffany Dennys or not, everyone looked for her in the trees and shadow fingers that crossed the valley, relieved help from outside had arrived to save them from talking.

Tiffany came over the bridge with the sunset coppery at her back. She'd gotten caught up with jerks from school that'd missed her, she said, but "voila!"—and she twirled around the hole before the group with her arms raised, then wilting dramatically, then reaching again higher. The dance exposed a slit of skin between her white shorts and top, which only John missed, who instead watched her hands flutter against the jet trails carved into the pale sky.

Josué clapped and sent the last of his Halloween candy around the circle—a hefty grocery bag—to sustain this positive spirit. He hadn't cared for trick-or-treating or Día de Muertos back in his hometown. Particularly men dancing in skeleton costumes startled him easily as a child, and the thought of the veil between worlds becoming flimsy, useless, made him feel faint, which caused his six aunts to tease him for acting like a sissy. Was he not the man in their house? Two years in America had hardened him. He'd made trick-or-treating his quest, setting out several times during the day dressed as a cowboy defender from the old times, until he'd reaped most of Palos Hills. His goal was to amass a trove to last an entire year. As of yet, his efforts hadn't been enough. Sometimes he had to hide from the older bullies, or rain clouds hung in the sky and brought nighttime early, and the streets lost their familiarity, and the yards sprouted heads of monsters and their limp, dismembered bodies left to rot, and going on meant facing an endless pageant of demons and the screams of innocents begging for salvation. And when his aunt who always had a limp cigarette in her mouth came in from the balcony, a marigold in one hand with the petals plucked, half her face painted as a skull, and said, "Ya estuvo, vaquero?" it felt to Josué like a betrayal. But last Halloween, he'd braved the night and walked into his home with a garbage bag of sweets slung over his shoulder. Little Santa he was called, earning the laughter but also the praise of his aunts, whom he later caught tearing into his stash like vultures; vultures he privately enjoyed pleasing with his labor. To the group's happiness, he similarly wanted to contribute. If for no other reason, very much did he want friends in school so that they might watch each other's backs, even strange ones like these.

Doug then opened his book bag and passed around candy bars. He'd bought two for Tiffany and him and U-turned back into the store and blew his allowance to appear generous. This quality seemed to have impressed the girl yesterday. Doug wagged a bar at her, and Tiffany said she'd just eaten, but would share one if that was OK. Doug laid his hoodie on the log for her to sit on, and she came around beside him. The tangle of sunny hopes and deeply plotted maneuvers and end-of-the-world disappointments that'd tortured him all day seemed worth that moment when she thanked him and his lungs again filled with her sweet cherry aroma, and her bare, darkly tanned knee nestled against his clammy thigh, and she asked, "Did you like my dance?"

"Very nymph-y," Doug said.

"You guessed it, genius," she said, and they smiled.

The kids spent the remaining hour in the woods before nightfall, snacking between excited talk about friends of friends they shared, about two notable fistfights that had gone down in the halls that day, as well as highlights of the unusual amount of teacher outbursts in the last few weeks that they'd witnessed or heard rumored. There was also Coach Atkins, who'd been killed last night. He wasn't murdered, just plain dead, and most teachers and the groups' parents seemed relieved by the news rather than upset when announced this morning. Mr. Atkins had been initially indicted in Erika's murder, as it'd come out that he'd occasionally given her rides to away games and allegedly she'd come out of his car once reeking of alcohol. Under interrogation, he'd admitted to the drinking incident but denied any sexual misconduct and killing the girl. The night of her murder, he'd been carried home, blackout drunk, from the Pump Room, a local bar, where he'd made an ass of himself in front of plenty of witnesses, and so had been released from custody. But his coaching and teaching career was finished, which was just as well at that point in his life, having lost John H. Walker, then Erika, then his wife and child from the scandal. The school had been allowing him to finish the baseball season, Palos's first without their star, but had suspended him from teaching. If he wasn't a killer, he was a drunk and a child predator, and that made him about as bad as one. Coach Atkins died having smashed his car into a tree at the corner of 115th and Harlem.

"It's almost safer out here," Greg said. He looked around the circle like a kid half his size for someone to agree.

"The police said the walking trails are safe, at least," E. added.

"As long as a killer is at large, no one is safe anywhere," Alex corrected, recalling the silly scare up on the train tracks yesterday, and decided not to jeopardize the investigation by sharing an unsubstantiated suspicion of being followed.

"Are you kidding me? This place? It's never been safe!" Tiffany threw back her head and cackled, shielding her smile loosely with one hand.

Greg ducked his eyes, feeling the shame Tiffany did not. But it was a very sexy cackle, he thought, how she broke the great stone silence of the moraine and finished in an ecstatic gasp.

"The only reason the cops reopened this place was to let the surveyors in," she said.

"Surveyors?" Alex asked.

"The land people," Tiffany said. "They're all in cahoots now. Don't you know anything? The police, the mayor, the developers. My dad's one. A developer. They'll be hacking trees within the week, he says. But here's the thing: he's a dumb fucking bastard, too."

They all laughed. Their conversation swept on, each seeking common ground unconsciously, enjoying the company, and feeling a little less alone.

Josué wanted to communicate the lightness in his heart, at last welcome and safe someplace away from home, as Greg had expressed, because the people there accepted and appreciated him. These kids weren't family. They had no responsibility to care for him. This fact heightened his joy. "Josué?" the girl named E. said handing him a fresh bottle of water. He hated the taste of water, which sat in his gut as though liquid rock, but he drank a gulp with great pleasure in front of her because she'd used his full name instead of just "J." and pronounced the name the right way, leaving its character sublimidad or apasionado, as his aunt had said of it after he once vented to her his frustrations with life in America. None of the kids in the group poked fun at the name after she used it, as jerks liked to do during study hall whenever the teacher, a well-meaning white lady, entertained herself by speaking to him in a robot-sounding Spanish. All he could do to thank E. was smile and give her a thumbs up, which made him feel less like a person, but some dumb cartoon, his fear of speaking poorly threatening his joy.

Attempting to speak even bad English with these kids would be a perfect opportunity to improve, he knew. But it was too late to start now because they would notice the change, and then it would be weird, and Josué could not stand the embarrassment of being singled out in that way and maybe ostracized for the difference. Instead, he withdrew from the group with his paint markers in hand, which he sometimes used for tagging desks and bathrooms, and he began to draw on the Big Tree where the bark had been dented and peeled away to expose a smoother skin. He drew Erika as he remembered her.

She used to pass him many notes during English class. These were comic drawings of the teacher, mostly, but sometimes of the author or class topic. Erika was easily the funniest girl he'd ever met. Josué still smiled when recalling the time she had rendered a likeness of the teacher's face in the ass of a horse and how she'd made it wink, which had forced him to tap his forehead against his desktop a long time to restrain uproarious laughter at the mere thought of the image. Sometimes she would speak to him about her life in these notes, about the friends she had and confess the trouble she'd gotten into over the weekend, which wasn't always funny, but her sharing was always appreciated. Sometimes she asked questions about his life, although Josué was too busy with family to get into much trouble. "I wish I had your life," she'd once written. He didn't think much of her words at the time. It was naive, a joke. Then her desk stood empty one day, and the next, too, and then he heard his mother on the phone speaking of otra pobre güera muerta and his world went black except for those six words that returned in Erika's loopy handwriting, so wide that each at first appeared as a deranged insect until painfully clear.

Her absence created a yawning gap in his life, as if a trapdoor had opened beneath him, and Josué fainted. He woke to his youngest aunt, Althea, bent and pinching his cheek to rouse him and to the sound of his mother calling his name, "Josué! Josué! Josué!" as if his revival were being cheered on. He went to the funeral alone and seemed the only boy who cried hot tears upon seeing the face of the harmless-looking girl in the casket, eyes shut forever. He then felt unmanly and went out to the parking lot where a gang of boys heckled him. He came at the hijos de putas full force, cracking fools' jaws and stealing the wind from their bellies with impassioned punches he didn't know he had in him, until, outnumbered, they beat him flat. His head cracked the asphalt and the fury fled him. He now recognized his pain and lashing out as selfish. He didn't like this quality in himself, so he imagined how special she might've been to the other fighters, though they didn't deserve his empathy, and how their anger might also be a kind of mourning. The effect of Erika's death was all that was left of her. He imagined the joy she would've brought to people, how that was gone. His joy, too. And her own. And then the precious memories, bubbles of laughter, moments of perfect happiness in his mind. Would they go, too? It was all very sad. This left Josué determined. Not soon would she be forgotten.

"That's pretty great," Greg said from behind the kid. J. stepped back from his drawing and revealed Erika. In a familiar floral dress with her hands relaxed at her sides, she floated peacefully as if on her back in someone's pool. Greg's heart stung, wishing she were alive. The picture wasn't at all sad. The way she smiled … It was as if Erika were right there, seeing them and happy; still here. "She's great, man," he said again. The boys nodded at each other and gazed back at the drawing, remembering, admiring together.

When Josué and Greg turned around, the whole group was risen behind them in silence. They joined the ring of figures, all filled with adoration and love, and standing against the coming night.

10

The kids hiked on sore legs down to Bachelor's Grove and up again every evening until, come Thursday morning, getting out of bed for school had never been more of a pain and the Big Tree side of the creek had been completely plowed for leads in the case. The kids had accomplished the feat as a team, digging and then filling ten-foot sections of earth, sifting the contents for a murder weapon or some clue as to what Erika and/or her killer or killers had been searching for. The group shoveled and heaved and bent and sweat. In times of weakness, their eyes rested on the dead girl drawn on the tree trunk. As much, they relied on some faith in the Dead Man and his own steadfastness. Yet after three days of hard labor, not a single solid piece of evidence had been discovered. All but John struggled to believe in The Work.

Even E., who had helped the boy most in his quest, more than she'd helped anyone ever, hoped that John would at last proclaim, "We've done our duty. We're going home," no longer because she thought his moral character overrated or false, but so that the group might forget the woods and explore their friendships elsewhere. John displayed no doubt whatsoever. Whereas at the start of the endeavor he might go an entire evening without having said but a handful of sentences due to, E. believed, the intense effort spent in masking the effects of his illness, in the last two days he'd become gaunt but also more animated and critical. Instead of losing hope, he scrutinized their methods, revised them hourly, and more than once he'd hinted at plans for scouring the other side of the creek. Occasionally he became frustrated. The boy's gaze then lingered upon the original hand-dug hole, perhaps as a reminder of what he worked against—the grave, time—and of why pushing forward was crucial, for Erika's legacy and his own, for dignity in death.

These moments of relent were brief, yet E. didn't miss one. Her sympathy, a palpable and self-consuming command of attention and concerns she never knew she possessed, had irrefutably and irrevocably latched her to the boy. It was only a matter of time before John would spot E. eyeing him. She appeared miserable from imbibing his struggle, and he strode over, speaking out of earshot of the others:

"It means something," he said defensively. "The hole—your sister's fingernails—all this junk we're finding. I'm not crazy."

"No one's given up," E. reassured.

He took a half-breath—deep considering the abrasive bodily pain, as if a clumsy doctor were using a nail file to rid the cancer from his bones. "You're right," he said with a sigh.

Five minutes later, the boy was back to the dig or implementing a fresh idea. E. imagined that her reassurances allowed John to refocus on the task at hand rather than on the fact his time was running out.

To feel necessary, needed by him, renewed her vigor for a little while longer. The intermittent unearthing of fascinating objects helped, too.

They marveled for a few minutes at a small gray arrowhead Greg had found buried along the creek. The kids passed it around and naively guessed to name the people who'd called the area home for thousands of years. Near the Big Tree, more recent history had begun to surface. These finds included two more .38 shells, a gnarly crowbar, and a wool fedora. Then Josué tipped the blade of his shovel to the group to display three notched bones. Alex took pictures without comment, first categorizing the find among the rest of the detailed photographs and notes—which, Alex was certain, would be pivotal to solving the case—and confirmed, holding the tip up to the fading light, the bones as a single human thumb. Erika had been buried complete with all her digits, E. assured the group. She recalled her sister's clean hands crossed over her chest in the coffin. Who then was this nine-fingered victim?

An unspoken consensus settled over the group that John had been right about more being in these woods than they'd imagined, as well as a general reluctance to uncover any more details of the place's brutal past. Only one of them was thrilled by these discoveries. Alex had begun researching Bachelor's Grove nightly and told stories during their now regular circle gatherings. Local gangsters had literally torn their rivals apart in the valley, the Grove being the spot where the infamous Al Capone had tortured and stashed the bodies of his victims.

"Hey, so you think these killers were after like, Capone's treasure or something?" Greg suggested that evening.

"Maybe," Doug said. "Maybe they were just burying crap."

"Like, these killers had their own gold or cash or something they were stashing?"

"No … crap—their shit."

In disgust, Greg threw the sifting pan he was repairing, and Tiffany gasped with a laugh and said, "Good one, genius." The girl's encouragement made him feel a foot taller, sharp-witted, brave. Her rebellious spirit came out somewhat snarky and bitter through him. Doug wasn't sure if adopting her candor and crudeness would damage his rapport with the others, and right now he didn't care so long as Tiffany thought him more clever and assertive, overall manlier than he really was, and he vowed never to miss an opportunity to criticize the Dead Man's endeavor.

"Improbable," Alex said. "Let's say for the sake of argument that it were true—about the treasure, not the human waste. The killers learned of a great treasure buried here—how? Again, this is very improbable—and so they made Erika—a close friend, someone with whom these kids could entrust the secret—dig with them into the night. This hypothetical treasure would likely be buried deep. Why the dirty nails then? Why not use shovels, like we're doing—"

"Greed was their motivator," John said.

"That's what I was saying." Greg smiled triumphantly.

"So why not bury the body? Not even an attempt made at hiding the evidence? No, this detail rings louder than greed to me. Our suspect lacks shame—the mark of a true sociopath. Or worse—they were proud."

Alex wasn't sensitive about Erika's death, and Doug noticed E. staring into the hole dug by her sister and/or the killers, the bottom of which could no longer be seen in the deepening shadow. She stood beside the seated Dead Man with her hand on his shoulder, like his caretaker. However, weakness showed in her slouchier-than-usual stance and in the way her hips curved toward John as if she might

113

collapse but for his support. Sure, the guy's health was shit, but his spirit had annoyingly doubled, and when he wasn't going on about the "will of the woods" or some other bizarre jabbering, he scanned the faces of the kids intently, creepiest at dusk when his eyes appeared gray.

Doug thought how difficult it must be for E. to visit the site daily. He couldn't recall having seen her cry once about losing her sister, which he'd thought unusual. Then again E. wasn't normal, which was what also made her so damn special. Likely, she wasn't doing OK, and the Dead Man certainly wasn't in any condition to help. Ready to depart this plane of existence, the guy had his sights set on something higher than love. Which was totally dumb, as love and closeness and comfort were all that seemed to make anything matter.

"Maybe we shouldn't talk about … it. Here," Doug said.

"It's fine," E. said without a hint of sadness. She continued as monotonously, as if hypnotized: "We have to know what happened."

"What if they got scared?" Greg went on hypothesizing. "Maybe the kids just freaked after they killed her. I would've."

Alex looked at Greg as if he'd shouted in their faces. "Would you have?"

"Any kid would've. Come on, A."

"Stop saying it was a kid already! You don't know if it was or if it was somebody's grandma trying to bake her into freaking gingerbread cookies," Tiffany said, disturbed that every theory Alex proposed implied her involvement, that Tiffany either knew the killer or was the killer. She'd already told the group what she'd told the police, and more. Though she had a lot of acquaintances, Tiffany had lost everybody that she would call a friend along the road to eighth grade due to being "too confident in who she was, or too real," or at least too sassy for anyone to handle but Erika, who'd introduced herself by saying that Tiffany was the "baddest bitch she'd ever met" and that she would do anything to be her best friend, maybe to achieve popularity ("Don't you mean infamy?" E. had interrupted, then immediately apologized) or maybe because she was actually "just the coolest." So she and Erika had become best friends, OK, but they partied at Bachelor's Grove a lot with a lot of different guys and sometimes Erika came by herself. Being incriminated by the girl, or boy or whatever Alex was trying to be, made Tiffany anxious that everyone was watching her, waiting for her to scream, "I did it! I killed Erika!" which made Tiffany uncharacteristically quiet and then pissed off until the comments kicked out.

"Or devil worshippers," Josué said. His two fingers curled into horns that sprouted just above his ears.

"Right," Tiffany said. "There's way more crazy adults out here than kids."

Alex flipped through notes, unmoved. "If E.'s observation about her sister's soiled fingernails is a fact—and I'm assuming here that it is—and Erika dug for the period of approximately six days, then it wasn't likely forced by an adult, but someone she trusted or someone whose trust she hoped to gain."

"For what?" Greg said.

"That, we don't know. More of what she wanted, perhaps. Esteem—love?"

"Who was she dating?" he asked, trying not to sound stalkerish.

"She was between boyfriends," Tiffany said.

"It could've been a friend," Alex said.

"Or maybe—" Tiffany took a breath "—some people—OK, maybe kids—just flipped out on drugs, like it was a total accident, and we're out here for nothing. How about that theory?"

"The friend-killer theory upsets you." Alex made a note.

"First off, you don't know anything yet. There's zero evidence. So let's stop pretending we're something we're not, like kid detectives. Second, I know you all think I did it, which is bullshit. You want to cast suspicions? It could've been any one of us. Maybe we should all go around and say our alibi. I'll go first: I was in my room, listening to music and crying my eyes out like an idiot because some dipshit I was seeing cheated on me. I'd cheated on him, so I don't know why I was crying. It's just, no one can ever really be trusted, you know? Anyway, I wouldn't come down for dinner. My bitch of a mother can vouch for that and the police who already put me through this. So, Alex, where were you on the night of the murder, huh?"

"Studying."

"Wow. Very convincing story."

"Sowing suspicion among friends isn't welcome here," John said.

Alex jotted another note, moved on. "Let's say we have a kid-killer on our hands that Erika knew—very probable, for the record. Why kill her? What was the motive?"

"I think they found it, the gangster's treasure. But the killer didn't feel like sharing," Greg said. "Like in that movie—"

"No," John said, "it's still here." He rocked back and forth as if tweaking after a pot of coffee.

"Aw, who knows, man."

"Look at it," Tiffany said. "No offense, but the stupid hole isn't even deep enough to bury all this treasure you're talking about."

"This is all speculation, of course," Alex added. "But if there is an item of great value buried here—if the killer still believes a treasure is to be found—one worth killing for—they'll most certainly return."

"Goodness—" John said horrified. He stared into the gray trees.

The kids scrambled up and faced that corner of the valley.

Josué's hands hovered at his sides as if to quick-draw his imaginary six-shooter. He stepped ahead of the others to confront Erika's killer, the group at his back. He saw nothing.

"It's late," John said. "We've stayed too late."

The kids had lingered in the woods longer than John had previously allowed, their restless conversation spurred by a desire to know their work meant something. Even the Dead Man's vigilance had grown lax. Despite the grisly history of the valley, the group's closeness had bestowed a sense of safety, and they'd worn their bond like an armor that just might prevent knife blades. John's constant warnings of not straying too far or remaining too late to avoid catching the attention of some nameless evil in the woods didn't feel quite real until now.

"Hide the tools back in the bushes," he ordered.

The kids did so without question. Effectively spooked, they clambered from the valley and spilled eagerly onto the streets of Palos Hills.

Doug, Tiffany, Josué, and Greg took the tunnel under the elevated train tracks, not keen on soon splitting up after the scare. On the other side, they walked the lampless, thickly shadowed suburban blocks, each wondering after their bravery and looking back on their work that week as absolute lunacy—plowing an entire crime scene without any weapons to protect themselves or adult supervision when a knife-wielding maniac might return to massacre them or, at least, track and slay them individually. The fact they'd been blind to the danger made them marvel at how they'd let John talk them into it, and seemed to explain why no other kids had yet come to party there.

If any place on Earth deserved the title cursed, it seemed to be Bachelor's Grove, and, as the four kids sloughed the woods' gravity, they began to struggle to conceive of a single good reason to ever return.

All at once they craved civilization and turned on 111th for the headlights and streetlamps and whir of steady traffic along Southwest Highway. Tiffany hopped on Greg's back, and the basketballer veered as if to take to the busy street running. A car honked, and their defiant laughs dispelled the last wisps of doom. At the Dunkin Donuts, the kids had milk and sandy donuts among the bums grimly sipping coffee, goofing off loudly as if the only people in the joint and talking about everything and anything but the woods. Loitering in the parking lot later, Tiffany lit a cigarette stolen from her mother, and each kid had a drag, coughing and dopily smiling because they felt like kids again, the kind to which death is an event that lies so far into the future that it is more likely a fib created by adults to encourage good behavior.

The feeling couldn't last all night (couldn't it?). Curfew nagged at every glimpse at the clock. The fact they were checking the time, like the lull in conversation, said it was time to part. The yet cryptic language of sexual chemistry had divided them. Tiffany didn't need Josué or Greg to stay. Maybe the dork? Both boys wanted to be upset, but they'd had too good of a time to call the night a loss. Regret would needle them plenty, later. They punched Doug's shoulder affectionately and with great meaning—*Don't blow this.* Greg swooped on Doug and headlocked him, really wished him the best, as even a tiny advance with the girl would mean success for everyone because they were still a group, after all, and maybe becoming friends, the kind who shared individual joys along with the hardships.

After Josué and Greg got their hugs and wandered home, and the cute dork stuck around, eyes a bit wet from choking on the smoke, readjusting his glasses with both hands as they slipped down his nose, Tiffany felt so free, like herself again, that she pulled this decent guy, maybe her first, close by the shirt pocket and said, "Get over here," and he did without any self-consciousness about having to rise on his toes to kiss such a powerful girl because he was so full of her at that moment, and only after they'd finished signing circles and waves and corkscrews with their tongues, a whole fundamental geometry of desire, and peered into the shop window to see the clock well past curfew, did they notice they'd been making out thirty minutes, and Doug hurried off with a sore tongue as proof he hadn't dreamed it, tripping on the sidewalk and looking back to see that Tiffany had also looked back and seen him trip—but she'd looked back—and they smiled and left feeling at last as if they'd accomplished something significant that week.

Though Doug didn't trust or agree with John's methods, and wouldn't start to, the guy had provided him this moment, an opportunity to belong, and actual belonging, a chance to feel like somebody, which wasn't lost on him as he ran home grinning.

But not all the kids shook the distress of the woods so easily that night. John and E. were followed closely by Alex as they wound through the many blocks of seemingly quiet, well-lit homes of upper Palos. Alex lagged a bit, composing a three-column list of all Erika's friends that E. could remember having visited their house: "During the last year," "Three months prior to the killing," and "The week of the killing." E. went through the girls' physical descriptions and names slowly and deliberately, but really sorting through hazy bits of birthday parties, sleepovers, hangouts, and phone calls. This included several aggressive fights between Erika and their parents over missed curfews and not checking in for hours after school, and the mostly fruitless interrogations by their mother about who Erika had "gone for a drive" with. All these incomplete recollections churned into two distinct impressions of her little sister: the girl's manner of speaking, as if cramming all her opinions on a subject upon a single breath, and a conglomerated image of her face, somewhat smug, but harmless, more happy than not. Starker than these moments in her sister's company were the gaps, the time she'd spent avoiding Erika, locked in her room or away at the library. E.'s loss—no longer remote, but crowding—overwhelmed her. All that remained of her sister was the steam of memories from a pot boiled down to empty, and a cheery, three-color drawing on a tree overlooking the site of her murder.

"I should've been there," E. said. It took the reserves of her restraint not to cry out the words.

No longer was she answering Alex's questions. The sidewalk was bleary. E. stumbled into someone's lawn who must've just watered because her shoes were wet. She didn't care and stopped without explaining why.

John took her hand. His slender fingers were cold. But they clung to her, and E. willed herself to love the coldness. Bent and silent, she pulled the boy closer. His other hand touched her back, delicate as a breeze.

"I'm sorry to need you right now." E.'s voice trembled.

"You've helped me plenty," he said.

"I don't want to make you late."

"Don't worry about that."

"Thank you, John."

"We're all here for you."

"That's right," Alex said and shuffled away the investigation notes.

They waited for E. to wipe her eyes and clear two lines of snot onto the lawn. Both were adamant about dropping her off first so she could rest up. Alex hugged her in the driveway, and John squeezed her hand. Then the boy waved and said brightly, "Goodnight, Mrs. Summerson." Her mother had flung open the front door in a panic to confirm that, though five minutes late, yes, her oldest daughter was alive.

"Was that John Walker?" the woman asked. She bolted the door and peeped through the blinds.

"Didn't think I could do as good as Erika?"

"Honey, stop. He's not your usual company, that's all."

"You're right," E. said.

"I'm glad for you." She didn't look it.

E. mounted the stairs for her room.

"You know I love you very much." Her mother moaned the words.

If E. didn't reach her bedroom quickly, a sobbing fit would ensue. Not over anything she'd done. Over what Erika never would.

"Even from a great distance?"

"What are you saying?" The woman started up the stairs behind her.

"Night," she said and locked her door.

E. struggled to sleep in peace. She closed her eyes on the feeble half-moon light only to slip and spiral backward into a much deeper, black-hole blackness that distended her atoms until she was nothing more than a vibrating string of matter. She woke from the dream terrified to sleep again. Then she fell asleep, had the same nightmare, and woke terrified to sleep ever. So the girl stayed up until after midnight and experienced a convulsing, existential pain at the base of her brain like a dying that would not kill her. E. lost all conviction in her emotional strength. She wanted to call out for John, her sister, her sister's murderer—anyone to end her suffering.

John didn't love her. Maybe he did. She knew his holding her earlier in the grass had been an expression of acceptance, no matter what she'd not done or not felt for her sister in the past, and that helped absolve some of her guilt about being withdrawn when she'd died. But his and E.'s relationship was too tenuous for her to ask for more. The boy wasn't in love with her, she knew—from his careful choice of pronouns to his lack of attempts to possess her—just as E. knew that only an all-consuming romantic love could keep her shielded from the reality that she would never see or hear from her little sister again. From a certain point of view, perhaps John's, she understood there was a gift in that, in allowing her to deal with the immensity of that loss on her own, for which she was grateful and angry, too. E. wasn't weak, but she was hurting and alone and without any experience in dealing with the pain, and all those books she'd read over the last few months about grief counseling and the various stages of coping were inert truths, flimsy facts, useless against it.

All night E. listened to grief claw around under her skin. It compelled her to pace the room deliriously, then to tear off all her clothes and lie naked on the floor and stare up at the motionless blades of the ceiling fan, and then to throw on a sweater to do it all over again. All the while, she whimpered pleas for release, until the sun rose from a strange angle.

She woke in her sister's bed, clutching the pink sheets. One arm snuggled Erika's favorite stuffed animal, a blue bear named Honey Bun. E.'s mother stood over her, heavy tears in her eyes.

The sentimentality of that moment was so cloying that E. actually felt sick to her stomach. Perhaps it was from anxiety or having eaten candy for dinner. She sat up in bed, as if to retch, when her mother caught her in her arms. E. gave in. She hugged the woman, who said, "Oh, baby … My baby girl …" She felt plainly and selfishly loved, as if for the first time because she'd at last let herself. They cried together for a long while over what they'd lost, and then, much later, they cried for what they still had.

11

Friday at Palos Hills Junior High was a half-day for teacher in-service. That morning, the halls were exceptionally vacant. Most students, it seemed, knew the day's lessons would be mindless worksheets and teasers of movies, and hadn't bothered to show up to pretend otherwise.

During classes, the group barely heard their teachers or school acquaintances. Despite yesterday's thrill over the discovery of the thumb bones and their last-minute dash from the woods, the building's emptiness resonated against the uneasiness each had woken up with. Although none of the kids spoke to one another at school—Alex's recommendation so they might keep from arousing suspicion, nor were any of them prepared to bridge the social gulf between the outside world and the woods—they caught each other's despondent gazes from across the lunchroom or while unable to focus on busy work in study hall, searching the face of the other for some answer as to why they felt so apprehensive about returning to what John called The Work. The sentiment went beyond their previous concerns about safety or usefulness. It had something to do with having experienced joy and heartache in their new relationships, what life beyond the mystery was like. Each kept dwelling on fond memories from their short time in Bachelor's Grove. Though creepy, the place was removed from the social expectations and general bullshit of junior high. What they were doing, their work, was becoming friends. But at some point, post-graduation or when the Dead Man went his way, their time in the woods would end, and they feared that would extinguish their bond.

That afternoon, walking down Oketo Street toward the rec center—no one admitting their worries, heads hung to watch the sidewalk slide beneath their shoes, or else squinting at the glary windows of the houses that floated by, allowing the group's momentum to carry them forward, no one saying a word—the kids spotted a white van, a shiny black car, and several dusty trucks parked around the walking trail entrance across the street. "Told you so," Tiffany said about the team of workers in neon vests. They assembled a tripod and unpacked tools from the vans. Two business people in construction hats stood back from the survey crew, near the decorative bushes that'd been crushed by the vehicles. One hitched his thumb, pointing deeper into the woods. The other laughed. Tiffany folded her arms and hid behind Greg. The kids weren't sure which was her father. The laughter trailed eerily as the group walked on, a wrongness in the man's pleasure that fouled the air.

Along their secret path behind the rec center, the group discussed the possibility of the woods being sawed and dozed. They imagined the entire stretch of trees erased from 115th to the moraine. Would the valley be spared? How fast could a crew clear-cut a forest that had existed for hundreds, perhaps thousands of years? Alex was quick to remind everyone that City Council's vote on the development had yet to be made. "Trust me, it's already gone," Tiffany said. Her surety made the land distinctly what it hadn't been all week—not theirs. For all its magic, the woods couldn't protect itself. The idea of strangers irreverently coming in charged the group with indignation, though of an ineffectual kind. They wanted to shout insults at the workers, City Council, but what could kids possibly do about it? They avoided the question. An answer would mean committing to a course of action.

Down in the Grove, they came upon a more upsetting sight. Their digging tools were ruined, shovels and rakes and sieves cracked in half and charred to sticks by a fire in the original hole. The toasted blades were plunged around it neatly in a circle. The discovery was alarming. They'd hidden their tools back in the bushes, leaving almost no chance of being randomly discovered. They'd been watched. Somebody was out here, invested in this place, and knew that others were, too. That person might even be the killer. The implacable emptiness that'd consumed them all morning returned, followed by the hollow frustration of defeat by a faceless tormentor. Greg kicked up the blades. Tiffany swore every few seconds. Josué slowly scanned the damage, then lowered his head as if he couldn't bear to look anymore.

"This was just some assholes being assholes," Greg said. "Right?"

"It looks deliberate." Alex roved the camp, alternately squatting and touching objects, examining the damage. "The work isn't chaotic. It's exceptionally dismantled. To me, it exhibits the kind of mind that could organize late-night rendezvouses with kids like Erika."

"Naw, maybe it was the construction guys just doing their jobs?" Greg said. "Like a warning to clear out."

"The killer," Josué said and pointed at the Big Tree.

There, E. vacantly stared up at the defaced image of her sister. Erika's eyes and smile had been filled with charcoal circles so that it appeared she had three spider-like eyes. Her body was cocooned in smoke.

They felt as though something were ending.

"We must be close," John said.

Alex nodded at his side.

"Yeah, close … to our deaths," Doug said before Alex or E. could begin agreeing with the Dead Man.

"Oh, shit." Greg faced the trees, as if expecting the killer at every turn.

John looked up at the canopy as he did whenever conversing with them, or maybe it was with the wind between the leaves. He'd never used the word God.

"What am I doing wrong?" he said.

Sick of his kookiness, Doug faced the group to try and reach them. Someone had to stop another kid from getting killed.

"Maybe we don't need to know," he said. "Not ourselves, on our own. I mean … this looks like the right time to call the police. Just— maybe we let the adults take over?"

Discerning that Doug was attempting to reason the others out of continuing the investigation, Alex came over and countered, "But it appears we're closer now than the police to discovering the identity of the killer."

"Maybe that's not a good thing … is what I'm saying."

"Yeah, no offense to anyone," Greg said, "but I don't want to die a virgin."

"You're still a virgin?" Tiffany walked away toward the creek as if totally creeped out by him.

"She is leaving?" Josué asked Doug.

"We all should—now—together."

"I'm staying," John said.

"Big surprise," Doug said.

"I'm staying the night. Tonight. He'll come back, and I want answers."

Doug really was surprised, then. "Dead Man—John, I mean—he'll kill you."

"I don't think he can. Anyway, I'm already dead, as you say."

"It's more probable that you'll leave us prematurely if out here alone," Alex said. "I can't let you make that miscalculation, sir. I'll stay with you."

"You want to confront a—a killer?" Doug said. "You two are … beyond—"

"It's the simplest solution to solve the bigger problem."

"You no fight alone," Josué said.

He stepped up to John and Alex. The three kids stood in a triangle and smiles broke on their faces as if the decision to throw away their lives to learn the identity of a madman before being gutted were the cause of great celebration.

"This isn't a joke," Doug tried. "The three of you—you can't take a kid … killer."

"How about four?" Tiffany said and brushed passed Doug. In one hand, she balanced a large stone with sharp edges lifted from the creek bank. "Sorry, genius. You're right. But I'm not here because I'm smart."

"Greg? Don't—"

"Ugh … I don't know, man."

"E.?"

The kids turned to E. She knelt at the Big Tree. She sobbed while scrubbing at the drawing of her sister with her shirtsleeve. In removing the charcoal, some of the colored paint had come off and left gaping holes in the girl's head and chest. These wounds caused E. to cry harder. Still, she didn't stop from trying to free her sister from the tormentor's handiwork, not even when she turned her head and noticed the others standing around her.

"Help me," she pleaded, her face deep red, "please."

Greg went to the creek. He wet his jersey to use as a rag. Josué passed out his paint markers. He and Tiffany began re-drawing the girl in an ornate dress. E. rendered her sister's face beneath a golden crown while Alex and John peeled away the gray bark to make the picture even larger and higher than before. The kids filled in the background with green hills and puffy clouds and a vast sky, the sun high above and, far above that, the darkening heavens, stars.

Doug kept away and watched the group bring Erika back to life, and E. back.

"Higher, Dougy?" She turned to him, her eyes still wet but hopeful.

"It can't go any higher than that," he said.

She gazed up into the boughs. "There's so much tree left."

"What goes above stars?"

"You tell me." She held out her marker. She was really looking at him, ready to listen.

"OK," Doug said. "Get me up there."

Greg and Josué hoisted the dork. Each supported one of his trembling, runty legs. Doug added the finishing touch. It disappeared up into where the bark began again: the tips of Erika's pink flats.

12

John had said the woods had said weapons were OK to bring in, but unnecessary. The group would be protected so long as they continued to treat the Grove as a sacred space. That evening, everyone came armed but the Dead Man.

Greg brought a stubby wooden club that was his grandfather's, who'd owned a bar on Archer Avenue and had sworn to his grandson that it'd long proved hard as steel. Josué brought two throwing stars that he and Greg lost within the first hour while waiting for the rest of the group to slip their parents. Tiffany was late again, but the jagged rock she'd earlier carried from the creek sat at the base of the Big Tree. Even Alex brought something: a pewter letter opener that resembled a dull knife, though a bit weak where the handle met the blade. E. brought a pair of handcuffs, which, she admitted, wasn't technically a weapon, but cuffs seemed practical and she'd assumed the others would do a better job in the attack department. She added that she hoped they wouldn't have to find out. The group agreed.

Doug came best armed. Clipped to a fraying army belt he'd received many Christmases ago was a flashlight and a hammer, and the first thing he did before saying hi to anyone at the camp was pick up the rusted crowbar from their evidence hideaway behind the Big Tree. Doug wouldn't set down the bar for a minute to help Josué roll over a few stumps from the old camp to make theirs more hospitable. Even when raising the weapon to adjust his glasses, nostrils flared, the kid almost looked intimidating. The haircut helped. When he'd asked his mother if he could spend the night at a friend's house, she'd made him agree to a haircut to look presentable to the friend's parents. Doug only weakly resisted because he did want to look good for Tiffany. His mother had taken him to Fantastic Hair, where a stylist whose nametag declared STAR ignored his warnings about what made his lumpy head look less like a fuzzy tumor. It didn't help that Doug began his usual stutter and blurt routine after noticing the bull ring in her nose and that, despite her nods and yeah-yeahs as he attempted the natural human capacity known as language, the girl was wearing ear buds—well, he first heard them in the form of tinny guitar shredding seemingly emanating from her eyeballs when she leaned over with the electric shaver and mercilessly buzzed him down to stubble. To be made repulsive on his first and most likely last night with a girl (if the haircut didn't end it, in all likelihood the murderer would kebab him—probably first, too) had put Doug in an awful mood.

He'd talked himself out of skipping the sleepover a dozen times. Doug had done a lot of thinking since locking lips with teen goddess Tiffany Dennys during their very meaningful thirty-minute make-out session. The meaning being: though total opposites, some potent magic was thrusting them together, and life was too short to worry about all the reasons they were a terrible match, so better to go along

131

with the thrusting. Whether that magic was love or genetic compatibility or dumb luck, Doug was sure he didn't want to know. Of course, the buzz cut wouldn't do him any favors. So, while the others gathered firewood and cleared an area for sleeping bags, Doug stalked the edge of the camp with a jerky gaze, praying for and dreading Tiffany's arrival, which lent him a vigilant demeanor. Perhaps this was why the Dead Man came over and said:

"If this night doesn't bring revelation, I won't ask anyone to come here, again. I promise. You weren't wrong, earlier. Ours is dangerous work."

"Then why—let's leave … now. I'll dig the other side of the creek if you … just—"

"Doug," John said, just above a whisper. His face contorted under the concentration required to explain. "They don't tell me everything. I think they're afraid I might not go on with The Work."

"Who … are we talking about?"

John pointed up.

A wedge of remaining daylight shot through the western trees and warmed the tops of their heads. Partially blinded, Doug tried to look, but saw only dust and other floaties in the beam. He recalled a quote his English teacher shared today about light being time thinking about itself. It didn't make any more sense now.

John turned his back. He faced the charred treetops over the old crime scene. Doug looked, too, but more at him. The guy's face went inky while the tips of his hair lit into a crown of burning filaments. John was a nut, a monster, and, if not kept at least ten feet away, his influence was stupefying. The Dead Man's arm came around his shoulders. It was thin, nearly weightless, almost floppy, like a short section of garden hose. Doug eyeballed the guy's fingers twiddling inches from his glasses. They were lean, the knuckles swollen and cracked. Doug couldn't move away, as if his feet were buried in the mud. Always a bit closer to the grave with John around, he thought.

"Thanks for being here," John said. "I know you took some convincing."

"I can't let … If something happened to—to everyone."

"You've a better reason than most to be here."

"Even you?"

"I have to try everything. This is my last inning, top of the ninth. If that means I go in the Grove, I'll be glad to have you and the group with me. Better than a sour hospital bed surrounded by nurses and the old doctor waving a light in my eyes while I lose consciousness like it's some damn alien abduction scene. Right, buddy? Who knows what forces are at work here. We could experience the real thing tonight."

John squeezed his shoulder. Doug was left to watch the radiant pink dusk die behind the hills. Color fled the trees. He was alone in the woods at night. He wasn't alone, of course. The kids had each other. But the Grove was no longer a refuge, their green and secret pocket from which they slipped back and forth to the real world. Still, he kept watch. After getting John and then E.'s approval, Greg and Josué started a fire in the dirt pit that Erika had made at the base of the Big Tree. It cast a dim glow that allowed Doug to discern where the woods thickened beyond the creek. An hour later, sheer walls of solid nothing rose all around them to the stars, making the boy claustrophobic and convinced that the portal through which they'd passed daily into the valley had sealed and left them captive until daybreak, maybe until the end of time. His imagination was speeding now. What powers and restraints did the killer possess? Why hadn't the group strung trip wires with cans full of rattling bits—some standard action-movie precautions to survive the night? Because they were kids.

The crickets were screeching and still no Tiffany. His grip on the crowbar tightened. What Doug felt wasn't bravery. If someone charged him or his friends out of the dark, he hadn't any faith in his ability to hit anybody or anything with the weighty iron bar. There was a possibility the girl would be slaughtered before she reached camp. No one else seemed concerned. The group sat behind him, a ring of firelight and laughter. Alex was cracking deadpan math jokes: "An infinite number of mathematicians walk into a bar. The first orders one beer. The second orders half ..." No one understood the punch lines, but they rolled sideways, saying, "Keep going!" Even E. laughed with skittering stops of breath. Doug was glad for that, and part of him wanted to share that moment with her. But E. didn't need him, Tiffany did. He judged the group's confidence in John's powers, or their own, or any power other than the ability to plunge a knife hungrily into another kid's flesh as naive, careless. He shook his head and turned his back on them. They weren't seeing what he was seeing because they weren't looking.

E. laughed freely, hair thrown back, not caring who was watching. Tonight, their tormentor would try what he might, stalk in and attempt to cut them down. But the spirit of the group, whether they'd face him united or divided, was in her hands. E. believed that the man who'd defiled her sister's image was the killer. E. also believed in her lone fury, that she could stop him if his strike didn't land first. If she had to, she would dig the sonofabitch's eyes out with her bare hands. Her rationale was simple: The living die. He was flesh and blood, unlike the lurking phantom he pretended to be, and therefore his body could be torn and spilled, even by a fourteen-year-old girl if her aim was true. E.'s strength was bolstered by her friends' willingness to fight beside her. John was prepared to give his life to the cause, though that had little to do with her, being guided by his messages from space. E. didn't believe that the boy communicated with some omnipotent god or received visions from a woodland spirit world. He was talking to himself, a very special part of his psyche not everyone knew how to access. She didn't and wanted to learn, to be less emotionally dumb, to have the courage to bring people together, not remain divided and thereby scatter them, maybe find peace with Erika gone. So when John had pronounced earlier that tonight would "yield profound revelation," E. believed him implicitly, even if she didn't understand him, yet. For once in her life, she understood faith. She'd always hated the word. Faith: When a supposedly intelligent organism believes a thing to be true despite an utter lack of logic and/ or empirical evidence. Perhaps E. had faith in her own development. Even then, zero belief was required. Effort, long hours at the library, had allowed her to know more than anybody her age about the human mind. What little good that had done her. Now she had something stronger—faith in her new friends, that they could be counted on when the moment called for it. Her faith was not all so grounded. Her understanding of spiritual matters was shifting. E. didn't believe in an afterlife, so how could she believe that her sister was watching over the group as more than a colorful drawing on a tree trunk? But she did. Erika's presence was a circle of buoyant happiness around the fire, binding them, bestowing purpose and a sense of belonging.

"Dougy!" she called to her old friend at the circle's edge, so that he too could feel a part. The boy came reluctantly with a frumpy smile and sad eyes because Tiffany hadn't showed. E. made him a spot beside her, and Dougy thanked her as Greg bragged about his

135

older sister, who was supposedly even taller than him, getting on the high school basketball team. Josué braved speaking some, too, about his favorite aunt, who took him to R-rated movies so long as they had hunky male actors and who was an exceptional horse rider and sometimes would take him along the moraine. And it seemed to E. that these weren't just a good bunch of kids, but some of the very best people on Earth. The epiphany threatened to break her heart with happiness. She let it.

"Look what I brought!" She patted her eyes and pulled tin-foil-wrapped potatoes from her bag, which didn't sound good to any-one. Potatoes without salt or butter? She stuffed them underneath the coals where they remained forgotten until fished out hours later. Their baked skins were charred in spots and their bodies steamed, moist and fragrant. Everyone praised her for thinking of them, and E.'s heart glowed warm as the coals at their feet.

A hush fell over the group as they ate. Their eyes wandered up the Big Tree, which loomed above the camp. Its most prominent branch stretched over their heads for a window of sky. The last quarter moon hung there like a slice of bone-white fruit. The kids were in the woods together at night. The exhilaration of this fact hit them all at once, and the profound liberty made their skin creep. They shared its charge around the fire, raised their bowed heads to exchange shy smirks. A few white lies and well-timed phone calls in front of their parents were all it'd taken. No one said anything, not wanting to scare away the moment—until they heard someone crunch up to the creek bridge.

E. broke the shackles of fear first and stood.

"Tiffany?"

The steps stopped. They redoubled, charging. The creek boards groaned and splashed under the runner's weight.

"Come at us, coward!" E. shouted.

The kids all rose. Everyone forget their weapons except for Doug, who held the crowbar in front of him as if wishing for someone to please take it and relieve him of the responsibility of defending real human lives.

"Coward?" Tiffany Dennys leaped into the light triumphantly. "No, no, hon. Not me," she said.

Tiffany shimmied among her spooked friends, as if trying to get a conga line going. She sang the school cheer in its entirety. The full attention of the group felt good on her. She enjoyed showing people that she was free to do whatever the hell she pleased and that she didn't give a shit what they thought about it, either. She'd come from tailgating at a high school game with this cheer girl, Diane. Tiffany didn't want to see old friends. She was starting over: new clique, new look, new outlook. But Diane said, "Hey, when did you start worrying about everything?"; they wouldn't see the old crew, her brother was playing a big game against Shepard High, and she knew a guy there who always had a bottle in his car. Maybe because of all the changes, the speed at which they'd hit her, getting fucked up sounded too good to pass up, a last hurrah. The guys were blah. They'd all sipped fumy vodka with the lights off in the parking lot and the windows cracked to keep from fogging. The windows did anyway with the faintest mist, the kids adrift on the buzz of the loudspeaker and circular stadium roar. When Diane wasn't drinking, her head dropped against the dash as if seasick. Tiffany was in the backseat with the guy's friend. He was older and cute, but wouldn't look at her even when she folded her leg to poke his with her bare knee. "You can touch me if you want," she'd said, tired of waiting for it or maybe to call his bluff, anything but an ounce of falseness. The guy went off, all offended. His hands flew up and hit the car top, saying he wasn't a pervert. Tiffany could see the hard-on through his jeans. Which was whatever, until Diane called her a whore. Tiffany had restrained from slamming the car door, but couldn't help flipping them off. These were the kind of phonies she needed out of her life. Hassling her … for what? Being real. Then all she'd wanted was to be back in the woods with her band of rejects.

"False alarm," Alex said, though that was clear. Maybe to get everyone to sit again. Not even Alex knew for sure, only that it felt better to have said it.

"Wow, E.," Tiffany said, "you get so fired up about stuff. Or is it only me?" Then her face blanked, seeing Doug. "Oh—"

He tried to explain the buzz cut. Meanwhile, his heart crumbled, crowbar sinking until it hit the ground, and he wished the killer would pop out of the bushes and end him already.

"Doug!" Tiffany rushed over and kissed him on the cheek. "God, I thought you were Rocky." She pulled away, conscious that the others had watched the kiss and were probably scandalized. She kissed the dork on the other cheek to show everyone she could kiss whoever she wanted as much as she wanted. She'd cared about crap like impressing people and rumors for most of junior high, which was long enough.

"You're … You've been drinking?" he said. The girl radiated booze, like his grandmother when she kissed his forehead and slurred, "Love ya, love ya, love ya.…"

"Damn, genius, nothing gets passed you." Tiffany flipped around her backpack and teased open the zipper. "I wouldn't leave my new best friends in the whole world out of the fun all selfishly." She pulled a large plastic bottle from her bag. Clear alcohol swashed inside.

"Whoa," Greg said. The others' less-than-enthusiastic faces curbed his excitement.

"I'm not sure that's allowed here," John said.

"Christ," Tiffany said, "sometimes I wonder if you're my good friend, Baseball John, or my goddamn … a hypocrite. No offense. But I do."

Tiffany's father would notice it missing from his office stash, would bark about her age, about consequences. The man wouldn't share a smile with his daughter unless drunk. Then he became another man. Master of inappropriate jokes, fifty bucks to say sorry, congrats, love you, hi baby, tie loosened and blazer lost godknowswhere—his closet an army of replicas—the running joke, "Daddy, where'd you lose your jacket this time?" "Oh, between drinks three and four...." Mr. Dennys's house parties of unwound business bores and official ass-holes ran late and often, so her father could hold a lot of liquor. On nights he'd had too much, a third man appeared. Once, this man gave Tiffany money to dance for him and two others in the coatroom on New Years Eve. They'd all pitched in to make her yes. Why did she take the money? Because she could do anything? "No—like this." He jerked her around to display her backside—or had she made up that part of the memory? She was eleven-ish. After that the man wouldn't stop coming at her with compliments around the house, even when he was sober ("My god, baby …" "Those legs and … wow …" "… not my little girl any longer."), teasing to yank her towel after show-ers, threatening to tickle a smile out of her, as if it were a game. She might've convinced herself it was, a long and relentless game in the shape of the world, if not for the nighttime visits. Sometime later— her timeline was a shit mess, she'd started drinking, etc.—sometimes, in the middle of the night, huffs of scotch crashed over her cool cheeks and collar bones and all down her arms and, instead of breaking hot with panic, froze the parts of her body left carelessly above the covers. Sometimes she would wake to the sickly sweetness in her lungs. Tiffany remained still as a corpse, so stiff and not-there that, if touched, she wouldn't know. Mornings after, she woke in a calm terror, not unlike when she'd heard Erika had died. A part of Tiffany was long and truly dead, an important part, she knew. Even if she cried, hard, she couldn't have it back. Why even wake up? What kept her outgoing, going out, going? Only when she thought about it did she not want to sing or dance or do anything for anybody, but be gone.

"He's only looking out for you," E. said. She was still on her feet, on guard.

"Oh, aren't they all," Tiffany said and sat in the girl's spot. She rested her head on Doug's shoulder for a second and then sat up very straight.

"For everyone's safety," E. said, "do you really think it's a good idea to be drinking out here?"

"You dorks kill me. I love you, but … trust me, guys—it's an old Bachelor's Grove tradition."

Tiffany tipped back the bottle. Afterward, she didn't breathe hard, only shook her shoulders, hair shimmering in the firelight. She was really loosening up and shook again to send the vibe down to her fingertips, and maybe out to those around her. She was wearing only one earring today—a dangly cross. It was a new thing she was trying, and it felt good to shake.

"You make that look easy," Greg said. Everyone heard him asking for it.

"Here she comes." Tiffany passed the bottle. "This helps keep you warm at night, too, guys."

"The reverse is factually true," Alex said.

"Oh. Well … it'll get you a wee bit shit-faced, Greg. But you may want to check with Alex on that point."

"Who's Rocky?" Alex asked. The name wasn't on any of the suspect lists.

"Nobody you want to know," Tiffany said.

Greg coughed after a sip. "Tastes like gasoline."

"Gas is way grosser," Tiffany said and winked.

Greg handed the bottle to Alex, who passed to E. without glancing up from the notes. E. held the bottle at arm's length and didn't pass. She looked as if she might dump it. Tiffany ignored the bitch.

"Hey, wouldn't you like a sip-a-roo, Alex? Hold up—is it really Alex? Or Alexandra? Alexie? I mean Alex is cool on a girl."

"No. Thank you. I would, however, like to know which school Rocky attends. A last name would also help."

"Take a sip, and I'll … tell … all."

"I also want to know where you first met him. And how."

"Bold—three sips—if I'm doing the math right. You'd know better than me."

Alex took the bottle from E. in both hands and sniffed the mouth suspiciously. "It's garlic-y."

"My bad," Greg said, raising a hand. "Pasta for dinner with that Texas toast."

Talk broke out about how good that stuff was, but hushed when Alex's eyes shut and the bottle upended. Alex took three even sips and one hot swallow that would likely impair critical thinking—a necessary sacrifice. In any endeavor, opportunity necessitated risk.

"OK." Alex sounded a little hoarse. "Speak."

Tiffany covered her mouth loosely with the back of her hand as she laughed. E. could see that the girl wasn't trying to appear modest. She looked truly ugly when she laughed. Tiffany's mouth and eyes tensed as if speeding a hundred miles an hour in a car without a windshield.

"Honestly, I don't know what school the kid goes to. I really don't. But probably Paragon Prep. You know, the delinquent school. But! I met him … over there." She pointed through the dark at the crime scene.

"In what way does he—excuse me—" Alex blinked, freckled nose wrinkling "—look like Doug?"

"Oh, he's got a buzzed head. The thin and pale type. Sickly. No offense, genius. I'd say too thin, though—like, stretched out. Doug, you're a short-thin, so it works on you. Maybe skeletal? Like the guy thinks he's a genius, some big deal, but all he eats is alcohol and pills and smoke."

E. passed the bottle around John—who rocked back and forth, either looking into the fire or eyes closed—to Josué, who also passed. Doug was stuck with it, then. He scrutinized the label like a connoisseur, stalling.

"What did he do to you?" Alex asked, not intending to upset Tiffany. It was a hardball question, the liquor talking. Alex leaned in and unapologetically stared across the fire at Tiffany.

The flickering light on Alex's face made the girl appear bewitched, Tiffany thought, almost sexy.

"I wouldn't let that bastard touch me. Once, he tried hitting on me by bragging he'd killed the principal's dog. The kid gives me the creeps," she said. "But he always has a lot of good drugs. I'm sorry, but he does."

"He knew Erika?"

"Hey! That's two more sips. Doug—" Tiffany took the bottle from his hands (thankfully), tipped it back, without making a show of it this time, and sent it around. Greg passed.

Alex took two deep breaths and two splashes down the throat. The liquid was developing a noxious aftertaste reminiscent of men's aftershave. Alex's body temperature had risen, and so the sweater vest got shed and cuffs loosened.

"You're really pretty, actually," Tiffany said and looked around the circle defensively. "What? She is. That's an observable factoid, my good friends."

"You know what I want to know," Alex said. "Is Rocky capable? Do you suspect him?"

"Are you kidding me? Everyone's a suspect. I don't know many kids who haven't come to the woods and partied. Erika and me, we'd meet a lot of weirdos out here. Some of them weren't kids, but older people who were perverts or maybe just bored. Mostly, it was parties, drinking, some drugs, and other stuff. Yeah, sex. Get over yourselves. Sometimes, though, shit got weird. This one time, I don't know what Rocky gave us. It was like acid or E." She smiled, no longer self-conscious. "E., you need some E. in your life, that's what I think. It was a candy cocktail that Rocky called Purple Rain. Though the candy wasn't purple. It was piss-colored with some black symbols on it. So we do the candy—Rocky calls his pills candy. 'You want candy, little girl?' He says it like he's some forty-year-old creepo and not some nerdball sixteen-year-old creepo. We do the candy—me, him, and Erika—we eat it—whatever—and the woods get streaky. Not like a blurry camera or whatever, but like the trees and us are trapped behind glass, and you can see smudges in the glass where God didn't do such a great job cleaning up because the fire is turned up so bright behind us. Erika—oh, man—she's totally naked. Because that's Erika.

She still had her neon gym shoes on and these white cotton panties, which is hilarious if you know her. Knew. She was jogging in place, like just warming up. Everything else was gone, until she sprinted in a circle, just like a blurry camera this time, where the light leaves tails in the air. She made a solid white ring around the fire. That's how fast she was. Give me the fucking bottle again, E. I don't know how she took her jeans off—unlaced her shoes, pulled off her pants, laced them back up? I don't get scared often. But there's this man standing there all of a sudden. I must've known it before. People come and go. I was pretty high. The guy was weird, but he was Rocky's friend. What do you expect, right? I'm on the ground when I notice him. I get the chills like it's eight freaking degrees out, which is why I'm laid out by the fire to thaw. Erika says something to me at one point, and I lift my head to see Rocky and this older dude, who just appeared out of nowhere, and Erika, of course, who's still tits-out but has her sweater tied over her shoulders like a cape, as if she thinks she looks very fashionable like that. You know. She just wanted people to admire her and all that puke. And the one guy—the older guy, he has a stubby knife out. Not like he's going to slash anyone to death. He's picking at his nails—I guess cleaning them—and he's got this big grin on. The guy really looked like a bum. He was kinda dirty, or more like dusty. And I remember thinking, 'That guy wears a lot of gray.'"

"How old was he? Twenty?" Alex asked.

"No. Way older. He cut his hand then, and … eh, it got too weird."

"Please," Alex said, "I need to know everything."

"You really don't. You're not as twisted as me. Only Erika could hang. She was a total bitch and the best friend ever."

"We need to know," Alex switched strategies, "to help her."

"I don't know, not really—was it by accident or on purpose? You couldn't tell because the guy still had this big grin. I was high, fucked up, so maybe none of it was all real. Blood ran down his hand, like how tears drip when you're bawling like a baby. And then—I was still out of it, seeing things, these albino bats flickering around the edges of my eyeballs that were more annoying than anything. Rocky drank some of it, the guy's blood. The guy'd made a fist, let it drip into Rocky's mouth. Rocky was stretched out with his hands behind his head, just kicking it, relaxing, you know, drinking this guy's blood. It didn't all get into his mouth. Some splattered on his nose, down his chin. So Erika had a lick. She crawled over on all fours and licked his face. I don't know if she did more than that. Blood makes me squeamish, so I think I vomited. She wanted me to do it. No way. Not even if it was on the face of a really cute guy. I mean no one should need to tell you that that's a majorly fucked thing to do. Erika was out of her mind. We all were, and everyone's done stupid stuff. So drop it, detective. I don't want to talk anymore about the past."

They waded through an awkward silence. Some expected Tiffany to wink or shout, "Suckers!" She set down the bottle and hunched at the waist. Her hair pitched over her head and waved dangerously close to the fire. She swept it out of her face and, miserable, stared at the flames.

John regarded the moon as if deciding whether to walk there. During Tiffany's story, E. had gotten up. She had her back to the group, arms crossed. The others didn't know what to do. They'd hardly seen Tiffany in any other state than raging excitement.

"I miss Erika," Tiffany said. "She was … just a kid, you know? I should've looked out for her. I didn't. I didn't and—I'm sorry. I'm really sorry—E. I'm sorry, guys."

"Don't do that." Alex came around to her.

"I know. I know, but—I'm sorry, you know?"

Greg made room for Alex. Tiffany closed her eyes and let Alex hold her. She hid her face in Alex's sweater.

Doug watched Alex hold on with no outward expression of sympathy, as if content to serve merely as a warm body, face stern if anything, protective, responsible for pushing Tiffany in the pursuit of adding two new suspects to the list—Rocky and the Man in Gray. Eyelids droopy, but not guilty-looking, either, it was late and Alex had had a bit to drink. On the other side, Doug put his hand on Tiffany's shoulder to say he cared. Tiffany didn't shrug away, so he didn't dare try for more and rub her in consolation. He didn't know how to care for anyone. When someone in his family got upset, they went to their room until it blew over. Doug had sometimes wished his family wasn't like that. To be able to touch Tiffany, even uncomfortably in that moment, made him necessary and, for the first time, glad to be in the woods.

It was past midnight. The fire was dying, and E. called time to bed down. They would rotate in pairs, she said, and guard the camp in two-hour shifts. A murderer was still out there. If anybody needed anything, call her name and she'd take care of it, she added. E. was playing the overseer, who acknowledged that others' physical and emotional needs required attention. She'd assumed the role partially out of responsibility for talking the group into the idea, partially out of necessity. John couldn't be relied on to manage matters of the material world, and their work in the woods truly was a matter of life and death. Her manner was only a role, affected. What knowledge or experience did she alone have that qualified her to lead? Tiffany's nightmarish story had proved that E. knew very little about what people—kids—were capable of. Her paper castle at the public library, though raised on pillars of wisdom, had served mostly as a defense against lessons from struggle, and, in her inexperience, E. was more of a child than Tiffany. This didn't make her envious. She was repulsed by Tiffany's behavior, yet humbled by her own ignorance. So, to keep the others strong, E. assigned the order of the watchers as if her plan to safeguard the camp was best and foolproof. Tiffany and Doug would take first watch. John offered to take the last. He didn't sleep much, he said. The kids unfurled their sleeping bags, zippers tinkling like tiny dull bells in some pagan rite to clear the air of ghosts.

The group lay down in the woods and closed their eyes against the night while the terror inside E. of losing one of her friends rattled her uncertainty about asking for their help. Naivete seemed to underpin her every decision. In assuming command, she'd imitated her dad whose shouting matches with Mom had returned now that the initial shock of losing their daughter had worn off. E. had long thought they'd be happier divorced. Instead, they kept waiting on her to get a little older to be able to better cope. Meanwhile, their bitterness grew and made any kind of relationship afterward impossible. Worse, it made her feel complicit in their misery. *They don't know what they're doing.* The thought echoed through her body and roused both sympathy and resentment. As leaders of their family, they were responsible for their actions—just as she was responsible if somebody got killed out here tonight. She was doing her best, as they probably were. Tomorrow she would have to dispel the illusion of her confidence in the group's safety so they could choose their own fate, free of her influence, she decided. It was the only way she could continue to believe they were doing the right thing.

Doug watched E. fold John into his sleeping bag. She sat up in her own a minute after that. Doug thought she might look up and say something. She zipped herself in behind John and spooned the guy. The Dead Man had won. He was Doug's better in so many ways, except for lacking the capacity to love her. It was obvious to him now: E. wasn't John's girlfriend, but his nurse. She lay at his side, corpse-like herself, vibrant red hair accentuating the dead white of her skin, content or at least prepared to tuck in the guy and say goodnight on the day he took his final rest. And after? Maybe she'd return. Go walking with Doug, arm-in-arm this time, kicking the autumn leaves along some sidewalk, maybe as soon as this fall, invite him up to her bedroom where they would look back at their crazy business in the woods and laugh in astonishment at how they'd spent the last days of their childhood. He couldn't picture her calling John a big mistake. Maybe a learning experience, a necessary encounter with death and dying. Would he take E. back? His imagination had already answered. Doug didn't want to think of her at all. He wanted to think about Tiffany and nothing but Tiffany, the way E. obsessed over John. He wished he were more grateful that she'd given them the first round of night watch. She must've guessed at what could happen, allowing them to stay up late alone.

During the first hour, he and Tiffany tended the fire and listened to the trees groan. They made up funny names for the animals that chirred and whooped and whistled around the ridge. Then they talked softly about all the reasons Tiffany had dropped out of cheerleading.

"I'm kinda running away," she said. "It feels good. Better than what I was doing. Which was letting people hurt me for as long as they felt like it. I'm staying away from the troublemakers. Like we agreed. Remember?"

Doug mostly listened. He asked questions to keep her talking. He was afraid of what he might say if she stopped. He asked who her troublemakers were and immediately regretted it. Hearing about all the things she'd experienced was excruciating. He knew, he just didn't want the barbed details about the various drugs and being intimate with athletes like John, Doug's betters except for their inability to care about her beyond what they could get from her sexually.

"Were you in love with them?" he asked. It was a stupid question. Something deep inside himself had spewed it, needed to hear her answer.

Tiffany said she wasn't sure she believed in love.

"I think people take what they want from you, or they sit around waiting for it to drop in their laps," she said. "We might be on their wish list, or not. Or be on it for a while. Then they get bored, want something new. Caring about someone despite bullshit and life, despite everything, is something our parents can't even get right half the time. Not mine. I don't pretend to be much better at it—love. Not at all. It's a goddamn shame."

If not love, Doug didn't know what she wanted from him. He wasn't sexy or handsome or smart or remotely funny. All he had was his laser-beam attention, a few dribbled words of affection, and a heart-shaped bucket full of love. Doug wasn't even sure that he could love Tiffany. Mostly he wished his worries would shut up before he blew a once-in-his-lifetime opportunity. A beautiful girl was treating him like a human being, and he was thankful for that and tempted that she was a girl who would go all the way. But she'd probably done stuff Doug couldn't even dream up, and that made him feel small.

Tiffany grew tired of hearing herself speak, think even, and stopped to let the genius get a word in about her totally fucked life. The dork nodded his head a long time. He went still and then she feared he'd fallen asleep. The kid was searching the stars with watery eyes magnified by his glasses as if mocking John or else really praying to God. She'd scared the shit out of him, she realized. Tiffany kissed him, rubbed his thigh, taking it slow to ground him. The kid was like a stone, and not in the way she wanted. He wouldn't touch her or respond at all. She unsnapped her bra to make it easier to forget himself. The trick always worked on timid boys, though wasn't much fun, handing herself over. Doug touched her breast through her shirt, tenderly with his fingertips, just the one.

He pulled away and apologized.

"What's going on, Dougy?"

"Don't—I don't like to be called that."

Dougy sounded too close to *Ducky*, the childhood nickname his parents still used. He wasn't grown, but didn't feel like a kid anymore. E. called him that, too, and he wanted to forget her.

Tiffany tried to reach him with a joke: "Don't worry. These babies didn't make it on John's list of commandments."

Doug couldn't laugh. He didn't want to hurt her feelings by saying the wrong thing or the right thing poorly.

Tiffany said to treat her right, damnit, and be straight with her.

"It's not how I wanted you," he said.

"OK. Well, how did you want me?"

"I wanted to feel … special."

"Welcome to the club."

"I know. I'm stupid."

"I'll say," she said. "I'm kidding. It's stupid because you are special, ya dope."

"I don't want to be anybody—just anybody, I mean."

"How do you think you make me feel when you clam up like you're doing? Newsflash: You're not the cutest guy I've been with. Not the least, either. You're cute in this frog-ish way. Like I want to put you in my pocket and take you to my room and pet you. That's not why I kiss you. I like that we can talk about stuff and be real with each other. That's rare. You know that?"

"Yeah. Like a friend … sorta."

"Right. I want a different life than the one I had. Right now, that means being with someone I can call my friend."

Doug looked up at Tiffany. Her smile was thin-lipped, cheeks taut and eyes scrunched, wonderfully so, a humanizing grimace of joy. Doug took her hand as she moved to cover her mouth. To see her happy because of him was all he could possibly ask for in life. Their eyes met. He hoped she was feeling something like that, too, and wanted to kiss. Otherwise, he didn't know where to drop his gaze. Her chest was still bulging inches from his hand, and even in the firelight, the translucent pink of her nipples showed through her shirt.

"Doug, I can give these babies to whoever I want, for whatever reason. Got me?" she said. "I'm giving them to you now for a very specific reason: I thought you cared about me. Me-me. Not just—" she lifted one breast, let it bob "—me."

"But I really do, actually."

"It surprises you, too, huh?"

"I mean—I do … care. You're—"

"The hottest girl you've ever been with."

"Yeah, but—"

"The only girl you've ever been with."

"Well, yeah."

"But funny as hell."

He laughed.

"And—?" she said.

"I'm sorry … for making you feel bad."

"Oh, god. Will you please just kiss me already?"

151

13

Tiffany woke at sunrise, underclothes damp and T-shirt clingy, not in post-coital baptism, but panic sweat, her heart pounding. She'd led the group deeper into the woods than Bachelor's Grove and gotten them murdered by the Man in Gray. They'd gotten lost after her assurances that a "really cool graveyard" was back there. They needed water badly and the Man appeared. A party drug he'd served made their concerns bubble ineffectually and fizz out of mind. Their bodies slumped as if their bones had become sandbags, as it slowly paralyzed them. Tiffany watched while the Man in Gray took his time kneeling behind each of her friends, happily, then greedily pushing a curly straw into their necks and sucking until frowns hardened on their ashen faces. He'd saved Doug for last. Tiffany tried to stop it, rolled a circle in the mud. She was too wasted to save even herself in the dream.

She sat up beside Doug, who was asleep with his arms at his sides and body as stiff as a board. Spending the night was cute—a first for Tiffany. She wondered if it'd happened too fast. Maybe fooling around was one thing and full-contact cuddling was another. She'd never slept with stuffed animals as a kid, the nap of their fur seeming to invade her mouth and smother her, and she was mildly impressed that she'd been able to sleep through the night. The boy was missing his large glasses, exposing his bare, placid face and a set of abnormally long, almost beautiful eyelashes. His sweet, resting eyes coaxed what tenderness Tiffany possessed. It wasn't much. Doug's overbite lent him the profile of a cartoon beaver and spoiled the sentiment. She didn't want it to. Placing her head on his chest, she listened for his shallow breathing, his heartbeat, something fundamental to love about him. The early morning crickets were loud, though, and the thought of their crisp bodies encircling in droves gave her the creeps. Tiffany got really scared, then, of what she was and wasn't capable of. Careful not to wake him, she slipped out into the cool morning air and stretched the cramps from her legs. Neither slowed her racing pulse. Doug was sweet, but not enough.

That's when she saw John in the fire pit—unmoving and gray as the dead in her dream. Out of guilt as much as concern, she screamed. Everyone woke. This included the not-yet-dead Dead Man.

John's joints were so stiff that the kids had to grip his icy flesh to hoist him out. He was filthy, arms and torso slick with ash. He clutched a chunk of mud that crumbled away into an old book. They wrapped him in blankets, rekindled the fire, and E. and Josué took turns rubbing his limbs until his jaw barely trembled. When he could speak, John told a fantastic story.

He'd been the last night watcher. The trees had quieted. If the killer had stalked their camp, he'd fled hours ago. Just before dawn, a light appeared in the branches of the Big Tree. It was red and blinked in the unhurried and constant manner of a passing airplane's wing tip. It spoke to John, not in the voice of the woods, he said, but as loud, and asked to be let inside of him. John closed his eyes against it. The voice quit. Still, its light bathed his face and hands and seeped through his eyelids. He called on all his strength and crawled to its origin—the hole dug by Erika. He watched the bottom. Red pulses rose and fell under the dirt, immense and deliberate as the breathing of a slumbering beast. John considered that he was dreaming or hallucinating while gazing into the campfire's coals. But the fire had died hours ago. And when he stuck his arms in to dig out the light, the ash was cool and soft. He dug a few feet until he'd discovered the hardback book, a diary, which he'd read by flashlight until passing out from exhaustion.

"Is it Erika's?" E. was the first to ask.

"No."

"Then …?"

John looked away as he handed her the book. E. hurriedly opened it and searched its pages. The group closed around her.

The diary was large and weatherworn to the cardstock. No dates topped the entries, written in a strange language with an intense, curling script. Only toward the end were a few words recognizable: "DIABEL," "SZATAN," "ANTYCHRYST." Though the text was old, several pages were freshly annotated in red ink. Cryptic notes and diagrams filled the margins. The diary ended abruptly, the last entry abandoned mid-sentence, two-thirds of the book left blank.

"Holy fuck," Greg said.

"You said it," Tiffany agreed.

E. calmly asked if John understood what he'd found.

The guy's squinting gaze faltered between the trees misting in the

154

daybreak and the whitening sky. He seemed suspended in his recollection of last night, struggling to fully accept what'd happened as reality.

"Abomination." He muttered the word, sadly and with failure.

For the first time, Doug wondered if John had killed Erika. It wasn't a nice thing to think about someone. But the coincidence of finding the book, any evidence at all on their last night before giving up and going back to regular life, seemed unbelievable, suspect. The cops had scoured the woods for months. Were they really so incompetent? John was rapidly losing his mind out here. That or he needed to cut back on the morphine, or both. And poof—a creepy book appears that he alone plucks from a nightmare. Maybe the guy had only made up the story to keep the group playing pretend with him a little longer, to feel needed, important. Doug could understand that. Though there wasn't a shred of shame in the guy's demeanor. There was guilt and dread. Something had happened to him last night. Mud grayed his arms up past the elbows, as if the Dead Man had been playing in his own shit. And the way they'd found him. The guy had looked as if he'd dug his own grave and died in it. If a game, it was a deathly serious one.

"It was here, in the last place anyone would look," John said without meeting the faces of his friends.

"It—this is ... oh, man," Doug stammered.

"Was the hole half empty or half full?" Tiffany said.

"On this point, we'd assumed incorrectly," Alex said.

"But what about ... our fires?... and the broken shovels?" Doug said. "It's too—"

"That was probably a scare tactic," Alex said, "a desperate solution to the problem of us. This place is important to the killer. He's attempting to return to the scene of the crime, and we're in his way. How then do we correlate Erika's dirty fingernails? Possibly, she and her killer, maybe others, were burying and removing this book nightly. To read it? Translate it?"

"What are the chances of that?" Greg huffed.

Alex eyeballed him suspiciously, then continued, "Tiffany, do you remember any strange books appearing during one of your woodland soirees?"

"What's a woodland soiree?"

"A party in the woods."

"No. Guess I wasn't cool enough to get the invite. I'm kinda offended."

Alex leaned over E.'s shoulder. "These notes could be the—"

Josué then snatched the diary and stepped out of the circle.

"Erika—she die over this?" He reached into his pocket and pulled out a paint marker. He threw it aside, reached in again, and pulled out a lighter.

"I highly recommend not doing that," Alex said.

"Dude, J.," Greg said, "I'm equally pissed. But I think we got to know what that thing—" he pointed at the diary "—is. Right?"

Greg looked back at the group for validation. Their faces, gathered together, showed conflicting emotions. They trusted Josué, and they hated whoever had killed Erika. They wanted to know the truth, and no one wanted to relive the details.

"La obra del diablo." Josué sparked his lighter. A flame crawled up the back a few inches before extinguishing from the earthen dampness. He flicked at the wheel. The lighter wouldn't keep a steady flame.

Doug watched for John's reaction, some confirmation of his involvement. All sense had gone out of the guy's face. He seemed to

156

barely notice the commotion. He hunched like an old man and stared exhaustedly through the trees at the original crime scene, as if he regretted talking the group into coming out here. Beneath the singed tops of the thin trees around the old fire pit, green buds of new growth showed around their midsections and had started to obscure the site.

"It's proof." Doug stepped past Greg. "… of what happened here."

"Evil, yes?"

"Evidence of it—of who's involved … just maybe."

"Yes," Alex came toward Josué and attempted a non-threatening posture: shoulders raised and palms upturned, but arms stiff in the sulky manner of a scolded child. "Listen to Doug."

"I'm upset … and really scared, too," Doug said. "I want to stop him—whoever. There might be a clue, see? So we can get them—him—the killer."

"Do you want to solve this case?" Alex said.

"Con justicia," Josué said.

"Me too," Doug said.

Josué looked the puny dork up and down, from the bad buzz cut to the too-clean rubber of his shoes, taking stock of this kid who claimed to fight on his side. He looked like a child. Not too young for his age, he looked exactly his age, no hint in his clothes or manner or features that foreshadowed maturity. Josué imagined Doug might always appear helpless, as a child does, much the same as Josué's uncle James, who jo-jo-joed for the family at Christmas Eve for as long as Josué could remember, costumed as Santa Claus. The man's youthfulness made the polyester beard glaringly false, and the deflated red coat flapped around his slim frame. Each year Josué would express his frustration to his mother, saying that his uncle was too puny, better suited to play one of the Kings, and that he was ruining the mystery of Santa Claus by exposing himself as a fake and making Christmas into a big lie for all the cousins who still had many more years to enjoy the mystery. "When you were their age, did you see your uncle as this 'big liar?" his mother would say and then tell him to shut up about it already. And why the obsession with Americanized holidays? an aunt would add. He was watching too much TV. Josué could say little in return because he did not remember the specific moment he went from believing to not believing. He knew only that he wished he still did believe the world was a place of magic, and—yes, foolishly—he blamed his uncle's youthfulness for stealing his wonder. The association with his uncle made Josué trust Doug less than he already did. For the first time, however, the kid's voice had some fight in it. Where was the little man's fire when Josué was getting knocked around at school? Josué nodded, to himself really, thinking he sometimes possessed too much faith in the deep-down goodness of people, and he gave Doug the book.

"It can't leave the woods," said the Dead Man. He stood in front of the fire with an eerie uprightness, Greg's blue blanket toga-like across his chest.

"It can't?" Alex said.

"No. And the book can only be read at night," he said, relaying his pronouncements from another world. "It's too dangerous, otherwise."

The kids scanned the woods, aware again that they weren't alone.

"True—" Alex paused to jot a note, looked around for dissenting opinions "—our work would be for nothing if this evidence chanced to be discovered by someone else now, including the police."

"Well, I want to read it," Tiffany said. Satanic kind of crap reminded her of that night with Erika and Rocky and the blood, how sticky as syrup it'd been on their fingers and faces. "Or try to," she said.

"Maybe she left it here for us?" She meant Erika. None of the group needed clarification.

"Tonight then?" Alex looked to John.

"It has to be," he said.

John beckoned for the book. Doug gulped and glanced at the rotten cover. He'd helped secure it because, for a moment, he'd wondered if John had wanted it burned. Maybe he'd not led them out here to uncover evidence, but to bury it forever. Doug looked past the group. The sight was frightening, all the earth they'd churned under his command, nearly the entire valley. The book could be all that was left. John couldn't destroy the evidence now. Could he? That would give away his guilt. Or was it all a sick game? Doug looked back at the group—he seemed to be the only one who suspected anything. He handed over the book reluctantly.

Pulling the blanket around his shoulders, John went to the Big Tree and put his hand on the bark and held a brief conversation with himself, speaking to the sky in impassioned whispers. No one else paid him attention except for Doug, who believed he was witnessing the triumph of a crazy person who'd convinced others his delusions were real and to spend another night with him in Bachelor's Grove with the object Erika had supposedly died over. The Dead Man disappeared around the trunk to secure the find in their new hiding spot.

Whatever being out here meant to John, Doug decided, it wasn't a game.

Greg and Josué and Tiffany and E. began to discuss the lies they could tell their parents to manage two sleepovers in a row without raising suspicion. Doug felt the whirring energy in their chatter, as if something important were beginning. He stepped back from the group, refusing to be swept up in the lunacy. Tiffany offered several pro tricks, including jumping from her bedroom window. "I mean, we're not children. How many times a night do your parents really come in and check on you?"

Tiffany enjoyed the approval of their laughter, mattering for the experience she possessed, not in spite of it. She noticed that Doug wasn't laughing, however, and came over and asked if he was still OK after last night.

"Why wouldn't I be?" he said.

"You look like you're thinking too much about it."

"I'm not, really."

"Ugh, Doug, don't bullshit me."

"I'm happy about that." He smiled, though weakly, too anxious to feel anything but an ache like a hole in his stomach. He imagined John at night, preaching over Erika's prone body. Too drugged to escape, she watched him close the book and pick up a long knife—

"What else?"

"I'm worried about us," he said.

"Just have fun and don't take it so serious, OK?"

"What if John wrote the book?"

"The book of love? What are we talking about here, genius?"

"The one we—that he found. What if he wrote the book?"

"He is pretty good at speaking gibberish."

"Right, the guy's insane. I'm afraid that he … What if … he was the one …?"

"You're sounding pretty crazy yourself right now. John's weird, I get that. But he's all right. I mean, if you think the Dead Man's scary, truly scary, you haven't met scary, yet."

"Don't you think—"

"You think too much sometimes," she said and squeezed his hand, but didn't kiss him.

Doug almost went to tears. The feeling came from a yet unnamable pressure. He willed away the discomfort, telling himself not to think about what her halfhearted gesture meant right now, to not "take it so serious," as she'd asked him to do.

When they separated at the trailhead, Tiffany said she had to stop by a friend's before going home, and she flashed him the same wave she gave the others before skittering around the rec center. He tried not to think about what that meant, either. Instead he headed east down 115th to take one of the alleyways home, while in his mind he traveled back through all the times the group had let John direct the course of their activities and they'd just gone along with it, glad to play their part for him, for Erika, and for their new and better friendships. The Dead Man had become a puppet master, pulling the strings in some screwed-up drama that seemed likely to end in their guts spilling under the Big Tree.

Doug stopped in the street and clutched his belly. Even Alex, who really was a genius and should be smart enough to know better, had fallen for his act. Or otherwise knew and similarly feared John hacking them to pieces. Or otherwise was complicit, his Yes Man or Yes Woman or whatever, and couldn't be trusted. Alex might even know that Doug knew, and together—

Woot-woot, yelped a police car. It slid to a stop so closely that Doug stumbled back after meeting the officer's face. The window was rolled down, an older woman in wraparound sunglasses behind the wheel.

"You know not to be playing in those woods, little man," she said.

"We shouldn't. We don't, I mean."

"We?" she said.

"Me and my—my best friend."

"What's the friend's name?"

"Eh ... John—ny. Jonathan."

"He still in the woods?"

"He's at ... He's home, already."

"And where're you headed?"

"I want to go home."

"Where's that?"

Doug blanked. He couldn't think of any place, but the woods.

"You ever see anything strange in those woods?" the officer asked. She removed her sunglasses, her kind, hazel eyes narrowed at him. She had a shell of soft hair like his mother, but her face was craggy.

"I don't know," Doug said.

"Anyone or anything," she said. "You can tell me."

"I—I really don't," he said.

"Next time I see you here, I'm going to take you down to the station. And I'm going to call your parents." The officer threw on her sunglasses. "And don't walk in the street."

As the police car rounded the corner, Doug puked into the drainage ditch. He was empty to the pit. His sinuses were stuffed, which muted the world beyond his discomfort. He went up the alley, aware of little except the crunch of the gravel beneath his sneakers and the four spaces between his fingers where Tiffany's had been.

A block from his house, a cook in a beard net came out of the back of the new Middle Eastern restaurant and did a double take, seeing the boy lean against a neighbor's back fence as if hurt. He set down his trash bags and called to Doug. Only then, the boy became self-conscious enough to wipe the spittle from his chin. He didn't acknowledge the man. He didn't ask his parents for help once home.

He went to his room and didn't message Tiffany or E. and stress his suspicions about John. Doug lay on the floor for a long time. He listened to himself gasp until his heartbeat slowed. He told his mind to stay as blank as the ceiling above. He had to pull himself together by nightfall. He had to warn his friends when the moment came to act.

That evening, Doug's family had dinner together in the living room. Never really together. TV bombarded their faces in ghost white flashes like paparazzi photographing dead movie stars. During commercials, he answered his parents passably about "the sleepover at Josué's," playing the role of a partially engaged fourteen-year-old. He even managed to smile when some funny nothing involving two characters having slept with the same woman happened on screen. Doug's brother huffed, and his mother went, "Oh, no—oh, no." His father held a beer absently and looked off into a corner of the room as if a small man down on the carpet called his name.

"Ducky, you feeling OK?" His father faced him now. Once a year, the man had the uncanny ability to sense when Doug really needed to talk.

"Yeah—OK, Dad."

"Haven't seen your girlfriend around much lately."

"My friend," Doug said.

"Your friend. How's Emily holding up?"

"All right."

"Well, good."

"She's OK," Doug said.

"Well, tell her we miss seeing her. Unless you're sick of seeing her. Then, you tell her to stay the hell away," his father said affectionately. He sipped at his beer and smiled at his family. "We care about you and your brother more than anything, Duck."

"I know, Dad."

"OK, Duck-ster?"

"OK."

After dinner, Doug emptied his backpack of all but the long-handled hammer and a flashlight. He sat on the edge of his bed and waited for his family to go still in theirs. He held an old paperback to provide an excuse for sitting up so strangely in case they looked in, which—Tiffany was right—they didn't. Doug wasn't chancing it. The book was *Franny and Zooey*, E.'s favorite when they'd met. She'd read it several times. Doug couldn't understand how any book could be so good that anyone would read it even twice. It would be the same story you remembered, unless maybe the story was so confusing she'd reread what she'd missed to make sense of it or to get at the deeper meaning, neither of which sounded fun. Doug flipped through the pages. He tossed the book in his trashcan. He'd been so excited when she'd retired her copy to him, believing it was a sign E. liked him as more than a friend. All this time he'd kept the book on his nightstand to be a little closer to her, certain that all he'd needed to do to become her boyfriend was exert masterful patience.

He was still a fool.

Doug didn't care if he was a nobody for the rest of his life. He didn't care about what others believed him capable or deserving of. He cared about E. He cared about the wellbeing of the group, too. And he was proud of his patience, which seemed the most requisite trait as he considered two things: (1) If he had to, could he kill the Dead Man? and (2) Could a dead man be killed?

Doug relied on an ambulance's wail to mask the sound of slipping out of his window just after 10:15. He didn't bother to lock his bedroom door, yet he'd been deliberate about taking the book he would never read out of the trashcan and returning it to its dustless corner on his nightstand.

14

Smoke rose from the valley.

Doug coughed under the arched gateway of half-dead trees to Bachelor's Grove and pictured his friends spit-roasted, crisp. Without a flashlight, he braved the steep path. He didn't want to give away his approach. His fingertips strained for familiar landmarks in the dark—a remnant of fall leaves overhead, a V of trunks worn slick. The rough corridor of stone handholds guided him into the clearing. He'd been right about John, and it was time to act. He only hoped he wasn't too late.

In the murk across the creek, a fire glowed under the Big Tree. Had the group gathered early and made a wild bonfire? The firelight was not trapped by the pit, Doug saw. Waist-high flames licked up the trunk of the Big Tree. He stopped and squinted against the light, unable to spot his friends anywhere. Smoke billowed heavenward and shadows quaked in the high branches. He searched the edges for the silhouette of a bent and emaciated figure, the Dead Man's shape.

Doug flipped his backpack around and wore it front-wise like armor. He did so frantically, not thinking too much about it, needing to unzip the bag and slip his hand inside for the hammer's rubber grip. There was something instinctual about the security brought by the drawn weapon. He couldn't even dwell on how terrible he was at video game combat. His senses strained and amplified his leaping heartbeat, the margins of the darkness, and the sharpness of the wood smoke.

Doug stepped from the trail toward the burning tree. His elbow trembled though the evening was not chilly. He was going to kill someone, beat in their brains like in a zombie movie until the twitching stopped. Or an athletically superior killer was going to down him, separate him into two pieces, as Erika had been separated.

Life isn't a videogame, he thought and was slowed to a pace that would take him an hour or more to reach the fire. His fear manifested as a swift current, and it took great effort to move upstream. Doug considered the finger of glacial ice that had pushed through the valley a bazillion years ago, clearing out all remains of plant and animal life or trapping the most insistent in a similar hell. His was the same battle, another life form against nothingness.

Take another step and you'll be a plucked little ducky, fear said.

Doug lowered the hammer. He stopped and shielded his eyes to spare the world from the humiliating tears that rushed forth—

But not before he saw a figure step out from behind the Big Tree. Amorphous fabric billowed against the flames. A long blade glinted in one hand. The cloaked figure stalked through the trees toward the original crime scene. It could be John, though the confidence and power in its stride was unfamiliar.

Doug coughed. He'd drawn a breath of smoke and spittle, and

couldn't help it. He clamped his mouth with one hand and stepped back. A branch cracked under his heel. The black-sheeted ghost scanned the valley. The figure had a wavy outline from the flames that made it difficult to tell if it creeped away or closer. No—the figure was stopped and faced in his direction. It'd spotted him.

Doug collapsed. Someone tackled the boy from behind. Ran into him, really. But the impact felt like a tackle, and he shrieked and kicked at his attacker—for the distance and time to—groping for—on his feet—the hammer rising—on Tiffany and Alex.

"Whoa, what'd you do, genius?" Tiffany laughed. She and Alex jogged ahead to assess the damage.

"Stop! He—it—Tiff!" Doug called after them.

They crossed the creek bridge. The girls were seconds from their death at the campsite.

Doug lurched forward. To face off against the Dead Man, who'd stolen his best friend and was leading the others to an early grave, was one thing. But it wasn't John. Was it? Terror broke Doug to sniveling just to think of the knife-wielder's nearness. His imagination ran: it was an enormous man; John seated on another kid's shoulders; a lean devil with neatly folded wings. His nose leaked hot strings that stuck to his shirtsleeve like melted cheese. He wiped his face over and over to regain composure, knowing he had to help his friends. Tiffany and Alex were at the fire now. He didn't see the cloaked figure. With painful clarity, Doug did see that he didn't love Tiffany Dennys. If he did, he couldn't have let her go ahead without him. Only alone, knowing the killer could be anywhere (even right beside him), did he go to them, not in support, but cowardice.

The fire wasn't as bad as his imagination had painted it. The flames licked high, but the Big Tree's trunk hadn't caught. Logs crossed at its base had been left to burn. Tiffany and Alex separated them with fallen branches and pushed each carefully into the fire pit. Doug turned a circle as they worked, watching the bushes for movement, his hammer out limply.

The trunk of the Big Tree was scorched black about eight feet high. The image of Erika was charred, as well as vandalized—where her abdomen used to be, two deep, deliberate cuts marked the tree in the form of a steeply sloping peak, like: / \

"By the state of these logs," Alex's quizzical eyes lifted to the shadows around them, "the fire was started no more than ten minutes ago. The killer could still be here."

Tiffany cupped her hands into a bullhorn and cried, "You better run!"

"I saw him," Doug said.

Alex asked where exactly, unfazed by the news. Doug pointed at the ground beneath his feet.

Noticing his blotchy face, Tiffany took his hand.

"Who were these kids, genius?"

He said it was just one person "in a cloak."

"A cloak?"

"Are you positive it wasn't a baggy hoodie?" Alex asked.

"I think so. He had a long knife—"

"Shit. You sound like John right now," Tiffany said.

"Which hand was the man holding the knife in?" Alex asked.

"The left. No … I don't know, now."

The rest of the group arrived soon after: John and E. together, and Josué and Greg together. Doug described the cloaked figure. There was talk of hunting for him in the trees. If still nearby, he was likely well hidden, perhaps watching from a perch along the valley's ridge. The book was missing, stolen from their secret spot behind the tree.

"They're trying pretty hard to scare us," Tiffany said.

"They feed on fear." John's back was turned to the group.

"Correct," Alex said, "that's what our tormentor would have us believe."

"It's fucking working," Greg said.

"Why attack Erika, again and again?" E.'s voice faltered, though her eyes were dry. "Why not come for us?"

"We outmatch him," Alex said. "Or them. Probably we're not the only ones who are afraid."

"But they've killed somebody before," Greg said.

"I saw the knife," Doug said. "It had to be—"

Tiffany hugged the dork how a parent preemptively embraces a fallen child. Doug didn't cry. The shock didn't wash from his face, either.

•

Alex shrugged. Each shoulder lifted awkwardly, independent of the other, at different speeds and directions, until approximately similar in height, simulating disaffectedness. Only simulating because Alex had a theory—a fine working theory along a reasonable timeline of events both confirmed and speculated—of what the previous group, the ones who had come before them, had wanted, how they'd operated, and what had soured relations between them. The sole remaining mystery was the identity of the perpetrators, and to let on now wouldn't be conducive to solving that mystery, as the entire group had not yet been ruled out as collaborators or informants: Josué, little chance. E., little chance. John, probable. Greg, probable. Doug, not very probable. Tiffany, not very probable, either, having phased into the negative an hour ago. What of the likelihood that this deduction was influenced by personal feelings? Not probable at all, but one hundred percent certain.

Tiffany had spent all afternoon with Alex. The girl appeared at the Karahalios residence not long after the group had adjourned from the campsite that morning. Alex's mother answered the doorbell, not an uncommon enough occurrence to disrupt Alex's social media research on one Rocco "Rocky" Lordes, who'd been expelled from Palos Hills Junior High and sent to Paragon Preparatory after multiple sexual harassment incidents, acts known as "sharking," and finally, it was said, he'd set fire to an American flag and sprinted down the hall with it toward the principal's office to deliver him the news that the world was "good and dead" (before reaching the office, the janitor had doused him with a mop bucket of dirty water). By then, the laughter coming from the Karahalioses' living room had reached the volume of an authentic disturbance, and Alex was forced to investigate.

"Alexie, your good friend is here!" Mother said in singsong.

She and Tiffany occupied separate ends of the white leather couch, their legs tucked similarly. Both wore tight fitting sweaters with white bottoms, Mother in Capri pants, Tiffany in shorts, probably a trend. Alex looked back and forth between the women. They showed teeth as they smiled. Alex assessed their camaraderie as high and began to calculate the odds that Tiffany Dennys and her mother were azygotic clones.

Tiffany gave a short wave. "Hey, kiddo," she said. Her eyes scrunched, thrilled by her own surprise visit.

"Mother, what's going on?" Alex sensed another plot deepening.

"Gosh, you're a Sensitive Sally today," the woman said. "I swear, the most obvious things remain invisible to her—the unkempt hair, that dowdy sweater. Then the school friend she's been hiding all year appears, and suspicion abounds." A lawyer, Mother packed an argument into every observation.

"I'm here to see you, silly," Tiffany said.

"See?" Mother said. "I need to finish up some work, girls. So why don't you two talk in your room. Alexie, you really should have more good ideas of this sort. And open up a window in that dungeon. A draft of spring air would do you well. I'll fix cappuccinos. You do drink cappuccinos?"

"All the time," Tiffany said with her back to Mother, who didn't see the girl wink and mouth the word "dungeon."

Then Alex and Tiffany Dennys were alone together, with the bedroom door shut and cappuccinos, which Mother never made for Alex. Tiffany rifled through the short shelf of paperbacks beside the bed.

"I wish I could be like you," Tiffany said. "Even the stack on your desk is in alphabetical order. Eh … no, I don't. But I respect it—a lot."

"Why were you trying to make a good impression on my mother?"

"To get us some time alone, Silly Sally."

"Sensitive Sally."

"Be whatever you want, Alexie."

"I want to know what you're after."

"Sit with me." Tiffany pulled Alex onto the bed without waiting for an answer. "I want to ask you something. Wow, it's hot in here." The girl fanned herself for two seconds, then pulled off her sweater.

Alex's gaze lingered on Tiffany's bra, radiating neon pink through her T-shirt where the curves pressed tightest. If working for the killer, a direct threat or attack would not serve her well here. Tiffany was clearly enacting a stratagem. Her weapon of choice? Her body. Connecting the Xs and Ys to figure the problem of what she could be after, however, proved difficult. Alex's brain began to misfire, interrupted by curiosity of a sort inconsequential to the case.

The girl told another long story with the same earnestness she'd exhibited last night. She hadn't returned home after the woods today. She was feeling awful, she said. Greg had invited her to lunch with Josué, but she didn't want to go anywhere with those boys, any boys. Not even Doug, who, she insisted, was not her boyfriend, so not to worry. They'd had sex last night, which had only made it clear that she was done with boys for now, you know?

"I have no interest in boys," Alex said. "What I want to know is—"

"So that's what I wanted to ask you." Her hand landed casually on Alex's thigh. "How do you get by without anyone? Boys. I'm not trying to be a bitch here."

"I—" Alex wanted to discuss the case. More interestingly, Tiffany was asking questions that'd been there before she'd posed them. "I don't want boys."

"Want to date them."

"Correct."

"Or to fuck them?"

"That follows."

Tiffany moved her thumb in a circular motion on the inside of Alex's leg.

"I think I understand," she said.

Sensual touch was unlike the rush of dopamine released after winning a state math competition or working through a problem said to be beyond one's age or ability. It was a fine, firming feeling, warm and almost funny.

Alex stopped her wrist when it rose further. "You don't."

Tiffany went stiff. Her neck blushed through her tan.

"I don't mean that to hurt you," Alex clarified.

Tiffany pulled back the hair that curtained her eyes and laughed short. "It's all good," she said. "I've just never been rejected like this before. Rejected period."

"By females?"

"Easier to kiss than boys."

Tiffany watched for Alex's reaction. Tiffany's eyes became hollow with desire, a second offensive. Suspended in waiting, she again asked to access Alex's body in the form of a kiss.

"Fine. Pure experiment. Then you answer my questions," Alex said and leaned in.

"Well, jeez." Tiffany got up. "Now I'm all nervous and shit."

She rubbed her hands and reseated closer. She stroked Alex's legs, and they kissed.

They mashed lips with a split of pain. Apologies were exchanged. Then Tiffany came in slowly and edged Alex's mouth with patient kisses. After a while, her tongue coaxed her partner's lips to part, prodded inside, and both widened their legs and mouths. Alex met the wetness of the girl and understood then that sex was about opening. There was some exquisite pleasure other people experienced in baring their insides, a ritual of great labor, it seemed, to feel right with the world. The act was empty of import for Alex. The result was no greater intimacy, no opening, nothing except for the terror of incompleteness, of maybe not having anything special locked away inside.

"This is doing nothing for you," Tiffany said after a minute.

Cross-legged on the bed, Alex looked down at the gap between leg and lap. She took Tiffany's hand. "I appreciate that you want to make out with me. I know it's how you express yourself. But there's something wrong with me."

"Nothing's wrong. You just want … something else."

"No. You were right. I don't want anyone."

"So? That's freaking amazing."

"It's not normal," Alex said.

"OK, it's not," Tiffany said. "But who wants normal?"

Alex's thinking seized up, refused to entertain the hypothetical.

"Talk about not normal," Tiffany said, "I want to quit wanting everyone. Wanting them to want me. Wanting in general. Seriously, it's like a curse." She rubbed Alex's arm, for comfort this time. "We're both cursed."

"The ends of a spectrum," Alex said.

"… hate the game."

"… middle is bliss."

"Hey, I tried to meet your middle."

They laughed, and their eyes met. Each shared genuine affection for the other for the first time.

Alex's mother knocked and the girls jumped and straightened their creased clothes. She poked her head in and asked could they handle another cappuccino. Coffee aged a young lady's teeth and nerves, but the addiction was requisite to keep ahead of the wolves, and they might as well start running now. Both were still working on their first, they said and thanked her. When the door had closed, they talked in whispers.

"What did you want to ask me?" Tiffany said.

"Would it be all right if we lay down?"

"Hell yeah—I mean, of course."

The girls lay facing one another on the bed. Alex advanced until their foreheads touched, limbs and fingers entwined, holding on.

"How does that feel?" Alex wanted to understand the difference between their experiences, what made Alex not Tiffany.

"This is weirdly intimate," the girl said.

"It feels secure to me."

"I make you feel secure? That's a riot."

The blood hummed under their skin from the caffeine or something else. As soon as they wondered about it, the distinction didn't seem to matter.

"You didn't kill Erika," Alex said.

"How do you know?" Tiffany said. "Maybe I'm not happy to see you. Maybe that's a knife in my pocket."

"You're happy to see me."

"Hold me tighter, yeah?"

That was it, Alex's defense for Tiffany Dennys—the girl's affection, her candor and compassion, an authenticity beyond what Alex had read was possible for sociopaths. And a true sociopath had been at work in the woods, amassing kids to perform old rituals, evil magic. Real or imagined, that wasn't of consequence to the case. Maybe it was, but Erika Summerson's murder felt so much less important this close to Tiffany. Alex's brain warmed and dripped contentedness, thick as honey, down the back of the throat, going for the heart. It was terrifying. Alex swallowed, pulled Tiffany nearer. Intelligence demanded faulty paradigms be shattered. For now, that meant accepting that a friendship could be worth more than renown for one's genius. So far, Alex had been careful to keep members of the group at a distance to prevent attachment from mucking up an objective view of the facts. It was obvious now that no accurate judgment could ever be made without intimacy with a subject. Alex remained dedicated to the case, having gained, during that languid afternoon in bed with Tiffany, a greater notion of why it mattered.

So, yes—Alex had shrugged when Greg implied that the ability to kill proved the killer's fearlessness and Doug admitted to having glimpsed the potential murder weapon. For one, if everyone who cared about something also knew the fear of losing that thing, the killer did, too. Even if that were the loss of his own life. Otherwise, why return to camp night after night to search the grounds for the strange diary? And two, a detailed description of the weapon was of far less use to the investigation than noting the reactions of the potential suspects after its mention.

•

Alex's indifference made Greg sweat like never before. She'd shrugged—the group's math whiz, whom he'd watched rise to lukewarm applause during so many school assemblies and be given enough blue ribbons and engraved plaques to decorate an entire team of brainiacs, as if thinking too hard were a sport. The group's work had made Greg uneasy from the start. Between John and Alex and the dork they called the genius, Greg worried that the group might actually find a trail of evidence that led to Erika's killer and be hacked to pieces for their heroism.

And now Alex shrugged as if it didn't matter. And the Dead Man stood with his back turned like he was giving up, too. The guy retreated into the shadows behind the tree. Instead of relief, Greg was on the brink of heartbreak, as if losing Erika all over again.

He and Josué had talked about her all afternoon. They'd eaten enough McDonald's french fries to stuff a small mammal, then hit Penny Park to shoot hoops. Josué wasn't bad. He put up each shot too stiffly and with great force, and the ball bricked off the backboard the same way each time. Even after a few games, the kid never limbered up. Some guys didn't have it. But J. smiled a lot and took the losses better than any kid Greg had ever played against, always making it a point to hand Greg the ball after the winning basket and to shake his hand and say, "Was a very good game."

Each win made Greg feel worse. Not for J. For her. For the fact he'd never kiss the girl's glossy pink mouth. Never feel her breath or run his fingers through her hair courtside on a hot summer night. He'd never hear her say, "Greg … Oh, Greg—" Because the girl was cold in the dirt at Resurrection Cemetery. He knew this because he'd been there, twice already, stood over her grave and all that weak shit, hands clasped in front of his hips all formal, then behind as if waiting for a game from the sidelines. Neither position felt right. What do you do in a cemetery but imagine weird shit, like speaking to the dead, her voice seeping from the headstone, "Greg … Greg …" Tiny, thin as the breeze. Then the night of her murder. The voice choked or shrieks.

Greg turned up the music in his headphones until he couldn't hear their gym shoes grind the asphalt or J.'s bricks off the backboard or his own thoughts. He wanted Erika out of his head, to bury her for once and for all, to move on. He began to regret following the Dead Man into the woods where he was constantly reminded that the girl he'd been obsessed with, maybe even loved, didn't exist anymore. He'd even asked Tiffany out to lunch today to help him forget Erika. She'd said no. That hadn't been an easy thing for him to do or hear, especially since she was the only girl but his mom that he talked to regularly. Pretty fucking defeated was what he felt, so Greg had to hand J. the ball and sit down on the curb and catch his breath. He was panting too hard for an easy game.

J. had noticed the guy's heavy breathing, of course, and said, "Better if Tiffany were here, no?"

"It's fine. Fuck her. It's … whatever."

"Genius … He's a real genius, eh? Tiffany—oh, man," J. said to bring Greg out of his sadness.

"Girls are messed up like that," Greg said. "Erika was the same way. Running with guys who treated her like garbage. The genius is a fine dude. But look at him. Against you or me? It doesn't make sense. Do they have eyes? Girls drive me fucking crazy. Give me a shot. I'm a nice guy. I am. Like a nice guy for once. I'll worship you. What more do you want? All I want's a nice, pretty girl to eat with and see movies with who won't judge me, won't think I'm nothing and never will be something, won't give up on me. Know what I'm saying?"

Greg wasn't thinking of Tiffany, but his mom. Neither she nor Greg respected the guy she'd remarried. He had a stable job and he paid for things. Yet she was cheating on him, and some nights would take Greg cruising with her boyfriend, who they picked up from the YMCA parking lot, and they'd all see a movie. The guy carried an old Chicago Bulls duffle bag and wore stained T-shirts and jeans like a deadbeat, but he was OK. He let Greg smoke cigarettes when his mother wasn't around and, unlike his stepdad, didn't ask him to do shit around the apartment, like take out the garbage and shampoo carpets when the untrained dogs unloaded hot piss in the corners, stuff that a man was supposed to take care of because it's his house. Greg missed his real dad, a burly man with a blonde beard and a hairy belly soft as a teddy bear. His dad didn't look like a deadbeat. He was one because of his drinking. But he'd never disrespected Greg and always said how much he loved him and his mother, would never abandon them. If the man had ever threatened her, it was because she'd refused to see him through tough times. Instead, she ran off with the first guy that could support her, then to a boyfriend to keep from regretting her poor life choices. It was pathetic, no different than Tiffany running to the dork, who was a wimp, a loser, a nobody.

"Yes," Josué said. He didn't understand all that Greg had said, as he'd spoken quickly. Josué watched the boy talk with great passion on the subject of women and nodded in sympathy. It seemed he had been hurt by Erika and still he felt this. All Josué's aunts were very smart about relationships, so much that their boyfriends, which changed like the seasons, never dared to argue with them. Josué believed women always knew more than men on the subject of love, more than he or Greg would understand. Women would do always what was best, and sometimes that was you and sometimes that was a short, pale pendejo with an overbite. There was no point in crying over it, as if shaking one's fist at the rain. What could bring happiness always? This came from a place inside. He'd been told so by his religious aunt who had more cats that followed her around than lovers. Josué didn't know where inside exactly and understood that trying to describe it now would not help Greg.

"It's not easy," Josué continued in sympathy.

"Did you want her real bad, too?"

"Tiffany?"

"No."

Josué recalled Erika's laugh in English class. It sputtered when she held joy inside for too long. That sound was hers and had made him happy. That was gone.

"Yes," he said. "Bad."

"Same, man. And now …"

"It is not right. It's sad."

"Would you kill for her?"

"Sí," he said.

"Yeah?"

"In defense? Oh, yes."

Greg could laugh—how insane these kids were, with their quick and thoughtless superhero talk and phony detective crap. Were they using their heads? They would all die out there. Greg didn't laugh, though. He listened. He really tried to hear J., as the kid somberly listed all he'd loved about Erika, all that was good and unique to her, his mouth a determined line daring the world to say otherwise. They shared the same hurt. The only difference was that Greg wanted to exorcise the pain of wanting Erika from his heart by hating her. He wanted nothing more to do with her or the woods. J. and the others could throw away their lives on the dead girl; he was going to despise and bury and forget. He was going to live. A guy couldn't always do the right thing to survive, and Greg couldn't see any other game plan to beat his misery for the good life he deserved.

"I want to hurt somebody," Greg said aloud. The kids around the campfire looked up immediately. The flames roared at the hearty logs in the pit. Greg wished no one had heard his blurt, his accident, though it felt as if he'd never said a truer thing his life.

"Me, too, amigo," Josué said, more to the group than Greg.

"Fucker hasn't taken everything from us." Tiffany pointed at the image that remained on the Big Tree, the portion that Doug had painted, Erika's pink flats breaking beyond the dome of stars into the heavens.

"Not yet," Alex said.

"Right," Tiffany said.

•

"We're all at risk of becoming a victim," E. said. "Everybody who visits this place is at risk while that monster—while evil is out there. So … we can fight back." The group could hear E. deciding her life was worth the endeavor. The comment remained a choice for the rest of them. She wasn't leading the group to battle or asking for their help.

Supporting John through chemotherapy that afternoon had finished the transformation of E.'s life study. She'd biked him home as she'd done all week, the boy perched on the handlebars not drunkenly smiling today, but sunken in his too-heavy coat like a sick bird shunning the morning glare of the white sun over the streets of Palos Hills. In his driveway, he'd touched her tensed forearm and asked if she had time to accompany him to the hospital and "know him outside of the woods." She told herself to quit imagining that his affections were warming on her and said, "Please." He'd been there when she'd needed him and wouldn't again let a cry for help go unanswered. "I'm here however you need me," she said with a little embarrassment, trying on the words of a caretaker, visited by a purer sentiment akin to what John had once said about love being bigger than the word. "I knew I could count on you," he'd said, then warned it wouldn't be easy.

John's mother had her purse over her shoulder and keys jingling in hand when they shuffled into the house. The kids were disheveled and dirty and stank of woodsmoke. Beside a trophy case in the foyer, they waited for her to comment. The shelves were full of propped plaques and medals and wide-mouthed cups alongside photographs of the boy in action or posed, grinning with a bat over his shoulder on sunny days or shaking hands with adults in suits. His accomplishments were furred with dust.

"You've about made us late," the woman said, the blame in the "you've" part directed at E. The look of the young girl made his mother's mouth dry up—a weakling child, bookish, redheaded, and those black clothes, poorly fit to hide an awfully full chest for someone her age—not the quality of person she'd pictured being the first flower her son brought home. "Johnny, sweetheart, I'm happy you're getting out of the house. But this Boy Scouting—you need your rest if you're going to beat—"

"Mom," John unzipped his coat as he passed, "E's my friend and she's coming with."

E. trailed him into the kitchen.

His mother stopped in the doorway and looked in at her patronizingly, as if the girl had misunderstood the nature of the appointment as anything that might resemble a date. "Dear, you don't want to go to a hospital."

"If you want me to continue—" John took two gulps of orange juice from the container while clutching the refrigerator door handle as if he'd otherwise collapse "—she's coming."

John's mother didn't challenge him.

It was terrible to watch the nurses work. They put two wide-mouthed needles into the boy's arms, clicked a gray button on a machine, and pumped a brackish liquid inside him. His hands made boney fists as his veins burned without the aid of painkillers. He needed to keep his mind clear, he'd insisted.

"Why are you being so difficult about this?" his mother said. After ten minutes of reproach, she left for the waiting room. Not before glaring, heavy-lidded, at E., distaste showing in the lower whites of her eyes. E. sat bedside with the boy. The blanket slid down his legs and his chair creaked as he writhed side to side.

"You're very brave," she said.

"I'm not."

"You've risked so much for my sister when you're …"

"I won't live."

"Don't say that." E. was quiet for a while, unable to think of one good reason why he shouldn't. His calves and biceps were thin belts strapped to his bones, and his skin was see-through. Ornate webs of blue veins decorated his temples and chest. He could go at any time. "If someone had told me two weeks ago I would be here today, I'd never have believed it," E. said. "Or how proud I'd be. You brought us together, got us to care. That's an amazing gift."

"I try because I'm scared," John said.

"To me that's enough."

"I want this to mean something."

He gritted his teeth against the burning.

"It does to me," she said.

"What?"

But after half a bag of treatment, he couldn't stand the pain. John asked for E.'s hand as a tall nurse stuck him with a morphine drip that vaulted his mind out of the room. "I don't … Don't …" His head tipped back, grip loosened. E. watched him float in silence for an hour. The boy was still beautiful. She studied the patterns in his vein-threaded forearms; the dimple in his chin, yet hairless; his wide, cracked lips; his fine eyelashes and their brush-like tips—the marvelous minutiae behind the force of John's charisma. He was more than that, too. E. closed her eyes, still tethered to him, his hand laid in hers, lukewarm and light as a nesting bird, and she listened to him breathe, to the cord of life being pulled in him, threatening to break, soundlessly, irreparably. Until she heard him, what he was saying by bringing her here.

"I'm fighting," E. said to her friends around the fire. She smiled as if having shed a great burden.

"No," Doug said.

E. met his disapproving glare and her buoyancy did not falter.

"The killer, he'll put one of us … there, in the fire … You next maybe."

"I know what the monster is capable of, Dougy." E. spoke past him, to the group. "We all do. No one should stay here for my sake. I'm not saying that. If something did happen … I couldn't take another loss like that. Serious things have happened here. You're right. He'll kill again if we let him. I can't let that continue. I couldn't live with that, either."

"Then let's get help," Doug pleaded. "Tell them … the police—everything. They'll catch him for us—arrest him … lock the killer up." Doug checked John's reaction to his plan, still unconvinced that he hadn't somehow been the figure in the cloak and Erika's killer. The guy was a mere outline beside the Big Tree.

"The genius is right," Greg said. "Isn't he?"

"Obviously," Doug said.

"Nope." Tiffany prodded the logs, which shot up an arching flare of sparks. She threw her poker into the darkness and looked at the group meanly. "I'm not afraid of some little shit dressed in a cloak.

185

And I hate cops. We've done a better job than them, anyway, in getting close to this guy. Haven't we?"

"Correct," Alex said.

"But the risk … dying," Doug said. "The police can do the rest."

"This decision, we all need to make," Josué said, "together."

"Also correct," Alex said.

"So which?" Josué said. "The cops? Or we fight?"

The kids each knew what path they wanted. They stared into the flames, waiting for someone braver to voice it. On both sides, there was doubt. They hoped an argument would be made to dissolve their fear, even if it wasn't the safer option, or to convince them otherwise.

"Fear," John said, "or freedom."

The boy looked over his shoulder at the group. One of his hands gripped the stony trunk. In the flickering light, it appeared to quiver under his touch like a living thing. His words didn't move their hearts to action. Indecision showed plain in their folded arms and downcast eyes.

John disappeared behind the tree.

•

"The guy … he's not right … in the head." Doug whispered to the group.

He adjusted his glasses and went over to where the Dead Man had been standing. The tree looked like any regular tree. He touched the bark to be sure. He looked again at the two slashes hacked into the blackened middle. Closer to the blade than he wanted to be, Doug withdrew his hand. The soot stained his fingertips.

"Spirits, or whatever … telling a kid—a killer to get other kids together … digging in the woods … at night. Sound familiar to anyone?"

"Whoa," Greg said.

"C'mon. You don't believe that," Tiffany said.

"It makes sense," Doug said. "Not total sense, but—"

"Then what're you still doing here?"

"I won't—I can't let him hurt you," he said.

"I'm a big girl, genius."

"Anyone … Please," he turned to them, "we have to leave this place … now, or—"

"I hope you make the choice to stay, Dougy," E. said. She squeezed his arm as she walked by. "You're wrong about John." E. stood at the head of the circle, the Big Tree at her back.

Doug kept away from her, from the group and the fire. "If it's John … or some other crazy person, like Greg said—the killer has killed before."

"So we'll have to be scarier than he is," Tiffany said.

"Scarier than the devil worshipper?" Josué said.

"War." In the orange glow, E. spookily smiled.

"That's what he wants," Doug said. Whether he meant John or the killer, not even Doug was sure anymore, so certain he was that they were walking into some monster's trap.

"I like this idea," Josué said. He and Tiffany high-fived.

Greg kept his head down, burdened by conflicting emotions about Erika.

"We're just kids," Doug said. "We're kids—kids …"

The more he said the word, the less true it sounded. The word recalled all the time they'd shared in the woods, how inexperienced and friendless they'd arrived, kids bearing the weight of being nothing special in a world that promised they could be anything. Here was a chance to be something. They were on the brink of it, and only a breeze …

Hearing the treetops rustle, Greg lifted his eyes.

"I—"

The kids saw movement high in the branches of the Big Tree. It wasn't the wind. A boy was up there.

John Walker found his footing on a thick limb that projected over their heads, thirty feet or more above. Slightly bent in the moonlight, the boy shed his clothes. The articles fell on them as graceful and quiet as the shadows of nighthawks. His shirt and a sock were lost in the fire. He stood upright and his thin body shown softly radiant. He took a bold step forward. One knee wobbled. The tremor coursed his torso and rattled his bony shoulders. The boy appeared to make jazz hands at an invisible audience in the sky. The group said nothing, were barely breathing, transfixed by the sight. John seemed to sense their awe then and stood straighter. Without looking down, he took two surefooted steps toward the stars. The tree beneath him was lost to shadows as he neared the end of the bough. The already vague outline of its leaves dissolved around him. The boy appeared to stand in the night sky. It was hard to say for how long John was up there, cheating gravity, death, disbelief. His arms hovered at his sides. He lifted them in a V.

"These are our woods," someone said. It didn't matter who. It could've been any of them, except Doug.

E. joined hands with Alex, who reached for Tiffany. Tiffany took hold of Greg. Greg gave in, accepted the hand of his good buddy, J. Josué and E. offered open hands to Doug to close the circle around the fire.

He joined them.

Doug didn't gawk in reverence at the heavens. He watched their faces flicker red against the night. Their wide-open mouths and up-turned eyes made masks of ecstasy and rage.

II

1

Doug Horolez would never forget one basketball game down at Penny Park starring the lanky Greg Dombrowski. The guy wore a parrot green jersey. Doug didn't follow sports, but it wasn't the school's colors. Greg wasn't on the team. He could've been. The way he moved on the court was unforgettable, feigning and slinking past other kids as if they were mannequins, soaring to the net, layup after layup. Greg remained stone-faced between roars of struggle against gravity and his body's limits. That was the feeling of watching him play—a solo performance with no other purpose but the enactment of grace to the end.

Greg showed the same surefootedness during the ritual, the Friday after John's. The boy's naked body towered on the limb of the Big Tree. He took three strides, going for the open break in the canopy.

They all had to walk, the group had decided last week. The Dead Man proposed it once he'd scaled down the rock wall behind the tree, naked and shivering, but also grinning with some embarrassment and pride. They put a blanket around his shoulders and hugged him. They high-fived in celebration, as if the guy had hit an out-of-the-park home run. Nothing had changed except their outlook on the danger ahead. They huddled together and discussed plans for reclaiming the woods. The ritual would be their "purification process." John spoke with what appeared to be great concentration, eyelids pressed tight, verbalizing cosmically ordained rules he alone could hear:

"We, each of us, must be fearless. The ritual will prepare us to confront the devil in the woods."

The group had yessed and nodded enthusiastically as the fire hissed and popped louder than the hushed voices they'd suddenly adopted. Whispering in this way, it was decided one or two ritual walks per week could be managed without arousing the suspicion of their parents and jeopardizing their work in the woods. Greg stood first when the question of initiation order was posed. Doug was the last sitting. Warnings died, strangled in him. The group giggled as if an inside joke had been made. Josué noogied him until he got up. They joined hands around the fire again and vowed in a low chant to finish all seven rituals before the moon was "pregnant with light."

Silently, Doug made a vow of his own: to save the group from themselves before then, preferably before his own walk. He understood their bond as a temporary insanity, born of desperation. He knew they were good people who could be returned to reality. When they didn't wake up doubtful the next morning or the next, Doug knew he had to keep his promise. He followed the group across an invisible boundary into another world. Somebody had to. He couldn't let John win, shepherd E. and everyone else into the woods until there was no one left to love him.

There was no talking to Tiffany about the dangers of confronting

a cloaked murderer that wielded a knife the length of Doug's forearm. On the night John walked, she'd curled asleep with Alex. In
the morning, she left camp early with Greg. While Doug rolled his
slippery nylon sleeping bag, trying to get it small enough to bind,
he watched Tiffany who'd only yesterday taken his virginity recede
through the trees with another guy. She sassed Greg, and he started
after her in mock chase. They ran around the trail bend and left only
their coupled laughter to echo in Doug's heart, empty as ever, ringing
as hollow as a tin can lost to the wind.

"The wind blows in our favor now," John said above him. It
sounded as if the guy had read his mind and spoke directly to him.
Doug didn't look up. The walls of whatever contained his emotions
felt thin. They trembled and threatened to crush.

"I feel it, too," E. answered warmly. She doused the fire's coals.

Doug unrolled his sleeping bag and tried again, one clumsy fold
at a time, uncertain if he were doing it right. Despite the insanity of
last night, he failed to think beyond himself. He focused on the labor
of his hands while his mind unpacked what he was losing, which
was nothing, as usual, except the potential of having something with
somebody. Even if dating someone, there was the threat of heartbreak, sure, but not after many deeply fulfilling moments to make the
potential (inevitable?) loss worth it.

Doug's hands ached now, and the sleeping bag was still too bulky.
He undid it and restarted. How long would he have needed to date
Tiffany or E. to break even with loneliness? A whole week? Months?
Fifteen years, like his parents? Nothing short of forever seemed
enough. Doug was alone inwardly, as in his sense of rightness, which
alienated him from the group. He wanted to feel strong and determined always, as he had when preparing to face an evil John Walker.

He wanted to put that power to use, to save his friends, be the sort of hero unconcerned about his fragile inner self, only the actions necessary to do good.

Whatever strength remained in him allowed Doug to pack his belongings and leave. He didn't cry in front of E. and the others. He got the bag rolled OK. One side funneled out wider than the other, but he was able to jam it into its drawstring sack, mutely wave, and hurry home, where, alone in his room, Doug sobbed into his pillow to keep his family from hearing.

The kids spent all week setting traps around the Grove's perimeter. Trip lines and stumbling pits camouflaged with sticks and leaves were strategically placed on the other side of the creek. They retraced the course the killer had run, as reported by Doug, through the crime scene and into the trees. They found trails zigzagging in razor thin lines up the valley's steep sides to the high ridge above. They booby-trapped these as well. The next day, they found their new hiding spot rooted up. Rations, tools, and supplies had all been reduced to ash and char in the fire pit as before. The failure of their juvenile defenses against the killer, who was more like a force of erasure of everything they loved, brought a humbling quiet over the group. After a day of strategizing, research, and rummaging their parents' sheds, garages, medicine cabinets, and junk drawers, they returned and built deadlier traps, starting up the ridge and working backward as methodically as their enemy: punji bear traps and reinforced steel trip wires, as well as common handholds and low-lying branches armed with the real consequences of sharp-ended sticks and spreads of nails, needles, and razorblades.

Doug didn't voice opposition to the work. He didn't say much all that week. The others noticed—his gawky smile swapped for lowered eyes, his usual criticism absent whenever the group discussed plans to defend the Grove. Each in turn asked if he were sick, if he were still shaken up from seeing the killer, if he'd had some trouble outside the woods, if something wasn't the matter. They questioned Doug while prepping weapons to maim another human being. Sure, a murderer, but maybe random kids who would return to the Grove to revive its glory days. Believing himself incapable of more than one stand against John's influence, Doug withheld his concerns, waiting for the right moment, a slip of doubt from one of his friends about the group's intentions. They were careful, determined. As the week marched on and the rift widened between their unity and his silent resistance, Doug began to wonder if they suspected his dissent and his desire to stop them.

That Friday after school, they toured the traps to ensure Greg's ritual would go undisturbed, making repairs and adjustments to askew armaments and loose wires. They walked single file through the breath of the woods, a muggy midday heat, uncommon for early May. They went slowly but confidently, swatting mindlessly at mosquitoes and intently mimicking the kid ahead of them. Alex led the group through underbrush, over humps of stone and dirt by way of detailed notes, stopping often to instruct where to place footing and which trees to grasp to safely venture from camp. All but John were coatless. Everyone but Alex wore shorts. Tiffany wore a striped dress. All of which would make a wrong move painful, if not lethal. Unlike yesterday, the nearest traps remained intact. The group paused to admire each, revealed by their guide like deadly spiders with exotic, gorgeously patterned backs, strung between trunks or nested in ground holes, awaiting a misstep. It seemed wild now to the kids that they were their makers. The woods were covered with them. None of the well-camouflaged tops of the punji traps in the middle of the trails had been broken. Just a little way ahead, one of their trip lines sagged, had been snagged out of the earth. Along one of the thin trails further up the ridge, they discovered a spiked foothold crushed and crusted in dried blood.

"We got him," Greg said. He landed congratulatory handshakes on the rest of the group. Winning smiles broke their anxiety. All but Doug looked relieved.

In a few minutes, the traps were adjusted and carefully reset, and the kids returned to camp as cautiously. They struggled to contain their excitement and traveled in an effervescent shuffle that resembled a conga line fleeing a room with a sleeping baby. Back at the tree, they yipped and howled at the trees. They clapped in triumphant pops and cracked jokes that portrayed the killer as an idiot, bumbling around last night, catching his goofy cloak on nails, tumbling cartoonishly into trap after trap until, too fearful to take another step, he was forced to give up his marauding until morning, stuck petrified in the woods alone for hours before scrambling to his perch up on the ridge.

"We've won one round," E. said over their trailing laughter.

Her eyes softened. Her lips remained a wavering line. To Doug, she looked a bit crazed.

"He can be afraid, like us," John said, not at the head of the fire pit, where E. stood, but walking up from the creek. He'd been crouched, cupping up enough water to slake a great thirst. His chin was glossy and he wiped it with his sleeve as the group turned. "He can leave us this place."

The others whispered yesses in their group voice.

From his things, John withdrew a disassembled fishing pole with line and a pouch of hooks. He put them in Greg's hands and said, "Do good work."

Driving pegs for trip lines yesterday, Greg had talked about fishing with his biological dad on the Cal-Sag River. The sun making pink fire in the black sky over the trees. Car tires thumping lazily across the bridge overhead. Greg full of purpose and the potency of the man's bitter cologne. John must've guessed at the story's significance and asked Greg to catch a celebratory dinner for them to fry after the ritual—three fish, no more or less—and to teach Doug.

Doug lagged at first, resisting John's order to play the child as Greg strode down the creek. Soon enough, though, he tried to match the guy's every footprint, unable to recall where he'd set his own traps, let alone others'.

The valley narrowed and sloped gradually until the ridge above both boys was lost behind the treetops. Over rocky steps, the creek snaked down through the dense woodland, quickened by smaller run-offs. One slender waterfall slapped the stones like hose water.

The land leveled. The hike became less strenuous. The creek widened and deepened. It bent calmly around a muddy embankment and the black corpses of several fallen trees. It was nothing new for Doug to be disoriented, yet it was disturbing that he couldn't discern from which direction the whir of traffic was coming, just above the water's trickle, on what was probably Willow Springs Road. The world beyond culminated into a slow roar, like an ever-cresting wave. Why that sound? If there was a god overseeing all things—good, evil, and mundane—it could've been anything, like a bell.

"Here'll do," Greg said.

Greg scanned the green surface while they talked about the likelihood that the stream emptied onto the Cal-Sag River. A fish flashed from the hollow of a submerged tree. Greg dropped to one knee and showed Doug how to overturn rocks to dig for live bait. Greg looked over at him after every step, not continuing until Doug glanced up to acknowledge his instructions. Maybe he emulated the father that he'd spoken of with nostalgia, and felt necessary, like somebody. The guy's confidence was irritating. Needing a break, Doug pulled a plastic bottle of pop out of his backpack and took a swig. He offered the pop to Greg who dumped it, pulled a stubby knife from his pocket, and sliced the top off without asking. He tipped a few worms over the jagged rim. The last he slipped bleeding onto his hook.

"Now we can get some work done," Greg said.

Doug followed him out onto the water, and the boys balanced on the soggy tree trunks, loose like basketballs underfoot. Doug played fisherman's apprentice, holding the squirming bottle away from his body while recalling his own assertiveness when the group first began to dig for clues at Bachelor's Grove. Having Tiffany on his side, the support of someone skeptical of John's judgment, had made him tougher. That version of himself seemed faded and false as a dream. To watch that power alive in Greg wasn't easy. The guy had stolen his girl and his best self.

"See that shady spot?" Greg pointed up the stream. He cast the line. Greg fumbled the reeling, but the bait sunk right on.

"John talk to you about how we could live out here, all of us? Grow our own food," Greg said. "Wouldn't that be something."

Doug looked down to hide his revulsion. The guy's gym shoes were so big, the tips protruded over the water. A part of Doug wanted to shove him in, watch him drift—safe, but gone forever.

"Did you really see him? The killer?"

"It sucked," Doug said.

"You couldn't see his face at all?"

Doug shook his head.

"I mean, if you saw him—if he passed you on the street—you wouldn't even know?"

"Probably not. I blew it … like everything."

"No way," Greg said. "You've come closer than anyone to this guy. That's cool, man. And you were ready to brain him with that hammer of yours? That's tough."

"Thanks," Doug said, too upset to be grateful.

The pole bent in Greg's hands.

"I got you," he cried and leaned in. He cranked at the reel, yanking the pole up and down against the catch. His body wobbled, angled sideways of the taut line. He readjusted his footing. Overstepping, Greg tipped forward—

Doug seized and held firmly to his waist, keeping the tall boy steady.

A minute later, they were out of breath and rested on the bank with a long, lean fish between them.

"Thanks, genius," Greg said. "I don't usually do teamwork."

Doug nodded. Still he wouldn't meet Greg's gaze. He felt like a toddler beside the adult-sized basketballer, and he watched the dead fish as if for another round of spasms.

"I should've asked you first, about Tiff—Tiffany," Greg said. "We got burgers the other day. She actually talked about you. Said you were the best dude she ever met. No shit. She said you two weren't dating. I still should've asked first. That would've been the right thing to do, right? Today we went to the park, hung out on the swings. You know … I don't know—I thought maybe she was flirting. Maybe that's how she is. I didn't touch her or anything. I wanted to. You'd have to be crazy not to want to. I mean, the girl is … She's not Erika. She tells you what she's thinking, in a good way. Doesn't hide anything. I like that about her. But, hey—you got dibs on her, man, and I'm not messing anything up. Shitty people do shit like that. It's easy to. That's not me. So, what's up? Is she your girl? Did you two date or what?"

"No," Doug said.

"That's what you wanted?"

"It's just … what it is—was. It's whatever. Nothing."

To face the others back at camp as a blubbering mess would make Doug look even less manly beside Greg. So Doug watched the stiff trees on the other side of the stream and waited for their branches to wave in a breeze. It was difficult to say if he would've rejected the ritual and the vision of the Dead Man as a real-life Christmas tree angel if Tiffany had taken his hand instead of Greg's that night. Maybe because of it, he couldn't hate Greg. He wanted to. Then again, Doug doubted Tiffany would ever be anyone's girl but her own. Which was good for her. But Doug expected never to have anything he wanted. Greg might get hurt worse.

"It's fine," he said.

"Yeah? Think I got a shot?"

"More than me."

"Right on." In a jump, Greg was on his feet.

The guy offered his hand. Doug took it. The boys returned to their spot along the stream. Greg showed him how to throw a line and tug up fish. They lost a few worms and several times nearly slipped into the water. Doug almost enjoyed hanging out with Greg. That'd likely been John's intent all along, to remind them of their friendship to prevent a break in the group. By reassuring Greg that he'd done no wrong, Doug had once again dumbly played into John's masterminding. It wasn't the Dead Man's fault that Tiffany had gone cold after Doug had pleaded with the group not to confront the killer, but it felt good to hate him for giving her another reason to. Doug didn't want to hate John or anyone. He wanted the guy to quit ruining his life and vanish already. The Dead Man wouldn't be wished away. Doug had tried, many times. Now, with the rituals, he couldn't be waited out, either. The single course of action left was the most difficult. Emotionally exhausted, without Tiffany or E., if Doug wanted to keep them from dying, he would have to break John's mind control with words.

"Are you seriously going to? … walk tonight?" Doug stammered.

"We all are."

"John wants us to … obviously."

"You don't want to, man?" Greg said.

"It was John's idea—just saying."

Doug snagged a line, and Greg took the pole out of his hands. He pulled and the line popped.

"It kinda was." He reeled in swiftly. While he tied another hook, he said, "It's sorta dangerous."

"Right! I mean, yeah—this whole thing is dangerous."

"We all swore to do it," Greg said. "We swore to each other."

"John had us do that, right? But what if you fall? Or Tiffany? Someone could be hurt—I mean, seriously die."

"There's way more dangerous things out there," Greg nodded upstream, "that we could be doing other than playing in the woods."

"But we're not playing," Doug said.

Greg stole the sawed-off pop bottle. He shook the extra dirt around the bottom, aggressively fingering for worms. It was empty. His mouth opened before he spoke, inhaling in frustration. He looked straight at Doug.

"You're scared." His voice trembled like a plea, then toughened. "I am, too. But I won't let these guys down. Not Tiff or John or J. They're doing it, I'm doing it. You're going to do it, too."

He left Doug on the water to find more worms. But he paused on the embankment and said:

"We're becoming a family. You don't turn your back on family like a total shithead."

Doug adjusted his glasses. He looked downstream, big feelings expanding. Small round leaves dappled against the sunset like scattered puzzle-pieces. The intensity of the cars on the nearby highway rose above the stream for a moment. Doug wanted to run. He felt beaten, not by Greg, but the Dead Man. It wouldn't be hard. He could escape back to the real world, save himself. He couldn't ever return, might never see these friends again. E. was already lost to this other world, a priestess of a strange tribe, a stranger to him, and Doug began to feel stupid to have believed he'd ever had a chance against John. If, during the ritual, Greg and E. and the rest fell from the high branch, it wouldn't be Doug's fault. It wouldn't, he told himself. It wasn't enough to absolve his concern for them, who were on the whole smarter, stronger, and more able to change the group's direction. If only they'd seen the cloaked killer in the dark—

A hiss sounded at Doug's feet. The thick, knotted body of a water snake lay piled at one end of the trunk. He couldn't tell where the creature began or ended. Doug searched the churning length for a face. One blunt, seemingly eyeless end jabbed forward, elongated up the trunk toward his legs. Doug couldn't breathe. He couldn't will away his weakness, the familiar, paralyzing fear of impending death.

The snake was inches away. He stepped back. The trunk dipped under his shifting weight. The snake sloughed into water, then himself.

The stream wasn't deep. He kicked at the slippery stones, frantically clopping for the embankment. Greg's open hand waited to help him up. Doug didn't accept it.

"Did you see that? A huge snake …"

"No, man." Greg gave the water a skeptical skim. He called after Doug: "Where you running?"

"I'm warming up at camp."

"But John said—"

"Go ahead. Walk for him, bark for him," Doug muttered.

He trekked back, wet and alone. His heartbeat raced at the thought that the Dead Man was only getting started in his plans.

The group laughed when they saw Doug sopping. He mumbled about falling in. Josué welcomed him with a place at the fire he was building. Tiffany bent and kissed his cheek, then wandered down the creek for Greg. E. brought a blanket. "Same old Dougy," she said. The group smiled, relieved that their jester had returned.

"You're a good person," he said to E.

Her gladness shifted with discomfort. She'd started to put the blanket around his shoulders and froze, caught off-guard by his sincerity. He took it from her hands and wrapped himself. To check that she wasn't suspect of some wrongdoing, she met his eyes, which pointed up at her from behind his thick glasses.

"You sure you're OK, Dougy?"

"Doug," he said without blinking. "Just Doug."

"He's named the fire in his soul," John intervened. The guy sat straight-backed at his place in front of the Big Tree. He didn't have to raise his voice for the group to hush and heed him. "We can all respect that."

"I didn't mean … Of course," E. said. Whether to John's request or his own, Doug didn't know. He wished he did.

She returned to the cookout equipment. She glanced back once, as if to verify that the ripple between them had originated not from her, but him. Then she crouched in the deepening shadow to prepare dinner, and her face blanked.

From across the campfire, Doug felt John's gaze commanding him to acknowledge he'd been granted a favor by his power. Doug focused on the fire and the liquid-like current beneath the logs. He heard the burn's hollowness, much like the ribbed streams of gas that blew in the body of his parents' furnace. They kept the thermostat low all winter, and though he often huddled over the living-room floor vent to keep warm, a comforter pulled over his head and resembling a lumpy ghost, Doug was invariably sick two or three times a cold season. He'd never spoke up to his parents about changing it. But, at his age, he could say something.

"Did you and Greg get along all right?" John asked.

E. and Josué didn't look over. They slowed in their labor to listen.

"I thought you knew everything," Doug said.

Josué chuckled. He quit as soon as he'd started.

Doug refused to look up and mark John's reaction. He had that power at least.

2

John's number-two performed the ritual on Saturday night.

Alex stooped and hugged the trunk at the top, struck motionless by the height as badly as Yiaya, who refused to trust escalators at her favorite department stores or to climb stairs to attend the cries of grandchildren. The result: a whole elevated world the woman couldn't access owing to an exaggerated fear of human failure.

Closing one's eyes didn't help. The group seeing you naked was also of last concern so high up. Below, a ring of vague, upturned faces shone like six candles. Alex braved a peek at the sky. The moon was new—was dark—wasn't there. In its place, Saturn oversaw the ritual. The amorphous glob of faraway light resembled how Alex felt, indistinct of form and lovely because of it—all the sentiments Tiffany had expressed last week converging into fact. The compulsion to walk along the bough of the Big Tree wasn't Saturn's doing, however, but the great space beyond's. Alex and the Earth were put into perspective thanks to the planet, their solar family, to which every atom of one's body and mind was related, linked distantly to those twinkling cousins way out there, and the incalculable, no, unfathomable space above and below that was part of one's being, too, which Alex fathomed, inwardly and outwardly, endlessly, striking awe, which was everything and—up there—enough.

3

Doug found the first note in his locker on Monday morning:
LET ME IN, DOUGYDEAREST. WHAT'S GOING ON
UNDER RED MOUNTAIN?

Left and right down the hallway, no one paid him attention between classes, as usual. Still, reading the note, he had the creepy feeling of being watched. He sighed, exhausted by the cryptic nonsense that'd appeared in his life since John. Doug crumpled the note and jammed it in his pocket.

His science teacher lectured the class about graduation, coffee in one hand, the other fixed to her hip like the handle of a much larger cup. Ms. Whitehead was a prim, gray-complexioned woman with a pouchy double chin and owlish glasses. She had an operatic voice that blared out of her peephole of a mouth. Today she warned that after next week's graduation ceremony they would no longer be eighth graders, and in four very short months they would be high schoolers. Their worlds would be turned upside down. Mixed among students from neighboring junior highs, some better prepared and many much worse off, they would be given the opportunity to start their social lives afresh. Some were already undergoing transformations she sincerely hoped the public school system had equipped them to face. It was a confusing time that would only become more so as the repercussions of each choice lay ahead. They might not understand this, yet, but their attitude in facing these challenges would determine their character for the rest of their lives.... The woman opened class at length about changes in status and cliques and hormones and temptations too remote for the class to care about with summer vacation so near, certain to be just another well of timeless days spent lazily, generally inconsequential, and later hazy, indistinct from previous summers, but for rare amorous moments with equally transient special-someones, and, though a couple of students mindlessly scribbled notes as if the material would show on the big test, the break couldn't come fast enough for them—all except for Doug, of course. Before then, he'd have to rescue his friends from becoming permanent residents of the woods.

E. was in his class. The girl sat severely straight, having adopted John's holier-than-thou bearing. Really, she wasn't in the room at all. She stared passed her classmates' tottering heads with a faint smile at the overcast sky beyond. Doug guessed she wandered under the broad arms of the Big Tree, an outline of lesser darkness, receiving arcane transmissions from John H. Walker, who rattled about their work in the woods like a blind and mad prophet. It made sense to Doug now. The woods, John—these were replacements for her library hideaway and the wisdom of greater authors. More immediate, more distracting, maybe, but a similar kind of distraction, or abstraction. E. had longed to live in another world of immaterial substance. If John had beaten Doug in melting a cavern in E.'s icy heart, it was not because he was handsomer or stronger or wiser, but because he'd carved her dreams into existence, secrets and imagination and words of power, the only place the dead can live. Maybe she was truly happy. If so, she was stupid. Doug was the butt of the real world. He'd suffered rejection and humiliation more than anybody. He wasn't running from it, though. Not anymore. His entire life, he'd been resigned to its mediocrity and to his own, he'd accepted the blows it doled out, accepted that the world couldn't be any other way. Because he was afraid. A nobody that speaks out and stands ground, aware of the consequences, against the consequences, who Doug could be, there was no script for that role. E. could be that free, too, here, where it wouldn't cost her life, where she was good enough to be loved, was loved. And Doug meant to tell her so. He had to try.

DEAR E., WHEN I SAID EARLIER YOU WERE A GOOD PERSON, I THINK I MEANT GOOD ENOUGH TO BE HAPPY. ~~TO NOT RUN AWAY.~~ PEOPLE WHO DON'T WANT ANYTHING FROM YOU ~~UNLIKE JOHN~~ LOVE YOU HERE. ~~I STILL LOVE YOU. I MEAN AS A FRIEND. AND MORE. BUT MOSTLY,~~ I CARE ABOUT YOU, AND YOUR LIFE IS IN DANGER. HELP ME HELP THE OTHERS ESCAPE THE WOODS ~~BEFORE SOMEONE ELSE GETS KILLED LIKE YOUR SISTER ERIKA.~~ PLEASE ~~WAKE UP. WITH LOVE,~~ DOUG, he wrote in an inky, redacted fury on a tear of notebook paper.

"Douglas—" the chemistry teacher reproached beside his desk.

The class rippled with laughter.

She ordered him to share the letter covered by his hands, what was apparently more important than his present company.

"Ms. Whitehead? It's ... personal."

The class went silent. Doug wanted to believe it was from the shock of him standing up to a teacher, to anybody. More likely, they were eager for a glimpse of the private life of the dork, if only to laugh about later.

"I'm not asking, young man. You know the rules. Share your disrespectful scribbling, or you'll spend the afternoon at the principal's office."

Without knowing it, Doug's teacher had presented him a way out. He could tell his story and be out of the woods forever. The end wouldn't be entirely his fault. The group couldn't blame him for that. He had to follow the rules of this world still, didn't he? His burden of responsibility lifted. As if he'd been holding his breath, Doug's lungs freed and swelled. He re-envisioned a future without John's puppetry, likely as soon as this summer. They would all get in trouble. Better than getting killed. Well, Doug could only speak for the living. His chair legs raked against the floor as he stood, surprising the teacher, who took a reserved step back to allow room for a public reading.

Doug held the note close to his glasses for some time before he said anything. He couldn't focus on it, except to watch his fingertips quake against the tight paper. His confidence drained as fast as the blood from his face, and he glanced at E. for confirmation that he was doing right. She gave him her full attention now. E. sat very still and looked as if she wanted to mouth the word "no" but was afraid to startle him, not concerned for him, but fierce and frightened of what he might say. Doug wanted to be brave for them both, then, to read the entire thing, crossed-out words included. Each had been methodically desiccated, a string of inky pits just beyond recognition. Having begun the note with his feelings about her seemed so sure to fail that he considered reading the lines in reverse. He looked at E. once more. She was no longer scared. Threat flashed in her eyes.

"I understand, Ms. Whitehead." Doug balled the slip of paper. "But I can't do that right now." He popped the note into his mouth, chewed, and swallowed. For once his excess of saliva was a perk.

Doug exited the room to an uproar before she could find the words to excuse him. It didn't feel like a victory.

Minutes later, Doug was again on the verge of confessing. Principal Pope paced his office and probed the eighth grader for an hour about this acting out. He inquired about his home life and friendship with Erika Summerson's "troubled" sister. The principal rephrased and reintroduced questions with anecdotes from childhood, himself raised in a modest town, not a suburb, not Palos, bigger, not in terms of residencies per square block, the streets cleaner and houses broader and lawns greener, each on a hill, it seemed, and no crime but for those who didn't belong or chose not to, so that pride was never the ambition of its residents, but the foundation, a place like what Doug began to imagine the contractors would deconstruct the woods into. He listened to the man reminisce under the guise of reaching a boy in the dim office and after forty-five minutes hadn't uttered one complete sentence, which Principal Pope must've realized then, too, because he stopped as if stunned before the slatted blinds overlooking the faded slashes of empty parking spots along the street, having talked himself into a stupor from which it took a minute to discern that he wasn't fourteen and home again, but with a boy on the road to becoming a troubled young man, and a bit embarrassed that he'd confessed so much and couldn't remember the student's name. He raised the blinds. Yes, he was still here, many years later, in a town where young people who mattered died of cancer and deviants snuck out at midnight to do terrible things to themselves and others in the woods, like Lucky, his German Shepherd whom he'd brought home to make life separated from his wife more tolerable. A rescue, she was old, old Lucky, lucky at last to have a stable home, as miserable in health as he'd felt, and maybe she'd only wandered off his front porch to die and it was coincidence that the police's investigation of Ms. Summerson's murder had turned up that mass grave of dogs behind Homerding Hill, just a sixth sense, or maybe the deathly quiet called canines to the spot, or otherwise they were snatched for Satanic sacrifice by individuals who lived in opposition to the Pledge of Allegiance, the values of Palos Hills Junior High School, and plain decency. Somehow that, too, was Doug's fault, the fault of deviants of the kind Doug would become if not purged of his rebellious spirit, and then, remembering his case exactly, the principal looked over the boy with distaste, as if he'd rather not go another minute alone with him. An admission of guilt was imperative to this child's salvation, and Principal Pope clamped the back of Doug's chair with both hands, fell silent, and waited for a response. Pressured into giving the principal something for his time, and despite an inexpressible loathing for the man, or maybe just his musky odor, Doug began to talk about his father's recent layoff and his parents having more disagreements lately. He went on for several minutes, astonished from where inside he'd stowed all these worries, to the point of wondering if they were completely fabricated, until he said, "Maybe they'll divorce." He stopped, stunned by his own admission. The boy was hollow. He didn't belong anywhere. The principal prescribed an after-school club to output his stress. "Start a chess team," he'd said. He gave more sincere advice with the zeal of public service warming his otherwise stern face, but Doug hardly listened. He recalled the fanaticism in E.'s eyes. If he debunked the grandeur of John H. Walker too quickly, he would lose her forever. He now doubted he could live with that. Maybe. Even for her own good, he hadn't the heart to betray her.

In the lunchroom later, Doug found himself staring at a long motivational banner on the back wall. It sagged in the middle and was clearly several sheets of printer paper taped together. It could've hung there for months and he was just now noticing it. "Never Settle For Less Than Your Best!" it said, followed by a graphic of a light bulb. Doug chewed, reading the banner so intensely that it took a moment to hear his remaining two tablemates. They'd shared their summer plans and were asking about his. "Not die," he answered and continued to repeat the poster's advice, slower each time, until the words mucked into a mantra: Neversettleforlessthanyourbestexclamationpointlightbulb. He knew why. Even that knowledge didn't help. He wanted a light to go on inside himself. The tablemates didn't return after dumping their garbage. They sat with the leftover assortment of geeks and weirdoes that'd regrouped elsewhere. The cheese sat alone. If he left the group, this would be his life.

After school, he found the walking trail entrance on Oketo Street swarmed with white vans. Reflective vests flashed through the trees. Land developers roamed the woods in packs and hollered in booming, yet incomprehensible voices. Along the wooded side of the street, several graphic posters were staked. Large digital images of glassy condos built around a nine-hole golf course were superimposed on a fat diamond of woods nearest the rec center. The project would leave few original trees but for lone decorative specimens. "VOTE FOR THE FUTURE! PROP#1!" each said. These posters made Doug uneasy and made the woods' erasure real in a way it hadn't been before. Dozing the place was the easiest solution to ending the group, he told himself, but couldn't believe it, deeply ashamed, as if he'd wished the images into existence by wishing John out during his visit with the principal, except that each house did not sit on a hill, though the buildings were as stately and streets as clean perhaps, and definitely as sad, as both were pictured empty, uninhabited. Of course, people would light all those windows (wouldn't they?). This new Palos looked so much fancier that rich folks would have to move in from elsewhere, from outside, Palos Park maybe, or much further north. Doug considered for the first time that the entire town might similarly be redeveloped. His home wouldn't be his, it too erased eventually, inconspicuously at first, from the edges, the woods, and then— Where would the people go? His family had been outsiders at some point, immigrants. What'd happened to the ones before them? And the ones before that? He vaguely recalled a lesson on Manifest Destiny, something about violence and identity—just a jumble of dates and battles in his head. He hadn't hurt anybody, was the victim (right?). Still, his guilt persisted over not wanting to stop the development of what felt like ruin. Doug continued down the block, dazed by his glimpse of one possible future. He tried to think of a single, positive force at work in his life, in life period. He immediately quit, mind adrift in a lingering fog of sadness. His only distinguishable emotion, he felt numbly, firm beneath his feet, yet at a distance, on the other side of his gummy shoe soles: hope that he and everyone weren't cursed to forget what'd come before as if it had never existed.

At the end of the block, four of the group called from the playground beside the rec center. Among the colored slides and bridges and tubes, they grimly squatted and scoped like vultures. The workers in the trails would make it difficult to go back and forth by day, Josué assessed. Tiffany confirmed that they would hang around all week, sizing up the job and laying plans, and that going unnoticed wouldn't be easy. Greg suggested taking the train tracks further into the woods and cutting across that way. Alex agreed to all points.

John and E. rode up. John seemed distracted and approved the plan with a twist of his hand, as if screwing in a light bulb. E. was quiet and attentive to her friends as usual, but she didn't look happy. She didn't acknowledge Doug at all. His first thought was that she'd told John about the note and his being sent to the principal's office. If questioned in front of the others about what he'd written, Doug would lie about nearly bringing down the axe. The woods were their dream place, after all, where they could be what they weren't in real life. Even Doug had been granted his wish there: he wasn't nobody. He let the group sweep him through the tall reeds of the overgrown ditch that ran along the elevated tracks. He was who they wanted him to be.

Greg helped John up. They climbed to the fist-sized stones that topped the wall and Greg slipped. He would've dropped the Dead Man but for E.'s save. The group laughed it off—Greg the graceful—then followed the rails through the woods to find another way down to Bachelor's Grove. When they didn't stay on the railroad ties, the stones clacked beneath their shoes like giant marbles. They stopped before the train bridge that spanned the Cal-Sag River. On the other side was the next town over. On the left, below in the tree line, they spotted a lightly used trail. They followed it in roughly an easterly direction toward the moraine. Several miles and many assurances later, the group came out huffing on a high ridge that overlooked the valley. Low clouds slid as smoothly and soundlessly as ice across glass above the split in the earth scabbed with trees. The leaves were in full bloom from the unusual winter rains to defend against another relentless summer heat wave.

Doug lingered a moment while the others followed the trail around the ridge. The view disoriented him, not the space but the expanse of time the moraine represented: long ago, but not forever. The woods had a remarkable history compared to his insignificant blip on Earth. It was just trees. They were pretty, emerald green and endless over the hills from this vantage. They were grand altogether, terrifyingly so, as if Doug beheld an entire labyrinth—one he was trapped in the middle of. Fear brought Doug into himself. They would be gutted together if he didn't change the course set by John and the killer, who were fundamentally the same. Whether the guy murdered or got people murdered, their disregard for others was indistinguishable.

"That's it," John said behind him.

The Dead Man's hood was up against a chill that only he seemed to feel on bright spring days. His arms hung at his sides, but his fingers were outspread and made Doug anxious while on the edge of the ravine.

"It's … something else," Doug said.

The Dead Man lowered the hood. Newly shaved, his head was egg slick. Blue veins branched up his skull like fractures. The guy came beside him and scanned the valley.

"It's home, Doug."

The Dead Man set a hand on his shoulder. John didn't pat him in the fatherly manner he had when they'd first met. The hand perched there, nimble and light. His fingers drummed, full of the potential to thrust Doug forward. Doug sucked a single breath into his tight chest. He'd never been in a fight before. All he could think to do was clutch John's hoodie and take the Dead Man with him.

"The Grove as it is can be yours forever." John continued intently, as if testing him with each line. "It soon will be. If we listen to the voice in the trees. For all of us. Do you understand me?"

Doug wanted to scream to shut the guy up. His throat was tight. All he could peep was, "I … It can't last."

"Your perspective needs readjustment," John said patiently. The hand squirmed like a tarantula and reseated closer to Doug's neck. Doug didn't look at it, couldn't. "You're right about Nothingness. But wrong about Forever," John said. He leaned in, still watching the moraine without lowering his voice, which added to the intensity of what he said next. "I need you listening, of all people. What remains when they take everything else is—"

"Is this even the right way to go?" Tiffany called to John. She ignored Alex's affirmations that the course was positively correct.

John hesitated. He released Doug's shoulder. "We'll finish this conversation later." He rejoined the group. Doug followed at a distance, convinced that, if John wasn't the original killer, he'd become capable of anything to see his plans realized.

John claimed to have spotted the Big Tree. No one else recognized it below, but they followed him around the rim of the valley. The trail was worn to the mud, a bike-tire wide. Wild growth made it impossible to see around each bend, and the group walked single file, slowly and cautiously, listening for the killer and the developers. They swatted at mosquitos buzzing in their ears. The lean path broke underfoot. John waved them aside to look down a less sheer face into the valley. It was only vaguely familiar to everyone else until Alex said, "This is likely the route the killer takes," and pointed out the gray stumps of the original crime scene visible just through the trees.

Josué stopped the group before they descended. He looked back over his shoulder, hand in his pocket as if prepared to draw one of his imaginary six shooters. Something red waved from behind a bush up the trail, like a flag, about waist high. He led them over to it. A strip of red plastic had been tied around one of the trees. It matched the markers used by the surveyors two weeks ago.

"They won't make it down to the valley. Right?" Greg asked.

John rested against a tree, back hunched, taking shallow hiccups of breath between which he said: "This will happen … to the Big Tree … in time."

"If we don't do something," E. said.

"Um, hell yes," Tiffany said and clung to E.'s shoulder enthusiastically. The girls smiled and immediately separated, weirded out by their comfortableness. Doug understood the moment—E. channeling Erika's rebellious spirit, Tiffany welcoming its return. "If it means screwing over my dad, I'm in," Tiffany said.

"The Grove—it can't fight for itself," Josué added.

"You said it, man." Greg pulled the red band until it snapped.

That afternoon, they devised additional plans to beat back the developers: removing and switching their land markers, booby-trapping all routes to the Grove, sabotaging equipment when the time came. Tiffany promised to snap pictures of the blueprints laid out in her father's office if it would help.

The group looked to Doug, waited for him to remark on their priorities or the plan's effectiveness. He didn't.

E. then listed the items each would need to bring tomorrow to camouflage and equip a stakeout team to track the land developers' movements.

Doug noticed her studying him across the circle. He looked up and her gaze dropped into the unlit pit. Did she feel some shame at last? Doug hoped so. Honoring her sister was one thing. But battling the killer and now the developers? John was leading them to war, an illegal one, to defend what? Trees? Doug didn't want to see the woods chopped, either, though not at the risk of death or jail. They had long lives ahead to make something of. OK, not the Dead Man. Too bad. The group could find a better, safer solution to these problems if only they plugged their ears and listened to themselves, to their fear if necessary. They weren't ready, Doug reminded himself. He put his fingers in his mouth and chewed to keep from saying anything. The meeting ended, and he grabbed his book bag and ran home ahead of the others.

Doug reached his driveway when E. shouted his name. She burned a line of black rubber across the concrete and let his bike bounce hard as she strode over. Her cheeks were flushed from pedaling fast, having first carted John home.

"What did you write?" she said. "The note. Today in class."

"I really—I can't—" He wanted to tell her everything.

"If it's about the Grove or the group, it concerns us all."

She stepped in close. The kids weren't two feet apart. He could put his arms around her. To reach out and touch E. even tenderly would make her shriek. She wouldn't feel the concern that brimmed his heart. She was too upset over make-believe missions that gave her life the sheen of worth. Which it had already. To Doug. Because he loved her. He had, all this time, and his love was real. What John didn't have for her. Because the guy was using her for his cause. Doug only wanted her to be happy, finally and truly. His last and only friend.

"You can't write about it. You can't talk about it," she said louder. "Were you going to tell them? Say you weren't."

"I—no. But—"

"John was waiting for me after school today. He asked if I thought you could be trusted. It's like he can read my mind." Pained, the corners of her mouth downturned.

"What'd you tell him?"

"The truth. That I didn't know. He needs to trust you in this work. Now more than at the beginning. If he can't trust you, then …"

"What's he going to do? … to me? We're friends. Aren't we?"

"Dougy, yes, but you have to promise me you won't say anything. I need to hear you say that you won't."

She took his hands. Her palms were damp, yet cool. Her finger bones felt lighter and finer than in his fantasies. In all these years, he'd never touched or been touched by the girl so deliberately. Not a hug, nor a helping hand. He looked down and couldn't believe her hands were in his. A bit delirious, he half-circled the back of one hand with his thumb. She didn't pull away.

"I want to do right," he said.

He squeezed. She squeezed back too firmly. Her eyes didn't look glad, but round with fear.

Doug let go. "I can't promise."

"Please," E. said.

"If he's such a good person, then … I shouldn't have to be afraid of him."

"What are you saying?" she said, shocked and a bit offended. "John would never hurt you. He would be hurt if others learned about what we do and if protecting the woods came to an end. We all would be. Doug, I need this. I'm happy for the first time since … ever. For once in my life, I belong somewhere. Don't try to end it. Not for John or the group—for me."

E. resembled her dark-haired mother, maybe for the first time. Her brow drooped, burdened by loss. Her lips flattened against her teeth and quavered to restrain tears. A dozen ways to say he cared crossed his mind. Not one of them sounded like he wasn't jealous of John and wanted E. locked away again in her bedroom or at the library or some tower to have all to himself, for as long as it took her to love him.

"I would never—I couldn't hurt you … or anybody," Doug said. "Fighting a killer … those workers—it's too much."

"It's not enough, yet," E. said.

Her grimness confirmed his failure. He'd wounded her at school in being a few words away from disclosing everything. Now that he'd shared his concerns prematurely, he'd screwed up worse. Not prematurely—too late. He had feared that under John's influence she would turn from him, from reason completely. She was already turned.

"E. … I'm going to say something. I hope … Can you hear me? All this stuff—the woods—it can't last. It's not going to. He's not going to. The Dead Man—John—the longer he stays alive, he gets more twisted. The guy, he's like a monster—literally undead."

"He's not," she said fiercely. "John's so—he's a—"

"What? Mysterious? Deep? He's on painkillers and who knows what else. The guy's out of his mind. Just … Don't you see that? What happens next, when he finally goes? What do you do after he dies?"

"Continue The Work."

"You—no," Doug said. This was his last chance. His thoughts scattered and distended, were useless. Something underneath, like a stone hill, rose inside him. "I plan to still be here. Think about that, the future—real life—growing up."

E.'s fists clenched as if wanting to shake him to make herself understood. Likewise, this would be her last attempt to reach him. Above her plea, which wasn't forceful, but melancholy, Doug heard that most.

"You mean well. You want to do good. I know you do. So you'll wait, won't you? You'll wait until you've walked. Then you'll see he was right about us and everything."

"How can you believe that? Things are so much worse," he said. "I want to go back to how it was before. We can. Together. We were … happier."

"Doug, none of this—" with an arching wave she circled Palos Hills and the entire world "—matters, only what's inside you … and me … between us." E. took a breath and showed her damp eyes. Her ginger lashes were clumped into triangles. She must've sensed she was losing him in making John-esque proclamations about the meaning of existence. "If you don't—if you don't want to … fine. But wait until I walk the ritual Friday. I at least want to live that fearlessly."

"You can, without him. The ritual—it's dangerous."

"What're you so afraid of?"

"Losing you … obviously," he said.

"Act like you care about my feelings, then. Like you're hearing me. Like you're my friend. John does that."

"I'm doing that. I'm trying."

"You're failing," she said. "You were my best friend."

Doug became full of stone, the boldness he'd known with Tiffany Dennys. "No, he's the one—he wants us to all to … Can't you see how close we are to dying? He has nothing to lose. He's making us crazy—just like him. I care about you. I just—I won't follow in his shadow anymore."

"That's between you and you."

He thought to pull out the note left in his locker this morning. It wouldn't rattle her. Its cryptic message might have the opposite effect, and E. didn't need another crusade.

"I'm sorry," Doug said without conviction, his strength used up, insides vaporous. He should've described his love. Instead he'd fought her.

He went in for a hug, to show her by never letting go.

"Please—" E. planted a hand against his chest, pushed "—don't be anything for me."

She walked up the street. The breeze lifted her crimson hair, muddled it with the evening dark. Doug watched the front wheel of his downed bicycle spin so slowly it was imperceptible unless he stood perfectly still. Headlights streaked past; others' loved ones returned home from work. His opportunity to stop E. was gone. That wasn't all. The suburbs were quiet. With unmistakable and resounding certainty, he heard it. He'd lost her forever.

4

Doug went to the Grove the next day. And the next. With a pair of heavy binoculars, he hunted the flash of reflective vests through the brush. Crouched behind trees, he listened to the murky squawks of radios and jotted discernable words. He traced the courses of bobbing hardhats on an area map Alex had made, sometimes forgetting to record the time of day, but sure to mark the storage sheds, portable toilets, and machinery that blocked his route. By the end of the week, Doug had scouted the entire breadth of the woods on all fours, from 115th to the archway.

He hadn't said a word to E. since their fight. Knowing about it as he knew all things, the Dead Man had separated them. Doug was put on surveyor patrol with Greg, Tiffany, and Josué. Meanwhile, E. schemed each evening with Alex and John. Doug saw them—all Upper Palos kids—when he stopped at camp to refill water bottles between shifts. Maybe that didn't mean anything, though Doug was feeling pretty unworthy. Huddled beneath the Big Tree, the three of them talked nonstop, but didn't laugh. None of the group laughed as much as they used to, since accepting "The Work," which, so far, included the risk of assisted suicide and arrest for eco-terrorism.

Seeing her there, drafting war plans and making impassioned speeches under John's influence, he thought E. could go ahead and kill herself already, for the dead guy or her dead sister or to prove whatever to whomever still cared. He no longer did. Later, fiddling with his binoculars, on his belly, being eaten by ants, all he thought of was being by her side to save her from herself. And doing so. E. seeing the good in him. Then he wanted to quit her, finally and completely. She'd chosen. Doug had lost. It was her life to throw away. She was the stupidest smart person in the world. E. didn't deserve someone so devoted. But that devotion wouldn't accept his arguments and only seemed to reinforce why she so desperately needed him.

Was this love? It was sick. Doug felt diseased. Every hour without her near passed in agony, didn't stab his heart or plague his mind so much as threatened to end him, a bodily collapse. It was worst at night with his bedroom curtains open to an empty street and the humorless eye of a crescent moon. Her loss—his failure—made him curl on the floor, fevered and weak, as if a venom coursed his veins. He couldn't sleep. Finally, a few minutes of relief graced the boy. Sobered after a good cry, he pulled himself up to the windowsill, movements languid, though not lazy, as if not Doug, but something beyond him were in masterful control.

The solution seemed obvious. He would have to lose everything to move on. They all would. His friends' lives depended on it. Why did he have to do anything for them? The second-guessing and pain resurfaced. They didn't see what he saw. The responsibility was immense, and he couldn't forget it. As the days ticked to Friday, Doug began to will himself the guts to do what they couldn't—to tell his dad or a teacher or the police about the woods and once and for all stop John H. Walker.

Friday came and he'd done nothing. That night, their flashlights found the Grove's defenses battered from the ridge trail down to the Big Tree. The campfire revealed a second drawing left on the scorched trunk beneath Erika's shoes: all seven kids engaged in sex acts that composed a pornographic totem pole. What disturbed Doug most were the intimate details that the killer had used: Doug's glasses on the tip of his nose, genitals replaced by a tiny hammer, and walking blindly into—E. in a pointed witch's hat, nursing a skull with blonde hair as she looked up lustily at John, curled at his feet beside—Alex in nothing but a sweater vest, notepad in hand which read NUMBERS; and so on, topped by the Dead Man, his arms outstretched, face as haggard as a wooden Jesus. The vile drawing proved that the killer could identify each in public from having watched their gatherings, Alex noted—the observation obvious and infuriating to Doug, who'd warned about this from the beginning. Most likely, Alex added, the killer used binoculars from a safe vantage. Since the developers had arrived, the kids had been traveling in pairs or packs to and from the woods through the less public, but more dangerous route down the train tracks and across the miles of dense woodlands along the river. They quickly decided they would need to carry weapons, each of them at all times, in and out of the woods.

"Wait—this is supposed to be scary?" Tiffany said of the image.

"Dude, I'm scared," Greg said.

"That's clearly his intent," Alex said.

Tiffany kissed Greg. Then she kissed Alex, whose cheeks flushed after.

"Jealousy is a bitch!" she shouted to the cliffs silhouetted against a backdrop of stars.

"He is out there now, yes?" Josué said, hips pivoted, as if on a word he would sprint to find their tormentor.

E. dropped the half-burnt log she'd used to smudge out the image. "Maybe we should wait on the ritual."

"And let evil win?" John said.

E. glanced aside at Doug. Her face didn't reveal doubt. But her caution, that she'd even looked over, said she hadn't totally lost her good sense. "Maybe. At least until our defenses are back up, we—"

"Tonight's mine!" Tiffany called and bolted.

"Listen—" Doug jerked forward, tethered to her shoulder after a sudden grab.

"Don't." She looked back hotly and made his hand recoil. "Not ever again. Cool?"

"The killer—he could—"

"No one's stopping this bitch." Tiffany's top hit the grass, and she darted behind the tree as if to tackle somebody.

The kids backed away and spread around the fire. They locked hands, compelled by the ritual's momentum. This time, they glanced over their shoulders instead of up at the heavens, muscles tight, flinching against a slashing assault from the shadows.

Which would do nothing to slow his blade, Doug thought. *Do something.*

Tiffany must've been naked before she'd climbed. One moment, the tree limb was dreary and shadowed. The next, her body glowed there. She glided forward, one foot in front of the other as if on the balancing beam at school. Above their heads, almost past the fire, Tiffany's arms shot up, then her hips wriggled in a showy way. The kids couldn't tell if she'd almost lost control or if she writhed deliberately, aware of being exposed to those below and to the killer hiding in the dark.

In the slow, dance-y motion was a taunt meant to wound them, and her skin prickled as Tiffany was reminded that her body was a thing sought by so many people. Her heart pumped hard with the power of being here, beyond reach. She spent so much time reacting to what others wanted from her and returning pleasure or harm, as her father had taught her, that she didn't know if there was anything else, having thought so little about what she wanted from this blue whir of possibilities in outer space.

Doug was the first to notice the girl's shoulders slacken. Her arms remained up in the air, suspended as if from invisible wires attached to the stars. Only her hair moved. The perfectly even ends swayed in a wave, then straightened again. Her arms lowered. Tiffany stood in the tree for the longest time, alternately gazing into the void of space and at the pinpricks of light, back and forth, being with nothingness, until purple-bellied clouds lowered like a movie curtain over the view.

She came down still naked. Tiffany swept wisps of hair out of her eyes, clothes clutched to her chest, not guardedly, and said, "Ta-da!" The kids laughed. Doug couldn't believe their stupidity, as if in going through with the ritual while defenseless they'd accomplished something like a victory. Their laughter didn't stop short, but grew with every breath, Greg with his hands on his hips, and Josué folding over one of the logs that faced the woods, almost heckling the killer, until the group roiled as one body with aggressive lows and celebratory birdcall trills and splashes where one's breath died and rejoined the whole. It was an orgy of laughter. Doug hadn't ever been to an orgy, of course, but his idea of one fit the group's sanguine and lusty pleasure, embracing or half-embracing each other freely, until Doug thought that the killer hadn't painted a gross caricature of the group, but an accurate portrait of their souls.

With an arm around E.'s shoulders—who grinned up like a puppy at her master—John asked Tiffany to rejoin them around the fire and share her experience. She sat among them in her underclothes and talked enthusiastically about what it was like to be "up in space." Tiffany apologized if she hadn't taken it seriously enough and completed the ritual too quick. She was surprised when Alex said she'd stood in the tree unmoving close to fifteen minutes, the longest walk yet. "Really?" She made her wincing smile, a bit embarrassed, but proud, too.

Tiffany said she had a great idea and then balanced a half-full bottle of brown liquid on her palm. She apologized for the selection—it was one her father wouldn't miss. This confused the others because the golden label and square cap made it look regal, a treasure recovered from a Spanish ship bound for the New World. In appreciation of her fervor or caught up in the moment, E. took a sip. Only John and Doug passed. When it went around again, Tiffany reseated beside John, almost in his lap, and insisted he have one drink with her to celebrate. E. touched John's leg from the other side. Couldn't he? she asked. The guy refused, no explanation needed considering his illness, yet added that alcohol "fogs the mind." Doug took a gulp. No one noticed. He immediately felt awful. Not from the booze. From trying to make a statement to E. or anyone.

Tiffany said she could respect that and then thanked John.

"It's like I've been given the greatest gift, or something," she said. "Except ... I have less than I did before?"

"It's a taking away, not a having," John said.

"Wow," she said. "Yeah."

231

They all thanked John for making The Work possible. Then the four members of the group who had already performed the ritual confessed how the experience had broadened their understanding of who they were, who they'd thought they were. They'd communed with something up there, beyond words, each insisted. It really was something, at least from below—the firelight glistening their edges, bodies mostly dark but for a touch of celestial light on their chests and faces, eyes locked, as if following the call to join God on high with the soundless and surreal step of a sleepwalker. "Soon you'll see," they said with shining eyes. E. and Josué expressed excitement over their rituals drawing near, that they wished they could walk right now. "You feel this, too, yes?" Josué said to Doug, as if needing to hear that, if nothing else, they shared this common desire, and gave him the room to say as much, guessing he hadn't spoken up out of humility or timidity. Even if Doug had converted into one of John's sheep, the ritual would still terrify him. He was so clumsy that, if anyone would surely die up there, it would be him. If given a choice between the two, he would rather take his chances on the ground against the killer.

A stick snapped across the creek bridge. The group rose with bladed and blunt weapons. They formed a deadly crescent, prepared for frontal assault.

The breeze rushed in.

"Where is the fucker? I'll …" Tiffany started.

Alex popped on a flashlight. The yellow eyes of a possum met the beam. It scampered downstream.

"Anyone without heart couldn't do what we do." John motioned for his friends to sit before he did. In the comment, Doug heard criticism for his not acting thrilled about the ritual. "Like summiting a great mountain," John said.

"A red mountain?" Doug's question from outside the circle resounded with challenge. Even the boy looked surprised by what'd come out of his mouth.

John was muted by shock. He lurched forward as fast as he could.

Doug backed around the fire. "Huh?" he said, a bit buzzed from the liqueur. Neck hot and suddenly overcome, his face broke with upset.

"How do you know that?" John said.

Doug's eyes watered as he recalled the strange note in his locker. Spittle flew from his lips as he returned, "How do you?"

With the stiff, but forceful slam of a horror-movie mummy, John thrashed Doug against the trunk of the Big Tree. Everyone hopped up, said, "Whoa!" and other exclamations of concern. The group didn't know what to do. The guy's cool was beyond lost, and he grabbed Doug's shirt for another slam. He weighed no more than the boy, though, who twisted and brought John down on top of him. They rolled a few feet. The Dead Man seized his collar as if to shake Doug into speaking.

"How do you know Red Mountain?" he said.

Doug bit the guy's hand. John staggered backward with a cry, and E. went to him. The others remained passive on the sidelines, between the fighters. Their consciences battled what they knew to be true about both boys to figure out whom and how to help.

"Tell them," Doug said, propped on one elbow. He wiped the blood from under his nose. John's head had whacked him nearly senseless during the fall. "You left that note in my locker."

"What note?" John started toward him again. E. held his arm.

Doug explained that a note had been left in his locker days ago,

233

calling him "Dougydearest" and asking what was going on "under Red Mountain."

"You can prove that?" John said. "You have the note?"

Doug absently patted his hips. He said that he couldn't remember, that it didn't make any difference.

"Those two words were inside the book we dug up at this spot," John said, "the only two words in English I saw, in the margins, in red ink. No one but me ever had time to look over the book carefully enough before it was stolen—before you watched it get stolen and our camp was burned."

Doug curled to sit up. Josué stepped on his shoulder and planted him prone.

"Sorry, amigo," he said with pleasure.

"The only people who could know those words are me and the killer," John said from behind Josué.

"Hey—don't—it's you who—" Doug stammered, unable to conceive of a useful rebuttal.

Greg stepped up beside Doug's head. "It can't be the genius. Can it?"

Alex asked why not, why Greg thought the killer couldn't have been any one of them this whole time.

"You think?" Tiffany asked. "Could he really …? No."

"I'm asking Greg to give me one reason why Doug is beyond guilt," Alex said.

"I mean, no offense, but look at him," Greg said. "But who knows?"

Alex added that Doug had naysayed their work in the woods on several occasions, giving exact dates and examples.

"He could do it," Josué said. The kid's face was shadowed and unreadable above.

The air seemed to have chilled around Doug. They were going to hurt him. His righteous anger froze. "No, I have it … here—somewhere. I swear …" Doug felt his pockets. He couldn't remember where he'd put the note. He might've thrown it away in Ms. Whitehead's class. Doug checked his back pocket a second time. He found the note flattened. He offered it to Josué, who handed it reluctantly to John.

"Is this Doug's handwriting?" Alex waved E. closer to the fire. Except for his guardian, the group huddled away from him.

"I've never seen him write in all caps like this," she said. She walked back to Doug. Josué stepped aside. "It doesn't matter. I know he didn't kill my sister."

"How?" Alex asked, ready to record her response.

"He wouldn't do that to me." E. stood at his feet, not in an imposing manner like the others. Her palms were upturned at her sides. She spoke with great sympathy. "He loves us—us all—very much."

"I got carried away." John shook his head as he came over. "Doug, I want to be the first to apologize for doubting you. It was wrong. I've said it myself that no one here is to accuse a member of the group. Our faith in one another is our pact. Just those words … I want to rid the world of that evil—together." He extended his hand. "Tell me what I can do to prove my faith in you."

"Tell them the truth." Doug stood without his help. "You did it—the note. You made E. not trust me. You made up this whole thing so we would—"

"Buddy, you're still a bit shaken up. You're not making any sense. Why would I do that?"

"Alex was right." Doug kneeled at his bag and packed his things. "I think we should leave the woods. We don't belong here. No kids do."

"That's what the killer wants," John said. "This note you've brought us proves that. He'll reclaim this place and defile it again. His sacrifices … Is that what you want?"

Doug stood in front of him, backpack slung over one shoulder and slightly hunched, with the potent stillness of an enraged person about to charge. He didn't look the guy in the face. He spoke with intensity into the space between them. "I want things to be normal again, safe. I want to get help."

"I hear your fear talking," John said. "Life in the woods is more real than back in that bubble. You've already started down the path. Just wait till you walk the ritual. You'll see. We can be brilliant here. Together, nothing can hurt us."

Doug kept his head lowered a moment. He appeared beaten, drained in spirit, as if he might collapse under the weight of his bag, but also like he might strike anyone who touched him. Doug pointed at the smudged drawing on the tree.

"Nothing?"

John smirked. A thrill warmed his fatigue over something he saw in Doug. "I know the road is difficult to see," he said. "Walk with me a little longer. There'll come rain for both fires, inside and out, and the smoke will clear."

A kick of thunder. An all-consuming flash. In the x-raying white of the lightning, Doug saw through the Dead Man's skin to the decrepit skeleton beneath, gray and eyeless. Or seemed to. So when the others cried out in great wonder that the guy had said the word "rain" and heavy drops began to spatter their faces and chests through the canopy above, softening the earth, and they scurried home with their belongings, Doug left unfazed by John's feigned supramortality, fixed on that vision of what he'd become: death seeking an end to itself.

5

Doug didn't sleep well all weekend. It wasn't from the storm that beat the windows. Or the lightning that snapped rapidly without roar across the vacant house, lights out, the night of Tiffany's walk.

He'd stood in the hallway awhile, soaked, and listened for the footsteps of the killer, imagining his family strung up like cattle, wet with blood in the kitchen twenty feet away. Simultaneously, he hoped his mother would come down from bed to fuss at him about the time of night, usher him into the laundry room, and pull off his shirt. Neither happened. Doug stripped his clothes into the dryer, pressed a few buttons, and sat on the cool machine. The heatless fluorescent was bright overhead. The dryer lid warmed his shivering body. Doug hardly noticed any of it, so resolute he was never to return to the woods.

His dad and mom and little brother had been to the discount theater. They came in on him with a towel around his waist, headed to his bedroom, the hammer in hand, just in case. They didn't notice the weapon. They were too excited about the thriller they'd seen, a hunt for a serial strangler of college girls. Doug lingered and listened to the many near-fatal run-ins with the fictional murderer that'd kept his family on the edge of their seats, conscious that only an hour ago he wouldn't have been surprised to find them hanging dead from the ceiling. His dad noticed the hammer only as Doug walked away. He praised his son for being extra careful while home alone. "And smart," Mom added, "unlike that Summerson child." His dad chastised that it wasn't a fair thing to say of the poor girl. "Poor in judgment. In the woods with boys at night? And drinking." To which Dad accused her of "passive-aggressively bitching" about his drinking.

Doug retreated to his room. He'd become someone they didn't know, an effect of the woods' isolation, he was sure. The true power of a secret is to bind those who know it, which wasn't friendship, but something like alienation. He was kept awake in bed that night, imagining what the group would've done to him if not for E.'s intervention. While he stuck around for E. and questioned their actions, his life was in jeopardy. She might've endangered herself by protecting him.

That night he dreamed of the ritual. E. was radiant in the branches of the Big Tree. She wore her hair around her head like a crimson crown. The group circled the trunk, five in number, hands linked, unmoving even as Doug sprinted over the creek bridge in slow motion, as was his luck. He shouted her name to halt the moonlight baptism. There was no valley, just an endless gray plain, though he heard water slapping the side of a log or still boat. Nothing would come out of his mouth but garbled quacks and puffs of smoke. E. got up on one foot, frightened of the smoke as it rose and crackled with tiny lightning on either side of the branch. Doug's hands went numb when he touched any member of the group to break them. They kept their heads lowered, in prayer or asleep. Through the sparking haze above, E. walked the branch. Doug quacked again for her to stop. The smoke doubled. Unable to see, E. slipped. Her leg went over one side, and she grabbed a thin branch. Slowly she pulled herself upright and crawled forward on all fours. Then her body slid as if sucked through the gray sky. From her hair down to the pink bottoms of her limp feet, she disappeared into the clouded heavens.

The rain didn't let up Saturday, drizzled in the afternoon and poured again that evening. The group had better sense than to allow the girl to walk a slick branch. The rising creek would flood the Grove and make camping impossible. Doug thought up many reasons they would cancel E.'s ritual. Accepting that E. was in danger would force him to leave his room and attempt something bold and, probably, play into another of John's schemes, which Doug wasn't going to do. He was finished with John Walker and his followers in the woods.

Too anxious to lose himself in video games, Doug spent most of that day on his bed reading *Franny and Zooey*, the book E. had given him long ago. He missed the old E. and sought her in those pages. He found her in the character of Franny—a smart and odd girl, horribly depressed and desperate for answers, but too stubborn and withdrawn to receive them from the boy who cared about her most. Which was her brother. Still, the analogy lit like a lighthouse beacon across the fear that fogged Doug's mind, and he couldn't quit reading until he'd discerned whether or not E. was the kind of person who would risk the ritual tonight if John were to say she was meant to.

By 8 p.m. Doug was a wreck. He paced the room, hyperventilating, his heart flabby from nostalgia. Delirious, he gripped the exhausted book, as if to tear it in half. He gritted his teeth and squeezed as hard he could, unable to live without seeing her another moment, which did nothing but make his gums and fingers quiver and ache in both relief and pain. A moment later, he wanted to shout in her face for getting them involved with the Dead Man, which he knew wasn't fair. Stress stretched him beyond reason and back again. He passed two hours in this manner, waiting for his parents to finish what started as a dispute over the broken vacuum cleaner, their eyes on the television or the dishes or the book in Mom's lap, their voices never raising more than that of a placid observation about the weather, Dad stating they didn't have the money to buy a good one until he landed a job, and Mom remarking he was apparently too busy looking to fix anything around the house. "What else is broken?" he wanted to know, a beer or two later. "The entire house is falling apart," Mom said, which was why she'd be voting for Prop #1, to offset the decline in property value. Dad countered that she was being socially irresponsible if she thought a blue-collar town needed a golf course instead of those peaceful woods. Peaceful? Their bedroom door muffled the rest. Doug went out the front in his father's baggy raincoat.

The rear tire kicked up about as much rain as what fell on him as Doug biked to E.'s house, indignant now, ready to give her a final warning. He was going to tell everyone about the woods. She could get her story straight and save herself by agreeing with him that the whole thing had been John's idea, or she could go down as the guy's accomplice, obstructing justice and aiding a potential murderer.

From the street, her second-floor window was dark. If he rang the doorbell and she'd snuck out of the house, she'd be in trouble with no chance to choose her fate. He wasn't doing that to her after how she'd defended him in front of the group. *"He loves us all very much."*

Just you, he wanted to tell her.

She could have turned in early. Doug rode a figure eight in the wet concrete before her house as he pedaled away and back again, unable to leave without knowing. He hefted her father's aluminum ladder against the brick as quietly as he could and, for a minute, weighed the fear of slipping to his death against the amount of effort E. had ever made in being his friend, told it to fuck itself, and climbed the ladder up to the landing in front of girl's window.

He crouched and peered inside. His luck—it was too dark to see anything but a thin gap of light beneath the bedroom door. He cupped his hands over the glass. She was either lying very still or her bed was empty and she was walking the ritual at John's command, voluntarily killing herself in the same place her sister had died. What scared him most was that her bedroom had changed. The bookcases were missing, condensed down to a single shelf beside the door. Her walls were bare of posters with grandiloquent quotes. Her long mirror was gone, the rugs, too. The room had always been tidy, but for lack of clutter. It was ascetically so, now. She no longer called this place home. He barely knew her anymore.

On the sill, inches from him on the other side of the window, he spotted the gift he'd brought the week her sister had died. He'd never seen it unwrapped. He'd not seen it, period, since he'd abandoned it in her trash can, realizing the gift served no useful purpose on her quest for wisdom and had been in poor taste for several reasons. She'd never said anything about it. But here it was: a clear glass candle-holder in the shape of a skull. It was a morbid gift for a morbid girl's bedroom, and it looked out at Doug with hollowed eyes. A stubby red candle stuck up from the notch on top of the skull. Dried wax uni-browed the forehead and crusted in one eye socket like the bloody shit of a large bird. Icy pleasure shot through Doug's heart. He imagined

241

her unwrapping the gift, turning it in her hands, thinking of him, maybe kissing it while she daydreamed. Or cradling the head as she might her sister's, experiencing solace and a pang of gratitude to Doug for making some strange and momentary reconciliation possible. Or catching her distorted reflection while peering deep into the glass and stopping to reconsider how she was living her life, how she was treating the boy who'd only ever showed her love and respect. Or all those things. Or she'd just needed a candleholder.

The sliver of light beneath the bedroom door darkened—the shadow of someone walking by. It stopped. Doug turned away from the glass. He scanned the neighborhood, aware of how ridiculously visible he would be to a passing car, and told himself he wasn't brave. He'd already been driven crazy and should scramble down the ladder before he got caught. He needed to see her. Doug risked another glance. The shadow remained there, as if fumbling with keys, except E.'s door didn't unlock from the hallway. Maybe it was her mother, weeping alone or listening and waiting to be called out for. Like he was doing.

The girl didn't need them. She did, only she didn't think she did. Doug knew no solution for that except to continue with his plan. He would confess and let her face the consequences how she wanted, without the help of anyone who loved her.

6

WRITE ME HERE BY NOON DOUGYDEAREST OR YOU'RE NEXT I SWEAR. DID THE BOOK RE-VEAL THE RITUAL? WHAT MASTER DOES JOHNNYBOY SERVE?

This second note appeared in Doug's school locker on Monday morning. He twice prevented his glasses from sliding off his nose as he reread the familiar red capitals on crumpled yellow paper before the obvious cut through his stupor: he was holding a direct threat from the killer.

Doug threw the note as if a snake had fallen into his arms. He was being watched. Nobody seemed to pay him attention up or down the hallway. Students mingled, adrift, in no rush to first period during their last week of classes before summer break. With some hesitation, Doug took up the note again, evidence his life was truly in danger. He considered how to respond: *Don't kill me. Please? My life has been too short and miserable,* was all he could think to say. He tried to recall the first note, later pocketed by John or Alex—something about a mountain?

The first period bell rang. Doug ran past his science class to check that E. was alive. The girl's hair was dark and wet, skin glossy, as if she'd spent all weekend in the pouring rain. She looked over her shoulder at his empty desk. Doug bolted from the doorway.

In the restroom, he locked himself in the far stall. Doug let his bag hit the floor. He sank against the wall. He was sweating in his hoodie and shorts, and the cold tile stung his calves, so he drew up his legs and curled into a ball. Inside, Doug worked to convince himself that the notes weren't real. The killer couldn't possibly know he was the weakest link, on the verge of squealing. It was a cruel hoax, John's doing, the guy who'd orchestrated a secret dig and tethered six kids with friendship against common sense, who floated the hallways between passing periods enough to plant notes, who "knew things," got in people's heads and exploited their weaknesses. How would a threat like this get him to stay? The tormentor in the cloak with the long knife, backdropped by fire, was all Doug knew to be true. That person would reach out for kooky info and seek him at school, be closer than he'd ever imagined.

The bathroom door whined open. Heavy shoes clopped past the sinks. Doug didn't begin to cry like he might've two weeks ago from the mere possibility that it could be John or the killer. His nostrils gasped. Otherwise, he didn't move, to keep his sneakers from squeaking. He reversed his backpack and unzipped it quietly, telling himself a killer hadn't followed him in, he was only losing hold of what was real and possible. Doug withdrew the hammer.

He unlatched the stall door. No one barged in.

Doug breathed deep and charged out to end it, himself, the pressure of living.

A kid with a hall pass pissed along the row of urinals while fooling on his phone. "What the—?" he said, stopped mid-stream, and flashed a picture of Doug holding the hammer like a crazy person. The kid huffed, kept pissing.

Doug wanted to be a kid again. He was exhausted from acting disturbed and thinking disturbed thoughts. He didn't know anything about a second book or John's "master," only that he wanted the psychological torture to end that he'd been subjected to ever since John H. Walker pointed him out among so many less emotionally beat-up kids and promised answers in the woods. Doug had learned enough already. Something about good intentions never being good enough. He bagged his hammer and walked home.

His dad sat on the living room rug in his underwear, a pair of work goggles strapped to his forehead. The vacuum cleaner lay disassembled in his lap, the plastic casing removed and wires exposed. Electrical gizmos and were gutted between his legs. Dad sat, leaned back as if mid-rappel.

Doug had to call to him to break his focus. The man waved distractedly.

"I'm home early," Doug said.

"So you are."

"I'm not supposed to be."

"Doing any better now that you've skipped?" He glanced up from sorting wires. His mouth hung in a loose smile. He noticed his son's fatigue and frowned. "You really aren't feeling good."

Doug had run the whole way, and he slumped against the wall as if glued there. Unconsciousness crowded his periphery. He hadn't eaten much over the weekend, anxiety turning his stomach.

"It's worse than that."

"Aww, Duck, I'm sorry. I could use your help here for a second, if you're not feeling too bad. Then you go lie down."

Doug came over. His fingers grazed the furniture to guide his way, as he'd done countless times treading the dark out of Bachelor's Grove. He was handed an unopened can of beer off the coffee table.

"Throw this damn thing away," Dad said.

"Dad?"

"Yeah, son?"

He wanted to tell him everything. He would start with the child killer leaving death threats in his locker. An immense wave of shame slapped him in the face as he pictured explaining the woods and The Work and the ritual, all the sneaking out he'd been convinced at the time was brave, how stupid he'd been, and how he'd lost E. to a dead kid.

"You want this in the garbage or the fridge?" he said.

"Trash it. And the rest from the fridge. Then you get some rest, Duck-ster." As Doug turned, his dad added, "Maybe you're getting a little too old for me to be calling you that? What do you think about it?"

"Yeah." Doug wished he could smile back.

"Good. A new man," he said. "If you need me, I'll be right here. I'm not going anywhere—not for a long while." He dropped the goggles over his eyes and lifted a small hammer, claws-forward to pry at something.

"There is … something, actually."

"Yeah, son," he said and enthusiastically removed the goggles.

"How do you tell someone something?… that's really … not easy."

"You've got something important you need to say—to a special friend, maybe?"

"Sort of."

"Good—well, I was timid when I met your mother in college. So I wrote her a letter. She actually didn't get that one. Her roommate got to it first and told everybody that I'd written *her* a perverted love letter. Not because the roommate liked me—she hated me. She was obsessed with your mother. They had a really unhealthy friendship at the time, and I was a threat, you see. She actually held a kitchen knife to my stomach when I tried to talk reasonably to her. I swear she did. I wasn't Gandhi, either. After this friend trash-talked me to everyone, including your mother, about what I'd supposedly said in this letter, I hung back for a few semesters. Luckily, smart people like Mom don't let sick people hang around too long. My second attempt fared pretty good, I'd say. You know, I used to write her little notes and leave them for her to find all the time. Now, I don't say much of what I'm thinking. I mean to change that, too. You should write this person, your friend. I'm not going to assume what's bothering you has anything to do with Emily—"

"E."

"A girl like that would appreciate a good letter, I think. You can say a lot more things writing them down, even to somebody who really knows you. Relationships are a hard business. It's a project that never ends. Sometimes you need to let go of an unhealthy one. Time changes us, too. It's still changing your mother and me. But you've always got to speak your mind. Especially you. You've got a good one in that noggin. Tell her—this person—everything you're thinking. Not everything. Be kind. Just be yourself."

"Dad?"

"Yeah, Doug."

"Are we selling the house?"

Dad refitted the goggles. "I'm not going to let that happen."

Doug went to his room and drafted three letters. The first he addressed to E. He didn't want to lose her forever, he said, but she'd had time enough to wake up, and there was no other way to stop her and the group from sleepwalking to their deaths. The second was to his mom and dad, mostly apologizing for the lying, as well as for their last family vacation to the Wisconsin Dells, how he'd a knowingly poor attitude at the water parks and spoiled their good time when he should've been grateful to be all together. The last was to the Palos Hills Police Department, a description of the when and wheres of what they'd done, which was fuzzy in the middle and made him stop to rub his temples and say, "Think, genius!"

Doug dropped his pen in a cold sweat. He looked at what he'd done, what he was about to do. To fold and address the many pages seemed impossible. It would be real. Not the consequences of his confessions, but the fucked-up-ness of the experience that was and would forever be his life.

He lifted E.'s letter to attempt a crease.

There was a knock on the door. His dad pushed inside as Doug heaved his backpack onto the desk.

A hooded figure slouched in the doorway, not Dad. The hood lowered. It was John Walker. He was alone, not smirking and terrifying because of it.

"The weather has been something the last few days. Hasn't it? Nice in here, though." The boy scanned the room, not budging from the doorway, hollow-eyed as the glass skull on E.'s windowsill.

Doug couldn't recall when last he'd seen the Dead Man in the early afternoon. Doug had been writing intensely in the meager light that radiated through his closed blinds, his mind on nothing else. The hallway was dim. An overcast glare came through the bathroom window and monochromed John's right half. He'd changed so much since he'd first materialized in Doug's life, at school in front of the big window at the end of the hallway, the specter of a legend, misty white in the full noon sun. He was bald now with an anorexic sunkenness and fragility. Daubed in grays, John had gone from ghost to ghoul. A pitiful one, too, as if he were only the ashen remains of a boy who might at any moment be lost to the wind.

"Who told you you could just … come in here?"

"I know what's going on, Doug. The notes—" His arm rose as if weighted. He pointed through Doug to the writing desk. A corner of the killer's note flapped up beneath the backpack. "He's made contact with you again."

"So you know … I'm not lying."

"I'm grateful you told us. Now we can finish The Work."

"There isn't an end to it, is there?"

"That's up to you," he said.

"I'm done with the woods."

"I wish you could hear the trees." Beside his head, John twisted his finger in a rising corkscrew motion. "You're not," he said. "Not even close."

"I'm sorry. No—I'm not sorry. I'm telling you, I'm not coming back. I don't believe in your craziness like the others. It's no good … for anybody."

"Doug, you know better than most: Good things can happen … like that—"

The guy snapped his fingers. Across the house, the vacuum cleaner buzzed to life. Doug's dad woo-hooed and hollered, "He's back!"

"Use all your tricks ..." Doug reached for the backpack behind him in case he needed to pull the hammer. In doing so, his gaze shifted a second. When next his eyes fixed on the guy, John was upright in the doorway. He blocked what little light there was and stood very still. "I don't care anymore what happens down there," Doug said. "You can't make me."

"You don't care about E.?"

"Of course. But—"

"Of course you do. That's why I chose you. I know how you feel about her, and—if that's where your negative view of me is coming from—I want you to know, I don't love her. Not the way you do, the way you always will. I know you'd do anything for her because she's sharp and dear to you. But she's fragile, too. She's leading the group to war."

"That's what you want."

"Doug, you need to listen harder. You need to listen harder to her. You need to listen harder to yourself. Harder to the woods." The boy closed his eyes. "I kept this from you because I know how you get under pressure—you're the key of the group. All I did was get us together. I can't save us from ourselves."

"I know what you're doing. We're all in danger because of you."

John's eyes opened, plaintively, as did one hand, as if in offering, palm skyward. "Then stay by her side. Be her conscience. Be the group's."

"I can't follow her anymore ... not where she's going because of you."

"Not even to save her life?"

His mouth was dark. Doug would've sworn that its corners had upturned in a grin.

"What're you going to do?"

"If you're suggesting I could hurt one of the group, I have lost you."

"But you'd hurt me if I left? Is that it?"

"I already told you, you're not leaving us."

"I am—I have. That's what I'm saying. But you're so … full of yourself—so insane, you can't hear anything that doesn't fit your plan."

"No, Doug. It's because I'm telling you, if you don't come with me right now, E. is prepared to take your place in facing the killer. And she will lose her life."

•

Alex waited on the orange tongue of the playground slide outside the community center, hands buried in the pockets of a pair of khaki shorts, head bent in thought, and eyes focused on the sand beneath the boys' feet. The look was familiar to Doug: a difficult decision.

The Dead Man told Doug to relax and listen to Alex's story, withholding old resentments or judgment. Also, to remember to breathe.

Alex said nothing. They listened to empty swings creak in the breeze.

"So, where's E.?" Doug said.

Alex stood abruptly and led the boys to the elevated tracks. Without so much as a glance at Doug or seeming to notice the Dead Man, who wheezed and dragged himself zombie-like behind them, Alex watched the railroad ties pass methodically underfoot during pensive silences between a thorough explanation of recent events.

251

On Saturday and Sunday, Alex coordinated a surveillance team to confirm Rocco "Rocky" Lordes as the key murder suspect. Tiffany's druggie friend that'd partied with her and Erika in the woods had moved to the Major Potential Suspect List after Alex spent the last two weeks tailing members of the group with promising motives, just to be sure. These suspects' names would go undisclosed. Of course, everyone couldn't be observed on those nights that mayhem occurred at camp, but Alex was now eighty-five percent certain that the Grove's tormentor was not among them.

"What'd you two talk E. into doing?"

Alex stopped before the train bridge and pointed underhand across the wide canal. Finding Rocky's current address and the discovery of a back trail into the woods helped in reprioritizing efforts to uncover the killer. The high school boy lived with his mother in Palos Heights in a subdivision on the other side of the river, making the Grove accessible via a relatively short walk. This gave him the means to come and go unnoticed by the group, the cops, and other witnesses. Alex was tired of theorizing, however, and wanted proof.

"And E.'s your bait," Doug said. "Is that it?"

"Keep up, genius."

Alex scrambled down the trail and into the trees. The Dead Man stayed at the top of the tracks. He gazed down at Doug with a sad smile. He then looked sidelong at the water.

Walking hurriedly along the path that crossed to the moraine, Alex disclosed to Doug that the setting of traps around the Grove had provided a prime opportunity to map the area for vantage points that the tormentor used to gather intelligence. This suspicion that their tormentor studied his prey before striking was aroused by the continual uncovering of their hiding spots and by the appearance of the detailed drawing left on the Big Tree last Friday, then confirmed by the appearance of Doug's locker notes. The initial search of the surrounding area turned up a few lukewarm spots with no conclusive evidence of regular occupation. Alex then decided to test the theory that the guy was watching from much higher up and only ventured down to perform sabotage. Walking the entire valley rim overlooking the Grove led to this—

Alex stopped in the trail and nodded toward a hiding place. The cubby was barely noticeable behind the low-lying branches of a scrubby pine.

"E.?"

Alex waited while Doug pushed beyond the branches and inside. The space was no more than a few feet wide, and the end was hidden from the valley by a huge rock. Beneath the rock, the steep slope plummeted to the Grove—only one way in. The rock was large enough for someone to remain concealed if sitting or crouching. From up here, Doug had a side view of the fire pit in front of the Big Tree and, although far off, binoculars might easily allow a watcher to identify the shoelace color of everyone below. The outpost's position wasn't the only evidence of it belonging to the tormentor. Paraphernalia of a demented mind littered the space. Images of older women crudely torn from a glossy magazine had been duct taped to the rock. Their eyes and breasts were stabbed through, leaving black-rimmed holes, as if from a cigarette. Unusual geometric symbols inked the women's bodies. Knifed into the trunk of the pine was the same upside-down V shape that'd marked the Big Tree, above which, about shoulder height, a name was also carved, the first two letters struck through: DOUG.

"So." Alex casually took Doug's picture as he jolted, surprised by someone standing beside him. "Proof that he's had his eye on you. Likely after your first confrontation. Or you're the tormentor and left your mark, as John had accused. Which do you think is more probable?"

"I … didn't do this. Any of it. I—I couldn't have."

Alex snapped another picture, camera raised, of Doug with the Big Tree in the distance. "Maybe."

"Hey, stop." Doug shielded his face. "You set this up. Maybe you did it. How do you know so much about the killer?"

"The tormentor. Who is potentially the killer," Alex corrected. "Haven't you ever seen a crime show? I have less of a motive than you do. Which you would know if you'd spent as much time solving the crime as falling in love with suspects."

Alex came closer, within Doug's personal space, and took his left hand. His fingers were splayed and palm examined, then flipped, and his splotchy, bitten-down nails marveled at. For a moment, it struck Doug that he'd been a fool this entire time, to have chased E. and Tiffany when here was this nice-enough girl completely obsessed with him.

"You and Tiffany engaged in sexual relations." Alex clamped his wrist as he tried to pull away, made uncomfortable by the blunt comment. "Of course, it's perfectly normal behavior. I've been tempted, even. To get involved emotionally, that is."

Doug allowed his hand to be taken and lifted to the tree where his name had been carved. Alex abruptly dropped it to jot another note, systematically recording evidence, no interest in him other than as a suspect.

"So, where is she? John said—"

"Soon enough, there will be more important mysteries to devote my life to," the real genius went on. "After I've cracked this one."

Alex checked the time, then hurried back onto the trail and held the branches for Doug, ushering the boy forth, not toward the Grove, but back down the long trail to the train bridge.

Doug had to jog and duck branches to keep the pace. He felt swept up in a familiar and deadly current. Alex drove him on, but it was always the Dead Man and his woods they were lost in, all misbelieving they were on the path to getting where they wanted when they were all just groping for an end in the dark. Doug, too. He had to regain control or lose himself, maybe for the last time.

"You have to know who did it already—that I didn't, at least. If I did, which I didn't, or John or Greg or any of us, it doesn't matter anymore," he said, trying to reach Alex, "not if one of us dies."

Alex hmph-ed and slackened in stride. "Do you still believe that John—the Dead Man, as you've mocked him for months—is Erika's murderer?"

"You won't like what I think. I know you worship the guy, like everyone—"

"I don't worship a phenomenon. It necessitates study."

"You have to suspect him … even a little."

"You identified the cloaked tormentor as tall."

"Maybe he wore tall shoes? John's crazy. The guy's got nothing to lose. He's capable of anything—of faking everything."

"I'm asking if you've evidence that substantiates his guilt, not to criticize the mental health of a dying man."

"I—no," he said. "Which I know sounds like I'm just jealous."

"His single show of force came on only after you dropped top-secret information. I also noticed the words written in the margins of

255

the book he'd found. And, of course, we all saw the mountain symbol left in the Big Tree, tying our tormentor conclusively to the book, as well as to Erika's digging during the week of the murder—and to you. But I didn't say anything to the group, waiting for a slip-up. Which is to say, you were a suspect. Though an unlikely accomplice, there was a chance."

"OK, yes—but what he's done to us—just being here, we're in danger. The ritual, his wanting to be in the woods all the time, to die in them …"

"The way you would go about solving the problem would get us all in trouble, ending the most comprehensive investigation of the murder that will ever be conducted, thus leaving the killer at large. That, I can't let you do. It's not about the fame for me anymore—Kid Genius Solves Gruesome Woodland Murder—making headlines, earning more renown than John ever had. I want a confession and, yes, the satisfaction of success. But I also want to keep our friends. Because he's right, you know. There's something here, bigger than the death of one girl—an old evil in the woods. Or maybe we brought it here. It too necessitates study—and defeat. But John's wrong to think holding hands around a campfire will stop it. E. and I had to beg him to confront the tormentor directly to get the closure we need. Does that sound like your mastermind urging us to our deaths?"

"He made you believe that you needed to be out here in the first place."

"False cause."

"He's wanted this from the beginning—us to follow him mindlessly, so when he finally goes, we all fall with him."

"More speculation. Our decision to be here has relied on factors beyond his control—"

A sound stopped Alex, who shushed Doug's whining. A chainsaw buzzed in the distance, followed by a crack and the shouts of workers.

"The vote passed," Alex said, almost surprised. "The contractors will make room for larger equipment to clear-cut for the condos and golf course. A two-front war begins."

"See? You think you're smart enough to play him and get what you want. But he's playing you—all of us. He doesn't need to have stabbed Erika to have killed her. Another person getting killed out here is just—it's right around the corner."

Alex looked him over, enthusiasm gone and annoyed, hating to admit he was right. "On that last point, we agree."

As they neared the end of the path, Alex slowed and confessed to involving John and E. in a surveillance operation over the weekend that almost cost their lives. A lone investigator could only accomplish so much. So, on Sunday they'd tailed him to the woods. Alex had watched the potential tormentor's house, E. had watched the train bridge, and John had watched the outpost in the woods. Rocky lived in a brick house, the kind in a horseshoe shape, with long gray shutters on the windows and a well-manicured lawn. Alex waited in the rain, crouched behind a neighbor's bush across the street until the boy appeared. He didn't come out of the front door, as expected, but out of his bedroom window, headfirst as if the house were birthing him. Alex tailed the kid down the block, squatted behind parked cars and yard bushes, made easy because Rocky was wearing a canary-yellow rain jacket. He crossed through a waterlogged park with several pitcher's mounds like islands amid little green lakes. Alex lost sight of him around a high fence. Catching up, there was no trace of the boy across the wide parking lot beyond, which dead-ended into a power line tower and some scrubby trees along the train bridge. This creeped out

Alex enough to retreat into a nearby dugout and wait with the letter opener drawn and notebook hidden between the aluminum bench and the wall, to save the evidence in the event of being murdered. A long time passed, straining for the sound of the boy's slosh-y steps, before the cold command of logic returned and Alex called E. to warn her that the suspect might be aware of being followed. E. had her phone off. She waited, eyes closed—in a location that Alex would not yet disclose—listening for the tormentor's step, eyelids cracking only as his boots creaked the rail road ties, walking eerily slow for someone caught in the rain and who'd evaded Alex's pursuit. John held the most dangerous position: in the woods alone, across from the tormentor's outpost, barely camouflaged in a dark hoodie. The rain was warm, and he sat in the wet earth on the roots of a small tree, content enough to doze. His eyes never closed, he said, so attuned he was to the rhythm of the rainfall and the mud spattering his pant legs and the feel of the living earth all around and inside him that, he swore, he could see the killer slip down the train tracks to the trail, curse after stepping in a puddle up to the knee, then pause at the outpost for a rusted set of tools he'd hidden beneath the rock and test the path to the Grove for traps, disabling some but leaving when the rain began to fall in sheets.

If John's testimony wasn't proof enough that Rocky was their tormentor, Alex had faked sick today—in itself an elaborate story—and followed the kid from his house to the doors of Palos Hills Junior High, video recording the whole thing. He ended up at—drum roll—Doug's locker, mixing in with other kids and rushing out before Doug approached. He reappeared during recess, fiddled with Doug's lock for less than a minute and picked up the note that Alex had left for him.

"Wait—what note?"

"You're going to have to ignore the irrational emotional part of yourself, now. Everything depends on it," Alex said, looking back, then went out into the gloomy day and up the tracks.

At the top, the Dead Man still gazed at the water. "Are you ready?"

"I'm stopping this," Doug said as he climbed the slippery rocks.

"It's too late," John said.

"Watch me."

"You literally can't."

Doug started home.

"Before you turn your back forever on the people who need you most—listen to me," John said, his voice straining.

"That's what got me here in the first place," Doug shouted back. "I'm not stupid. I'm telling people about the woods."

"We used your notebook—your paper, your pen. We mocked your handwriting."

Doug slowed. He cringed on the knife of betrayal.

"The three of us—we decided to leave a very convincing note for the killer. Just in case of … this." John waited for him to stop before continuing. "If you tell anyone, it'll look like you were corresponding with the killer as his accomplice. Alex's video and photos would confirm that. It's something you would never do—I know, because I know you. The people you're running to don't. By the time you sort that out, E. will have confronted the killer and you can't let that happen. I'm sorry. Believe me, I didn't want it to happen like this. I wanted—needed you to help of your own free will. But your fear has been so great. I would take it on, but he chose you."

"You really did set me up this time." Doug was shocked. He

should've been used to being manipulated by John. He wasn't used to being right.

"We threw the pitch, evil hit. The ball is going way back to the fence. You have to make the catch and close the inning, be the hero. I know you want—more than anything, deep down—to be that. To save E., who is resolved to face the killer on the train bridge herself unless you make this play. The trees know my limits, buddy. You're up."

Doug hadn't turned around yet. No matter how hard he squeezed his hands into fists, his heart remained small and hard, no longer an egg, but a stone, paralyzed with defeat.

●

Doug waited for the killer on the train bridge until dark. He got up hourly, stepped with care across the gaps in ties that led to a long drop to the green water, and switched tracks to let the passenger trains scream by, and, later, the endless freighters. One way or another, John would succeed in getting him killed. After being so upset that Doug couldn't cry, a bit of sense returned and he laid his hammer out on his backpack. Occasionally, distant figures approached from the Palos Hills side, scrambled in midday heat lines. They vanished long before coming near enough to recognize. No one had yet approached from the Heights.

Doug had time to run, to flag a police car, to tell all. Meanwhile, what if E. died? The possibility that John and Alex were telling the truth petrified him.

Alex had promised they would keep watch from the trees along the canal. Josué, Tiffany, and Greg were likely with them now, passing the binoculars, maybe horsing around or talking about school or their parents, as if it weren't totally fucked that people who claimed to be his friends were convinced that him confronting a murderer was a good idea. Because they weren't his friends. And where was the best of them?

Doug peered over the sides to spot the girl. Not seeing her on the bank of the canal, he looked behind the rusted truss beams on both sides and found nothing. She was on the far bank, maybe. He felt as if E. were just behind him, close enough to reach out and touch. He called her name. He demanded she appear to defend how the death of her sister justified being so careless with others' lives.

Everything else came out, too. How long he'd waited to be good enough for her, smart enough to love her, only proving he was stupid enough to stick around. She'd been his best friend, but she'd never been a good friend. Why had she kept him around so long? Did he entertain her, like a pet monkey? Or did she enjoy how well he echoed her ideas, like a blank wall at the end of an empty corridor? Then Doug cried, really wailed. He said mean things. Like maybe he'd never liked her. Maybe he'd only liked the attention. Still, there was no one in the world like her, as challenging, as brilliant. He didn't stop there. He shouted about how he used to admire her quest to understand things, life, but that it'd taken her down this crazy-scary path he couldn't follow, or refused to. And here he was. Because he couldn't accept—for himself, not for the group or the dumb woods—allowing someone that he cared about to throw her life away. He admitted his fears about losing her to John, as well as his nightmare about the ritual and the smoke. To him, the dream meant he'd never stopped loving her. He loved her. That was the truth. Even the conviction she'd developed over the last few weeks to do good for people, he admired.

Just not her means, which were John's means. If only the guy were to leave them, Doug knew they could make great things happen and be happy, side by side. If only the Dead Man would die.

He lifted his head from where he stood in the middle of the bridge. Dusk pushed the last arc of cool blue heaven under the canal. Headlights shone on the car bridge around the bend—too far to be noticed no matter how high a boy jumped or loud he shouted.

Behind him, the night sky was clear, for the suburbs. Gazing at the stars, he no longer felt bonded to E., to his family or anyone.

Day became night. He was clean, solitary. That peace didn't last, though.

Doug couldn't remember when last a train had roared by. It'd been a long time. In both directions, the tracks led to darkness. He remembered Alex had agreed that very soon there would be another victim. Doug reseated his glasses. Wide-eyed, he scanned the tracks for movement. Even if the group were watching and, by some magic, could see him in the dark, how would they reach him in time to subdue the killer when he appeared? It occurred to Doug that the story about E.'s life being in danger out here had been a lie. For wanting to leave the group and to confess, he'd been fed to the Devil in the Woods. E. was probably under the Big Tree with the others, smile waning as she asked if anyone had seen Doug, her old friend—the only person who'd ever cared about him duped into never-minding, forgetting him until gone. No one needed help but himself.

A dark mass slid around the canal's bend. A white eye opened in the center of its body. Horror and awe stunned the boy. Creeping on the water was not a lurking monster of the deep, but a cargo ship. The rusted craft was a bulbous heap, stacked haphazardly with boxcars. Its spotlight swept up the Palos Hills bank toward the bridge. Doug backed from the edge, ready to run home and distribute the letters he'd written as soon as it'd passed.

"What aren't you afraid of, Dougydearest?" an unfamiliar voice said.

The speaker was not twenty feet away. A figure garbed in black stood between the tracks. By its confidence and imposing build, Doug recognized the knife-wielding tormentor who'd set fire to the Big Tree.

Doug backed and tripped over a rail tie. He clutched his twisted ankle that immediately began to swell.

The figure snickered. "You're just as I imagined you," he said, impassioned but satisfied, almost lusty.

Doug scrambled to his feet. The figure strode for him commandingly, the way he'd come around the Big Tree that night.

"Let's have a good look at you," he said. He reached for Doug's head.

The freighter's spotlight hit the center of the bridge and illuminated the boys. They froze for an instant. The figure spun behind a beam.

Doug crawled away on his hands and knees, careful of the gaps. He stopped and cursed himself. Exposure was exactly what he needed to avoid being killed. He stood and waved to be noticed by the freighter's crew.

"Fool! What're you doing?"

Doug flailed both arms and hopped on his good leg as the craft passed beneath the bridge. The radiance of its beam showed up through the slats. It hadn't seen him. A sprint home was impossible. Doug took up his hammer. He turned and faced the killer.

"If you come—come any closer, I'll—"

"I came to warn you against false prophets, not to sacrifice you, little lamb." The figure loomed a reach away. "*Dost thou know who made thee?*" he hoarsely whispered. Amusing himself, he laughed. He wasn't getting any nearer, though.

"Are you—?"

"The less you know about me, the better, kid."

The light beneath them went out as the freighter's beam swung up-river. In the enclosing dark, the tormentor's silhouette had the sheen of velvet. His cloak opened. Slowly and deliberately, he withdrew the long blade, which—there was no mistaking this close—had a serrated edge. He crouched, setting the knife lengthwise on a tie between them in the manner of an offering. Peace—parley at least. His gloved hands settled on his hips. He towered before Doug in a moment of heavy silence. The baggy hood that veiled his face shuddered in the wind.

"Why don't you put the hammer down," he said, voice syrupy, almost congenial, except for a hint of threat. "Let us talk—two simple men, both wronged by the one ringmaster."

"I don't want to hurt you—anyone—I don't want anyone hurt."

"Hush now. That's beyond our power in this moment. Rest easy in knowing your former master will soon retire to the great applause of his own undoing."

"Master?"

"The boy doesn't understand the true nature of the woods. That's why you're here. Isn't it? As if with X-Ray Specs you peered through the falseness of his parlor trick hocus-pocus, seeing it for what it is— good intentions and a minor deathbed enchantment, nothing more."

"John isn't my master."

"Let me tell you now what the others will never guess and what the Late One will never suspect: The woods, in which he trusts, are leading you to—"

The figure collapsed. A swath of black cloth doubled over at Doug's feet.

A girl stood behind it, clutching a long club. The downed figure moaned. Twice more she beat its head. It went still.

The others cried in triumph somewhere in the distant trees.

E. was in her underwear and batted the windblown hair out of her smiling eyes. "You came back for me," she said.

"You—I thought—I didn't know—" Doug stammered.

"I heard everything."

E. stepped over the figure. She came into Doug's arms and rested her head on his chest.

"Come on, Doug. Hold me, please?"

She nestled against him.

Doug hugged E. Her back was taut, spiky with goose bumps, her body streaked with soot from slipping up through the railroad ties.

Alex and John had lowered her onto one of the concrete bridge supports that afternoon, she explained, unclothed to move stealthily and unmarked by evidence, where she'd waited beneath the tracks all day for the killer to pass. She'd hoped that Doug would have the courage John and Alex didn't. Otherwise, she'd have climbed up to club him without the help of Doug's distraction—attempted to.

"You risked your life for me," she said.

"I still can't believe I'm not dead." He watched the figure, motionless at their feet.

E. squeezed him. "Can you believe that I love you?"

"No," he said. "Wait—you do?"

"Like family." E. looked up at him, searched his face for … Doug didn't know what, yet. "You've been trying for so long to make me feel more." Though close enough, E. didn't kiss him. She smiled, politely at first, next from the awkwardness. Her smile then softened into genuine affection. "I'm going to work on it, like I've worked on everything else. It's just like you said—we can be happy together, here in the woods."

III

1

The group was joined around the cloaked body of the killer. Or their tormentor. But conclusively a high school boy named Rocco Lordes who threatened them by mere knowledge of their existence. He shifted and groaned on the train bridge that night as they bound his legs in duct tape and fixed his wrists behind his back and his mouth similarly with a gym-sock gag. Working in silence, they dragged his booted feet thudding against the rail ties and log-rolled him down the bumpy slope to the wooded path below. His darkly garbed body landed in a cloud of white dust.

Rocky was fully conscious when the group reached him. He'd crawled ten or so feet. He sat with his backside crooked up a tree trunk. His legs were in the air and he sawed, frantically and uselessly, at the thick band restricting his legs against a branch. "Lose this?" Josué held up the knife near enough that Rocky kicked at him for it. Josué flattened him with an impersonal jab to the kidney. Greg swept in and delivered an arching punt to his ribs. A tuft of chalky dust shot up, and he flipped onto his back. He groaned, struggled to rise onto one elbow. E. toppled him with her staff. Tiffany sat on his chest, then, grunting, "No—no," and pounded against his weakening attempts at sitting up. Alex assisted, holding tight the baggy ends of his hood, blinding him until Tiffany relented, satisfied with her work.

Rocky lay still before them.

"He is not so scary now, eh?" Josué said.

He dragged the boy crudely by the feet to the trailhead. His cloak snagged branches. The cheap velvet ripped and caked with mud. Josué stumbled backward, left clutching a boot that'd slipped off. They huddled and decided that a body was best carried over one's shoulders, as in a war movie. Greg scooped him up without needing to be asked and remarked that Rocky was as light as somebody's kid sister. E. asked him if Rocky was at last being agreeable. Greg hefted the limp body. "Perfect angel," he said. They laughed, and the group hiked with their captive to camp. Without a flashlight, E. led them through vague, moonlit trails, down into the valley around their gnarliest, yet-to-be-sprung traps. Doug walked behind the girl in faith that she would bring them to safety. He looked back only once. John lagged far behind.

Alex engineered the binding of Rocky to the Big Tree, relying on Greg's muscle and materials brought for that purpose. In ten minutes, their tormentor was well fastened, arms behind his back in a sitting position. His shoulders slumped forward and his head drooped sideways. That Rocky could be unconscious after so much jostling seemed unlikely. It created an ominous sense that he was faking. But nobody dared draw back the hood.

They sat and waited for the boy to speak. The campfire burned close enough to his boots that he shared their circle. As fresh logs cracked in the pit, their hatred for him expanded and consumed them from inside. His presence fouled the night air, the strength of their bond, and the sanctity of the Grove, which filled with firelight and hatred. To even look at him was torturous. Yet their fascination was too great to turn away from the stranger for more than a moment. Here he was. They'd tied their tormentor, potentially the killer, to the same tree he'd defiled several times. But they felt no great relief. Its trunk, scorched coal-black from his fires, rose at his back like a high throne. All that remained of the group's original memorial were those pink flats well above him, as if flying from a hell to which he—and they too—were left condemned.

They had him. Rocky was helpless. His cloak, which they'd childishly pictured in daydreams to be composed of shadow itself, was shredded in spots and dusted white, which powdered the long smears of mud on his chest and arms and made him appear pitiful and clownish. Considering how much this one person had dominated their lives by luring Erika to the woods and then toying with them in the place of her death, and how he'd completely altered the course of their futures, who they'd imagined they'd be at the end of—what otherwise would've been, right?—another banal year of junior high in an ordinary American suburb—reflecting on all he'd done to them, the group couldn't shake the feeling that still he had them. His actions had transformed them, a change that, now at its end, felt like a deformation, their souls having twisted against each hardship and challenge. Because of his influence, they'd become what they were—secret, not normal, specters even by daylight, a group, forever marked as such—and they hated him for it, for dark thoughts like these that glowed like the head-lanterns of creatures at the bottom of the sea, illuminating their nightmarish faces.

"I wish you had let us know about ..." Greg jabbed a finger at their guest.

Alex started to list the many circumstances that'd made confiding in the entire group an impossibility. Greg and Tiffany and Josué weren't briefed until Doug was facing the killer.

E. lifted her hand, which until that moment, Doug had held as if an artifact made of precious stone in his upturned palm. Alex hushed immediately. "If things had gone bad for us up there," E. explained, "we didn't want you to feel responsible."

"Um, no offense, but what you're saying is total bullshit," Tiffany said. The night air was clammy and her arms tightened across her chest. "No matter what happens here, ever, we're basically all responsible at this point."

Josué nodded. "No secrets."

"Right," Tiffany said. "I'm here. We're all here now, aren't we? We obviously care enough to feel responsible no matter what. So don't take away my choice in ... whatever. Because you're not more special than me or anybody else."

"Yeah. It would've been nice to know." Greg looked side to side, not raising his head high enough to meet their eyes. "I thought we did things as a group. I could've been there for you guys." After each sentence he halted, as if having much more to say but unable to put all his racing thoughts into words. "I should've been asked. Told something."

Silence fell over the group. It ran deep and carved ravines between the kids until each became an island amid a sea of silence. They felt disparate, alienated, increasingly self-conscious of their bond's tenuousness, which hurt, because they loved being a group. Didn't they? The question echoed over the distance they felt. The reply was a shared shame, seemingly all that remained to bind them. The kids looked across the circle at each other for some explanation of why the victory hadn't united them. To everyone's relief, Tiffany and Greg's breakup became obvious.

Over the last two weeks, Tiffany and the boy had been inseparable. Greg had pulled her into his lap whenever possible or greedily slung his arm around shoulders. They sat apart now with Josué between them, who balanced Rocky's knife flat across his thighs with his legs sprawled out and touching the pit. Tiffany was perched at the very edge of her log, too stiffly to be in good spirits. She'd tilted to keep Greg out of her field of vision. Greg rubbed his eyes and alternated between crunching them as if about to cry and huffing through his nose as if ready to yell at somebody. Whatever they'd meant to each other, it hadn't worked out. Their conclusion brought Doug wicked and delicious pleasure, and allowed Alex and E. to rationalize that other issues were contributing to the group's unhappiness.

"I was wrong not to include you—all of you," E. said. "I hope you understand how personal and painful … how badly I wanted him here."

"He's hurt all of us," Greg said, not letting up.

"He did. Of course. You're right. We all deserve that he answer us."

"Sure," Greg said. "But I didn't ask for that. I wanted him to stop, yeah. But this …"

"He has to pay for what he did. What he did to us."

"Well, here he is—knocked out, beyond unconscious."

The hooded boy whimpered.

The group hushed. Their mouths hung open, anticipating remarks to come roiling out of their rival. His head lifted shallowly. It fell and bobbed. Rocky went still again, soundless.

"He's injured?" Josué asked with as much concern as if curious whether it would rain.

"He has to be fucking with us," Tiffany said.

"It is possible," Alex said.

"Right," E. said and ordered Josué to rouse him.

He put the long knife through his belt. It slapped goofily at his side as he went to the boy. Josué stood over Rocky, one hand against the Big Tree. He stooped with the nonchalance and open-heartedness of a man confessing everyday sins.

"Wake him?" he asked before proceeding.

"Yes," E. said.

Rocky's roped torso absorbed Josué's thrashing kicks. His body didn't tense against the blows, merely jolted on impact, then slumped same as before. "Hey. You awake?" Josué said. A groan sounded from inside the boy, thin and brief.

Alex stood, hands clasped in anticipation. "If I remove the gag, maybe we can begin interrogation."

"Let him eat it," Tiffany said. "I say we kick the hell out of him, instead."

"I don't disagree with you ... in sentiment."

The captive twitched. Alex and Josué jumped. Minor spasms coursed the cloaked boy's body. His head rolled back. From beneath the folds of cloth jutted his chin and mouth. The muscles of his jaws tensed with an athletic springiness as his cheeks strained against the gag for air. His chest convulsed against the ropes, and the group wouldn't have been surprised if Alex's calculated work tore away like string cheese. As in the case of John Walker, they weren't certain of all that Rocky was capable of.

Doug looked to the Dead Man, expected him to rise and convince the group to silence their captive—before he could say too much about John's complicity. The boy averted his eyes. He didn't want to see it.

Rocky didn't have strength enough to struggle for more than a few seconds. The hood fell back as his head leveled, and unveiled his face. Both cheeks were reddened, one bruised. Dried blood plugged one nostril and crusted his duct-taped mouth. The other nostril wheezed a hard, straw-blow exhale and sucked a desperate and wet inhale.

"Speak of devil," Josué said.

"It appears he's experiencing difficulty breathing," Alex noted.

"That's what he wants us to think." Tiffany gazed at their captive skeptically. "Choke on what you did. I'd like to see it."

"I need to hear him confess," E. said.

"Let him choke." Greg sat up, all his grief bared in his reddened under-eyes and curled mouth. "He's wearing the cloak. He's got the huge knife. He's the guy—case closed."

"We should be one hundred percent certain of his guilt," Alex said.

"If he's not the killer, who the hell is he?" Greg went on. "Look at him. Think about it a second. Then dump his body off at the police station with a sign around his neck that says, 'Hello, I'm the killer,' and forget him. I just want this all behind us, man. Ya know? Anyone?"

"If he has something to say for his crimes, we deserve to hear it. Before …" E. looked around the circle for support. She appeared small beside the sturdy club she clung to like a wizard's staff. Her features didn't crack with emotion this time. She paused at every face around the circle. The girl possessed an enduring strength—the desire to re-unify the group through a shared purpose. She'd put a baggy T-shirt on and, having accidentally dropped her pants into the Cal-Sag River, had Doug's hoodie tied around her waist, her thin and dirty legs exposed. With her hair tousled from the scramble on the train bridge, E. appeared witchy, though she had a stoic, almost queenly bearing. She'd been teased since her sister's death as a "Sataness," one of the long-rumored devil worshippers in the woods. Perhaps a vision from her critics' nightmares, she wasn't trying to be anything anymore, trusting her feelings to guide her.

"He's most positively suffocating now," Alex said.

Rocky's head was plum-colored. Though shut, his lids squirmed over his eyeballs, which swam back and forth.

E. tightened her grip on her staff and used a different tack. "I'm not afraid of him. Is anyone here afraid anymore?"

"Ugh," said Tiffany. "Fine. Can we choke him later, though?"

Greg stammered a few poor rebuttals. He found himself unable to think clearly while facing E., who embodied her dead sister's boldness.

From across the fire, John rose to his feet, slowly, achingly, further delaying Alex's removal of the gag. Even upright, he seemed shrunken. He clutched his hoodie to his chest as if freezing. He hadn't said a word since the train bridge. The group had almost forgotten he was among them. The missing force of his leadership during the kidnapping had created a void of influence. The kids had immediately tried to fill the vacancy with their squabbling. Only Doug expected his rival's return to lull the group into submission. John's presence grated their minds. Like a parent that interrupts a child's game, his warning nagged their consciences:

"Watch what moves inside you," he said. John looked down and away, at no one.

E. nodded to Alex, who cut the tape behind the captive's ear.

Rocky gasped for breath, choking. Saliva spewed down his chin upon removal of the soaked gag. He hacked until his head drained from violet to crimson and paled again, tipped back against the Big Tree. The group had a clear look at the young man while he caught his breath. The sides of Rocky's head were buzzed short like Doug's. A knot of hair topped his head, not long, but askew and disheveled as if chewed by goats. His eyebrows were uncommonly thick, like two brown caterpillars drinking from the corners of his eyes. They hadn't ever pictured the boy behind the mask, not consciously. Coming from the rich-kid suburb of Palos Heights, they might've expected the face of a handsome villain: healthily complexioned, haughty, magnetic in a John Walker way. The boy looked sleepless, raw, years older than he was.

"You've been tormenting us for exactly three weeks now," Alex started, crouched just out of reach.

Rocky was unresponsive.

"Why has it been important for you to return to the scene of the crime?"

Despite the lack of compliance, Alex didn't become impatient. The group could see how long Alex had waited for this moment, content to squat there indefinitely, fully focused on the boy, mouth open as if after a subtle gasp, altogether sincerer than ever, believing absolutely in the necessity to prove several well-worked hypotheses about the murder true.

Josué slapped his face. The boy winced.

"P-please," he murmured.

Alex repeated the question.

"Out ... side," Rocky answered.

"What is?"

The clot in his nostril began to run thinly with blood. "Time ... You ... returned."

"You aren't speaking straight, Rocky. You have to speak straight."

"Bo-ok," he said, blowing a spit bubble. The pinkish sphere swirled and gleamed at the corner of his mouth.

"The book—good. The one you found." Alex pushed on when he didn't answer: "You found the diary here, in the ground. You studied it, you and your group, nightly. The margin notes were in your hand-writing, one of several reasons you were desperate to retrieve it. You thought the book contained secrets worth killing for. Which is why you got angry when Erika hid it from you."

"We ..."

"Yes. Others were involved. You and Erika. And others."

There was a buzz in the air, a sense that Alex was really doing it, nailing the suspect with the firm but suave coercion of a TV show detective, the thrill of danger but also success. Every accusation astounded them, how much Alex had uncovered and deduced. They'd started the investigation together—isn't that what they'd been doing under John's leadership? Alex had finished it and, if conscious of doing well, didn't break focus.

"Where are they now? Are any of them here with us? Or do you see only victims?"

Josué gripped the boy's plug of hair with the resigned displeasure of taking out a wet trash bag. He turned the head to scan around the fire. Rocky's busted eye had swollen monstrously, as if a rubber ball were stuffed under the bruised top lid. The other blinked with the ineffectual fluttering of a dying butterfly. Instead of sliding down, the spit bubble had moved up his face onto his cheek.

"No? Maybe later?" Alex said.

Josué released him. The head tipped sideways.

"Erika was in charge of hiding the book from the others. Every night. Digging it up again before your rituals began. Explaining her dirty fingernails. Until she hid the book from you. Or, she was reading it behind your back. Either way, she was done with you and the woods—I don't know why and don't need to. I know it made you angry. So you killed her. Is that what happened, Rocky?"

With his head lowered, the bloody bubble slipped to the tip of his nose. It hung there, shuddering under the mild wheeze of the unplugged nostril.

"No."

"But you were there. You have the murder weapon." Alex leaned in. "You know who did kill her."

"Yeah," he said. The bubble popped.

Alex gave the boy a minute to breathe. In labored increments, his head raised. He looked shakily at the kids around the fire. He would name someone among them as the killer or his accomplice. Whether or not it would be the truth, the moment made them tense and vulnerable, being seen here, unquestionably what they were, by another person, an outsider. He wasn't one of them and never would be no matter how many nights spent watching, as evil as he was nocturnal. Rocky's mouth opened. His head again fell back. He swallowed. It was a hard swallow, they saw. His spit-glistened Adam's apple squirmed uncomfortably in his throat before it bobbed.

"Who did it, Rocky?" Alex prodded.

His face scrunched and trembled as if from a terrible itch.

"Th-the group," he said with malice.

"Oh, my—fuck you, Rocky." Tiffany stood and spit in a single motion.

The boy didn't wince or turn. Her spit clung to his not-swollen eye and that cheek. Rocky's mouth cracked slightly wider. He licked up what he could reach in laborious strokes with his toady tongue.

"Tiff," he said. "Bubblegum. S-sweet."

Greg came around the circle, head tucked like a boxer. Driven by jealousy, knowing it, welcoming hatred, he was ready to smash in the other half of Rocky's face. Not fully understanding the freak, not needing to, either, he knew the guy was making a smartass comment about Tiffany's mouth or taste or—

Josué got in Greg's way with his hands up in little shields. He looked to E. for the final call. Alex rose behind Josué to help block Greg from their captive.

Rocky goaded the group now: "Greg—could you? Kill me?"

His cheeks crinkled, like a child's the instant before crying. Rocky was smiling, attempting to.

E.'s arm snaked to the top of her staff as she stood. The bark was the same prehistoric gray color of the Big Tree, slim but for a thick knot around which her hand tightened. Seeing it up close, Doug recalled his nightmare—through the blinding smoke, E. slipping in the high boughs, him trying to help, achieving the opposite, the girl clinging to a lone branch, ascending. That was just a dream (wasn't it?). The entire group was on their feet now and heated, except for Doug, hiding in her shadow.

"No," she said. "Not yet."

Greg huffed. He stepped away from his friends and the campfire to cool down. His retreating footfall cracked sticks in the dark around them.

Rocky had committed his biggest transgression against E., the group knew, which gave her the biggest stake in parsing justice. E. hadn't said anything until then, only observed, measuring the character of her sister's killer—potential killer. His disrespect disgusted her, that a thing such as murder could be joked about here, considering the brutality, considering all that she was worth to so many, considering the vandalism and arson and slander, considering the boy's situation.

"Careful," John piped, at the corner of their minds, voice washing to gravel as it rose.

Rocky's features again tightened into a gruesome smile. He flinched from the pain of contorting his busted face as he looked across the rising smoke at John.

"I know you," he snickered and coughed up a small cloud of blood and spittle that bathed his own face.

There was challenge in the way he smiled, drunkenly and almost radiantly, unyieldingly gazing at the Dead Man. The group didn't need to understand Rocky. They saw what he meant. John curled in on himself, wouldn't look at him, wouldn't strike back in words. Whether in defeat or reflection, the boy appeared crushed under the tormentor's heckling. Their pride and sense of righteousness felt debased, then, as if fools in the hands of a charlatan, no more than a handful of Erika's guilt-ridden enemies who'd never known the power of forgiveness, compassion, and honor, no better than Rocky. The group looked to E. to redeem them.

The girl wore hot tears like reflective war paint down her cheeks. Not frailty or sadness, but E.'s determination blazed forth, the desire for closure over the greatest loss of her lifetime. She glared down at the captive. Her disgust alone said she would not allow him to best them. The group imbibed the power they witnessed. Regaining their sense of purpose, they sat or stood a little straighter. They were fighting to honor Erika, for a world threatened by a brutal child killer, for goodness itself. Their individual desires to beat and break him, to spit and curse, or to turn and run bent to E.'s lead, eager for a single act that would bring closure. When at last she spoke, a surge of confidence rekindled their commitment to make the woods right again.

"You killed my sister," she said.

Rocky didn't feign ignorance well. A corner of his mouth turned up, entertained by the entrance of a new challenger.

"Who?" he said.

"If you had the arrogance to take Erika's life, you can own up to it. Or are you that ashamed of what you did?"

"Sh-she wanted … to … be dead."

"Josué," E. said, ignoring his taunts, "show him the murder weapon. Jog his memory."

Josué squatted at the bound boy's side. He turned the knife before Rocky's face. Its long, serrated blade looked a hundred years old— older, three hundred or more. It hadn't a color as much as a texture, rough as a flat stone, patchy with rust, though the knife retained a fused and immutable strength from tip to heel. Overall it was dull with the unconquerable blackness of oil, yet the blade flashed as it caught the firelight. Josué patted the side of the blade against the boy's cheek tauntingly.

"Un-tie. I'll tell." Rocky's humor went flat, his gargled response uncharacteristically frank, joyless.

The group searched each other's faces, shiny from perspiring around the fire:

What do we do?

Should we?

Don't listen to him.

But maybe?

End him—now.

He might know something.

Nothing he says can be trusted.

He's watched us.

What choice have we?

He knows too much.

"Talk. Or we'll hurt you," E. said.

Josué raised the blade, edgewise, against their captive's cheek. Rocky mock-yawned. He blinked with the one eye and looked around as if concerned he'd missed an important turn in the drama while nodding off. Josué smirked, impressed by his enemy's cockiness and with mild respect for his tenacity—a small admiration bullies had never shown him. He pulled the knife in a slick swipe down Rocky's cheek. Blood coursed his neck and into his collar. The flow became heavier when the boy clenched his teeth. Josué stumbled back, surprised by the leap of blood. It collected on Rocky's jaw in drops and spattered onto the front of his cloak.

"Still think it's fun to hurt people?" E. asked.

Rocky tensed for another mocking smile. The pain was too great.

"Confess," E. said. "Or we kill you."

"How would we get rid of the body?" Tiffany asked.

"Burn him."

Alex's head shook in disbelief. "No, no. We'd have a ID-able skeleton on our hands."

"Bury him, then. Alive. We won't have to worry about blood—more blood."

"Damn, E.," Tiffany said. "Just when I start hating your guts, you go and say something great like that."

"The hole would have to be deep, eight to ten feet," Alex said. "It wouldn't attract animals that way. Probably."

"Not here," Josué added. "The Grove is sacred. And for cops—they will look here first."

"Correct," Alex said. "On the other side of the tracks, then. It would have to be soon. If not tonight, tomorrow evening at the latest. My notes don't show Rocky has a curfew, but we wouldn't want—"

"The little shit comes and goes as he pleases," Tiffany said. "His own mother won't miss him."

"We have a plan," E. said. She hadn't looked up from their captive. "I don't want to make the same mistake I did in bringing him here. All of us have to agree on it. The killer talks or his arrogance kills him. Objections from the group?"

The conversation had turned so quickly that Doug wasn't sure he'd heard her correctly, what was being asked of him. E. was a victim, of Rocky, of the Dead Man's influence, they all were. That's what was so wrong here. Why then was John meekly studying the faces of his friends and not stomping his feet, shouting, "Yes! Kill him!" Because he didn't have to? John's withdrawal infuriated Doug more than E.'s proposition because it made the boy wonder if he'd been wrong about the guy. He no longer controlled the group—E. did. How long had she been? Doug's mouth shrank tight.

Greg had returned, on the outskirts of the circle and hazy in the darkness. He came nearer, gradually, after every few words. "Are you guys sure about this?" he said. "I mean, are you serious about maybe killing the guy?"

"I say we give him the night to think about it," E. said, "and we act tomorrow night."

"The guy's acting like he's dying. He could be dead by the morning."

"We don't know that for sure. We know he's been messing with our heads for weeks. Now he wants us to believe he's dying after a few punches. What do you think he'd do the moment we cut those ropes if he had his knife?"

"I hear you," Greg said. "But—what if he does die? Are you—is everyone here—gonna be cool with that? Dougy?"

The others looked for Doug behind their leader. His glasses glinted white with firelight.

"It's the least he deserves after what he did to Erika," E. spoke for him.

Greg rejoined the circle. "I want it to be over. Erika, him, all of it."

"It soon will be."

"Yeah," said Tiffany.

"Further objections?" E. said.

They shook their heads, grim, resolute.

"John?"

But for Doug and the tied-up kid, John Walker was the last left sitting around the fire. He talked with his chin dropped, head turned to one side. He didn't raise his eyes, which made it impossible to discern whether they were open and pensive or clamped in pain.

"The trees hold their breath," he said.

The woods were silent, breezeless, as if they too waited for a thunderclap, some divine threat of doom or cleansing flood because of their pact. Intense quiet pressed in on all sides. The group wondered if it were simply too difficult to hear anything over their pounding hearts. They searched the dark and returned to each other's faces, firm in their decision and unfazed by the possibility that there were no woods at all. They might have been at the bottom of an ocean trench or on a high tower on another planet or beyond space and time altogether. They were a ring around a steady fire, the air between them charged with a bond impossible anywhere but this place that was their own, and they were not afraid.

"Tomorrow," E. said, "we'll make our own fate."

The group re-gagged Rocky. His brows furrowed, and he protested in muffled barks. His chest swelled against the restraints. He shook, futilely. Sucks of breath and a hearty, muted ha-ha-ing followed, the captive either wildly amused by his misfortune or determined to belittle his captor's advantage. As they packed to leave, without trying to acknowledge him, not their slightest movements seemed to escape Rocky's wild, wide-open gaze.

It was decided someone should remain to stand guard overnight. Greg volunteered. Tiffany said she'd stay to keep him company, presumably to talk over the breakup. When John said that it was better he himself stay, having already delivered an excuse to his parents for not returning home, no one protested. Their former leader seemed to need some time alone in the woods. Alex, who'd made a similar excuse, insisted on keeping watch with him, however, as if harboring doubt of his loyalty. Josué agreed to relieve them in the morning.

"It's ditch day tomorrow, no?" he said.

The group's conversation lightened. Tomorrow was eighth-grade ditch day, though the rest agreed to go to school to avoid suspicion, and how awful would it be to sit over an hour on the hard bleachers during a bogus award ceremony for people who tried too hard to be liked—no offense, John—and thank god it was the last week before summer break or otherwise, Tiffany said, she just might die. They decided to celebrate their total freedom this weekend after the completion of the rituals, when all had walked in the sky alone so that they would never have to be alone again. They would potluck and drink and dance under the full moon.

"Kinda sad, though," Tiffany said. "It's the end."

"No," E. assured her, "the Watchers of the Grove are just beginning."

2

"We're not actually going to kill the guy. Right?" Doug said to E. on the other side of the creek.

They'd caught the killer. This fight was over. No longer a need for traps, the others ran ahead to disarm them with Alex's help and to mark a path around ones not easily disabled. The kids went shoving and laughing, excited for tomorrow's celebration. What Doug didn't feel. The eyes of their flashlights flew through the trees. Their bodies merged with the night. Their laughter shimmered across the valley.

Doug looked back at the captive, bound across from John. Rocky watched him and E. with serpentine focus. His narrowed eyes were glossy.

E. deeply exhaled. She jabbed her staff into the ground and patiently took hold of Doug. Not by the hands as on the train bridge. She clasped his arms.

"I know our plan sounds wrong," she said. "It's not one hundred percent right. But you see—he's not remorseful." E. gestured openly at the captive. Rocky's head was hung now. He coughed on the gag. Strands of phlegm spurted out the sides and dangled. "He never will be. You know that's true. Even if he does admit to it, can we let a monster like that loose? He killed my sister. He's evil. He'll kill again. Locking him up won't right his wrongs. Not for me it won't. Ridding him from the world is the only way we can be free. And, after another kid is found in the woods, the developers will be forced to go away. Nobody will want to live here but us."

"That's not you talking. John—"

"It's me." E. pulled him close. Her arms snugged around his shoulders. "If you meant what you said on the bridge, about me marching to my own drummer, how can you think differently now?"

Doug couldn't think of the answer. He felt E.'s breath, smelled the smoke in her hair. The girl he'd wanted for so long. His glasses slipped down his nose and he inched back to fix them, scared of what was happening but not wanting to miss anything. E. reached the frames first. She set them on his head.

She examined him fully and said, "Handsome."

Her affection felt real. It was. Doug wanted to cry. Not because it had been so long in coming. He wasn't sure he deserved it.

"When we fought in your driveway," she said, "you asked me to think about what would happen when John's gone. I have. We all have. He's gotten us a long way from where we started. But we don't need him, anymore. That was the point of the rituals, learning how to stand on our own. The train bridge was your walk, Doug. You faced your fear and beat it. John would never say it, but the Big Tree doesn't matter. John wouldn't say or do a lot of things. You know, he wouldn't help us against the murderer? You proved that you're braver than he is. That's the truth about you and why I need you. To take his place at my side. You want that, don't you?"

He nodded.

"You love me."

"I really do," he said.

"Then if you love me—me-me—here I am."

She kissed him. Her lips moved over his, sipped him at first, then opened, wider, tasted him, took him inside of her and didn't spit him out. That primal gesture, the bliss of being accepted, cleansed Doug of his concerns about the captive, that he'd ever worried about anything. It didn't last long. The feel of E. and her stilted advances were so different than with Tiffany, and Doug struggled to appreciate the details. E.'s much fuller chest squashed against his, smotheringly. And instead of meeting from opposite ends of the world as equals, E. seemed to work away at his face, as if steadily devouring him head-first. Doug was soon sweating hard and no longer wanted to be in her arms, unless it was to break down and cry. For the first time since Tiffany had left him, he was grateful for their time together, for learning how to make out, as it allowed him to perform the act without having to lead with his heart. The boy tried to lose himself in the moment, but his sexual desire kept edging the high-adrenaline terror of being in the passenger seat of a car that E. was steering off a cliff. The killer— maybe it was Rocky, but maybe not—had almost gotten away with Erika's gruesome death, so why wouldn't seven much smarter kids get away with a clean, well-planned murder for a good cause? Doug caught the thought mid-slice through his mind and was stopped still, literally left stiffly clutching the back of E.'s T-shirt, benumbed by how killing another human was so simple. Maybe it was a symptom of the woods, living away from the world so long. He tried to imagine himself back in the regular world, a year from now on an average day among the rows of a high school history class, taking notes, preparing for a test as a young man who'd killed somebody, as a killer-killer. Not just in that moment, but every day, for the rest of his life, going through what everybody does—driving, having sex, losing jobs—as a killer. For always. He wouldn't be alone. He'd have the group to suffer guilt with, to lean on in moments of excruciating regret, E. to help him sleep, to tell him he was OK, that they were all OK and that he'd done good, as she did now, stroking his arm (you're OK), putting her lips on him again (you're good), and sharing her body (you're one of us), drawing him out of his thoughts.

"Eeeeeee! Eeeeeeeeee!" the others called from up the path. They needed her to help locate a lost punji trap. She went ahead with her staff. Doug offered his flashlight. Stopping to check, he'd forgotten his things at camp.

"I don't need one anymore," she said traipsing backward. She smiled and faded to black after a few steps. If bravery made it possible for her to pass through the trees unburdened by the potentially horrible consequences, Doug still didn't have that. He turned back to camp for his stuff.

Rocky nodded, as if having anticipated Doug's return. Doug ignored him.

Behind John, a triangular stack of logs waited to keep him and Alex warm overnight. The Dead Man hadn't set any on the fire, which had gone to coals with a smoldering underbelly. He didn't acknowledge Doug. He faced the pit but stared into the darkness up the creek with the faraway look he'd worn on the train bridge that afternoon. Doug hunted around his seat for his backpack three times. That he was disturbing the Dead Man during a moment of reflection was confirmed when the guy lowered his head and, with a shudder, sounding irritated, told him the bag was where E.'d been standing.

Doug had beaten the Dead Man at last. He'd gotten the girl. Despite his many shortcomings, he'd won. But he didn't feel good about it. He felt responsible for John's melancholy and almost thanked the guy, not for the help, but for not dating E. simply because he could've. Any way he framed the words in his mind ("Thanks for having the compassion to reject this girl who's been everything to me"), he either lowered E.'s worth or raised John's to uncomfortable levels. Just the thought of talking personally with a kid who'd had his own mortality on his mind for over a year made Doug shrink inside with shame. His romantic feelings for E., the biggest thing that'd ever happened to Doug, was pathetic beside the guy's life-or-death bout with cancer. Doug considered apologizing for having reclaimed the girl's affection, an even stupider sentiment. Then he almost owned up to coining John's unfortunate nickname. Doug lingered beside the fire, irritated that he cared what the guy was feeling. He unzipped and dumped his bag, searched it for the flashlight, and found it immediately. Then he repacked the bag and pretended he'd lost something else he badly needed.

Over his shoulder, the captive called his name through the gag, "Dhhhhk. Dhhhhk!"

Doug turned his back on him.

Rocky laughed with a wet munching sound, as if chewing the gym sock as a late-night snack, his last meal.

John couldn't be upset about losing E. He was the one who'd avoided taking their relationship to the next level. Why then did he look so miserable? Doug felt amazingly dumb. It was as if he hadn't understood the guy from day one. He'd gotten the group to devote their lives to the woods, to never leave his side. What more did he want? To live forever? John's gloom spoiled the sweet, wet straw scent of E. on Doug's skin. He needed to hate John now. No matter how much he wanted E. to be the girl he'd first fallen in love with, despite her insistence that wanting Rocky to die was smart and just, Doug had to admit she'd been altered by the Dead Man's influence, corrupted by his ritual, his Work. Doug had defeated the leader of the group he feared only to start dating the leader of the group he feared. Like some twisted magic act, the joy in getting what he wanted most had disappeared. That was John's fault.

"You should be happy. You got what you wanted," Doug said bitterly, not caring whether John would misinterpret him or be hurt.

Doug properly re-stuffed his bag when the comment didn't earn a reaction, not a single lift of his chin or tilt of his head, no sign the guy had heard him. John wasn't sleeping. Doug could see his open, unblinking eyes. Doug zipped up the backpack and strapped it to his front, how he wore it when feeling vulnerable, and clicked on the flashlight to leave, pestered by the thought that he might've actually lost something after dumping the bag repeatedly, when John jolted and asked:

"Would you still be here if E. didn't want you?"

"I love her," Doug said. "I can't just turn it off. I've tried."

"I know," John said.

"You know everything. Sorry. I forgot for a second."

"If it were up to you, what would you do with the captive? If E.'s opinion of you wasn't your only concern."

"Whose opinion should I be concerned about? Let me guess," Doug said. "You know … I'm so—I'm done fighting you."

"You must be as tired of it as I am."

"I don't want things to be this way. I don't want to do anything. That's the thing. I'm not a fighter. But you keep coming at me, asking me to do things I can't, to be things I'm not."

"You're fighting yourself."

"Stop it," Doug said. "I meant what I said. I'm not listening anymore. I don't care about you or this place. After tomorrow, me and E. are going to be together."

"Someone has to die to make that happen," John said, not a decree. He was putting into words what Doug couldn't say.

"You started it. Don't come asking me now to do something because you feel bad about what you did."

"You're right."

"I am? Right. I'm right, and I'm going home. Then I'm forgetting everything you made us do here."

"Listen to yourself. There's time. You can fix this."

"Bye, John."

"Forgetting is a battle you can't win."

"I beat you, didn't I?"

John looked into the fire. His back curled worse and he planted his elbows on his knees. The guy began to cry. Not a hard sob. He didn't make any noise at all. His eyes moistened, shined, but didn't shut. A few tears dropped into the dust at his feet. Doug had wounded him, though not this much. Maybe he was upset over losing control of the group. If as wicked as Doug had believed, he would scheme revenge, not slouch with pained eyes at a dying fire. There was more going on inside the guy than Doug had cared to imagine, and his conscience, not wanting to leave John broken to pieces out here, kept him from running ahead with the others, from starting over by forgetting the guy completely.

"I can't care about you," Doug said. "You've lied to me too much."

"I never lied about your importance," John said. "You were always our most valuable player. You still are."

"Have you ever … I'm sorry, but maybe it's the meds or—have you thought …? Maybe you're wrong."

"All the time. About everything we do here. That I do—that I've ever done." John laughed despairingly. "I've doubted you. I'm doubting you now. But the trees never have. You were meant to be here," he said, again serious. "And you have a life after this."

"You do, too. Right?"

"I'm not going anywhere," he said. "I wanted all of us to stay. No one's ready. The game's not over, but it's my last inning playing in it."

It was the loneliest thing Doug had ever heard in his life. Leaving John that night wasn't easy, alone with the killer, across from one another like chess pieces locked in eternal stalemate, waiting for a big hand to knock one of them down, one much larger than Doug's.

3

The awards ceremony was held each year on the half-day before graduation. Whatever the original purpose, the ceremony decorated the most freakishly talented and popular kids at Palos Junior High with medalled ribbons and embossed certificates testifying to their superiority, typically before a large number of empty rows, as it was also eighth-grade ditch day. This year's ceremony was atypical in several respects. For one, the rows became so tightly packed that, as full classes continued to stream in from homeroom, Mrs. Shepard shrieked her whistle and directed kids to form additional rows on the floor, doubting the constitution of the creaking bleachers built well before she was born. Also, John Walker wasn't present, which sent waves of jocular concern over how Principal Pope would announce the biggest awards, having never paid attention to anybody else. There was a current of anticipation that this ceremony would be different, not to be missed, heightened by the restlessness of so many kids crazed by summeritis and a forecast of light rain for the rest of the day.

Amid this sea of four hundred adolescents sat the group—not next to one another, of course, to maintain the illusion of ordinariness and preserve their secret lives to the very end. Tiffany and Greg were mixed on one side of the bleachers, E. and Alex on the other. Doug got put on the floor. The group alone seemed to suffer under the smell, perhaps owing to weeks in the open air. So many junior high kids crammed into the bleachers gave the gymnasium the palpable moisture and stink of steamed hotdogs, a beefy, salty odor unique to pubescent youth of the American Midwest. Distracted by the scrambled echoes of their peers' inane chatter—snippets of graduation party plans and summer vacation plans, first dates and impending breakups—the group couldn't think much about their plans to kill a kid later that evening.

The ceremony opened with the introduction of teachers and staff whom everyone already knew and/or would prefer to forget. Seemingly never-ending, laudatory speeches were made. Finally, the award pomp began and, as predicted, the crowd sensed something unusual and very wrong occurring. Students whom nobody had ever heard of were decorated. They belonged to the school, but not to its social fabric. Their names sounded foreign when announced, granted renown by the crackle and blare of the speakers to fabricate an alternate history of winners and losers. These were average kids in the graduating class who'd plodded along in their studies and respective sports and clubs with the work ethic of the unexceptional-though-tenacious, and after three long years their moment to shine had arrived. As they shuffled forward, other students began to recall, but only vaguely, that a few had been on the award stage before. The difference was that no big stars had risen today to blot them from memory, as if administrators were leading a pogrom against popularity, to which each winner also fell and receded, as, altogether, the most talented and hardworking stood beside one another in their ordinariness, only to rejoin their classmates as audience.

Equally unusual, Doug didn't feel ordinary or unremarkable today. If a wide picture were taken of the gymnasium, he'd have bet on his head looming three times larger than other kids', slightly greenish, sick and swaying like a balloon tied between his shoulders, swollen with the guilt of something he hadn't done, yet. The group was going to kill a boy tonight. Doug risked glances at his friends above him in the bleachers, needing to feel like he wasn't the only one second-guessing their plan to exact justice or vengeance or pragmatism. None returned eye contact or appeared deeply troubled. Bemused by the triviality of the ceremony, they wore faint smiles to keep outsiders from seeing through to their disgust with meaningless customs observed outside the woods, truly possessed by what they were, the Watchers of the Grove, which made Doug feel ultra-unordinary. Even among the outcasts, he didn't fit in.

Applause washed around him, rhythmic and facile as waves lapping and retreating from a distant shore. He focused on the sound to drown out what he was going to do—but each round hit like clock ticks in slow motion, incalculable in intermission and duration, which returned his thoughts to the boy whose time was running out, whom they'd tied to a tree. All morning, guilt had crashed inside him. At home, he hadn't been able to look his mom or dad in the face. Another life passing away, receding in time—and it would be his fault. That's all it was, he told himself. Erika was a name, like John Walker was a name and these awardees were just names, and names come and go, if not now, then later, but eventually, inevitably. How many names would Rocky erase from history if left alive? Doug could almost convince himself that was the meaning of life: a light in the branches, then no light. Simple and strange and lovely, as it came and wasn't. In fearing for E. over the last few weeks, he'd come close to understanding why life mattered. He tried not to answer and to focus on the clapping. There was no stopping his friends, short of telling the police. Big feelings made life worth something. There was more to it than that. Following the question threatened to make his head burst. More than the kindness of choosing to not inflict pain on another kid, necessary and silly as the awards themselves—a pact that things mean anything at all. The values of the outside world, however, didn't reach the vacuum of the woods. What Doug knew for sure was that he mattered there. Though he'd feared them, the group hadn't ever turned their backs on him, even after he'd attempted to do the same. He pulled at the spiky hairs along the back of his neck as though he could yank out the doubts and focus on joining indivisibly with E. tonight. What was the point of torturing himself? Rocky was basically gone already. Nobody here would miss him. He was a creep, a psychopath. It almost didn't matter if the boy were the real killer. His dying would purge E.'s soul of her demons, so she could move on, with Doug. They would all move on (To where? And then?) at last. After graduation, not one kid here, but for the group, would re-member Doug had ever existed. By allowing Rocky to die, he would only be treating others in kind.

The announcements of the two biggest awards were no shocker. Alex Karahalios earned the gold-colored medal for overall academic excellence. The acceptance was interesting in that Alex, the youngest person in the building, wore a tweed jacket like a college professor and sidestepped the principal to the podium to deliver a concise speech, never before attempted by a student. With wisps of blue under eyes that appeared frantically awake, as if from some grand secret procured overnight in conversation with the killer and the Dead Man, Alex thanked the mathletes coach for the opportunity to teach the team "a few new tricks," and then paused dramatically before saying, "Expect to hear great things from me soon," which garnered awkward giggling and a few slow claps. The school pride award was given to Damien something-or-other. The kid had been involved in a long list of collaborative artistic endeavors with obscure, embarrassingly earnest, and/or pretentious titles that no one mentally recorded, and, after a brief guitar performance riddled with mic squeals and deafening feedback and broken strings, followed by perfunctory applause, students and teachers stretched to leave, as there were no more awards to give away and everyone was eager to get home early, until Principal Pope silenced them to announce the inauguration of a new award.

His speech began about a boy they might recall, an exceptional boy who should long be remembered, and the crowd got the creeps. Their rising discomfort crested into a wave of nausea as he recounted the achievements of alumnus John H. Walker, including the boy's hall-of-fame-worthy t-ball record and a list of state and regionals he'd led. John was more than an athlete, the principal reminded, as if they needed reminding, and recounted the kid's years as an assistant coach of the school's Special Olympics team and the other service work and fundraisers he'd started or been integral to, not because John was ever asked, but because he believed in giving back to the community that had celebrated his potential. The award Principal Pope had created was not for the boy, but in honor of his legacy. He held up the plaque, as if rather proud of it, made of wood with an austere square of dark metal, the boy's name and the award's details inscribed in cursive. No one clapped or even smiled. His former classmates didn't want to think of him, let alone honor him. He was the past and they wanted the present, and maybe the future. Yet here they were, transfixed by the sight of the plaque, rounded at the top like a gravestone. The John H. Walker Memorial Award would be given each year to a student who exemplified not his unparalleled successes, but his virtues: good character, teamwork, and a positive spirit. The first would be given to John, who couldn't be with them today, so instead Principal Pope asked students to bow their heads in a moment of silence, to reflect on the good times they'd shared with the boy, the inspiration, the light above Palos Hills, he said, as if the kid had been dead a year already, which was weird, but weirder in how comforting it was, particularly to the graduating class, for whom this chapter of their lives couldn't have ended more poetically.

The group warmed with esteem, hearing John praised. They knew him no longer as the legend of sterling reputation and towering ego. He was their friend, larger-than-life, yes, but not flawless. During the principal's recounting, they recognized John's virtues, thinking back on the last few weeks in the woods, and they were proud to have played on his team in the final game against the killer. Though his failing strength made him no longer useful as a leader, their belief in his power—now and forever entwined with the Grove's—persisted. John would never die, not in those woods. The thought assuaged their guilt of already having accepted his death, as well as gave them hope. And with their heads high and eyes wide open, the group saw the Dead Man walk in through the gym doors.

His shuffling sneakers first gave him away to the back rows. The gymnasium was that quiet in remembrance. The sixth graders on the floor, more familiar with his name than the physical manifestation of the boy, turned their heads up in religious-like awe, as if one of their prayers had finally worked, phoned a higher power and manifested what was lost before them. Could it be …? He scanned their faces, the room, as if about to speak. He went for the podium, not showy or in a hurry, but determined. He stepped through the field of whispers with a lightness that made kids imagine the cancer had eaten his bones hollow, cleaned him in a way, maybe his organs, too, preparing him for a saint's death, so that his body might too ascend, accompany his soul to heaven. He wore his old baseball cap, the Pirates logo dusty and the maroon bill frayed, screwed low to cover his bald head. There was no hiding his condition. The kid looked terribly sick—his skin waxen, his cheeks sunken, his eyes dull. Yet, for having spent all night in the woods, he was immaculate. His shoulders glimmered from the light rain outside, and the body itself bathed and powdered and in fresh clothes—a shirt and tie under his rain jacket, stiff blue jeans. They could've buried him in the outfit. The rest of his venerable aura was secured by his lifted chin and forward gaze.

"John Walker, everyone!" the principal shouted from his gut to crescendo the moment.

The astonishment in the room was too great. The audience needed the release of hellish clapping. But no one did. His name boomed, echoed, and died against the huge lights in the rafters as they followed the simple vision of him, persevering against terminal illness, against rumors he'd been dead for a month. Those nearby were fascinated enough to reach out and touch him, to be imbued with John, his potency to endure. They were terrified of it, also, of being cursed to share his fate, cut short too soon and soon enough.

John rose to the stage as he'd done countless times, only more laboriously. He didn't glide up. Each step required attention, which said enough. Principal Pope put the award in John's hand as the boy came forward. John accepted it as a means of reaching the podium, his momentum unrelenting. The principal reluctantly backed from the microphone, blabbered about his joy, what an honor it was, too much of a believer to deny the boy command of the room and eager as the audience to hear what had compelled Mr. Walker to come before them after so long.

John began without clearing his voice.

"I haven't been around much this year," he said. "Many of you tried to keep in contact. Especially you guys on the team. I failed you, then. I don't feel good about that. You know I hate losing."

A handful of kids in the audience tested nervous, sympathetic laughs. John's face was difficult to read between the hat and the microphone. His voice was steady and clear.

"It's been a difficult time.

"Tomorrow's the last day in this building for the eighth graders. Look around." The bill of his cap pointed to the back corners of the gym. "You know now what it's like to be at the end of something. But your story is just starting. You'll be in high school next year. You won't have classes anymore with kids you've known your entire life. It might feel like the good parts—the friends, the familiar places that feel like yours now—are gone. They won't be. Your world will be getting bigger. You'll have to get bigger, too, and keep going. You've probably heard a lot about what that'll be like. I hope it's the best of those things."

He smirked. It wasn't handsome and revealed the illness beneath, and the hardship. For the first time his peers saw that the boy was really going to die.

"It's not easy, saying goodbye. This is the last time I'll be seeing most of you. The award ..."

He lifted the plaque and paused over the inscription. He tugged the bill of his cap lower. His voice sounded hoarse when he spoke again.

"I couldn't win my own award."

He laughed. The crowd joined him. The remark wasn't funny, but they needed release, if not by laughter then by heartbreak. This could be his last joke ever. The room waited for an explanation as to why he'd come before them today, what he needed from them, one and all attuned to his words. There was a sense that John knew it, too, that they sat charmed, eyes subdued, bodies lax under the spell of his image and words, like the old days, when, for a magic moment, time moved in breaths, not seconds. Even to a crowd, his voice poured silver into your ear. It was just you and John. He was almost everything. So much that you could love him for it. So much that he could love you. This would be the last time.

John's good humor faded. His head dropped as if ashamed. The audience mimicked with a churchy hush. When he looked up, he stared out at them, dead serious.

"Don't be a stranger to yourself. I was a stranger to myself until recently," he said. "I've been there to help others who needed it. Honestly, I never thought too much about what I was doing. I never asked if it was enough. I didn't wonder if it was the best way to help or if maybe I was part of the problem in other ways. Asking questions takes strength of character. I still struggle in that. It's like a sport—some out there were born with the ability and the rest have to put in the work. I've learned something about it, though. Either way, the work never ends, and the ones who keep playing are the winners."

John took a deliberate pause. Gradually, a smile relit his face, lukewarm but steady, reminiscent.

"I owe my wake-up call to a good friend out here today. And I'd like to give this award to that person, who really deserves it."

John looked for an approval from the principal, who shooed him to continue, brow lumpy with mild disappointment at the derailment, yet saying John could do with his award whatever he wished and secretly hoping the awardee was himself. The boy peered into the audience, scrupulously searching for the person, as if it were absolutely requisite before disclosure to witness the reaction of being named, as he and those before him had been named. With heat and light, his gaze swept over the kids, and their hearts expanded and hummed. They wanted to be named. Even if it didn't make any sense, if they'd only ever said hi to John or met his glance once in the hallways, they believed it could be them. They recalled the good things they'd done, miniscule things, picking up a classmate's pencil up off the floor, lending paper to the kid who never brought a notebook, seemingly insignificant acts of kindness they'd not have remembered otherwise, and the big stuff, too, apologizing after school to a girl they'd teased, helping their lousy moms and dads to bed, daily heroics that made each half-believe they'd inspired John Walker to be a better person, that they should've.

"Doug—Doug Horolez," he said.

Hardly anyone clapped. The eager clappers quit as the name thudded without currency, not any of the school's preps or jocks or nerds or freaks or anyone of talent, useful or otherwise, but a guy whose name they would've preferred to unlearn, if such a thing were possible, so inept, so clumsy and personality-less and pathetic and awful-looking a guy that, many realized then, a "Doug Horolez" had long been an archetype in their subconscious for all things unexceptional, subpar.

Doug felt the room ice over. He didn't dare move for fear of being

305

mobbed by kids who believed themselves more deserving. If he stayed perfectly still, maybe John would move on, think him absent and select another lamb for the sacrifice.

John paused, vaguely homing in on his direction in the audience. He lifted the bill of his cap. The guy eyed him like a fresh batter stepping up to the plate.

"I can't do this alone, buddy." He smirked to break the tension. "This is the last time I'll ask for anything. Promise."

Until he stood, Doug hadn't realized he'd been holding his breath. He let out a spurt and expected his body to deflate and curl like a rubber snake on the floor. He remained on two legs. He stumbled and apologized through kids who began to part for the anomaly, sure that he would receive the blunt end of a joke that John would soon and hard deliver. Sneers lined Doug's path. Even he thought it absurd that the word "buddy" had stirred his heart and strengthened his limbs. Still he came on. The Dead Man had again put him into a situation nearly impossible to refuse. Doug was certain he could've—gotten up, turned his back on him and the others too, pushed that far by the group and their conditions for acceptance and E.'s conditions for love. This time, John's proclamation felt genuine. By publicly admitting their friendship and alluding to The Work, he'd defied the group's vow of anonymity, and the cool, electric freedom packed into the transgression was infectious.

Doug got onstage and suffered judgment before four hundred sour faces. Principal Pope looked ready to tackle him if he did one stupid thing. John beckoned to join him at the podium. For once, he felt safer beside the guy.

John returned to the audience, gleaming with inspiration. He described how they'd met—"around town," both "basically friendless."

Maybe the Dead Man had conned him one last time. Maybe he'd stood up only to be slayed before the entire world—the audience wanting blood without knowing why, John's command that masterful—to allow him to finish what his disciple had failed on the train bridge.

"Doug took pity on me," John said. "Not over my health. For what I was deeper than that."

He dropped his arm around the boy's shoulder. The room audibly gasped.

He told them to look out—for one another, as a team does, and other things Doug could no longer hear, stunned by the lights and the micro mushroom-cloud field of blooming confusion trembling under reach of John's resounding voice, which touched all, assuredly and godlike, vaulting from the waxy floor to crash against the bleachers, bathing bodies and all in foam-soft words that penetrated their beings with the crude penetrability of lava.

Through all of that, Doug was unable to name a single vaguely familiar face in the room. He tried. Couldn't recall his own name. Or the speaker's. At the same time, each kid looked more real than ever, more close-up—leaning in to understand, their necks craned, chewing lips, fingers knotted or forgotten in their hair—more themselves. Adrift until the finale, until he was certain the guy wasn't talking about baseball. As Doug almost had in class, John edged on exposing their work in the woods:

"Chasing wins, I lost touch with how I was winning. I forgot what matters. You matter. If you don't, I don't. We're leaves of the same tree. That goes for everyone outside those doors, in Palos and past that, during our toughest games, when we're lost in the woods.

"It was Doug who showed me that," he said. John put out his hand to shake. "So, thank you."

It hit Doug like a hot and stiff wind—he'd been wrong about John Walker. The guy wasn't the undead leader of a bloodthirsty cult in the woods. E. was, spurned by loss, emptiness, and rage. John wanted peace. Maybe he hadn't always. The score didn't matter now.

Doug shook John's hand.

He braced for heckling and boos. The gym burst into cheers. The force of the blast reflected that something monumental had transpired. It didn't involve the audience, yet couldn't have happened without them. The aftereffect? Students felt inspired to take on high school and more: their deficient personal lives, the future, all their hopes and dreams. None might've been able to explain why a dying legend shaking hands with a nobody meant so much. All felt the reconciliation—the living and the dead, the center of the universe and dust, all and nothing—forces that couldn't have collided without rapture.

John smiled, half surprised by their acceptance, half satisfied. Doug smiled with him, not in the Dead Man's chilly shadow—at his side. Maybe not as his friend, but that hadn't ever been possible with John. The guy had wanted friendship, maybe more than anything. His speech told of great isolation. He'd had it all, and everyone, except for feeling a part, equal. Fame and his egocentrism had brought him followers instead of friends. Even among the group, the boy was a symbol, a spectacle, a prophet. Doug had never worshipped him, though his unease was a type of reverence. Their conflicts aside, John wore a bubble of self-importance that would've prevented their intimacy. Its root was also fear. If he was regular like everyone else, he would have nothing, he would be nothing. Nothing special, at least. Doug could understand that. If fear had made John recoil from the town and disgust had made him retreat to the woods, love made him return. Because he wasn't a tyrant. Or because, on his deathbed, he wanted to be remembered as more, a person, a boy who wanted to do good and be loved.

In humanizing himself, Doug ascended, maybe not his equal, but nonetheless integral to the success of an exalting moment.

Until John whispered in his ear: "You hear the trees?"

Doug barely heard the guy. He basked in the joy of a different life: celebrated by his peers, wishing the applause to drown on after he descended and onward, the soundtrack to a new Doug, to a new sense of himself, his specialness never more positive, firmer, affixed in time, how the group had described feeling after the ritual in the Big Tree. No, opposite. He felt purged of the woods and the drama of the group. Why think of it? That's what John's question did, of course. It recalled the tormentor, whom Doug had allowed to be beaten and left tied up overnight. His having treated another boy cruelly, no matter what Rocky might've done or was capable of doing, metastasized through Doug and ate at his fulfillment. He tried to wish the ignorance to return. He wanted to be as large and as worthy of love as he felt right now, before the entire world, eternally. If he helped to kill Rocky, his shame would never again allow him to accept it. His break with E. would be total and complete either way. He'd be no better than Rocky. That wasn't entirely true. He'd be no better than John— the old John, the monster of undying ego, the Dead Man Walker. A familiar pit of emptiness opened beneath Doug's heart, his very being, and threatened to wholly consume him. He would be the guy he'd most hated.

Maybe his posture straightened. Maybe his eyes brightened behind his glasses like short charred wicks that at last took flame. E. must've recognized a change in Doug across the gymnasium. She raced down the bleachers, through the crowd for the side doors as the principal excused everyone and then blurted the necessary instructions for the graduation ceremony tomorrow, only to give up over the tumult of mass exodus and teachers who rushed the stage to tell John his speech was wonderful or else to say goodbye. For E., the speech hadn't been a restoration, but a declaration of war. The doors popped. She was the first out of the building, headed to the woods to keep anyone from altering the captive's fate.

Alex was nowhere to be seen. A head taller than the rest, Greg pushed through the kids who bottlenecked into the building. Tiffany's blonde head pinged through the crowd in front of him. Doug watched Greg measure the effort to get to the stage, not to embrace Doug and John in celebration of a new life together, in a mutual desire to do good, but rather to see if it was easier to run against the current and stop the dork here and now or to race him to the Grove. Doug's heart skipped. Tiffany pulled Greg's hand. They followed the red flag of E.'s hair out of the building.

Mobbed before he could vanish, John stood on the stage stairs ringed with admirers who talked loudly, mostly about themselves and all at once. He spoke kindly, patiently, to each by name. He looked up at once, fully attentive, however, when Doug called his name and said that E. and the others had left to—

"We should stop them."

"Is that what you want?" John asked.

"Yeah," Doug said. "Yes."

"Then you should."

The gym doors had shut behind the others. The effort of going that far and opening them seemed herculean.

"You can," John said.

Doug Horolez burst through the rear doors. The impact hurt his shoulder. He fumbled his bike lock combo several times. Then he pumped at the pedals with all the oomph his meager body possessed and crossed town to beat the group to the Grove. He sped Oketo downhill, avoiding the less public side streets they would favor to gain a few minutes. His bravery dried up as he pictured the confrontation: Greg and his long legs overtaking him on a dead sprint down the train tracks, E. clubbing him unconscious to be tied up, Tiffany pounding at his face if he whimpered or squirmed as the group hauled him to camp, another log for the fire. Doug was racing to his death.

His pedaling wound down. The momentum of the hill pulled him yet faster down the street past rows of houses framed identically as to be indistinguishable at his speed. Their windows reflected a furious young man streaking across the black-silver surface, otherwise disrupting no one and nothing—the placid lawns of sprinkler chirp and dog yip queries, the mismatched siding and peeled awnings and saggy porch steps, a ball left in a yard under a tree riddled with dry rot, the cracked and variegated sidewalk alongside him—all whipping by on an overcast afternoon that stunk of impending rain, the day not dark, just a diffuse gray over everything except for a single cloud peak, high and far above the rest, with an expansive base that swelled into a battered purple bulge soon to wreak lightning. Where were the stay-at-home parents, the retirees, the babysitters, the out-of-workers, the peace officers, the help for kids lost between worlds?

Doug was that help.

On 115th, the trees had already been cleared thirty or more feet back from the street. Construction workers in neon orange vests mobbed the entrance of the main walking trail, imposing in their wraparound sunglasses. Doug saw his one chance and double-backed down the only path that would allow him to stop E. and the others.

He swerved hell-bent through the worksite, around barricades and trucks. Hardhats turned, swears flew. If Doug stopped to explain, it would be too late. One wiry guy with copper sunglasses gave chase down the main trail. Doug biked far beyond that.

He soon couldn't feel his legs. He spun gears regardless. If the group took the train tracks, at most he'd have ten minutes to work out the rescue. The Grove's archway came in view. He hit a stump and flipped over the handlebars.

Doug landed hard. He sat up mute for a while. His glasses were split down the center. They came off into his cupped hands as if his eyeballs had fallen out of his head. This was the least pain he would experience if caught as a traitor.

He stumbled on, half blind through the archway. He strapped his backpack to his front-side and let his body be drawn by its weight down the steep, rooted trailway. His shoulder clunked a young trunk and set his body spinning counterclockwise. Doug nearly tumbled the rest backward, and scraped his forehead on a low branch. He told himself to ignore these distractions, so close to the valley floor, and kept on through the woodland blur, watching for low-lying branches, as if that were more important than his footing, when his leg disappeared through the doors of a punji bear trap.

Doug pulled his gnarled limb out by the knee. His foot hadn't thrust down far enough to be punctured by the rusty nails sticking up from the bottom, and the gum of his shoe sole had prevented his foot from being iron-maidened. But his ankle had been shredded on the way down by nails along the sides of the trap. He refused to examine the mess. He tried to stand. Something was excruciatingly wrong. Doug peeled back his bloody sock. One of the longer, stubborn nails had come off inside him.

"Crazy … Sick …" he cursed through gritted teeth.

As if stabbing himself in reverse, Doug pulled the nail from the thick of his trembling calf.

Anger drowned his pain. Though slowed, his will intensified. He limped through the passage of sheer stone and into the Grove.

Through the trees, the creek cheerily babbled. The captive was still bound to the Big Tree. Doug saw no one else at camp. He kept low and hobbled over, remembering to watch his step.

Rocky lay on his side. He was trying to slip under the ropes. At Doug's approach, he inched upright and joyfully called, "Dhhhhk!"

Faint strings of smoke rose from the campfire. There were no flames, but somebody had tended the bright coals. Josué was supposed to be on guard, Doug recalled. He was relieved the kid had gone home.

Rocky "Mmhmm"ed at Doug's bloodied leg like a steak dinner had been set in front of him. Doug said to hold still and undid his gag. He fished the gnawed gym sock from between the kid's wide teeth.

"Bravo!" Rocky cried amid a coughing fit. "I knew you were the dark horse. The Master would've come … but only as they were flaying the skin from my bones! He never misses a good show."

"I'm not here because I like you," Doug said.

Rocky gave one last, pleased huff and cleared his lungs. He spit a gob in a high arc that landed sizzling in the fire.

"Let me go, and I'll tell you who killed the girl."

"There's no … deal. I'm just—" Doug unzipped his backpack and with the hammer's claws began to hack tape and rope "—I'm saving you."

Rocky grinned as a draught of power reentered him.

"There's always a deal."

The restraints were no joke. Doug paused several times as he wrangled the series of elaborate knots. Were they loosening or tightening? The minutes ran fast. His nerves didn't help. If only Rocky's knife were nearby.

Doug saw the boy's grin go out. A runner's footsteps crunched around the fire pit.

He wheeled around. Josué charged with the knife.

"Sorry, buddy," he said and tackled the dork.

Josué pinned him and Doug lost his breath. His head had smacked something shockingly hard on the way down, and he rolled onto one side.

When he could think, Doug clutched his guts. A terrible pain coursed through him. He craned his head.

Josué stood up, horrified. He wiped his nose, and tears pooled his eyes.

"I didn't mean …"

The handle of the knife protruded from Doug's backpack—the blade lodged deep in his guts. He would die exactly as he'd feared from the start.

"I want the ritual," Josué said shakily.

He reached to yank out the knife. Doug raised his arms to stop him from making the pain worse. They both noticed Doug's hands weren't smeared with blood. Josué drew out the long knife, and it too was dry. They looked at Doug's belly. A gaping hole was punched through the backpack. Doug put a hand inside and it withdrew miraculously clean but for some notebook shreds and uneaten lunch muck. A ruined textbook slid out like an afterbirth. He'd been granted the grace Erika hadn't.

With astonishment frozen on his face, Josué sank to his knees.

Rocky stood over them in his ragged cloak. He'd struggled free and had cracked Josué in the head with one of the fire circle stones.

"Pathetic," Rocky said of his unconscious jailer. He tossed the weapon to undo the ropes still lashed to his arms. "He was going to kill you over that do-nothing ritual. Do you know how hard it was not to laugh at their little drama last night? The 'Watchers of the Grove'!"

Doug wasn't listening. He was still recovering from not being dead, gutted as Erika had been. Then the suspected killer was looming over him, hands on his hips, fully freed. Doug was alive, but not safe.

Rocky eyed the knife where it'd fallen. His humor went out.

He lunged. Doug scrambled on his hands and knees and reached it first. He pointed the knife, and the high schooler reversed as Doug found his feet.

The two boys turned in a slow circle, until Rocky's back was to the Big Tree and Doug's was to the valley clearing and the trail to the regular world.

"I have in my possession a book of arcane secrets." Rocky tapped the dirt-strewn velvet over his heart. "There's so much to learn, Dougydearest. You could be my newest apprentice. Together we could pick through the entrails of our enemies. Or are you tempted, as I would be—as Erika had been—to strike me down and claim that power for yourself?"

Rocky's gaze, all lit up again, fiercely amused, challenged Doug to say otherwise.

Doug threw aside the knife. It clanged into the fire pit.

"I want everybody to stop," he said. "I won't kill you, or anybody."

Rocky heckled Doug's frustration with an abrasive *ha*. "You could under the right master."

Without Doug's prescription glasses, Rocky was a dark smudge. The smudge grew taller, widened. Rocky spewed riddles as he stalked closer. Doug was defenseless and too wounded to run.

"A firm and dominant hand is required to implement the mysteries revealed in the woods," Rocky continued, "and your Dead Man can't lead you to the peak of the mountain. You need me."

Rocky was close enough that Doug could see him clearly now. The disarray of his robes was no longer comic. It befitted his unrestrained wickedness. His hands rose, either to embrace Doug as a brother or to strangle him.

"You're crazy—" Doug staggered back "—just like them."

Shouts sounded from the valley's rim. The group was coming fast. If the boys were going to escape, they had to leave now.

"Save yourself and come with me," Rocky said, "or you too will die a calf for the coming slaughter."

"I'm going to the police. I'll tell them everything. We'll all go down. I'm OK with that."

Rocky didn't laugh this time. He gave Doug a dire look, the closest thing to pity he seemed capable of. "You're crazy if you think that world can protect you."

More shouting from above. The boys had been spotted. Rocky slinked up-creek to follow it deeper into the woods, and Doug went up the main trail.

"Wait!" Doug called back. He paused at the bridge. "Who killed Erika?"

Far off Rocky halted in the trees.

"Have time for a long story?"

The answer wasn't worth their lives, Doug decided.

All along the stone passageway and up the steep path out of the moraine, Doug heard Rocky's laughter. It echoed up from Bachelor's Grove, in the breeze, but otherwise directionless, bathing the trunks, drowning the leaves, overtaking the insects and birds, all animals, until the Grove, the entire valley was a sloshing basin of mad laughter, and Doug wondered if he'd done the right thing.

•

Doug limped down a longer, unfamiliar walking trail and soon was lost without his glasses, the pieces of which he'd pocketed near his downed bicycle. Part of him worried what his parents would say about smashing them, wanting to believe it would be the worst of the news he would deliver. He pushed his bike through paths untrampled for months, then blazed his own. His handlebars caught overgrowth every few feet. His calf cramped in pain. With his remaining strength, Doug pulled the bike through a mire thickened with biting swarms of insects. Then a clearing of dead and cracked saplings obstructed him further. His leg was failing, and he expected Greg or even Rocky to hear his cries for the damn road to just be there, please, and to impale him atop one of the jagged trees, gasping at the sky.

He heard the whine of old brake pads. Doug was looking out at 115th, the sky overcast. Not a drop of rain had fallen.

A police car eased by, vigilant like a sixth sense. It hadn't seen the boy in the tree line. Doug gave up his bike and tumbled into the runoff ditch. He struggled along the roadside, never happier to see a police officer. He chased and waved frantically, fearing that, if he couldn't reach it, help would be forever withheld. The brake lights pumped.

The older officer who'd stopped him weeks before put his bike in the trunk, despite his pleas to go, hurry, now. Doug swore through tears that he'd confess everything if she brought him home before hauling him down to the station. The boy must've looked as crazy as he felt. She didn't press him with questions.

The first thing Doug's dad asked was what'd happened to his glasses. Even with the officer in the foyer, whose radio squawked between a dozen other officers in the area, Doug couldn't tell a word of it until the front door was locked.

Under the officer's glare, the story came out jumbled with parts too fantastic to have occurred in real life, to Doug of all kids. Maybe in a movie or a videogame. They said as much, and he agreed—it hadn't happened in the regular world at all, but deep in the woods where magic was still possible. They didn't know how to respond to that, other than to reaffirm he was safe. Doug banged his fists on the kitchen table and scolded himself, "I should've … I should've …" His dad had never seen the boy like this, which he told the officer. Feeling language unhinging, becoming inadequate, Doug ran upstairs and grabbed two of the letters he'd started before John had coerced him not to tell the truth. Even these his dad reviewed skeptically and said, "It's quite a story, son," embarrassed to see his boy acting deranged in front of another adult. The officer assured him that any "shenanigans in those woods" would be seriously investigated if related to the Summerson murder, and together they went over the details, again and again, until Doug began to lose focus of the specifics, including the name of the tormentor. The major events went to fuzz, and then all he knew was that he'd experienced enough fear to last a lifetime.

Dad touched his shoulder. Doug had his forehead on the kitchen table. He couldn't remember for how long. The officer was still in their home, across from him in a creaky leather jacket. She wore a pair of reading glasses at the end of her nose for taking notes. The boy sat up and her pen went down. The officer looked tired and disapproving. There was concern, too, pity from a distance. Doug had the terrible feeling her expression characterized all the sympathy he would get for the rest of his life. Lightheaded, he took his dad's hand. He couldn't look at him. It seemed as if the kid would pass out. He showed his leg. It was an awful crusted mess. Hoping the wound was somehow the source of his son's strangeness, Dad excused the officer—who ominously assured they'd be hearing from her again soon—and rushed him to the hospital. As Doug rested back in the doctor's chair, he thought he might lose the throbbing limb. What sympathy would he get, then? The doctor gave him a tetanus shot, a loose handshake, and said to keep those bandages clean.

A few hours later, he closed his bedroom door on his parents, who were arguing, not with each other, but over the phone with lawyers and counselors to ensure that, if their son had gotten involved in the Summerson case, he wouldn't be going to a juvenile detention center and that, either way, he would have the best treatment to "recover from this mix-up." Doug kept his light off. The sun breached the dense clouds on the horizon. It shot liquid gold over Palos Hills, then used the lingering gray sheet to radiate a wistful aura of cotton candy and powder blue before all darkened beneath the beat of long clock strokes. Doug ripped up the letter he'd written to E. and stood dumbly with the pieces for a moment. Dumb on the outside. His insides roiled with discomfort, left him dazed and incomplete, wanting to whine, as a dog does, for something he sensed though could not name. He dropped the letter into the trashcan, then the paperback she'd given him—it felt like—in another life. He mutely took stock of the childish bedspread print that matched his window curtains, the desk littered with keepsakes and junk in the corners, the scarred dresser topped with toys he hadn't touched in years, and the bare white walls. This was his room. It felt like someone else's, whom he remembered as a meek and simple boy. The thought made Doug sad, and he lay on the bedcovers in his clothes and shoes. He looked inside then. There were few illusions there. It made seeing himself easier. He was still nothing, a nobody. He was afraid, too. He cared about E. and the others, though he doubted his actions would wake them. He believed it was possible in time if they were separated. Doug surveyed what he was, without mistaking that more was hidden someplace, and watched the light fade in descending slants on the ceiling. Everything was ending. All lives. His in particular. It hadn't meant anything before, but hit him full-on now. He wasn't a child anymore. The morning cartoons, street games, classroom pranks, the pleasures dependent on the privilege of drifting through life half in a daydream, without consequences or responsibility, were gone. They were buried in the woods where he could never return. Doug would never again be that boy. He'd leave junior high as he'd stepped into it, without lifelong friends, no longer achingly so, but singular. He might go on for the rest of his life like that. Doug didn't know for sure. He couldn't, of course. But he knew some things. He was a teenager. He was going to high school. He was growing up.

4

Doug woke in the night believing the woods a dream. His parents had been right. Those bad memories hadn't happened, because childhood never happened like that: kids killing kids over lost loved ones, over territory, over ritual.

Something had woken him.

The wind had picked up, and it rustled the bushes beneath his window. Debris flicked the pane.

Do it, Doug told himself.

He slipped out of bed. His legs almost buckled. His guts ached, too. Doug went to the window with a sleepwalker's faith. He didn't lift the curtain. He lifted his shirt. A head-sized bruise marked his abdomen where he would've been knifed to death.

The boy backed from the window. At one point, the woods had made him nuts enough to climb the side of E.'s house in the rain. The group was capable of far more. Would E. come for him alone? Doug was hoping, again. He didn't know what he'd feel seeing her. And the others? He imagined them in cloaks on the other side of the curtain, five in the shape of a sickle moon, to spill him in the name of justice. He imagined Rocky's laughter, the boy's head pushing through the curtains, chomping them, his gray Master waiting in the wings (with wings?). Or them all outside—together, against each other. Doug in the middle, either way. Weaponless, he thought to cry out for his parents, as if eight years old again and having risen from the crash of a nightmare, mind still under its delusive spray.

Grow up.

Doug pulled the curtain. He was prepared to shout the words through the window at E. and anyone else. The bushes were still. Maybe the wind hadn't picked up. He couldn't see if the treetops swayed against the sky unless he pressed his face to the glass. The yard was empty. The street glared in the near-full moonlight. Doug inched forward—

The window shattered. An object—obdurate and hate-flung— burst through the pane.

Doug's parents rushed into his room. They'd remained stiff but sleepless in bed, kept up by the frighteningly cohesive amalgam of fantasies their adolescent son had confessed to partaking in beyond their supervision. They'd projected those experiences decades in time, onto the adult man he would become, whom they'd failed.

Standing before the window, now a web of cracks, Doug put his arm around his mother's hips. He took his father's hand reassuringly, in consolation of the future self he'd already accepted, as they discerned the object that looked up at them from the bedroom floor.

Doug understood the glass skull to mean things had irreversibly ended between him and E. He was OK with that. He'd lost the girl he'd loved weeks ago.

•

At 6 a.m. an unidentified caller placed the location of the murder weapon in the investigation of Erika Summerson in the locker of the recipient of the John H. Walker Memorial Award. Who that was exactly—the principal and several teachers were consulted before anyone could remember, other than that the boy had a rather unfortunate name—was identified, and the evidence confiscated from his locker was more or less confirmed as the murder weapon a few hours later. The call had conveniently incriminated Doug Horolez as the killer, which he regarded—bearing the news silently, almost nobly—as the group's last effort at human sacrifice. Following his arrest, an anonymous email arrived at the police station with notes, photos, and video that connected Doug to a disturbing overlook near the scene of Erika's murder and to the delinquent Rocco "Rocky" Lordes. A picture taken of Doug wielding a hammer in one of the school's restrooms, snapped by a random student, simultaneously leaked on social media and seemed to corroborate that the boy wasn't all right in the head. Doug spent more than a few hours at the police station believing the group had successfully punished his betrayal and secured their survival. He'd expected to be framed, the group having planned for it, and Doug answered questions as if he no longer cared what happened so long as his time in the woods had ended.

Doug's preemptive confession proved his saving grace. Later that day, all the kids were hauled in for questioning.

None of the group walked at graduation. Emily Summerson was found at 9:10 a.m. in Resurrection Cemetery. She recited a poem to her dead sister's tombstone, revising the lines as she repeated them like an incantation. She didn't seem to notice the officers calling her name until one took her arm, when she yelled, "I'm not finished!" The girl bit his face and had to be subdued via Taser. At 9:40 a.m., Josué Ortiz was torn, weeping, from the hips of his religious aunt. "Aún verde y sin cortar …" she said over him with her heavy arms crossed. She did not weep. Greg Dombrowski was picked up at 10:15 a.m. in Penny Park, attempting to sink over-the-head half-court shots. Music loud, he didn't hear the cops until they charged up the middle. He faked by and ran, until left strung by his shoelaces from the top rung of the fence he'd attempted to hop. Alex Karahalios was led out of Palos Junior High by a police escort before commencement at 11:55 a.m. Alex waved to the teachers and gowned lines of eighth graders in front of the gym doors, as if paparazzi, shouting, "It is my job to know what other people don't!" Tiffany Dennys walked into the police station at 12:20 p.m., oversized sunglasses on and still a little buzzed. The girl gave testimony to every crime she'd witnessed or been victim of during her lifetime.

The suspects' stories about the murder didn't add up. They first accused Doug. An hour later, it was a high school delinquent named Rocky. Thirty minutes after that, each began to suspect one another, and eventually admitted to being responsible for Erika's death one way or another, though the whats, wheres, whens, and hows didn't fit the facts of the case. There was, however, enough evidence to place them at the woods over the last month, performing an illegal investigation past curfew, at best. At worst, they were cultish co-conspirators in the murder of Erika Summerson and guilty of the attempted murder of at least one other child. Doug dropped the allegations of attempts on his life when he realized the trouble they faced.

Rocky was picked up and questioned later that evening. He cried half the time, still recovering from the duress of torture. That's what he said, at least. He confessed to drug use and breaking curfew. As confirmed by the video, which the police had never mentioned, he claimed to have reached out to Doug after witnessing the group's "irreverent rites." He'd wanted to help the boy, though knew he should've called the police. Rocky answered every loose end. The murder weapon, clean of his prints, he'd never seen before except when the group had cut his face open. The Man in Gray had been the drug-induced hallucination of a girl with a history of sexual abuse by older men. The groups' stories were tangled lies, delusions. Investigators showed him Alex's photos of the hideout with its profane pin-ups and demanded he tell the truth because a mountain of evidence linked him to it (a bluff, as the scene had been torched in the night). The work of the group, he said. His mother, a Palos Heights City Council Alderman, was livid they would implicate her son, a terribly misunderstood boy playing with kids who were the obvious threat. On the night of the Summerson girl's murder, he'd performed a private magic show for her and her adult friends. She invited investigators to search his room. They found no book, no cloak, no cigarettes. His brutal wounds were photographed, and Rocky was released with a stern warning about his direction in life.

The development of the woods into golf course–townhouse residences halted immediately. Public outcry renewed for closure in the case, and the search for evidence in the woods resumed, aided by the trove of data Alex had amassed. As election season neared, a solution to the moral corruption of Palos's children was demanded of City Council if the murder hadn't anything to do with perverts, gang violence from the inner city, or the many Muslim families moving into town (though these suspicions persisted among countless, mostly white residents). Few regarded the "Warlocks of the Grove"—as they were dubbed in the press—as proactive and unlikely heroes who'd at least found the murder weapon and two potential suspects. Most regarded them as the town's mistakes, the consequence of bad parenting, of liberal schooling or the repression of conservative values, of pop culture and the degenerated social fabric of America, or of genetic mishap. Altogether, enough rhetoric appeared in the media to tangent concerned citizens away from what'd happened and to allow the old mayor a slim victory, owing somewhat to nostalgia, over an upstart eighth-grade social studies teacher, and then to allow developers to recode and seize most of the land by the summer's end, a final solution City Council approved with relief, to civilize the woods as if they'd never existed. Voiced opposition came only from local trail walkers who were forced to migrate to Orland Park Mall. Though, before the woods were fully dozed, already they'd begun to wonder why anyone would want to hike so far without soft music and A/C.

John Walker's involvement was received with no little amount of skepticism. Under interrogation, when asked what'd initially drawn them to the woods, if they weren't a cult, why come together and get involved in solving the girl's murder, the group invariably responded, "John knows," the boy's name dropped casually, almost as an afterthought at the end of their testimonies, as their guide to the woods. Police entertained the kids' statements enough to call the Walker residence and inquire as to the boy's whereabouts and explain that he was being incriminated as a scapegoat. It was discovered then that John wasn't in his room and hadn't gone to commencement. An APB was put out. For several days, the boy was nowhere to be found. In that time, they combed the woods with dogs and volunteers. The group was again interrogated, this time as suspects in his disappearance, which didn't add up except in terms of circumstantial evidence.

These were desperate people at a desperate time, cops who'd learned more about criminal investigations from a child than from years working the streets, and whose esteem was plummeting daily in the eyes of the community they were committed to serve, and eventually in their own eyes and the eyes of their families who suffered beside them through the long nights, false starts, bum leads, dead ends, and an increasing number questions seemingly without answer about what human beings, children, are capable of under watch in a small American suburb. John wouldn't be found in the woods by daylight, if at all, the group asserted unanimously, their eyes glazed over. They seemed to know more but refused or, more accurately, were bound by reverence or terror to a code of silence on the subject of the boy. This was exactly the kind of supernatural nonsense that needed to be surmounted if progress were to be made and justice served, investigators insisted among themselves. At the same time, a part of them came to believe, as members of the group had suggested, that at last John Walker had truly and transcendently vanished.

•

After John reappeared a few days later, it was decided by the groups' parents that their children would be separated. The Summersons filed for divorce that June, and E. went west with her mother. After her father's sentencing, Tiffany lived with her grandmother and enrolled in an all-girls private school on Chicago's North Side at her own request. Josué moved to Phoenix with one of his aunts and attended a STEM school. Many years passed before he drew again. Greg went to trade school in Cincinnati, but dropped out at sixteen to change oil. Alex spent half a semester at Palos Community High with Doug and another at a local community college before starting over on the east coast.

So, for several years, Doug was the only ex-member of the group who heard other kids remark offhandedly before exams, performances, driving tests, and so on, not to "John Walker it." What they meant was: Don't screw up and kill yourself or your reputation. Students from Palos Hills Junior High who wanted to appear tough and other local high schoolers used the phrase, which some sad child that wasn't Doug must've invented. Some kids claimed to have witnessed the boy's epic demise firsthand. Others insisted it a sick rumor, that John was still very much alive, successful though humbled after winning his bout with cancer. This split over local historical fact owed mostly to the private debates of residents and their neighbors after his return as to whether John had been Palos Hills's savior or its bane all along. Not as Erika's killer—though fringe individuals spun that urban legend for a while—but in the sense that the celebration of the boy's potential had led to the neglect of other, more fragile-souled children, the mental health aspect of national school tragedies being popular discourse at the time. Deliberation over John's fate and his role in the story, their story, inevitably led folks back to the known details of the Summerson girl's murder and her friends' unfortunate intervention, which caused the subject to crest and curl back in on itself, a question without answer that roared (from what point?) for a good while (to what end?) and proved only one thing: John H. Walker had been a wonder. As time rolled on to claim that remainder of the boy's legacy. And the woods were fenced up or paved over. In the world and in the minds of those who told the story. And at last in the minds of the group. But never for Doug, who wondered, nights behind a heavy

curtain inside his home, peeping at the glare of the full moon light,
What ever happened to that kid? To the kids we'd been?

EPILOGUE

*T*he fire pit was cold. A column of impenetrable darkness loomed
over it and the boy in the night, unmistakable from the backdrop
of lesser darknesses outlined in a shimmer of starlight. He'd come to
see the last ritual performed. The woods were his home, and, without
flashlight, familiar steps and handholds had guided him down into the
valley, stiff-limbed but sure.

The boy climbed the Big Tree alone like that.

He perched above. The full moon hadn't yet revealed itself. Sightless-
ness gave a spherical shape to the cricket chatter, the illusion of being at
the center of the universe, as if he were that center and the Big Tree's limbs
creaked his name.

Dead Man Walker, they'd called him. The boy wasn't dead, wasn't a
man (yet). He'd run, a great distance in record time. He was tired.

To stand against the oncoming wind, the boy would need strength,
more to walk the bough and set things right. Until then, he huddled, eyes
closed. Or were they? Such little difference, anymore, he being too weak
to discern if only in his mind's eye a camera pulled back from him and
everything—a boy in the woods, as if made of woods and the woods were

him all the same, as if written by god because what he saw was all-known, watched from above in the guise of a wide-eyed moon.

Below, doubt stretched in long shadows. The world wasn't a better place. The Work had amounted to what it was—another human endeavor. Not even in the sacred Grove ...

Where Erika Summerson was. Cross-legged at the foot of his hospital bed. No longer. Never again. At the end of the high bough, the girl's specter smiled, kind and big-hearted, where she'd risen months ago.

The boy's head ached. He couldn't remember when last he ate.

He thought about failure, redemption. About what the dead leave behind. Stories making stories.

He was too high to come down.

The canopy rustled, dropped a lunar spotlight, and a hundred billion fans cheered as Walker tottered up to the plate. Or was it crickets, again? Or his friends, fearless at last and rushing back to him? Or the tormentor skulking for corpses like a carrion bird? Or the town seeking him and answers and unable to discern the difference?

A sacrifice fly was easy if a guy had the guts to take a loss. A clean miracle was better—to fall like an eclipse over the woods, make them vanish to fools and fanatics as if they'd never existed. By not existing. He'd wanted to free others, not make them more lost. Best to keep the lesson of the woods kindling in those with the potential to be more than just potential for when the big game comes.

Expire in a hospital bed? Nah.

John swung hard and ran like hell.

The last play of the last inning of his last game on Earth. The boy left the field. He soared over the moon, over the fences of both worlds. He went back, back, way back beyond the stars. All the way.